TO KILL A NIGHTINGALE

TO KILL A NIGHTINGALE

MATT HARDMAN

DOUBLE✝DAGGER
— www.doubledagger.ca —

Copyright 2023 Matt Hardman

All rights reserved. No part of this publication may be reproduced or transmitted in any form or by any means, electronically or mechanically including photocopying, recording or any information storage or retrieval system, without prior permission in writing from the author.

All of the characters in this book are fictitious and any resemblance to actual persons, living or dead, is purely coincidental. The events, dialogue, and opinions expressed are solely the product of the author's imagination and not intended as expressions or representations of the views of the United States Navy or any agency, organization, or government described within.

Library and Archives Canada Cataloguing in Publication
Hardman, Matt. author
To Kill a Nightingale / Matt Hardman

Issued in print and electronic formats.
ISBN: 978-1-990644-53-5 (soft cover)
ISBN: 978-1-990644-57-3 (kindle)
ISBN: 978-1-990644-58-0 (epub)

Editor: Jennifer McIntyre
Cover design: Paul Hewitt/Battlefield Designs
Interior Design: Winston A. Prescott

Double Dagger Books Inc.
Toronto, Ontario, Canada
www.doubledagger.ca

**K-561 *Kazan*
05 December 2022 | 0155 Local Time
Black Sea**

Captain Ivan Sergeyevich Korov stepped into the attack center of the *Kazan* and let his eyes take in the myriad of information presented to him. This was a force of habit developed over his two decades of submarine service. His pale blue eyes scanned every panel, display, and readout in the space. The information contained on each screen, gauge, and dial was being relayed to him verbally, each watch station using clipped phrases to communicate the status of Russia's newest cruise missile submarine.

But I need to see for myself. Always.

"Contacts?" Korov's voice was gruff. He didn't like this mission. The *Kazan* was a Yasen-M-class cruise missile submarine. It had been designed and built to shower fleets and land-based targets with the new Igla-M cruise missiles. It was not a special ops boat. It wasn't designed to ferry troops into battle. It could do that, the captain knew. It was capable of such missions, but Korov did not like risking his new command, an eight-hundred-billion-dollar collection of technology, running special operations troops to shore.

Or anywhere else. Fucking brown-water ops.

Korov scowled as the *Kazan*'s sonar officer, Senior Lieutenant Yevgeni Stepanovich Belyaev, reported. The man's voice was barely a whisper.

"No subsurface or air contacts, Captain. Several surface contacts. All cargo ships. One is the *Brixton*, a British merchant hauler. One is the *Istanbul*. Turkish registry."

"Very well. Keep your ears open, Yevgeni Stepanovich."

"Yes, Captain."

A hand fell on Korov's shoulder and he turned to see a short, overweight, balding man smiling at him.

"It is almost time, Captain," Mikhail Gregorovich Alexandrov said cheerfully.

Korov went back to scanning the displays and gauges in the attack center, trying to ignore the man. Willing him to go away. Alexandrov was not a sailor. In the Soviet Navy, he would have been the political officer, a man assigned to ensure that every sailor on the ship remained loyal and committed to the Communist Party. Though the job title was missing, Alexandrov's job was little changed. He was...

What do the Americans call such people? Snitch?

"Is something the matter, Captain?" Alexandrov would not be ignored.

"Nothing, Mikhail Gregorovich. Everything goes as planned." Korov forced a smile.

"You do not like the mission?" Alexandrov asked.

Korov paused, choosing his words carefully. "I would choose to make this approach with another class of submarine. One that is less valuable to Russia." Korov saw Alexandrov's brow knit in confusion and explained. "These merchant ships are clumsy and ignorant. Having this one stumble into us is a risk."

"Ah," Alexandrov exclaimed. "But leadership in Moscow knows this and they have chosen *Kazan*. It is our most technologically advanced ship."

Korov grimaced inwardly, but did not speak.

Alexandrov's hand fell heavily on his shoulder again. "Trust in Moscow, Captain. They know best."

Korov watched Alexandrov walk away and shook his head.

Idiot.

Korov looked around the attack center, searching for the one man who was clearly out of place. There. By the scopes. Dressed almost completely in black. A heavy beard. A dark, knitted, woolen watch cap rolled above his ears. Korov did not like the man and knew that his assessment was unfair. He didn't know the man. They'd not spoken more than ten words at a time for the past week. The man in black—Korov didn't even know his given name—never spoke without need. He just stood there, with his eyes scanning and a peculiar expression on his face. Korov disliked the look more than the man, because he thought he knew what the man was thinking.

He thinks he's better than me. Than us.

Korov thought about that.

Maybe he is. At some things. But that arrogant bastard needs us. And he probably knows it.

Korov checked his charts and the various weather reports resting on a nearby clipboard. He did not envy the man or his team. December in the Black Sea was cold as hell. Enough to make even the most stolid Russian shiver.

And these men will get wet on top of that.

Korov shook his head, smiled, and motioned the man over. "It's almost time. Are your men ready?"

A nod. No verbal response. Korov looked at the electronic chart and at the chronometer mounted next to it. He turned back to his guest. "Fifty minutes."

The man in black nodded again before turning and walking out of the attack center. Korov watched him go and thought again about how much he hated this tasking. It wasn't particularly difficult or taxing. His crew had the training and skills to carry it out easily. As did the crews of almost every other submarine in the Russian fleet. And that, Korov thought, was precisely what made his job tonight stupid.

Driving a cruise missile submarine right up beside one of those clumsy cargo ships. Mother of God. Who thought this shit up?

But Korov knew the answer to that. And he knew why. A cargo ship, or any other vessel, could transport the silent man and his eight companions to within striking distance of the *Brixton*, but two relatively large ships in such proximity would cause navigational problems. And questions. Tonight, there could be neither. That meant a submarine.

A good one. With an expert crew and a captain who was both skilled and trusted. And that is why you're here, Ivan Sergeyevich.

The *Kazan* had completed her annual wargames the previous month and she'd done well. Exceptionally so. The *Kazan* had single-handedly decimated a goodly portion of the Russian fleet. She'd done exactly what she'd been built to do. She'd stalked her targets, showered them with administrative ordnance, and disappeared from the face of the earth.

Victim of your own success, Ivan.

Korov was not flattered by the assignment. Easy as it was, there were risks. A collision at sea wasn't unthinkable. Cargo ships were awkward vessels, ungainly in the best of conditions. All it would take was a single inopportune turn by the hauler's crew and the submarine would be crumpled like an empty soda can. If the merchant was large enough, as the *Brixton* was, she might not even notice. Korov knew that from experience. Two years earlier, he'd been trailing an Iranian diesel boat that had stumbled into the path of one of these behemoths. Korov and his sonar department had listened to the crumpling noises of the destroyed submarine and watched as the surface track had wandered off, oblivious to the destruction in her wake.

With that memory, Korov decided that the planners for this operation hadn't completely lost their minds.

At least they hadn't used a ballistic missile boat. *Be thankful for that, Ivan.*

Korov and his submarine were involved because they could get to within yards of the noisy British tanker and drop off the submarine's guests undetected. After which, Korov could take the *Kazan* back into the depths of the Black Sea and disappear. It was a simple and largely uncomplicated task, work for which his crew was proficient.

Korov checked his watch.

**ced
Neptun Deep Natural Gas Platform
05 December 2022 | 0200 Local Time
Black Sea**

The alarm went off, a combination of the pleasant and the grating. The smooth sound of a Tom Petty track contrasted with the irritating vibration of a cellular phone bouncing around on an aluminum shelf. On the bunk next to the shelf, a figure stirred and rolled towards the competing noises. After a few cycles, a hairy arm reached out from under a stiff, white sheet. The hand at the end of the arm fumbled and poked at the phone blindly before connecting with one of the device's buttons and plunging the room back into an eerie silence.

The portion of the sheet over the figure's head moved and the man in the bunk forced his eyes to open. It took a few moments for Jonathan Evans to remember where he was. The ceiling above him was decidedly foreign. It clearly wasn't the plain white he'd gotten used to seeing above a long line of hotel beds during the past few months. Nor was the ceiling the boxed-frame design currently installed above the king-sized bed in his Bethesda, Maryland home. The thirty-year-old systems engineer blinked in the dark.

Pipes.

Jonathan's eyes began to trace the chaos above him, a spaghetti-piled mess of piping that zigged and zagged before disappearing off into the darkness. His brain worked on the issue for nearly a minute before settling on an answer.

The gas rig.

It took a few more moments for Evans to remember where the rig was and why he was there. He reached for his phone and looked at the time. It was two in the morning. He chewed over that information, digging through a mental list of tasks from Exxon's home office. He had an evolution to observe. In thirty minutes. Jonathan groaned, flipped on a fluorescent light, and fell reluctantly out of bed.

M/V *Brixton*
05 December 2022 | 0205 Local Time
Black Sea

Oliver Wallace peered out the large windows on the *Brixton*'s bridge, looking ahead into the dark night. The night was clear, the velvety blanket of black sky broken only by the twinkling of billions of visible stars and a nearly full moon. The Black Sea was relatively calm, its dark, rolling waters distinguishable only by the occasional whitecap visible in the bright moonlight. He smiled, took a deep breath, and—as usual in these solitary moments—reflected on the path his life had taken.

Wallace was sixty-five years old and, if he was being honest with himself, nearing retirement. He loved what he did, but was reaching the point in his life where his body sent him hourly reminders that it did not approve of the steel decks, steep ladders, and constant rocking a ship at sea offered. He woke up every day to new aches and pains—his knees and back were particularly bad—and stoically told himself that it was all worth it. For the most part, the aging mariner believed his own lies. Sure, the swollen knees and abused back were unwelcome, but what better sight was there than a cloudless night at sea?

Maybe a sunrise?

Wallace smiled. He was a short, barrel-chested man with a bushy mustache and a pair of what his grandson called "chicken legs." A veteran of Her Majesty's Royal Navy, Wallace was a former destroyer sailor who'd spent a portion of his early twenties aboard the HMS *Coventry*, trying to inflict as much damage on the Argentine Navy as was humanly possible. He'd been immature then, convinced of his own immortality. Back then he'd viewed war, despite the grave warnings of his father and grandfather, as an adventure. Something serious, but not lethally so. Not against Argentina, anyway.

Sub-Lieutenant Wallace's opinions regarding armed conflict had changed on the afternoon of May 25, 1982, when a foursome of Argentine A-4 Skyhawks descended on his flotilla. His captain, the *Coventry*'s crew, and the sailors from his sister ship, the HMS *Broadsword*, had fended off the first pair of fighters while Wallace looked on from his position on the *Coventry*'s small bridge. Even now, Wallace could not remember feeling vulnerable. He remembered watching as the first pair of attack planes veered off. He'd felt a deep sense of pride seeing that one of the Argentinian Skyhawks was trailing thick, black smoke. He also remembered the next few seconds, when his pride had turned to icy-cold fear. The rapidity of the change still amazed him. Mere seconds, if that. Just a scream from the lookout and the turn of his own head.

Wallace had watched the second pair of Skyhawks race toward his ship, coming in low and fast. To him, it had looked like the fighters were skipping across the water, as if some warring giant had bounced a smooth stone across the wavetops. He'd frozen, hearing nothing but the sound of the captain's voice. Unable to track via radar, the captain had ordered a blind surface-to-air missile launch and a hard turn to starboard. As the ship heeled over and tried desperately to race out of the line of fire, the approaching Skyhawks had kicked their bomb loads loose. Three of the weapons hit the HMS *Coventry*, but Wallace only knew this from the after-action reports of other ships.

The first bomb had ripped into *Coventry*'s hull just aft of where the ship's operations center was located, and the resulting blast threw Sub-Lieutenant Wallace through the bridge's starboard-side hatch and off into the sea. The force of the blast had knocked him unconscious and he'd been saved from drowning only by the life vest he'd donned before arriving at his battle station. When Wallace had regained consciousness, he was greeted with the sight of his capsized ship, the *Coventry*'s keel and propellers clearly visible above the surface. Wallace was eventually rescued, pulled from the water by a boat crew from the HMS *Broadsword*.

He'd spent months in a series of hospitals recovering from a pair of broken legs, a fractured skull, and a partially flailed chest. Between surgeries and therapy, Wallace found himself with time to think. Hospitals were good for that sort of thing. Once you've watched every channel on the little television and read every periodical, there's not much else to do.

He loved sailing. He'd known that all along. From the very first time the *Coventry* had cast off all lines and slipped away from her pier in Portsmouth to the moment he'd been thrown into the sea by that bomb's blast, he'd wanted to do nothing else. He loved the open sea. The sights and sounds and smells that could not be found anywhere else. He'd discovered a freedom at sea that he found impossible to describe to those who'd never left dry land.

War was another matter entirely. Wallace had been forced

to admit that his father and grandfather were justified in their warnings. His crooked legs and battered ribcage were proof of that. War was something to be taken seriously. Since he'd survived it, and would walk again, he had taken that lesson to heart.

The logical convergence of these two trains of thought eventually led Oliver Wallace into the employ of the United Kingdom's Merchant Navy. He'd finished his physical therapy regimen in late 1983 and had immediately set to work to obtain a position as a merchant sailor. He'd worked hard, spending his first full decade in the service perfecting his craft with twenty-hour days. By the end of 1996, Wallace was reaping what he'd sown. He was given his first command that year.

Wallace rubbed his aching back, smiled, and peered forward into the night.

***Neptun Deep* Natural Gas Platform**
05 December 2022 | 0215 Local Time
Black Sea

Jonathan Evans walked into the office he and his team were using on the rig, cup of coffee in hand and a smile on his face. Despite the early hour, Evans was happy. He loved his work.

Especially on days like this.

He worked for Exxon Mobil, an occupation that had caused grumbling over the past year. Not because of who he was—in the big picture, he was a nobody. The average Joe or Jane didn't care who he was or what he did for a living. Ninety-nine point nine percent of the world's population did not care about him. They, most certainly, did not understand that the test Jonathan was about to witness would place this rig online. They didn't care that placing the rig online, getting it into production, would provide access to enough natural gas to serve half of Eastern Europe for the next eight to ten years. What they did care about was much simpler. Pocketbooks and bank accounts. Bills and income. They cared about the cost of heating their homes and cooking their dinners.

And, Jonathan knew, they cared about the source of the gas they used for both. Those people, regular folks going about their regular lives, cared that this rig, and others like it, would mean energy independence for countries not far removed from Russian rule.

The grumbling about Jonathan in particular revolved around principles, or, more precisely, a perception among the masses that the thirty-year-old systems engineer just didn't have any. The perception was false, he knew. He had morals and ethics and principles up the yin-yang. His parents and grandparents and aunts and uncles had made sure of that. They'd raised him "right," an expression Jonathan had always found odd. But the uproar wasn't about Jonathan's upbringing, and none of the people attacking him had bothered to ask his opinion on anything. Rather, the public, fueled by media outlets that straddled the whole of the American political spectrum, had gotten bent out of shape over who signed Jonathan Evans's paychecks. He was cast as a greedy prophet by people who believed Exxon Mobil to be one of the great evils in the world.

Jonathan could deal with that. It didn't really bother him; as he did with most contentious issues, he viewed the issue as pragmatically as he could. He was well aware of the climate issues related to his work and the work of his company. That anyone spent the time and energy to complain about his lowly position in the worldwide conglomerate was, to him, borderline ridiculous. That his employment hadn't been questioned before was, he thought, probably an oversight by the public. He'd been with Exxon Mobil since leaving college and it was only in the last twelve months that he'd become famous.

Or was it infamous?

Whenever Jonathan wasted time thinking about that, all he could picture was Martin Short explaining the word's meaning to the rest of the Three Amigos.

Not that any of that mattered. Jonathan Evans wasn't famous— or infamous—of his own accord. If he was either, it was because of his uncle. The man who'd taken a hard line on drilling, fracking, and oil and gas exploration. The man pushing clean and renewable energy legislation through Congress. The man who currently resided at 1600 Pennsylvania Avenue in Washington, DC.

"Johnny-boy! How's it going?" The youngest member of the team stood to greet his boss. Jonathan rolled his eyes. He hated being called Johnny. It was something his mother could get away with. Sometimes. Even his uncle, the sitting president of the United States, avoided calling him that.

"Greg. We ready?"

A nod. "Yep. Foreman called earlier. Everything is set up and on schedule."

Jonathan looked at his watch. "Well, let's not keep the man waiting. Time is money." He immediately regretted the last line. It sounded like something his dad would say.

Doesn't make it less true. Just…

Everyone refilled their Styrofoam cups of coffee, donned hard hats and safety glasses, and followed Jonathan out onto the rig's catwalks.

M/V *Brixton*
05 December 2022 | 0225 Local Time
Black Sea

Oliver Wallace checked his watch before cracking open a bottle of aspirin and downing four small, white tablets. He could feel his knees aching and longed for his watch relief to show up early. He didn't normally subject his body to the strain of standing bridge-watches for this length of time—not unless it was some special evolution. There were others for that. Good, well-educated and properly trained crewmen whose sole purpose in life was to take care of things like this so that Wallace could focus on running the entire ship. The problem tonight was simple. One of those individuals, the man who was supposed to be on the bridge for this watch, was in his rack right now, fighting off a stomach bug that Wallace prayed was just related to the evening's less-than-stellar dinner.

If it's contagious…

Wallace shook the thought off and went back to work. He scanned the horizon and glanced at the radar display.

Not much out there. Just other cargo haulers. Seven of them, to be exact.

Wallace continued scanning. Engine displays for the big Colt-Pielstick diesels. Electrical displays. Damage control readouts. Navigation radars. Weather broadcasts. He took it all in and let his brain process it all while his hands worked to knead the muscles in his lower back.

Just thirty-five minutes, Oliver.

Wallace grinned despite the aches and pains and began scanning everything again.

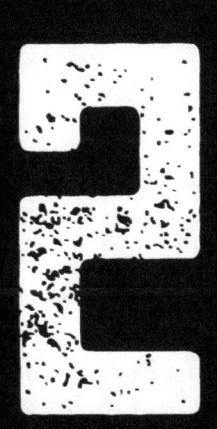

***Neptun Deep* Natural Gas Platform**
05 December 2022 | 0235 Local Time
Black Sea

In the control center for Exxon Mobil's *Neptun Deep* natural gas rig, Jonathan Evans watched readings flit across a flatscreen display while sipping from a fresh cup of coffee. He knew that, at the console behind him, Greg would be copying down the same readings, creating a paper backup just in case something happened to the digital log Evans was watching. Jonathan smiled at that and let his mind wander for a few moments.

Everyone on the team hated taking the paper logs, himself included. It was archaic, something from the previous century. But they did it. Because it was theoretically possible that the computer would shut down. Or that an erroneous coding line would translate a series of meaningful pressure and temperature readings into complete gibberish. The software engineers who'd programmed this system had calculated the probability of such events to a fraction of a fraction of a percent. It was unlikely. But it could happen. And if it happened, Murphy's Law dictated that it would happen at a critical moment. Likely at one of those junctions in engineering operations when a degree this way or that or an extra pound of pressure here or there could send a volatile system spiraling towards a catastrophic failure. Not that keeping paper logs would prevent something like that; that was nearly impossible. But keeping paper readings made it easier to reconstruct the events leading to a system failure. It would give investigators and engineers a touchstone of sorts. Just some data that would inevitably lead them to point the finger at a specific person or event as a cause or contributing factor. Because of that, and because of the need to ensure that catastrophic failures didn't repeat, Jonathan's team took readings the old-fashioned way.

On reflection, Jonathan admitted that there was another reason. Computer systems and software could miss something. A simple programming glitch could transmit an incorrect signal. If that happened, the automated safety system might not shut down the rig properly. That signal could be detected by near real-time trend analysis. By looking for the piece of data that didn't quite fit. By recognizing that certain critical readings were heading in the wrong direction. And that was another reason a team of human beings were tasked to painstakingly scribble data into a series of labeled boxes and note the time that each reading occurred.

Better safe than sorry.

"Pressure is coming up," the foreman announced. That was a formality. Everyone could see the readings scrolling across an impressive array of screens mounted on two of the room's four main walls.

Jonathan smiled again as he continued to monitor the data in front of him. He was thinking about every aspect of the test. He imagined he could see the test team, each man or woman in his or her place. Most of them were safety observers, people designated to watch over very specific portions of the rig and report at the first indication of an issue. But there one person out there—an experienced field engineer with thirty years of work on her resume—who was actually making things happen. She was elsewhere on the rig—actually less than one hundred feet from where he stood drinking coffee—and she was artificially increasing system pressure. She would continue to raise the pressure until three things happened. First, within fifteen percent of the rig's designed maximum operating pressure, an alarm klaxon would sound and the relevant readings would begin flashing red on the giant displays in the control center. Next, if no actions were taken to correct the over-pressure condition, a series of safety valves would automatically shift position to relieve the excess pressure. Last, if the valves and human intervention failed to reduce pressure in the main, the control computer's safety program would shut down the entire rig. That was what Evans and his team were here to witness. A successful test of the automatic safety systems was the final hurdle in placing the rig online and moving portions of Europe away from their dependence on Russian energy.

K-561 *Kazan*
05 December 2022 | 0245 Local Time
Black Sea

Ten kilometers due east of the *Neptun Deep* rig, Captain First Rank Ivan Sergeyevich Korov turned to his sonar officer and raised an eyebrow.

"All clear, Captain. Just the *Brixton* and several other surface contacts. All civilian traffic."

Korov nodded and took the three steps into the attack center. The *Kazan*'s navigator, a twenty-eight-year-old senior lieutenant, greeted him with the expected report.

"We're in position, Captain. Periscope depth, three hundred meters off the *Brixton*'s port quarter."

Korov clapped the man on the shoulder. "Very good, Dima. Keep us on station. No closer than this."

"Yes, Captain," the navigator answered. Korov noticed the man was sweating.

Well, why shouldn't he be? They were sitting three hundred meters from a tanker so some prima donnas could play their little commando games. And some political hacks could stir the pot.

While Korov didn't know exactly what the silent man and his team had on their agenda, he could hazard a guess. Korov didn't regard himself as a politically astute man; his job required too much of his time and energy to waste much of it on the political games played in Moscow. But he did read the news. Moscow and Washington and London had been flexing their muscles lately, mostly over Romania and several of her Black Sea neighbors.

Romania, working with Western energy companies, had recently made public the discovery of a reservoir containing more than thirty billion cubic meters—a highly conservative estimate, according to Russian intelligence—of natural gas. The nearest well to the *Kazan*, Exxon's *Neptun Deep*, was ready to swing into full production. When it did so, Korov's intelligence briefings stated that it would supply Romania, Ukraine, and several other European nations with something they badly needed. Something they'd almost entirely depended on Russia for. Those nations would become something the world knew as "energy independent." Korov remembered his political theory from school. With energy independence came a whole new economic lifestyle. An energy-independent nation could find itself flush with cash. Cash enough to buy new friends.

And discard the old ones.

Korov picked up a nearby handset and gave his next set of orders.

M/V *Brixton*
05 December 2022 | 0248 Local Time
Black Sea

Oliver Wallace looked at his watch for the tenth time in as many minutes and suspected it might be broken. The numbers didn't seem to be changing, or weren't changing fast enough. His knees and back were screaming at him and a saying from one of his American friends, a retired Navy commander from Texas, popped into his head.

I'm too old for this shit.

Wallace smiled and went back to scanning the horizon and his displays.

Fifteen more minutes.

***Neptun Deep* Natural Gas Platform**
05 December 2022 | 0250 Local Time
Black Sea

Jonathan Evans knew leaning forward had no bearing on the test he was running, but he couldn't help himself. The test engineer had raised system pressure past every safety set point except one, and Jonathan's leaning closer to the display was an instinctive reaction to the situation. Intellectually, he knew what would happen when the pressure increased just fifty additional pounds per square inch. He wouldn't miss anything. Not if he was one inch from the screen and not if he was ten feet from the screen. With the pressure fifty pounds higher—forty pounds now, actually—the rig's extensive safety programming would dispatch hundreds of shutdown signals. Pumps would stop. Valves would shift position to reroute excess pressure to safe locations. Alarms would sound. Then everything would go nearly quiet. It would happen soon and Jonathan would witness the event. He'd sign for the test. And the *Neptun Deep* rig would be fully operational. It was exciting. The culmination of years of hard work and headaches. So, he leaned into his screen in much the same way kids did when they were trying to find the hidden killer in a horror movie.

One of the operators called out. "Max pressure shutdown!"

Before the man had finished speaking, alarms sounded and Jonathan's eyes followed the events on the display in front of him. He saw warning lights for pump shutdown and watched as the digital map displayed the valve shifts that rerouted excess pressure safely away from the main. Chatter filled the room as technicians acknowledged each alarm and took no other actions.

That was part of the test. The rig had to put itself in a safe condition and it had to do so with no human intervention. That process took precisely three minutes. The displays changed. Over-pressurized portions of the system that had been flashing red before now indicated green. Digital pressure readings were compared with analog readings at more than thirty locations on the rig. Pumps stopped by computer commands were verified stopped by the technicians who maintained them.

The control center on Exxon's *Neptun Deep* rig went dead silent for a full fifteen seconds after the final verbal report was radioed in. Twenty pairs of eyes checked and rechecked every reading and display. Then the cheering started.

**M/V *Brixton*
05 December 2022 |0252 Local Time
Black Sea**

At the *Brixton*'s stern, a lone figure slipped over the ship's railing and crouched on the deck. He scanned the area through the sight of a suppressed AK-74M. Satisfied that his intrusion had gone unnoticed and the area was clear, he announced that fact over a small, waterproof radio.

In ninety seconds, he was joined by the remaining eight members of his team, the last man ensuring that the wire-rope ladder was firmly secured in place. He checked his watch, got a nod from the last member of the team, and gave the order for his troops to begin their deadly work.

Colonel Ilya Gregorovitch Chernitsky and Sergeant Sasha Ivanovitch Vorobyov were assigned to the ship's superstructure. They were the first team to move off, heading for the tanker's bridge. They needed to move across the cluttered deck and up the superstructure to take control of the vessel's bridge crew and, more importantly, the communication systems located there. This, both men knew, needed to be done silently and fast. Once that was done, the rest of the team would scour the ship and execute all aboard.

Chernitsky and Vorobyov moved forward in the shadows of bulk containers and deck gear, each man taking smooth, exaggerated steps and keeping a wary eye out for both movement and possible trip hazards. Ships, as a rule, were noisy places and cargo ships were doubly so. But a ship's crew developed the ability to subconsciously ignore routine noises and focus on sounds that were something other than ordinary. Tripping over a wrench or a chain left on the deck would announce the Spetsnaz team's presence as surely as an air raid siren.

Halfway to the superstructure Chernitsky spotted a single crewman walking through the stacks. He pressed himself deep into a shadow and signaled for Vorobyov to do the same. They watched as the sailor approached, a flashlight waving back and forth in a lazy arc that simultaneously announced the man's boredom and his confidence that all was as he expected it to be.

Chernitsky signaled to Vorobyov and went back to scanning forward and to the sides. He felt movement at his back as the experienced sergeant shifted in place behind him. Chernitsky knew what was happening without looking. Vorobyov would have secured his rifle using the chest harness and cloth strap designed for the purpose before drawing a suppressed MP-443 Grach 9mm pistol. They would wait, invisible in the shadows, as the sailor's tour brought him to within arm's reach for Vorobyov and then...

The sailor stepped past both Russians without seeing either of them, his flashlight in one hand and a cigarette in the other. Chernitsky felt movement to his rear and forced himself not to look.

Vorobyov moved with the speed of an attacking snake. As the sailor passed, he stepped quickly from the shadows and clamped his muscled left forearm across the man's neck. He took two steps backwards, dragging the startled sailor behind him as his right hand brought the suppressed pistol up towards the back of his victim's skull. As soon as the pistol made contact, Vorobyov squeezed the trigger once and sidestepped, dragging the now lifeless body into the alcove where Chernitsky still hid, providing overwatch. Vorobyov laid the body in the shadow and confirmed the absence of a pulse. Satisfied, he holstered his pistol, unslung his rifle, and squeezed Chernitsky's shoulder. The colonel remained still for a one-count before moving forward to the next row of containers. It took the two men ninety seconds to clear the remainder of the deck and climb the metal stairs leading to the bridge.

♦ ♦ ♦

Oliver Wallace looked to the radar display and then back to the engine readouts. He noted that the readings on one of the *Brixton*'s huge propulsion diesel engines were slightly abnormal. The oil pressures and temperatures were running hot. Nothing major, just a few degrees above what was the norm for the vessel's current speed. He had just picked up the phone to call the *Brixton*'s engineering officer when movement to his right caught his eye.

Two men were entering the bridge. The first swung in and

pivoted left. The second moved in a moment later and pivoted right. Wallace watched each man scan the bridge through the top-mounted sights of a rifle, too fascinated by the sight to recognize the danger.

◆ ◆ ◆

Chernitsky followed Vorobyov into the bridge, pivoting to his right as he did so to clear his sector and knowing that Vorobyov was busy doing the same thing to the after portion of the *Brixton*'s wheelhouse. It took less than two seconds for Chernitsky's rifle to present a sight picture of a sailor with a telephone handset in one hand. Chernitsky's right index finger depressed the trigger of his rifle twice, discharging two rounds into the man's chest with a sound no louder than the pop of the powder charge and the mechanical clack of the weapon's bolt. Chernitsky saw the man go down and continued scanning until his sector of the bridge was clear.

"Clear!" Vorobyov announced.

"Clear," Chernitsky agreed. He scanned the entire room one more time before transmitting to the seven members of the team still waiting on the after deck. "All teams, go."

It took less than thirty seconds for the Spetsnaz teams to begin reporting portions of the ship as cleared. They were moving smoothly and methodically, performing a well-rehearsed ballet of death as Vorobyov dogged the bridge hatches shut and the colonel familiarized himself with the bridge controls. They'd been briefed on what to expect and were pleasantly surprised to note that the information was almost completely accurate.

Chernitsky located the ship's voyage management controls and began the process of programming in a series of waypoints that would lead the vessel to her final destination. After double-checking the data, the colonel handed navigation control of the ship back to the computer and began shutting off every safety system on the ship. Chernitsky finished his task by securing power to every external light on the vessel. When he was done, he looked to Vorobyov.

"Time?"

Vorobyov checked his watch. "Five minutes. Two teams complete with their sweep. One sector remaining."

"And the packages?"

Vorobyov grinned. "In place. Wired with the timer set."

Chernitsky nodded as reports continued to broadcast in his earpiece. He took one final look at the voyage management controls.

"Move, Sasha."

The two men undogged the bridge's portside hatch and began retracing their path back to the vessel's stern. In ninety seconds, all nine Spetsnaz operators were at the railing and beginning their descent back to the rubber craft waiting below.

Neptun Deep Natural Gas Platform
05 December 2022 | 0315 Local Time
Black Sea

There was no alcohol on the rig. A few bottles of champagne to toast the rig's success might have been just the ticket, but corporate rules prohibited such things. It was a rule that most of the team agreed to be archaic, but it was a rule nonetheless and running a natural gas rig was far too dangerous to jeopardize in that way. Besides, they all agreed, a cooler full of ice-cold sodas wasn't a bad consolation prize.

Jonathan Evans grabbed a fresh drink and popped the top open. They'd already transmitted the test results off to corporate and he suddenly found himself without much to do. He clapped a few members of his team on the back and stepped out of the rig's main control room and on to a catwalk.

He leaned against the railing, sipping his drink and looking off into the darkness. He really did enjoy this work. It was true that drilling into the earth was not without risks. Only a fool, he told himself, believed otherwise. But in this case, he thought the risks justified. After all, without this rig, the majority of Eastern Europe would remain dependent on Russian companies like Gazprom to fulfill their energy needs. Jonathan wasn't anything close to the politician people assumed he had to be, but he understood the economic impact energy independence had on countries like Romania and Ukraine.

He peered out into the darkness and continued enjoying his drink. There wasn't much to see or hear out there. The lighting on the rig all but destroyed night vision, and the rig was a noisy collection of piping and machinery that drowned out the otherwise peaceful sounds of a relatively calm evening at sea.

Evans was raising his can of soda for another sip when he heard his name called over the rig's loudspeakers. He took one last look at the darkness beyond the lights and walked the forty feet back into the control center.

"Someone call?" he asked, suspecting that Exxon HQ had transmitted a message acknowledging the successful test.

The rig foreman waved him over to a console. "Sir, we got a ship inbound."

Jonathan cocked his head to the side. "Really?"

The foreman nodded and pointed. "Here, sir. Just picked it up on radar."

He leaned forward to look at the screen. He wasn't familiar with radar systems and was having trouble interpreting the data shown on the large display. "Ships pass here all the time, right?"

The radar operator answered. "True, sir. But usually not this close, and this contact hasn't changed course or speed for several minutes."

Jonathan turned to the foreman. "What's that mean?"

The man shrugged his large shoulders. "Could be disabled. Adrift." The foreman turned to the next desk to his left. "Comms? Have you tried hailing that ship?"

The woman seated at the communications console nodded. "Four times, sir. No response."

The foreman turned back to the radar operator and ran his fingers over his shaved scalp. "Distance and speed?"

"A little over two nautical miles. Thirteen knots."

Jonathan had been cut out of the conversation. "What's going on?"

The foreman turned. "What's going on is that we've got a vessel out there headed straight for us that is unresponsive to communications and appears to have lost steerage."

"What's that mean?"

"It means we have one hell of a problem." The foreman turned to the radar operator again. "Do you know what ship that is?"

"The *Brixton*. UK registry, sir. Container ship."

The foreman swore and Evans looked at him. "What?"

"That's a five thousand TEU hull."

"In English?"

"It's a big damn boat and it's heading right here."

"How big?"

"About as big as one of your navy's aircraft carriers."

As Evans processed that information, the foreman took three steps to a nearby bulkhead and slammed his massive fist into a large red button, setting off a massive array of sirens and rotating warning lights.

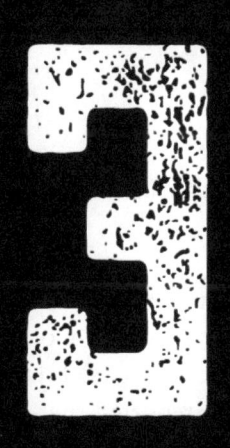

M/V *Brixton*
05 December 2022 | 0318 Local Time
Black Sea

Oliver Wallace tried to push himself off the floor and failed. He collapsed, landing face-down in a pool of his own blood. He'd been shot twice in the chest—the intense burning told him that—and a distant part of his mind reported that he probably did not have long to live. He was having difficulty breathing and his mouth was filled with the coppery taste of blood. He'd watched the two men who'd entered the bridge hover over the ship's controls. Wallace did not know what they'd done, but he was certain it wasn't good. He told himself that he needed get up, to look at what they'd done and broadcast an emergency call. He knew he was running out of time.

Wallace tried using his arms to pull himself across the now slippery deck. His legs weren't functioning and he could feel his body weakening. A strange, almost euphoric feeling crept over his body and his mind told him it had to be shock. His breathing was labored and he began coughing, his lungs trying to expel the blood pooling there.

Wallace was able to pull himself to within arm's reach of the control console. He reached up. His body had begun to convulse, and frothy, pink blood dribbled down his unshaven chin. His hand closed around one of the chrome bars affixed to the front of the console. He pulled with all the remaining strength he possessed, but it was not enough. Oliver Wallace collapsed on the deck at the foot of the ship's control console, pulling the handset for one of the *Brixton*'s expensive radios off its mount as he tried to stop his fall.

Eyes closed, Wallace lay sprawled against the console. He recognized the feel of the handset in his fingers. He held it to his head and tried to speak into it. His voice was weak and raspy. He heard nothing in the earpiece. He tried to speak again and realized that the cable leading from the handset to the console was not taut. He ran his free hand down the curled black cord, coughing and sputtering as he did so. When he reached the end and held it up, he saw the frayed wiring and his eyes went wide. The overhead, lit by bright, fluorescent bulbs, darkened quickly. The last sensation Oliver Wallace felt was a massive shudder as the *Brixton* pushed hard into a rolling sea.

Neptun Deep Natural Gas Platform
05 December 2022 | 0320 Local Time
Black Sea

Jonathan Evans stayed with the foreman as the alarm klaxons threatened to deafen him. They'd gone out on the catwalk, each man holding a pair of binoculars. Before racing from the control center, the foreman had ordered all lighting on the seaward half of the rig turned off. They both began scanning the horizon, frantically trying to get a visual on the ship.

"What the hell good does this do?" Evans had to yell over the blaring sirens to make himself heard.

"Doesn't do a damn thing!"

"Then why the hell are we out here?" Panic crept into his voice. He could hear it.

"Just trying to get a look before we ditch. Maybe it ain't gonna hit. Radars can be wrong, you know. I want to be sure before I tell folks to head for the boats. That water down there is cold as shit."

"What?"

The foreman pointed down. "Sea ain't exactly calm, and it's not exactly the easiest thing in the world to keep a ship on course. Even a heavy monster like the *Brixton*. If I put folks in the boats and this thing ain't gonna hit…" His voice trailed off.

Jonathan nodded and looked around. Behind him, he could see dozens of people scrambling towards the lower decks and the life rafts there. The foreman had sent word for the crew to head that way, just in case. It looked like everyone was taking the matter seriously. He turned back to the foreman.

"How long do we have?"

The foreman started to respond, but stopped. Binoculars still to his eyes, he extended an arm and pointed. "There she is."

Jonathan looked through his binoculars. At first, he couldn't see anything. He kept looking, scanning to his left and right without leaving the general area that the foreman had indicated. He was about to ask where when he saw it. A massive black shape that occulted the stars beyond, given away only by the frothy wake at what had to be the bow. He felt his heart drop and his blood run cold.

"Holy shit!"

The foreman got on his radio and ordered everyone to abandon the rig. He grabbed Jonathan by the arm and dragged him along the catwalk. "Move!"

Jonathan began racing along the metal gratings as fast as his panicked legs could carry him. He stumbled twice, the sharp, skid-resistant grating of the catwalks ripping through his pant legs and shredding the skin on his knees and shins. The two men reached the end of the walkway and sped down the steep stairs, taking them three steps at a time.

◆ ◆ ◆

The *Brixton*'s one-hundred-and-twenty-thousand-pound bulk pounded through the waves, heading directly for the *Neptun Deep* natural gas rig. Without a crew to steer it or disable the autopilot, the ship proceeded on its programmed course as if the rig wasn't even there.

The massive container ship plowed into the rig, the bow driving straight through the abandoned control center and slicing into the main portion of the structure. The screeching of metal-on-metal contact was deafening. Below the waterline, the ship's hull buckled several of the legs supporting the rig, snapping them like particularly fragile bones. The decks of the rig began to sag and bend out of the way as the ship continued driving forward. Piping fractured and massive electrical cables were ripped apart as the bulk of the ship kept pushing through, driven by her powerful diesel engines and colossal propellers.

Several small fires started as the *Brixton* pushed her way over, and through, *Neptun Deep*'s collection of pipes, cables, offices, staterooms, and catwalks. Machinery and gear throughout the rig were dislodged by the violent passage of the hull and thrown aside, crashing into the water below. As the debris fell, the crew of the rig scrambled to get clear. Some people dove and jumped from the lower catwalks, and some were thrown, along with the debris, into the sea and on top of the staffers and rafts already in the water. Two rafts took direct hits from large pieces of piping and sank, everyone aboard killed instantly by the impact. Two individuals who'd donned thick orange lifejackets were trying to swim away from the rig and were crushed by flying debris. Dozens of others saw this, shed their jackets, and dove to avoid similar fates.

◆ ◆ ◆

Jonathan found himself holding onto a stanchion for dear life as the whole rig shook. He'd been halfway down a catwalk when the *Brixton*'s bow had plowed into the rig. The force of the impact had thrown the foreman into the sea below and Jonathan had only been saved by the fact that the portion of the catwalk he'd been racing through was partially covered by a lattice-work of white painted metal that looked like the front of every gym locker he'd ever had. He'd been thrown against the metal lattice, and instinct alone had caused him to latch onto the nearest object and squeeze before he toppled into the water below.

He tried to pull himself up, tried to swing a leg high enough to get a foothold as he felt his grip weaken. His heart was pounding. He could feel it racing away in his chest and he could hear it pulsing in his ears, somehow drowning out the horrendous screech of ripping I-beams and shredded piping.

The shaking was getting worse as the *Brixton* continued its passage, the widening hull continuing to shove portions of the cleaved rig away from the ship. Jonathan grunted and stopped struggling long enough to take a deep breath. Then, he pulled with all his might. His jaw clenched down so hard it felt like his teeth might crack. His muscles strained. His forearms burned. The sharp, damaged edge of the safety cage tore into his chest. Slowly, he began to move upward. When his waist cleared the edge of the cage, he took another breath, gripped the stanchion tighter, and kicked his legs to the left. One of his boots caught and Jonathan dug in with his heel. He took another deep breath and strained again, pulling himself fully onto the destroyed catwalk and using his feet and arms to brace himself.

♦ ♦ ♦

Fully one-half of the *Brixton* had passed through the rig when the devices set by the Spetsnaz team reached time zero. In each case, a short electrical impulse traveled just a few inches to RDX-based blasting caps. All but one of the caps exploded. The spiderwebbed trunklines of Primacord exploded next, each line sending an explosive signal downstream at nearly eight thousand meters per second. Each line terminated at an explosive charge placed by the Russian commandos to ensure that the *Brixton* could not stay afloat. These charges went off nearly simultaneously, blowing massive holes in the hull and destroying the integrity of the twelve-inch seawater cooling mains on board the 120,000-ton cargo ship. Every major compartment was instantly vented to the sea. The icy waters of the Black Sea rushed into the hull, racing through every room and passage with the force of a freight train. The Spetsnaz team had shut down every damage control system on the ship and had disabled the vessel's emergency power generators. They needn't have bothered. It took less than thirty seconds for the rampaging seawater to find and destroy the ship's main power distribution switchboards. Within seconds, the entire ship went dark. Two minutes later, the *Brixton* was already down twenty feet at the keel and listing heavily to port.

◆ ◆ ◆

Jonathan Evans had just gotten himself onto the narrow ledge when the *Brixton* exploded. Geysers of flame, debris, and water shot through the air just below the young systems engineer. He saw none of this. He was thrown off his latticed perch and towards the icy sea and the pools of burning fuel there. He had time for one short scream that stopped when his body slammed into the surface eighty feet below.

Frigate *Admiral Makarov*, Russian Navy
05 December 2022 | 0330 Local Time
Black Sea

Fifteen miles east of the carnage at *Neptun Deep*, Colonel Chernitsky stood on the flight deck of the *Admiral Makarov*, a Grigorovich-class frigate assigned to the Black Sea Fleet's 30th Surface Ship Division. He borrowed a cigarette from the aft lookout and lit it. It was, he knew, an awful habit for someone in his line of work. He knew he'd have to quit eventually, but there was something about smoking that his body loved at a time like this. They'd completed their part of this operation and all that was left was to sink the raiding craft and sail away. They'd taken no casualties—not that he'd expected any—and the only injury had occurred when one of his team had nicked a forearm in the *Brixton*'s engine room. Success, he'd always thought, warranted celebration. Vodka, Chernitsky reflected, would have hit the spot, but that vice was frowned upon at sea. So, he sated himself with smoking. He'd had a doctor explain the chemical processes involved in burning and inhaling nicotine at his last annual physical, but it was not something he'd cared to remember. Chernitsky took a long drag and held his breath, savoring the rich flavor of the Turkish tobacco. He exhaled and leaned over the wire and steel flight deck nets.

"Sasha Ivanovitch! My mother can do this faster."

Sergeant Vorobyov finished placing a small explosive charge and looked up. He laughed. "*Da*. That's probably true. But she's been doing this longer. She is three days older than dirt."

Chernitsky shook his head and smiled. "For that, I should leave you in the boat with your explosives. How much longer?"

Vorobyov looked around, running his eyes over the arrangement. "I think it's done." He walked to the front of the rubber craft and began climbing the thin wire-rope ladder to the *Makarov*'s flight deck. He reached the top and Chernitsky helped him over the top rail of the upright safety net.

"We're good?" Chernitsky asked.

"*Da*, Colonel." Vorobyov checked his watch. "Five minutes."

Chernitsky flipped his cigarette into the sea. "Good. Cast off the lines. I'll let the captain know to get us out of here."

K-561 *Kazan*
05 December 2022 | 0331 Local Time
Black Sea

Two miles south of the *Makarov*, Captain Ivan Sergeyevich Korov read the message he'd just been handed and smiled. To anyone else, the note was gibberish, just a collection of letter groups that translated into a few unrelated words. To Korov, the seemingly random words meant freedom from a task he'd hated from the very first. It was an acknowledgment of a job well done and permission to take the *Kazan* back into the icy shadows where she belonged.

Korov smiled again and ordered his submarine to reverse course and descend into the depths of the Black Sea.

USS *Key West*, United States Navy
05 December 2022 | 0332 Local Time
Black Sea

Five miles east of the *Kazan*, the USS *Key West*, a thirty-six-year-old Los Angeles–class attack submarine, hovered just below the thermocline layer. With relatively warmer water above, the American submarine was able to hide from surface contacts in the Black Sea's Cold Intermediate Layer, an anoxic basin of water that available intel and an array of expensive sensors indicated was just above freezing.

Commander Scott Reynes peered at the waterfall displays. "Talk to me, Chief."

"I don't know, sir. It's a mess up there. Surface contacts all over the place." Chief Sonar Technician Jerome Hughley concentrated on his screen. "Lots of tankers. A warship. Grigorovich-class frigate, I think. He's moving off to the north. Something smaller near there for a few moments that dropped off. And that mass of noise there." The bulky chief pointed at the screen. "Mechanical transient. Like metal breaking."

"And the explosion," Reynes added.

Hughley nodded. "Yessir. And that." He paused. "It's a ways off. Maybe thirty-five thousand yards."

Reynes did the math. "Twenty miles, give or take." He patted the chief on the shoulder. "Good work. Keep listening."

Reynes stepped into the attack center. USS *Key West* was, he saw, rigged for battle. Each member of the crew was at his or her battle station, sent there by his order after the explosion had been reported. He scanned the space, taking in the data from each display, dial, and gauge.

"XO?"

"Battle stations manned, Captain," Lieutenant Commander Will Sandler reported. "We're stopped."

"Thanks, XO." A pause. Reynes turned. "Sonar, bearing to the explosion?"

"About two-nine-five, Captain. Almost due west. A little north." Hughley paused. "That's just an estimate. Should be pretty accurate, though."

A nod. "Thanks, Chief." Reynes looked over at his executive officer. "That's over by the offshore rigs, isn't it?"

"Pretty close." Sandler paused. "Some kind of accident maybe?"

Reynes shrugged. He was about to respond when Chief Hughley's voice cut through the thick silence.

"Conn, Sonar. Submerged contact. Bearing two-seven-two. I got hull-popping noises."

Reynes head snapped around. "Where'd he come from, Chief?"

"No idea, sir. Just showed up." Hughley paused. "Bet he was up above the layer, Captain. Up in the surface noise. Designate

Sierra-Twelve."

"Distance to contact?"

A lengthy pause. "Shit. He's close, Captain. Less'n ten grand."

Reynes pursed his lips. "XO, get the tracking party on it."

Sandler started to acknowledge the order when Hughley's voice cut through the space again.

"Conn, Sonar. Explosions. Small ones."

Reynes and Sandler exchanged a look.

"Where, Sonar?" the captain barked.

"Same line of bearing the frigate was on. About three-one-zero. About ten thousand yards."

Reynes scowled. "What the hell is going on?"

4

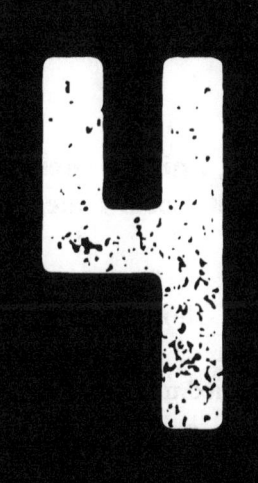

USS *James E. Williams*, United States Navy
05 December 2022 | 0400 Local Time
Black Sea

Chief Petty Officer Brian Thompson tore his eyes away from the computer screen in front of him. He leaned back in his chair, rubbed his eyes, and listened to the noises around him. There were the usual sounds of an office. Behind him, sailors who'd just come off the 2200 to 0200 midwatch hacked away at keyboards and chatted. A phone rang and was answered. Chairs scraped across the deck. A printer was whirring away. Brian was amazed that he could hear any of it. It wasn't that he was losing his hearing, though eighteen years in engine rooms had surely done some damage. The reason he was surprised he could hear anything at all sat almost directly to his left. The engineering log room's air conditioning unit roared as it rammed hundreds of cubic feet of cooled air through a collection of sheet metal ducts and loose diffusers. It was, Brian thought, like working in a wind tunnel.

"Jesus."

"What's that?"

Brian turned to the man at the next desk over. "Evals, sir."

Lieutenant Walker, the chief engineer for USS *James E. Williams*, snorted without looking up from his own computer screen. "A hundred wrench-turning mechanics putting words on paper. What could go wrong?"

Brian waved at his screen. "It'd help if this was in English."

Walker turned. "What?"

"Evals aren't English. Well, not exactly."

"Meaning?"

Brian grabbed his mouse and scrolled. He read. "Led twelve junior sailors in completing twenty major repairs and forty maintenance tasks and saved the Navy…" Brian stopped. "It goes on like this for five lines with no punctuation. No commas. No periods or exclamation points. Just word salad."

Walker laughed. "It doesn't have to be Dumas, Chief. Or Dickens or Dostoevsky or whatever the hell it is you're reading this week."

"Gogol this week." Brian grinned and turned back to his monitor. "Shit, sir. Right now, I'd settle for Peanuts or Far Side. This hurts my brain."

Walker leaned back in his chair and stretched. "What's on your plate today?"

Brian ran his hands over the keyboard, editing the comment he'd just been criticizing. "Chief's Mess meeting this morning and another watch later. You?"

"Gotta talk to the captain about Caldwell and that debacle at his EOOW board."

Brian turned his head. "What for?"

"Captain is in a weird place on that one. Caldwell has to get that qual to move up in the surface navy. He had a chance before and missed it. This might be his last shot."

"It'd help if he knew what he was doing," Brian said.

"Yeah," Walker agreed. "Still, you were a bit rough on him at the board."

Brian turned back to his screen. "Maybe, but that's stuff every junior engineer knows. It's simple crap."

"He's never going to stand the watch, Chief," Walker pointed out. "You know that."

"I don't give quals away, sir," Brian said. "Especially if they're never gonna actually stand that watch."

Walker was about to respond when a voice interrupted the conversation. "Chief?"

Brian turned in his chair and saw one of his sailors standing by the door. He waved the sailor over. "What can I do for you, Faulkner?"

The sailor looked nervous and Brian found that odd. Normally, Faulkner was an energetic and confident young man. As he stood there in the doorway, his eyes searched the floor and he didn't seem to know what to do with his hands. Petty Officer Derek Faulkner was one of the rising stars in Engineering Department. He was a gas turbine mechanic with operation and repair skills that Chief Tim Guillory routinely bragged about. This was odd, Brian thought. He glanced at Walker and raised an eyebrow.

"Umm, Chief. Can we talk in private?" Faulkner didn't look up.

Brian nodded. "Sure. Let me clear the room out." Brian turned to Walker. "Sir?"

Walker started to rise. "I'll get everyone out."

"Umm, sir? You might want to stay. Maybe you and the chief can help me."

Walker nodded. He turned to the rest of the sailors in the space and shouted to be heard over the air conditioning unit. "You folks mind stepping out for a few?"

It took a few minutes for the room to empty. When the last sailor out shut the door, Brian turned to Faulkner. "What's going on?"

"Well," Faulkner shuffled his feet, "I don't know where to start."

Brian sat, waiting. Walker leaned forward. "Is it something here, or at home?"

Faulkner didn't speak. He shifted his weight back and forth nervously. The effect was pronounced as the ship leaned into a hard turn.

Whatever Walker was going to say next was lost in a cacophony of gonging that blasted from the ship's 1MC speaker just above their heads. All three sailors looked at each other as a voice began broadcasting.

"General Quarters. General Quarters. All hands, man your battle stations."

Brian stood. "Shit." He turned to Faulkner and waved a hand at the speaker. "Come see me as soon as this is over with. Got it?"

Faulkner nodded and Brian noted a look of relief flashing across the kid's face. Well, he thought. Whatever was bothering the kid couldn't be that bad. Could it?

Faulkner left the log room and turned left, heading for Repair Five. Brian and Walker followed the young sailor out the door and turned right, heading for Central Control. It took twenty seconds for both to arrive and they found the ship's engineering nerve center in near chaos. As Walker took his place, Brian scanned the room. His console operators for general quarters were in mid-turnover with the two engineers who'd been on watch when the announcement had been made. The ship's Damage Control Assistant, Lieutenant Leslie Hunter, was already at her station, setting up comms with the assistance of four junior sailors. Everyone was pulling on flash gear—a fire-resistant gray hood and similarly capable cream gloves—and adjusting their uniforms for the event. Collars on coveralls were buttoned all the way up. Sleeves were rolled down. Everyone's pant legs were gathered and stuffed into tall black socks.

Well, Brian noted. Almost everyone's. He eyed the left sock belonging to his Electric Plant Operator—EM2 Chris Barton—and grinned. A black sock covered in emojis.

Brian turned to Damage Control Chief Quentin Kelly, the scheduled engineering officer of the watch, and listened to the man's rapid turnover. Chief Kelly, "Q" or "Chief Q" to nearly everyone on board, was one of the ship's new engineering chiefs. He'd reported the previous year while the ship was in the yards at Portsmouth.

"You got everything?" Q asked.

Brian nodded and pulled his own flash hood on. "I got it. You're relieved."

Q left the space and Brian resumed scanning. Everything was as he'd been told and, with all of the watch turnover complete, Central Control was settling back down. Brian sat and began tucking his own pant legs into his socks.

"CHENG, Any idea what's going on?"

"Not a clue, Chief."

Both men heard Hunter announce that the ship was rigged for battle. Walker turned.

"DCA, you know what's up?"

She shook her head. "No idea."

"Great," Brian grumped. "Last time we did this for real…"

The two officers nodded. Hunter, Brian saw, barely repressed a shudder.

Less than two years previous, USS *James E. Williams* had been involved in the interdiction of a stolen Pakistani nuke bound for the Indian port of Chennai. During the attempted boarding, an explosion in the ship's shaft alley had severely damaged the Arleigh Burke–class destroyer and one sailor had died in the resulting fire.

"Whatever happened to the contractor that installed the explosives?" Hunter asked.

"The Robinson bastard? Still awaiting trial, I think," Walker said.

"That's some bullshit." Hunter shook her head.

Brian stayed silent for a moment. He'd been the one to authorize Robinson's repair work, and he'd actually stood in the space and watched the man install a portion of the explosive charge. He hadn't known there were explosives hidden in the replacement parts, but there was guilt there. He told himself that he should have known, should have checked. The realist in him knew that was a garbage assessment, but whenever the subject came up, Brian's skin would flush and a ball of lead would form in his stomach.

"Should give him to us."

"Still want to keelhaul the guy, Chief?" Walker asked.

Brian shook his head. "Not with this boat. Divers scraped and blasted off all the barnacles and crap. Dude would just drown, and that's better than he deserves."

Brian leaned forward to note something in the log book when the 1MC crackled to life. Commander Derrick Allen's voice rang loud and clear.

"Good morning, USS *James E. Williams*. A few minutes ago, there was an explosion at a natural gas rig just a few miles from the Romanian coast. We don't have much info right now, but early reports indicate that a cargo ship lost steerage and propulsion control and rammed the rig. We have been directed to proceed to the location and assist with search and rescue operations."

As the captain continued his announcement, Brian leaned back to look at the map display above and slightly behind his head, wondering for the thousandth time who had thought placing it there was a good idea. He turned to Walker.

"What is that? Five miles?"

Walker was looking at the display. He nodded. "Give or take."

Brian closed his eyes for a moment, thinking. He said, "Think we're gonna need the boats?"

Walker swore. "Let me make a call." He leaned to his right and yanked a phone off its rack. As he punched in numbers, Brian scanned the engineering plant readings.

Walker hung up the phone. "They're going to pass the word to man the boat deck. Both boats." He turned to DCA. "Give the repair lockers a head's up?"

Hunter nodded and relayed the message. Walker continued. "Chief, boat engineers in the lockers today or will a space watch need relief?"

Brian had to think. "Should be in the lockers. Brooks and the new kid. Gregory."

Walker nodded. "You miss being in the boats?"

Brian turned away from the engine readouts. "Hell no. I'm too old for that shit."

"I remember a time when you wouldn't let anyone else touch them," Walker noted.

"I remember a time when no one in A-Gang knew a damn thing about those boats." Brian paused. "Or how to swim. They've changed a lot in the past year, huh?"

There were a series of nods as an order to man the boats was passed over the 1MC. Everyone felt the USS *James E. Williams* surge forward as the bridge pushed the throttles to the stops.

Kremlin Senate, President's Office
05 December 2022 | 0530 Local Time
Moscow

Russian President Dmitri Mikhailovich Barsukov strode into his office in the Kremlin Senate, a building that dated back to 1776. Barsukov was tall and thin, a pale man with angular features, a shaved head, and a short, well-groomed beard and mustache that was currently free of the gray and white hairs normal for a man in his mid-fifties. He was fit and athletic and he worked hard to stay that way. Barsukov regularly subjected himself to the demands of an array of personal trainers and dieticians. Not out of a fit of narcissism. Out of necessity.

Russia, Barsukov believed, had employed too many weak men. Too many fragile individuals had been elevated to the office he now held. They had projected their weakness to the world. On television. On radio. In newspapers. In person. And Russia had nearly died for it.

Barsukov thought about that as he removed his suit jacket and began rolling up the sleeves of a white cotton shirt. What had they expected? A nation like Russia, with its history and a long line of enemies, could not be led by weak men. But that was what had happened. Gorbachev had knelt before the world with his glasnost and perestroika nonsense. Chernenko had been a wheezing disaster, seventy-two years old with a failing heart when he'd taken over. And Andropov. Nothing on that old bastard had been working. His organs had fought each other for the right to kill him off. Same with Brezhnev, who had died of a massive heart attack. His own predecessor, a maniac at the end, had suffered a massive heart attack just days after being pronounced fit by an array of doctors.

Barsukov shook his head and muttered to himself. Russia could only be led by a strong man, someone who could, and would, stand up to the world.

Especially the Americans.

Barsukov jabbed a finger at his intercom. "Send them in."

The doors to the presidential office opened a moment later and two men entered.

Barsukov eyed both of them. "Report."

The shorter of the two was Admiral Fyodor Kirilovich Borshevsky. He was the Commander-in-Chief of the Russian Navy and was, the president noted, resplendent in the dress blue uniform of an admiral of the Russian Navy.

Borshevsky spoke. His voice was even and low, a rumbling sound that one expected from a much larger man. "Mr. President, the commander on scene reports all objectives met. The *Neptun Deep* rig is a total loss and the team is aboard the *Makarov*. As we discussed, portions of the Black Sea Fleet are now blockading the entrance to the Black Sea, and we will release the statement declaring that this is necessary for security purposes within the hour."

Barsukov nodded. "And the American destroyer, Admiral?"

"They arrived on scene fifteen minutes ago, with orders to conduct search and rescue operations."

Barsukov nodded again, a short bob of the head. He turned to the taller man. This man, Igor Romanovich Tolstov, was the head of SVR. He was taller and thinner than Barsukov. His sallow skin and deep, dark eyes gave him an almost undead look that the Russian president found unsettling. As good as the SVR Director was, something about the man made Barsukov distrust him. He was, the president knew, a man to be wary of. A man to be handled delicately. "And your part of the operation. Is it ready?"

Tolstov nodded. "Yes, Mr. President. Everything is in place. Both here and abroad."

Barsukov sat down without indicating to his guests that they could do the same. He ran through the operation in his mind and reviewed the necessity for such action. He smiled inwardly at the name of the operation.

Nightingale.

An old Russian folktale about a half-human, half-bird creature who could whistle up destruction and chaos in order to seize whatever it was that he wanted.

Nightingale the Robber.

Barsukov's eyes flitted back and forth between his guests' faces as his mind worked through his problems.

Despite more than a decade of progress under his leadership, the Russian economy was still vulnerable. Oil and gas represented sixty percent of Russia's exports, and that constituted a full third of the nation's GDP. Europe was Russia's biggest client and there was—had been, he corrected himself—little in the way of competition through the years. Russia had a supply of energy resources and Europe needed them. It should have been simple.

But it wasn't. New wells of oil and gas had been discovered in the Black Sea, and Russia had no claim on any of it. It was, he reflected, as if a new petrol station had opened in his neighborhood. The new station was more convenient and better suited to provide Europe with what it needed.

And if that happened? If Europe stopped buying from Russia? If they became truly independent? Then what?

Barsukov knew the answer. Everyone knew the answer. If Russia lost influence in Europe, if these nations developed a sense of independence, Russia would lose both financially and diplomatically. Independent European nations would worry less about making deals with America that might anger Russia. That concept was simple. But if Russia supplied a majority of the energy needs for Europe, then Russia retained power. Nations would not go out of their way to offend the provider of such resources because there were repercussions for doing so. What was the American saying? Don't bite the hand that feeds you. Barsukov smiled to himself. Not very poetic, but the point was valid.

Russia needed control of the Black Sea fields.

Russia could have taken the fields by force, but that would have meant securing the pipelines on land—and that meant a military invasion of several sovereign nations. That was something Barsukov believed Russia could do, but only temporarily. He did not see any situation in which Russia could invade a good portion of Europe without provoking a Western response.

Barsukov and several handpicked men had struggled for several months before a plan had begun to take shape. Russia needed to own the pipelines. To take them, but not by force. Russia needed undeniable legal rights to the pipelines, the rigs, and the vast fields of oil and gas they served.

It had become known that the companies who currently owned the rigs, like Exxon, were interested in selling, but proposals from Russian energy companies had been universally ignored in favor of Western buyers.

That fact, ironically, had provided Barsukov with his answer. It was simple. All Russia needed to do was scare off the other buyers.

The Russian president looked at the two men standing in front of his desk. "Nightingale may proceed on both fronts."

USS *James E. Williams*, United States Navy
05 December 2022 | 0600 Local Time
Black Sea

USS *James E. Williams* had been on station near the *Neptun Deep* rig for an hour before Commander Allen stood the ship down from battle stations and began focusing on search and rescue operations. Brian held the watch as EOOW for an additional fifteen minutes after that, waiting for the ship to finish launching one of its two MH-60R Seahawk helicopters to aid in the efforts. Once the evolution was complete, he signed the watch over and headed topside.

Brian emerged midships amid near-freezing temperatures and a gently rolling sea and scanned the area. The ship was trolling almost a mile from the rig and debris seemed to be everywhere. Brian walked to the starboard side and found the ship's Chief Bosun, a large bear of a man named Jason Roberts, leaning on the rails.

"Jason."

The bigger man turned. "Brian. You see this shit?" He waved a massive hand at the over the lifelines.

Brian looked over the side. Wrecked furniture, concave sections of sheet metal, filthy life jackets, and parts of what Brian guessed could only be mattresses bumped and rubbed against the hull.

"Jesus." He looked at Jason. "What happened?"

"Logan stopped by earlier. Said the same thing the skipper did. Cargo ship rammed the rig."

Brian looked out at the wrecked rig. It was a mutilated mess of piping and steel beams. It was almost unrecognizable as a rig. "Where's the ship?"

Jason shrugged. "Hell if I know. Sailed on by?"

"Maybe it sank," Brian offered.

"No way." Jason said. "Surface tracks say it was the *Brixton*. Hundred and twenty thousand tons. I looked it up. Too big to sink from something like this."

Brian nodded. "That's the size of a Ford-class carrier." He looked out at the remnants of the rig again. "Damn."

**Frigate *Admiral Makarov*, Russian Navy
05 December 2022 | 0605 Local Time
Black Sea**

Ten miles northeast of the rig, Captain Yuri Nikolayevich Dashkov read the message in his hand. He read it again. And a third time.

"Son of a bitch," he breathed. "We're really going through with this."

"Sir?"

Dashkov looked up, saw his operations officer watching him. He folded the message, tucking it into the pocket of his uniform trousers, and smiled at the younger man.

"Follow me, Lieutenant."

"Yes, sir."

The two men walked forward, heading up two ladders enroute to the *Makarov*'s cramped bridge. Dashkov looked around, saw everyone doing their job. They looked like professionals. Hell, he thought, they *were* professionals. They were well trained and disciplined. They always delivered. In drills. In exercises. This, Dashkov admitted, would be different. This was the real thing. He checked the nearby charts.

"Officer of the Deck. Sound battle stations and make your course two-one-zero."

The young officer acknowledged his orders and turned to carry them out. As the gonging started, the *Makarov*'s operations officer leaned close to his captain. He'd checked the charts too.

"The rig, Captain?"

Dashkov nodded.

"To do what, sir?"

Dashkov glanced at the man, saw the nervous look on his face. Gorshkov, he thought. The kid—he didn't look more than twenty—bore one of the Russian Navy's great surnames. Not by accident. He was distantly related to Admiral Sergey Gorshkov, a Hero of the Soviet Union who'd once commanded the Black Sea Fleet before taking over the entire Soviet Navy. Dashkov wondered if this child had inherited more than just a name.

"Pavel Stefanovich, we are going to pick a fight with the Americans."

5

USS *James E. Williams*, United States Navy
05 December 2022 | 0730 Local Time
Black Sea

Chief Petty Officer Brian Thompson walked into the Chief's Mess on board USS *James E. Williams*, a mug of coffee in one hand and a file folder stuffed with evaluations and notes on each of Engineering Department's nine first class petty officers in the other. Given the ongoing search and rescue operations, he did not expect the scheduled ranking board to take place—the Mess Association meeting earlier that day had been canceled—but he figured he'd show up anyway. He saw Logan Carrillo, the ship's command master chief, scribbling in a notebook and selected a chair next to him.

"How's it going?"

Carrillo looked up. "It's going." He pointed at the folder in Brian's hand. "Those for the ranking board?"

Brian nodded. "Yeah. Didn't figure the meeting would happen, but just in case."

Carrillo went back to writing. "You're probably right. How are the boats doing?"

Brian shrugged. "No idea. Haven't heard anything except the calls for the Oil King to set up for refueling."

"Really?" Carrillo looked up and blinked. "I remember a time—"

Brian cut him off with a raised hand. "I had this same conversation with CHENG."

Carrillo grinned. "Don't miss being in the boats?"

Brian shook his head. "Nope. With a torn-up ankle and a jacked-up neck, I don't miss it one bit."

Carrillo eyed Brian for a moment and leaned back over his notebook. "You're different."

Brian took a sip from his mug. "How so?"

"A year ago, you and I sat in here and had a screaming match about you trying to do everything yourself."

"I remember." Brian shrugged. "Times were different. It was just me and Tim and everything was falling apart. I've got a full complement of chiefs now." Brian paused. "I'm actually over par in that department, what with pinning the new one a couple of months ago. Two GSE chiefs."

"For now," Carrillo cautioned. "BUPERS will correct that little oversight in short order."

"You're probably right." Brian leaned over. "What are you working on?"

"Crap for the force master chief and some mentoring policy revisions." Carrillo looked up. "Shit, that reminds me. You talk to Faulkner?"

Brian shook his head. "He came to see CHENG and me before we went to battle stations. Told him to come back after it was over. Haven't seen him since. Why?"

"He stopped by here about ten minutes before you did. Asked where to find you."

Brian finished off his coffee. "Guess I better go find him. He say what it was about?"

Carrillo shook his head. "Nope. Why?"

"He seemed really damn nervous earlier. Wouldn't look at us. Shifty feet."

"That's not like him," Carrillo noted. "When you find out, let me know?"

"Will do."

Frigate *Admiral Makarov*, Russian Navy
05 December 2022 | 0733 Local Time
Black Sea

Dashkov stood in the bright blue lights of the *Makarov*'s combat control center, calculating the distances in time and space. *Makarov* to the American destroyer, the *Williams*, he reminded himself. *Makarov* to the American rescue craft. To the circling MH-60Rs. He glanced at the display to his left and calculated the distances from the Americans to each other. He picked up a handset and issued a series of orders to the bridge.

"Are we really doing this?" Gorshkov whispered.

Dashkov was disappointed in the young man, but he let it go, reminding himself that he'd been raised in the Soviet Union, however briefly, and that that upbringing made him a little different. The rest of his crew were too young for that. They'd not lived in a time when Russian sailors were feared. Their era was one dominated by American sea power. In the news. At the higher naval schools. The message had always been the same. Be wary of the Americans. Gorshkov's concern, Dashkov decided, was based in theory, not experience. Dashkov smiled at that.

"Yes, Pavel Stefanovich. We are. Is there a problem?"

Gorshkov's eyes flitted side to side and Dashkov saw him take a deep breath. "Won't they shoot, Captain?"

Dashkov shrugged. "That is possible, but unlikely." He pointed at the radar display. "They are here to conduct a rescue, not to fight. We are just forcing them off their spot."

"But how?"

"Did you ever wrestle, Pavel Stefanovich?"

"Yes, some."

"And how did you force another fighter off the mat?"

"Leverage, Captain. Leverage and speed."

Dashkov pointed at the display again. "Look. Tell me what you see."

Gorshkov scanned the display, his eyes dancing around. "I don't see it."

Dashkov glanced at a clock on the space's aft bulkhead before placing a hand on the younger man's shoulder. He had time for this. "Look again. Think about it. The strategies taught at the academy. The technique for a good takedown."

Gorshkov looked from his captain to the display and back. Dashkov merely smiled and watched the young man take another deep breath.

Gorshkov's head cocked sideways and he pointed. His voice sounded almost excited. "There."

"Very good, Pavel Stefanovich. Very good." Dashkov nodded. "Now tell me why."

"Center of gravity. Push the fighter off that, or get under it, and your opponent can submit or flee." Gorshkov looked up. "And you are sure they won't shoot?"

Dashkov considered the question for a moment. "Sure? No. I'm not sure. American rules of engagement do not permit such things. But that does not mean that such a thing is impossible. They could consider our, ah, aggressive approach hostile. In that case…"

"In that case?"

Dashkov turned back to the various displays lining the bulkheads. "In that case, we will sink the *Williams* and go on about our business."

USS *James E. Williams*, United States Navy
05 December 2022 | 0745 Local Time
Black Sea

Brian Thompson dropped his armful of notes and evaluations on an already cluttered desk and headed for Central Control. He stuck his head in the door and saw Chief Petty Officer Tim Guillory on watch as EOOW.

"Tim, I thought Q had the watch."

Guillory turned, his Cajun accent heavy, as it usually was during football games. "He did. Just relieved him."

Brian glanced at his watch. "Damn. Time's flying." He scanned the room, letting his eyes trace over the mass of information displayed. He noted that the ship was operating "split," one gas turbine driving each shaft. "Need anything?"

Guillory shook his head. "Nah. We're good. You?"

Brian nodded and turned for the door. "I'm good. Looking for Faulkner."

"Yeah, me too."

Brian stopped. "Did he say something to you?" That made

sense, Brian thought. Guillory was Faulkner's division chief.

"Say something?"

Brian nodded. "Yeah. He popped in right before battle stations and cornered me and CHENG. Sounded worried about something."

Guillory scratched his balding head. "He didn't say shit to me."

"Then why are you looking for him?"

"He's fifteen minutes late for watch." Guillory pointed. "Faulkner is supposed to be my Propulsion System Monitor."

Brian turned to look and saw a grumpy-looking sailor sitting on a desk with a set of logs on a clipboard resting across her legs. Her angry gaze shifted back and forth between the logs, her wristwatch, and the door to the space.

Brian turned to Guillory. "We got anyone off the watchbill qualified PSM?"

"Cruz. He's qualified up to both consoles."

Brian pointed at the angry sailor. "Get him and get her relieved. If Faulkner doesn't show up in ten minutes, call the OOD."

"Roger that."

Brian walked out of Central and paused. He tried to think, to put all the information together. His brain was racing.

"Fuck." Brian reached for his radio and depressed the button. "CHENG, Top."

A few seconds and a crackle. "Go for CHENG."

"Location, sir?" Brian could feel his voice shake, but he wasn't sure why.

"Log Room."

"Be there in two seconds, sir."

Brian let go of the button and walked around the corner. He entered the Log Room and found Lieutenant Walker in the middle of a maintenance spot-check with two junior sailors.

"Gents, can you pardon us for a few minutes?" Brian said.

The younger sailors nodded and stepped out of the space. Brian shut the door.

"What's up?"

Brian sat down. "We can't find Faulkner. He was at his battle station earlier. After that, he popped by the mess to see me. Master

Chief told the kid he'd tell me. I haven't seen him yet and he's late for watch."

Walker thought for a moment and picked up the phone on his desk. He dialed a number and waited for an answer. "Captain, CHENG here. Permission to have the OOD page Petty Officer Faulkner?"

Brian listened as Lieutenant Walker explained the circumstances. It frustrated him that you couldn't just call the bridge and have the word passed, but he understood. The ship's 1MC system wasn't for paging sailors—not on a five-hundred-foot destroyer, anyway. The system had been abused in the past few months by leaders too lazy to go find their troops. That he had been one of the lazy leaders who'd abused the system was, for the moment, forgotten.

Walker hung the phone up and stood. "Let's start walking. I'll start forward, you start aft."

As they left the space, the 1MC system blared with the order for Petty Officer Faulkner to contact Central Control.

♦ ♦ ♦

Commander Derrick Allen hadn't even taken his hand off the phone when it rang again. He picked it up.

"Captain."

"Combat, sir. We have a surface contact headed this way."

"Identification?"

"It's the *Makarov*, sir."

"On my way." Commander Allen hung up the phone and stood. He was out the door in five seconds and heading down the nearest ladder in ten.

Frigate *Admiral Makarov*, Russian Navy
05 December 2022 | 0755 Local Time
Black Sea

Dashkov stood on the bridge and rolled his neck. He took a deep breath and let his eyes close for a second. When he opened them, he glanced at the navigational display and nodded. He knew the capabilities of the Burke-class destroyer and its circling helicopter. They had to have him on radar by now, had to know he was heading right for them.

Well, almost right for them.

Dashkov turned and ordered a slight course change. On reflection, he ordered an increase in speed. Despite the bulk and speed of his ship, this was a delicate tactic that his fellow commanders had perfected during the previous decade. Race in close aboard and force the opponent to move. It always worked. American and British captains always backed away. Always.

Right before they called us reckless and irresponsible, thought Dashkov. He smiled to himself.

USS *James E. Williams*
05 December 2022 | 0758 Local Time
Black Sea

Brian made his way aft, past an athwartships passage leading to Shaft Alley, down one ladder, and past a space affectionately known as Three Gen. He crossed to the ship's portside through the horseshoe passageway and turned left, heading aft again. He stopped in between two doors. To his inboard side was the entrance to the ship's RAST machinery room, the gear that assisted with the capture and stowage of embarked helicopters. Since that space was secured with a cipher lock that Faulkner wouldn't have the password to, Brian turned outboard and opened the hatch to the steering machinery room.

Getting into Steering was always an awkward maneuver. Brian reached carefully across an opening to the ladder. With a grip on the ladder and the door, Brian moved his left foot to the ladder and followed it with his right foot. Secure on the ladder, he used his right arm to pull the door shut, letting go of the handle and snatching the locking arm in a swift, jerky motion that allowed him to pull the dogging arm as he began climbing down into the space.

Brian's feet hit the deck and he ducked under a low I-beam, stepping into a space awash with light and the pungent smell of old hydraulic fluid and grease. To his right, one of the power units pumped hydraulic fluid back and forth into the ram assembly, and Brian took a moment to watch the angle indicator swing back and forth over the zero-degree mark.

Brian began walking the space. He wriggled around the gear and ducked under piping. He checked the forward corners of the space. Those were places he'd found people sleeping before. He found no one and began working back between the power units, remembering a time when he'd found a yard worker tucked under the deckplates in the back.

Brian was just stepping over a loose five-gallon can of grease when the ship's 1MC system blared to life.

"General Quarters! General Quarters! All hands man your battle stations!"

Brian heard the steering engines strain and felt the ship heel violently to port. The unsecured grease can slid on the steel deck and slammed into Brian's legs. He felt the cracking pain shoot up his shins like lightning bolts as his body began to tip over. Brian threw his hands out, trying to latch on to anything to arrest his fall. His right hand brushed against a collection of electrical cabling and small, steel tubing without catching either. He caught an elbow on the handle of the emergency hydraulic hand pump. The force of that impact spun him sideways. Brian landed in a heap on the steel deck, the side of his head bouncing off the quarter-inch-thick plating. A thousand tiny points of light exploded in front of his eyes and his vision went blurry.

Brian lay there for a few moments as the pinpricks of light spun and danced and faded. He could feel burning at his shins, elbow, and the side of his head and knew that lumps had to be forming already. He tried blinking everything away when he heard a voice.

"Chief?"

Brian sat up. It was a slow process and his head was pounding. He blinked again and saw Petty Officer Coleman, a bosun's mate, staring at him. Brian rolled his neck and touched the side of his head. It stung like hell.

"Yeah?"

"You all right, Chief?"

Brian rolled his neck again. It felt like he'd pulled something. He started to speak, but his radio crackled to life.

"Top, Central."

It was Tim Guillory. Brian depressed the button. "Go for Top."

"You on the way? I gotta get to Repair Five."

"Yeah. Gimme a second. I'm in Aft Steering."

"Roger that."

Brian climbed to his feet. His whole body felt sore. He moved slowly, checking above him with one hand before standing fully erect. He paused. His vision went blurry again. His hearing went fuzzy, as if someone had stuffed wads of thick cotton in each ear. In his chest, it felt like his heart was racing. He felt a slight wobble in his legs and the world went black.

♦ ♦ ♦

"Captain, he's not responding." The officer of the deck's voice was shaking.

Commander Allen nodded. "Keep trying." He turned and pointed. "You, get MA1 up here with the dazzler."

The junior officer turned to a nearby microphone to carry out the order. Allen pointed again, this time at Chief Roberts. "Chief, contact the boat crew and get them back here, now. I don't want that Russian can between us and our RHIB."

"Yes, sir," Roberts said. He stepped onto the bridge wing to make the radio call.

"And tell the helos to keep an eye on them."

♦ ♦ ♦

Lieutenant, junior grade, Jeffrey Strater acknowledged the order and released the pushbutton on his radio. He glanced aft and could see the outline of an approaching ship. He looked to port and could see the *Williams* trolling through the outskirts of the debris field a few hundred yards away.

He reached forward in the RHIB to tap one of the sailors on the shoulder, careful to widen his stance as the small craft bobbed and bounced on the surface amid a wasteland of debris and burning puddles of fuel and oil. The sailor turned. Strater twirled his fingers in the air.

"Brooks, wrap it up. We gotta get back to the ship."

Petty Officer Brooks nodded. "Just this last one, sir. Gimme a hand?"

Brooks and the RHIB's SAR swimmer were struggling to pull a body over the boat's inflated rubber sponson. Strater worked his way around the console. He reminded the coxswain to keep the craft steady and reached over the side. It took one try to realize why Brooks and the swimmer were having so much trouble. The body, a man by the look of it, was limp as hell and coated in fuel and oil. What little clothing was left on the body was shredded and near useless as a handle.

Strater looked aft again. The approaching ship was closing. Fast. "Fuck it. Grab whatever you can. We gotta go."

Strater latched onto a handful of hair and pulled. Nothing happened. He checked aft and saw the ship growing larger. He could make out people on the bridge wings.

"On three!" He shouted. "One. Two. Three."

Strater heard Brooks grunting beside him and the RHIB listed to starboard as the body was lifted out of the water. Strater's foot slipped and he began falling backwards. His left leg shot out at an awkward angle and he felt a fiery pop in his knee. His falling weight, his grasp, and the efforts of Brooks and the swimmer pulled the body into the RHIB. It landed on Strater's damaged knee and he howled in agony.

"Goddamnit!" He was breathing hard. A red-hot, searing pain was throbbing in his knee and the smell of fuel filled his nostrils. He looked aft as best he could, peering around the port side of the console from his place on the deck. He could make out faces now, and something else.

"Coxswain! Step on it! Get us the fuck outta here!" Strater roared.

♦ ♦ ♦

Commander Allen watched in disbelief as the Russian ship slipped between the *Williams* and her small boat crew. He turned and began barking orders to maneuver clear. His brain raced through options as the *Williams* heeled over, turning away from the Russian frigate.

He wanted to open fire. Those were his sailors on the other side of the short, gray hull, and he had to protect them.

But could he? Could he start shooting at a Russian warship? One that hadn't shot at him? To protect his sailors? Maybe. But who was to say the RHIB crew was in danger? The Russians liked doing dumb shit like this. They were trying to start a fight. He couldn't take the bait. Not over a handful of sailors.

American sailors. My sailors.

Commander Allen slammed his fist into the side of the ship's control console. "Son of a bitch."

Frigate *Admiral Makarov*
05 December 2022 | 0800 Local Time
Black Sea

Captain Dashkov smiled as the American destroyer veered away. He turned to Lieutenant Gorshkov.

"You see?"

Gorshkov nodded. He looked pale as death. Dashkov turned and issued his next set of orders.

6

The White House
05 December 2022 | 0100 Local Time
Washington, DC

President of the United States Daniel Evans stormed into the Situation Room followed by his chief of staff and took his place at the head of the table. He waved everyone back to their seats, though he elected to stand behind his chair as the briefing started, too amped up by the adrenaline dump to even consider sitting down. He could feel the slight tremor in his hands. Every muscle in his body was on edge despite the early hour. He could feel his heart racing. *Calm down,* he told himself. *Calm down.*

He scanned the room, found the face he was looking for, and took a breath.

"Ophelia, what do we know?"

Ophelia Adams was the Director of National Intelligence, one of the president's principal advisors on all matters relating to national security and the head of the United States' Intelligence Community. She stood and cleared her throat.

"Mr. President, a few hours ago, a container ship—the *Brixton*—collided with this natural gas rig." Adams pointed to one of the wall-mounted screens. "This is the *Neptun Deep* rig. At the time of the incident, final testing was occurring to place the rig into service."

Evans nodded and pursed his lips, thinking. "And one of our ships was sent in for search and rescue?" He turned to accept a mug of coffee from an aide.

"Yes, sir," Adams confirmed. "One of our destroyers was nearby and was ordered to render assistance. They were on station and conducting search and rescue operations when the frigate *Makarov* drove in close aboard. Rear Admiral Gomez at the National Military Command Center reported that the *Makarov* forced our ship away from the accident site by maneuvering in close at speed. The commander on scene issued orders to maneuver clear to avoid a collision."

"Shots fired? By either side?" Evans asked. He took a sip from the cup. The coffee was hot as hell.

"There are no reports of shots fired." Adams paused.

"Go on," the president ordered.

"Mr. President, at the time the *Makarov* arrived on scene, our ship had a small boat team in the water as part of the search and rescue efforts. It has been reported that a Russian boat crew seized the sailors on the RHIB and transferred them to the *Makarov*."

"At gunpoint?" Evans asked. He could feel his pulse quicken.

"Unknown, Mr. President."

Evans put his hands on the back of his seat and squeezed. "How many sailors?"

Adams looked down at her notes and flipped through a few pages. "Five, sir. We're getting the names shortly. Rear Admiral Gomez and his folks are working on that."

The president paused for a few moments, looking down at a spot on the table with his brow furrowed. He raised his head. "So, bottom line, one of our ships was conducting a rescue and a Russian warship interfered, tried to play bumper cars, and then kidnapped five of our sailors. Right?"

"That's correct, Mr. President."

Evans nodded. "This is probably irrelevant, but do we know why the *Brixton* smashed into the rig? These are modern ships. Radar. Autopilot. The works. What went wrong?"

Adams shook her head. "We don't know, Mr. President. Probably an accident."

Evans nodded. "Occam's razor?"

"Simplest answer is usually correct."

"That's fair." Evans filed that train of thought for later. "What are we doing about this?"

The chief of staff, Leslie Barnes, stopped scribbling notes. "Ophelia, are we damn certain that this Russian ship took our sailors? I mean one hundred percent certain?"

Adams nodded. "There's video, Leslie. Shot from the long-range camera mounted on the ship's mast."

"And it shows what, exactly?" Barnes asked.

"The distance wasn't all that far. It shows American sailors on the fantail of the *Makarov* and an empty RHIB adrift."

Barnes turned. "Sir, we need to get Jack Burroughs calling people right—"

Evans held a hand up. "No. President Barsukov won't budge for SECSTATE. Not for this. This is a call I'll have to make. President to president."

Barnes shook his head. "Daniel, that's like throwing your trump card on the opening play. You start something like this at the lowest appropriate level. You know that. This a big damn deal, but—"

"So is kidnapping American sailors right in front of their commanding officer." Evans paused. "In international waters, no less."

"But sir, it's just five sailors…"

Evans shot the man a poisonous look. "That's right. Five sailors. Five of *my* sailors. Five American sailors." Evans could feel his temper getting loose, getting just a little wiggle room. "I am responsible for those men and women. All of them. Every last goddamn one. And I am not delegating that responsibility to someone else just because the head count is only five."

Barnes closed his eyes. "But Mr. President…"

"No, damnit," Evans snapped. "End of discussion. I'm calling Barsukov. Set it up."

The president headed for the door. As a marine in full dress blues moved to open it, Evans paused and turned. "What ship?"

"Excuse me, sir?" Adams asked.

"We sent a ship to conduct SAR operations and the Russians harassed it before kidnapping American sailors. What ship?"

"USS *James E. Williams*…" Adams started.

"The *Williams*? The same ship that…"

A nod. "Yes, sir."

The president left the room. Adams and Barnes collected their belongings and headed into the hall.

"What the hell was that about, Leslie?" Adams asked.

"Not sure," Barnes said, still walking.

Adams stopped. "Bullshit, Leslie. He's snapped at people before. It happens. He's the president and there's a great deal of stress and it happens. But that…was different."

"It's fine, Ophelia. I swear. It's just a Navy thing. He used to command one of those crews."

"You're a shitty liar, Leslie." Adams folded her arms across her chest, her briefing documents and notebooks tucked into one hand.

The chief of staff paused and turned. He walked the twenty feet back to the DNI. "What's your point?"

Adams could hear the stress, could feel it. "My point is that he's the president and he has a lot of shit on his plate. He's stressed and stressed people yell and bark and scream."

Barnes looked at his watch. "And?"

Adams softened her approach. She could see that Barnes was still on the defensive. "Leslie, he's yelled at me a lot over the years. It's never personal. I usually have it coming. We've dropped the ball a few times in the past year. He can't go to some entry-level analyst and rip his or her head off for missing something on an estimate, so he barks at me." She shrugged. "For people like you and me, it's part of the job. But the attrition, Leslie. Do you know how many senior staffers have quit in the last few months? I'm talking career service people. People with history here who decided that anything was better than getting barked at by the president for doing their job. Not for being wrong. Not for giving advice that was too far off his path. For existing, Leslie. Just for being the person standing in front of the president. He's shooting the messengers. A lot."

Barnes just stood there, blinking. "Is there a point to this? Or are you just being a mother hen here?"

Adams ignored the last remark. "It's not just the IC he's affecting. It's Treasury. State. Defense. He's turned into a screamer. He's becoming unreasonable. He's ripping people's heads off for minor things. Or nothing. He does it to everyone. Except you. Leslie, until today, he's never snapped at you." Adams paused. "Ever. Has he? Not in private. Not in public. Never."

Barnes bit the inside of his cheek and looked at the ground. "You're not gonna let this go, are you?"

Adams just stared at the shorter man.

He looked away, took a breath, and glanced at his watch again. "My office, Ophelia. Twenty minutes."

The Kremlin
05 December 2022 | 0830 Local Time
Moscow

Russian President Dmitri Mikhailovich Barsukov stepped up to the podium and smiled. He placed one hand on each side of the hand-carved lectern and felt the smooth, warm wood. He wondered briefly what kind of wood it was, where it had come from, and who had made it. It was elegant, he thought.

Barsukov looked out at the sea of reporters. He saw the bright lights operated by the television crews. He could hear the whirring and clicking of cameras. He even imagined that he could hear the gentle scratching of pencils on paper as the crowd in front of him scribbled notes and possible questions. His mind started to wander again, to wonder if the notes were in shorthand or not, whether they were even legible. He supposed not and reminded himself that now was not the time.

Barsukov raised one hand and the room fell almost completely silent. He looked to his right and saw his SVR director tucked away off stage, hidden from view by an impressive array of thick gold and crimson curtains. Igor Tolstov nodded, just a barely perceptible inclination of his head.

So, Barsukov thought, all is ready. Good.

The Russian president turned back to the reporters.

"As you know, a few hours ago a British merchant vessel rammed the *Neptun Deep* natural gas rig off the Romanian coast. I am here to report that this was a deliberate act. We have evidence that the captain of the vessel, Oliver Wallace, murdered his entire crew and programmed the vessel's autopilot to set the ship on a collision course with *Neptun Deep* before taking his own life. An American warship was then dispatched to the scene to muddy the waters, purportedly under the guise of conducting legitimate search and rescue operations."

Barsukov paused. He could see the men and women in front of him leaning forward and he almost smiled. Of course they were leaning forward. They needed to catch every word, to hear the nuance and inflection and to see the expression on his face when he spoke. Not because this was a sensational story. It was. No, he thought, they leaned forward and tried to get this absolutely right because that is what we tell them to do.

"Now, you may ask why a man would do such a thing. Why would someone deliberately drive a one-hundred-thousand-ton ship into a gas rig? Well, I will tell you." He paused, took a breath, and plowed ahead. "We have also obtained evidence that Captain Wallace was acting on orders from Western intelligence agencies." Barsukov held up a sheaf of papers for the cameras. "These documents prove that Captain Wallace accepted several payments from both American and British intelligence agencies to commit this…this atrocity against the people of Europe. And why? To what purpose?"

Barsukov put the papers down and moved his hands back to the polished wood sides of the lectern. "Russia has long been a friend of Europe. European interests and Russian interests have been intertwined for decades. The destruction of the *Neptun Deep* natural gas rig is nothing less than an attack on our European friends and allies. It inhibits access to one of the world's largest natural gas reservoirs and affects the ability of every citizen in Europe to live in peace and comfort." Barsukov paused again. He scanned the room. "As you know, Russia provides a large percentage of Europe's energy needs. While we are more than happy to do so, this demand places great stress on our own aging infrastructure. We cannot shut down for much-needed repairs without harming or inconveniencing our neighbors. It is, therefore, only a matter of time until our systems cannot adequately provide for Russian or European interests. It is only a matter of time until we let our friends and countrymen down."

Barsukov looked directly into the row of television cameras. "For these reasons, I have tasked portions of the Black Sea Fleet with the protection of these valuable resources. Proud Russian sailors are now standing in harm's way today to ensure the continued operation of these rigs. One ship, the frigate *Makarov*, courageously forced the American destroyer *Williams* away from the *Neptun Deep* wreck. Our navy has a proud and noble tradition, and they will remain on scene for as long as is necessary."

The White House
05 December 2022 | 0135 Local Time
Washington, DC

"Oh, this shit is gonna make his head explode." DNI Adams muted the television and put the remote on the desk in front of her. Across from her, Leslie Barnes was seated behind his desk, still staring at the soundless television, watching as the Russian president was escorted off stage, smiling and waving to the assembled reporters.

Barnes turned his head. "What the hell is he even talking about? Western intelligence agencies paying a ship captain to ram an oil rig? Why the hell would we do that? What possible purpose would that serve?"

Adams gestured at the screen. "You heard him during the Q and A. Money. Keep Europe paying energy bills and strain Russian infrastructure."

"Is he insane? They've already got, what, a third of the market there? What the hell else do they want?"

Adams leaned back. "Come on, Leslie. It's Russia. They want more. They've always wanted more. This isn't new."

"But the claim that we—"

"It's bullshit, Leslie. Pure bullshit. Plain and simple."

"But…" Barnes started to protest.

Adams held a hand up. "I know. It sounds crazy. But it happens. We've been dealing with this crap, domestically, for months now."

"What do you mean?"

Adams cocked her head. "The election stuff. The deepfake videos of Daniel. The forged certs. In this day and age, creating evidence out of thin air is child's play."

"Seriously?" Barnes pointed at the screen. "This is an awful lot to pull out of thin air."

Adams picked her phone up, unlocked it and tapped the

screen. She scrolled a few times, tapped the screen, and turned it so both could see. "This is a video of Daniel, Elvis, Jimmy Hoffa, and Tupac smoking weed together."

Barnes took the phone and watched the video, his eyes wide.

Adams leaned back in her chair again and smiled. "Look at Daniel's shirt."

Barnes leaned towards the phone, his nose almost touching the screen. "Does that say…" He trailed off.

"'Fuck the police'? Yeah. That's my favorite part." Adams grinned. "That was a song by N.W.A. about thirty years ago." She pointed at the phone. "That video is obviously a fake and it's had more than ten million views in the last two months."

Barnes handed the phone over. "It looks real as hell. And the other stuff you mentioned?"

"Same degree of sophistication. Looks real. With the right presentation and audience, it feels real. Feeds into what folks want to be told."

"But can't people just look it up? You know, check sources on the internet and find out it's fake?"

Adams thought for a moment. "You're from New York, right?"

"Yeah."

"Yankee fan?"

"Of course."

"Ever buy into stories about how awful Red Sox players are? About them being dicks to fans and whatnot?"

"In the past, sure. But that's different."

"To you, maybe. You've gotten above it. To Joe and Jane Sixpack, finding out the Boston shortstop stole some kid's sucker just feeds into the shape they need the world to be in. Doesn't need to be true or real. Just has to feel that way. To fit into their comfortable picture of the world. Who's good. Who's bad. Who's an asshole and who is the second coming of Jesus himself." Adams stopped talking. Her eyes drifted to the ceiling. An idea floated by and she snagged it. She looked at Barnes. "Son of a bitch. That's it, isn't it?"

"What?"

"The election stuff. The bullshit claims and videos. The constant harassment. The loss of support in Congress. Drops in polls. It's getting to Daniel. Little by little. Piece by piece. Eroding at his confidence. Putting him on defense. That's why he's snapping and snarling."

Before Barnes could answer, the intercom buzzed. Adams pressed a button. "Yes?"

"Ma'am, the president just called for a meeting of his national security council."

"We're on the way." Adams released the intercom button and stood. "I'm right, aren't I?"

Barnes stood and slipped his jacket on. "I've been trying to steer him away from that stuff, but…" He gestured at the television.

Adams headed for the door. "Yeah, the snarling is gonna get worse."

The Kremlin
05 December 2022 | 0900 Local Time
Moscow

Barsukov shed his jacket upon entering his office, pausing only long enough to hang it on a coat rack before taking a seat behind his heavy desk. He gestured to one of the chairs facing the desk.

"Sit, Igor Romanovich. Make yourself comfortable."

Tolstov did as ordered, a thin smile stretching across his face. "Thank you, Mr. President."

Barsukov smiled back. A thin, forced smiled. "The information on the *Brixton* was well done. Masterfully so."

"Thank you." Tolstov nodded. His thin smile widened. "I serve the Soviet Union."

A grunt escaped from Barsukov. He shook his head. "Can you imagine what it would be like if we'd had the same capabilities then? Everything might have turned out differently." His head shook again. "Thirty years wasted."

Tolstov knew exactly how his president felt about the preceding decades and he agreed, though not nearly as vehemently. He wasn't as certain that the good old days were that good, but he could temporize. "Russia, and the Soviet Union, did not have us to push them in the proper direction, Mr. President."

Barsukov let another thin smile work its way across his own face. "Flattery, Igor Romanovich?"

A shrug. "I'm not above it when it suits my purposes. The Soviet Union lost its way because of stupid, prideful men. Mostly."

Barsukov eyed him, the thin smile vanishing as quickly as it had come. "So, what is it you are flattering me for?"

"No reason."

The president was silent for a moment, watching his senior intelligence officer. "I know you better than that. What is it?"

"Just some information that might amuse you. Something that is both telling and useful."

Barsukov leaned forward, elbows on the desk. "And what is this information?"

"Remember the reason we began pushing disinformation about the American election and President Evans?"

Barsukov nodded and motioned for Tolstov to continue.

"Well, it would appear that there is an unintended benefit. We have been flooding the internet with disinformation. Videos. Leaked intelligence reports. News articles. We've been pushing this and that. Bot nets. Troll farms. Hackers. You name it."

"I remember," Barsukov confirmed. "Mainstream media picked it up. All sides. People we pay and people we don't."

Tolstov nodded. "That's right. The sheer volume of information we've put out feeds the political divisions in America and gives the Evans Administration's opposition material they can latch onto. At the individual level in the United States, there is a certain willingness to accept information that fits your own…narrative."

"I remember, Igor Romanovich. I remember. What's your point?"

"Mr. President, we started this cyber campaign to divide America. To push the wedge in further. To make it politically impossible to do much of anything. But we can do more. Much more."

"I'm listening."

"Mr. President, we have a young man who works in the Evans

Administration. I will keep his name to myself. You wouldn't recognize it and you don't need to know it." Tolstov paused and took a breath. "He sent a report to us that offers a unique opportunity."

Barsukov raised an eyebrow. "Go on."

"According to this man, our disinformation campaign is getting to Evans. He's not sleeping. He's snapping at staff. His temper is increasingly volatile."

Barsukov considered this. "And you think that we can exacerbate this issue?" He paused, thinking. "To cripple him politically and militarily?"

"Yes, Mr. President."

Barsukov closed his eyes and leaned back in his chair. He remained silent, running the information back and forth in his mind. After a full minute, he opened his eyes and looked at his visitor.

"Tell me how."

7

Frigate *Admiral Makarov*
05 December 2022 | 0945 Local Time
Black Sea

Captain Yuri Nikolayevich Dashkov walked into the *Makarov*'s medical ward and was immediately besieged by the odors. The air was pungent with a clean, antiseptic smell, one that spoke of alcohol swabs and industrial detergents. Dashkov hated that smell. He'd hated it since childhood, that time when physicians were terrifying monsters with needles that had looked like railroad spikes. He fought the urge to leave, to turn around and head back to his cabin. Or the bridge. Or combat.

Anywhere but here, he thought. *Coward.*

"Doctor?"

The *Makarov*'s medical officer stood and turned. He was a small, thin man with a narrow, rat-like face and round spectacles. Dashkov distrusted the man, but had no idea why. *Because of how he looks*, Dashkov thought. *Or because he is a doctor?*

"Captain, welcome." The doctor motioned for Dashkov to follow. They took four steps across the small ward and passed through a hatch on the inboard bulkhead to an even smaller room.

This was the ship's operating room and it doubled as the ICU. A man was strapped to the table in the middle of the room. A blanket—probably several, Dashkov thought—covered the man, with various wires and tubes and leads running off to a series of monitors and bags of fluids.

"How is he doing?"

The doctor shrugged. "Coma. Vital signs are weak. Bloodwork is a mess." He plucked a chart from its holder on the wall and started to read through the litany of medical concerns.

Dashkov held a hand up. "Will he live?"

Another shrug. "It's too early for that, Captain."

"Can he be moved?" Dashkov kept his eyes on the body, saw the faint movement where the chest had to be. Orders or not, he didn't really want a dead American on his ship. He *was* American, wasn't he? Dashkov had to admit that he didn't really know.

"That's the catch. A medical evacuation by helicopter or boat would almost certainly kill him. But he needs better care than this ship is equipped to provide. Still..."

Dashkov nodded and placed a hand on the doctor's shoulder. "Still, you will do your best."

"Yes," the doctor agreed.

Both men stood silent for a moment. The doctor turned and put the chart back in its holder. "It's odd, though."

"What's that?"

"This one." The doctor gestured to the figure under the blankets. "He's not with them."

"What do you mean?"

"He's not a sailor. Not American Navy, I mean."

Dashkov turned away from the patient. "How do you know?"

The doctor motioned to the captain. "Follow me." They moved back, out of the OR and into the main medical ward. The doctor turned and opened the hatch leading to his private office, a cramped space packed with records, cabinets, a small folding desk, and two chairs. The doctor opened the top drawer of the nearest cabinet and began rummaging through it. "When the Americans were brought in here, the other five were wearing uniforms. This man wasn't."

The doctor pulled a large plastic bag out of the cabinet and placed it on the desk. "These are his personal effects. Civilian clothes. What's left of them, anyway. Everything is shredded and burned." The doctor kept digging through his patient's belongings. "The other five haven't said a word yet. That's not surprising, I suppose. I wouldn't say anything in their position. Shock, I guess. Anger…"

"Doctor?"

The physician looked up. His glasses, with their round, silver rims had slid nearly to the end of the pointed nose. It made him look older and, Dashkov decided, slightly senile.

"Yes?"

"You wanted to show me something?"

"Oh yes. Sorry, Captain." He flipped over the remains of what appeared to be blue jeans and tugged at the pocket. "His wallet survived. I found it a few minutes before you came down. In the hurry to treat him, no one took it." He handed over a small, tri-fold leather wallet.

It had been light brown before, Dashkov thought. Probably coffee-colored. Well, coffee with too much cream, maybe. The dry portions were lighter brown and encrusted with a layer of salt. The rest was mottled, a soggy, darker chocolate color. Dashkov opened the wallet and began flipping through it. He was surprised to find nearly two hundred dollars in the billfold; he extracted the bills and set them aside. There was the normal array of credit cards—Visa, American Express, and what looked like a corporate MasterCard. In the left side, Dashkov found two pictures and a Maryland driver's license.

He looked at the license first, examined the red and yellow and white plastic and the photograph it contained. He looked at the print and saw that the name on the card was Jonathan Evans. That meant little to him. The same name graced each of the credit cards; the silver embossing on some of the letters was noticeably worn. Dashkov decided that there was nothing of interest and set the license and cards aside . He shuffled to the photographs.

The first showed a young man—Dashkov checked and noted that the face matched the picture on the license—and a young woman sitting on the side of a fountain. The photo was awash in sunlight, and the couple looked happy. Dashkov felt a twinge of sadness for the woman and recalled a similar picture in his own wallet. The time before marriage and children. He'd been young then, new to adulthood and new to his career as a professional naval officer. The two people in this picture had the same look.

Their whole life before them. Adventures that might not happen now because the young man was near death on a table two rooms away.

Dashkov shook the thoughts off and shuffled to the second photograph. He stopped cold. His breath caught in his throat.

Dashkov's mind raced. It couldn't be. This was some kind of joke. A trick. But it wasn't. It was there. In his hand. In color. On the Kodak paper. This man, Jonathan Evans, stood in a gray suit and blue tie, bundled in a heavy black coat and loose white scarf. Next to him, arm over the younger man's shoulder, was the president of the United States.

"Son of a bitch," Dashkov muttered, his voice barely a whisper.

"It's him, isn't it? In the picture with my patient. The American president?"

Dashkov looked at the doctor and began stuffing the man's personal effects back into the bag. "Doctor, who else knows of this?"

"No one," the doctor said. "I bagged up all of this myself after the patient was stabilized."

"The security team?"

"No, Captain. It was an OR. I kicked them out as soon as they placed the victim on the table."

"What about the orderlies?"

"No, Captain. As I said, I cleaned—"

Dashkov held a hand up. "Listen carefully. I want an armed guard in front of the OR door at all times." He paused to think. "And one at the escape hatch in the back."

"Yes, Captain. Can I ask—"

Dashkov collected the bag and headed for the door. "Not now, Doctor. Not now." He put his hand on the knob and started to open the door, then stopped. "No one passes the guards except for you and me. Do you understand me? No one. You are to attend this case yourself. I do not care how menial the task is, you must do it. You. Not an orderly, Doctor. You. Understood?"

The doctor stammered. "Yes, Captain. But—"

"Not now, Doctor. Not now. I will be back in thirty minutes. Get the guards in place and keep that man alive."

"Yes, sir."

76 | MATT HARDMAN
USS *James E. Williams*
05 December 2022 | 0955 Local Time
Black Sea

Chief Petty Officer Brian Thompson opened his eyes and winced. Dimmed as they were, the buzzing and flickering sixty-hertz tubes above him still sizzled his retinas. He closed his eyes again. He could almost feel his brain pulsing against the inside of his skull. It felt as if the ship's bosun had unleashed a team of sailors with needle guns in his head.

"Hey, Chief."

Brian turned to see the corpsman, a musclebound sailor with aspirations to join the Fleet Marine Force.

"Can we turn the lights down?" Brian croaked.

"That's as low as they go, unless I flip 'em off. How do you feel?"

Brian tried to sit up, but the effort doubled the pain in his head. "Got something for the headache?"

The corpsman hesitated. "How about I give Senior a call?"

Brian started to respond, but the sailor was already on the phone. Brian heard him talking to the ship's senior medic, a hospital corpsman who'd recently been promoted to senior chief petty officer. The corpsman hung up the phone.

"They'll be here in a few, Chief."

"Fine. How about aspirin or something?"

"We'd better wait."

It took several minutes before the door to the medical ward opened. The flash of light from the passageway sent fresh stabs of pain into Brian's retinas and he was briefly thankful for the comparatively dim lights in the medical office. When the door clicked shut, Brian looked around. Commander Allen was there. So was Lieutenant Walker, Master Chief Carrillo, and Senior Chief Martin.

Martin began checking Brian over.

"How are you feeling?"

"Could stand something for the headache."

Martin grabbed Brian's wrist, two fingers feeling for his pulse.

"I'll bet. And something for that knot on your noggin, no doubt."

Brian reached up and touched the side of his head, and a fiery pain shot through his face. "Shit... That's tender."

"It would be. You knocked yourself unconscious back there in Steering."

Brian thought back. He remembered the sliding bucket and the ship heeling over. "What the hell happened? I was climbing over a bucket and next thing I know the ship's rolling over."

"We almost got rammed," Allen said.

It took a few seconds for that to register in Brian's mind. "By who?" He paused. He remembered why he'd been in Steering. "Never mind. Doesn't matter. We find Faulkner?" Brian had his eyes closed and was rubbing the welt on the side of his head. He missed the looks exchanged by the other men in the room and didn't look up until he heard the scraping of a chair.

Commander Allen was sitting down. "Chief, did Faulkner say anything to you today? Anything at all?"

Brian resisted the urge to shake his head. "Other than he needed to talk? No. Why?"

Allen nodded, almost to himself. "Faulkner is dead."

Brian sat upright, amplifying the pain in his head tenfold and causing waves of nausea to wash over him. Senior Chief Martin moved to restrain him, but Brian shoved him away.

"What?"

"When general quarters went down—the second time, I mean—he never showed up. A pair of investigators found him about ten minutes after we got you up here."

Brian's pulse raced; the throbbing in his skull was nearly unbearable. "What the fuck happened?"

"They found him in a fan room. Faulkner hanged himself."

Brian could feel every beat of his heart. His vision narrowed and each pulsing beat seemed to rock his whole body. He felt his stomach lurch and, helpless to stop it, he leaned over the side of the cot as his stomach emptied itself in a series of violent heaves. When there was nothing left, Brian tried to sit back up, but his world went dark again.

The Kremlin
05 December 2022 | 1005 Local Time
Moscow

Anatoly Mikhailovich Shablikov sat at his desk and waited for his boss, thinking about the many benefits available to him as a special assistant to the director of the SVR. Transportation. Travel. An intimate knowledge of the inner workings of the Russian government and—Anatoly thought—the workings of various foreign governments. In this position, in this office, Anatoly's life had been comfortable for years. Comfortable. Not opulent. His flat in downtown Moscow was old and in disrepair. He did not have his own vehicle. But he collected a decent paycheck, and that, plus a small pension from a previous job, kept him fed and kept him looking presentable. He worked hard. He was loyal. He kept the secrets that needed to be kept and leaked only what his boss told him to leak—and even then, through various back channels constructed for the purpose.

But Anatoly was not comfortable now. And he was not happy. Anatoly Mikhailovich Shablikov was angry. And scared.

He'd taken his station in life for granted; he knew that now. He'd expected something other than what he'd gotten. He'd expected to be taken care of, and he was just coming to grips with how naïve that thought was.

Anatoly glared at the pieces of paper on his desk and felt his blood pressure rising. The paper on the left was a leave request for medical treatment. There was a check mark in the block labeled 'Disapproved' and the reason, in the director's flowing hand, read simply 'indispensable.'

Anatoly mouthed the word and thought about it. "If I'm so indispensable..." His voice trailed off.

The paper on Anatoly's right was a medical claim rejection. Like most Russian citizens, Anatoly relied on government-subsidized healthcare known as OMC. Also like most citizens, a portion of the cost for his treatments would come out of his own pocket.

And that was the problem. Anatoly smiled grimly. This wasn't a tooth extraction or some voluntary cyst removal. It was chemotherapy. A last-ditch effort which the government had decided wasn't worth paying for.

"Bastards," Anatoly muttered. He was simultaneously shocked and unsurprised. What had he expected? The doctor had made his chances clear, both to him and, probably, the review board.

Anatoly closed his eyes, thinking back to the previous week.

♦ ♦ ♦

"I'm sorry, Anatoly. There is nothing else to be done."

Anatoly had stared at the young doctor. He was at a loss for words, his mind fighting against reality. He'd known this day would come, had anticipated it for more than three decades now, but the finality of the doctor's pronouncement shocked him. He'd not expected good news. He knew the inevitability. But the time had come. The doctor had said so.

Thyroid cancer.

Anatoly had lowered his gaze, looking at a spot of white tile between his shoes. He knew the numbers, could recite the statistics. An explosion in cases of thyroid cancer mirrored unexplained rises in cases of aplastic anemia, leukemia, and a host of other illnesses and diseases that shriveled human beings into barely recognizable twigs. In Ukraine, thirty-six thousand widows received survivor benefits. Just shy of one million Soviet citizens had participated in the cleanup at Chernobyl. Fifteen percent of those were already dead.

Anatoly knew another number.

Thirty-one.

It was a random number, significant only because it came after thirty and before thirty-two.

Thirty-one. A statistic pulled out of thin air.

That was the number the Soviet government had given birth to in the years following the accident. That was the number the Politburo and all loyal Party men had quoted, an absurd attempt to convince the rest of the world that what had happened hadn't been as bad as the Western press made it out to be. Thirty-one people. Thirty-one souls who had, probably, believed in the Party and believed in Lenin. People who'd bought into the Soviet lie. People who had died in the days, weeks, months, and years following the explosion at the Chernobyl Nuclear Power Station. The Vladimir Ilyich Lenin Nuclear Power Station. The place's real name.

Anatoly shook his head. He thought of the two people, both buried in lead-lined, concrete-sealed coffins, who weren't on the official list, weren't buried at Mitinskoye Cemetery with the rest of the firefighters and powerplant workers who'd perished in the name of nuclear power and good communism. Moscow hadn't approved of them. They weren't official victims.

Official victims. Stupid idea. If there were official victims, there had to be unofficial victims. Right? What the hell was an unofficial victim?

Anatoly knew the answer. His brother and wife were unofficial victims. They were encased, sealed, and buried less than five kilometers from the power plant in a pair of unmarked graves. They were people who'd died and been forgotten. Ignored. Like they had never existed.

The young doctor cleared his throat.

Anatoly looked up.

"I'm sorry," repeated the doctor, the clarity of his Saint Petersburg accent contrasting sharply against the slurred Russian common in Moscow. "We've tried everything."

Anatoly nodded. "How long?"

"Hard to say. Four months. Maybe six."

Anatoly thought about those words. Four months. Six months. In that time, he would die. Finally. It would all be over. He would pass, painfully probably. Someone would discover his corpse and notify the proper authority. A doctor, like this one, would confirm his passing. Then he would be placed in a cheap coffin and buried in a state graveyard.

Anatoly looked at the physician. The doctor—Anatoly realized that he didn't even know the man's name—shook his head as if the patient's impending death was somehow personal.

Anatoly nodded. "It's done, then. The state has finally killed me."

"Anatoly," the doctor said, frowning. "The state does not exist anymore. We are just Russians now."

Anatoly looked at the doctor, trying to guess his age. Twenty-eight. Maybe twenty-nine. Certainly not in his thirties. He did some quick math. "And what would you know about the state?"

A shrug. "What I've read in history books. What I learned at university."

Anatoly dismissed the doctor with a wave of his hand. "Bah. You know nothing about the state. When were you born? Ninety-two? Ninety-three?"

The doctor cocked his head. "That's irrelevant."

"Please, Doctor. Humor a dying old man." Anatoly was taking out his frustration on this poor doctor and knew the kid didn't deserve it. After all, it wasn't his fault he'd been born when he'd been born.

"Ninety-three." A sheepish grin from the doctor.

Anatoly nodded. "Two years after the collapse. You know nothing about the Soviet state except what you've been told by some government-approved author."

"I know enough." The steely professionalism was gone from the young man's voice, replaced by the nervy chatter of someone who desperately wanted to get back to a more comfortable topic.

Anatoly leaned back in the exam chair. "Oh. So you know enough? Tell me how I reached this point. Stage four thyroid cancer. What caused it?"

Anatoly knew the doctor knew. He also knew the doctor couldn't say. Not ever. This illness and eventual death would never be laid at the feet of the state, even a now-defunct one. After forty seconds of silence, Anatoly threw the doctor a lifeline.

"Hold up that pencil." Anatoly pointed. "What do you see?"

The voice was nervous as it ticked off the parts of the pencil. "Wood. Yellow paint. Metal cap. Pink eraser. Graphite."

"Ah. Graphite. That's where it started for me." Anatoly watched the doctor furrow his brows.

"Anatoly Mikhailovich, graphite cannot cause thyroid cancer."

"Correct, Doctor. But what comes off graphite can. What you do with it can."

"I don't understand."

Anatoly leaned forward. "Doctor, my brother was in the control room for Reactor Four at Chernobyl when they tried to shut the damn thing down. When those rods, with their graphite tips, dropped back into that unstable pile of uranium and the whole damn building blew apart, it threw chunks of graphite in all directions. From the rods. From the attenuator blocks. From God knows where else. It ended up everywhere. Roof of the building. Tops of nearby buildings. In the parks. In the pools. On the streets. Everywhere. Each piece, every single one, firing off billions of invisible little particles called gammas. You know what a gamma particle is, correct?"

The doctor nodded. "Of course."

"So, you know what that means?"

"Well, medically, it means—"

Anatoly cut him off. "It means that that the exclusion zone was a battlefield. Trillions and trillions of invisible bullets rampaging around in all directions at the speed of light, colliding with bodies and destroying tissue cells. If you're lucky, you get shot by enough gamma particles to kill you. Not immediately and not without a great deal of pain, but soon. My brother lasted less than a week. My wife, just a few days more. Burns cover portions of your body, red splotches that look like you touched the surface of the sun. Cell walls break down. You bleed from everywhere. Pain so intense that no drug can kill it. That's if you're lucky."

"And if you're unlucky?" the physician asked.

"Ah. The unlucky ones live. Months. Years. Decades, even. Borrowed time, Doctor. Never knowing when the end will come, but knowing it must. The unlucky ones have to live knowing death is waiting. Knowing their bodies are time bombs."

Anatoly sat back in his chair again, eyeing the doctor.

"I can't help you, Anatoly. I can't."

Anatoly nodded. He knew. "Doctor, have you ever said anything against the state? Done anything other than what they tell you to do? Believed anything other than what they tell you to believe?"

"Certainly not."

Anatoly looked at the floor. "I did. Once. Just once."

"What happened?"

"What do you think? I was persuaded to see the error of my ways." Anatoly watched the doctor. Then he laughed. "And for that I was given a good job. What a trade, eh?"

"Anatoly, three irresponsible plant supervisors caused the explosion. Individual people, Anatoly. Not the state."

Anatoly shook his head. "Ah. The propaganda! You really believe that, don't you?"

"I do. You should too. The state isn't to blame, Anatoly. These things happen."

Anatoly stood. This was a pointless debate. The doctor was simply a product of the system. He'd been taught what he'd been taught. Learned what he'd been directed to learn.

"Maybe so, Doctor. Maybe so. But I know what happened at Chernobyl. I questioned it one time and I was lucky. I was not silenced by bars or bullets. They could have done that. They could have disappeared me when I questioned the cause of the disaster. Fed me to dogs or hanged me or just put a cheap bullet through my thick head. They may not have done those things, but they have killed me just the same."

Rubles bury secrets almost as well as a good pistol shot. So does time.

Anatoly could see frustration on the doctor's face as he spoke, clearly trying to get back to business. "As you say, Anatoly. If you have any further questions, please return. We will see you to discuss a last course of chemotherapy in the next few days. Is that satisfactory?"

Is that satisfactory? What a ridiculous question. Anatoly Mikhailovich, you will die in a most uncomfortable manner. Come talk to us about how best to go about it. Is that satisfactory?

"Yes. I will return next week."

◆ ◆ ◆

The office's outer door opened, bringing Anatoly back to the present. He stood unsteadily as Director Tolstov entered the room, brushing bits of snow from his hair as he walked.

"Director." Anatoly nodded.

Tolstov shed his coat and waved Anatoly to the door to his office. "Ah, Anatoly. Come. We have much to do."

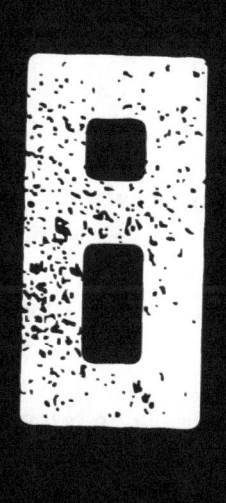

Frigate *Admiral Makarov*
05 December 2022 | 1022 Local Time
Black Sea

Captain Yuri Nikolayevich Dashkov sat at his computer and stared at the screen.

"Shit," he muttered. His voice was barely a whisper. The image on the screen, and the information below it, chilled him. And this was the thirtieth link he'd clicked on.

Dashkov leaned back and looked at the pipes crisscrossing the ceiling in his stateroom. "How much proof do you need?" He looked at the screen again. It was the same photograph he'd found in the man's wallet and the caption was simple. 'Daniel Evans, president of the United States and his nephew, Jonathan Evans.' The article attached to the photograph was irrelevant, an editorial hit piece targeting former's environmental record because of the latter's employment at Exxon.

Dashkov leaned sideways and snatched a phone from a bracket.

"Gorshkov to my stateroom. Now." After waiting for confirmation, Dashkov hung up and waited. He scrolled through more images and articles and found the same photograph attached to several more pieces, all in the same environmental vein. A knock sounded at the door.

"Enter," Dashkov barked.

Gorshkov stepped into the small room. "You called for me, Captain?"

"I did," Dashkov said. "Have a seat. I have something to show you and I want your opinion. Not some political bullshit."

"Yes, sir." Gorshkov nodded.

"You know what our purpose is here. You know what is coming, our next orders, correct?"

"Yes, sir."

Dashkov paused and then leaned forward and grabbed the monitor for his desktop computer. He turned it on the desk-mounted hinge to face Gorshkov. He pushed the wired mouse across the desk. "Here. Scroll through the pictures. What do you see?"

Gorshkov looked confused but did as ordered. His right middle finger spun the wheel on the mouse while the index finger clicked away. After a few moments he looked around the monitor. "President Evans and his nephew."

"Exactly."

Gorshkov looked from his captain's face to the screen and back. "Exactly?"

Dashkov flipped the photograph and license from Evans's wallet onto his desk. "Look at those."

Dashkov watched as the younger officer examined the documents. He saw the eyes flick back and forth between the material in his hands and the computer screen. He saw the eyes finally go wide.

"Well?"

"Captain," Gorshkov stuttered. "How… What…?"

Dashkov held a hand up. "We must tell Moscow. We have the nephew of the president of the United States lying half-dead in our medical ward. What will Moscow say? How will this change things?"

"They'll want to fly him off," Gorshkov blurted.

"Are you certain?"

"Of course, Captain. What else would they do?"

Dashkov smiled. "What if he's too sick to transport?"

"I don't know," Gorshkov said. "Is he?"

Dashkov shrugged. "The doctor says so. But what do I know?"

"What are you saying, Captain?"

Dashkov held his hand out for the photograph and license. Gorshkov handed them over and Dashkov sat back in his chair, looking at both items. "I'm saying that it was possible that the American ships out there will eventually open fire on us. Especially if we keep preventing their approach to rigs and harassing them. Our job is to cause chaos. To drive the more risk-averse clients away."

Gorshkov nodded. "*Da*, Captain. I know. Cause problems that drive buyers and investors away so that Russian corporations can purchase ownership of the rigs out here and, subsequently, the gas reserves they pump from. Moscow gave us the orders and target list. But—"

"But it was always possible that the Americans would retaliate. Freedom of the seas and defense of others and all that rubbish. But with the president's ailing nephew on board…"

Dashkov saw the young man's face light up. "We'd be untouchable." Gorshkov's voice was shaking. "Holy shit, Captain. We tell Moscow and they tell the Americans. Or better yet, Moscow tells the world."

Dashkov nodded. "Get the message prepared, Pavel Stefanovich. I want it off the ship in fifteen minutes."

Gorshkov stood. "*Da*, Captain."

The Kremlin
05 December 2022 | 1040 Local Time
Moscow

Anatoly Mikhailovich Shablikov looked at the notes he'd scribbled on the operational plan. "And we are to ramp up on all fronts?"

Director Tolstov nodded. "That's right. Everything. We want the American public so divided and angry that it is impossible for the government to get anything done. Protests. Counter-protests. Riots."

"I can do that." Anatoly made a few additional notes in the margins. They'd been feeding this particular monster for nearly a year. Twisting truth. Publishing outright lies. Distributing everything widely on social media. Letting the animal slip its leash at this point was, Anatoly knew, child's play. "Anything for me on the actions in the Black Sea?"

Tolstov began tapping the keys on his laptop. "That is proceeding on schedule. Captain Dashkov has his orders and his target list and timeframes." Tolstov stopped tapping. "You are certain about the data?"

Anatoly looked up. "The data?"

"The losses, Anatoly. The number of rigs we can destroy without affecting the operation's success."

Anatoly nodded. "Yes, sir. If you remember the report—"

Tolstov raised a hand. "I remember the report, Anatoly. I am just confirming your level of confidence in it."

"Yes, sir. My apologies." Anatoly looked down. He flipped through the pages in his lap. "And this last item on the operational orders? Pages twelve and thirteen."

"Hold on that one for now. The moment needs to be perfect." Tolstov paused. "Or as perfect as it can be. The president will green-light that at the proper time. Any questions, Anatoly?"

Anatoly shook his head and stood. He moved to the door, thought for a moment, and turned back to Tolstov. "Sir, if I may?"

Tolstov looked up from the mess of papers and folders on his desk. "Something on your mind?"

Anatoly pulled the denied medical claim from a pocket and handed it over. "This came yesterday."

Tolstov scanned the document and looked out at Anatoly over his reading glasses. "I'm sorry, Anatoly. How long?"

Anatoly stiffened. "The doctor says a few months. Maybe more. One last try with chemotherapy."

"Expensive?"

"Yes, sir."

Tolstov handed the paperwork back. "I'm sorry. Let me know if you need anything. Anything at all."

"Well, sir. I thought that maybe you could…" Anatoly ran out of momentum. He could hear how pathetic he sounded. Like a Dickensian orphan. *Please, sir.* His face flushed.

Tolstov leaned back in his chair and steepled his fingers. "Ah. Anatoly, you know I can't interfere with such things. The appearance alone."

Anatoly watched his boss, saw that the man wouldn't look him in the eye. He should have been furious and he knew it. But he wasn't. The shock of the words was too much. Anatoly just stood there until the director spoke again.

"Now, Anatoly, if there's nothing else…" The voice drifted off.

Anatoly turned, walked to the door, and started down the corridor, his face red and his knees shaking. He was still trying to get his emotions under control when Tolstov burst out of the office behind him, struggling with his heavy coat.

As the man swept past him, he called back. "Anatoly. Call the president's office. I need to see him immediately. Tell them it is critical."

Anatoly wondered what in the world could have changed in five minutes that he wouldn't have known about, and then picked up his phone.

The White House
05 December 2022 | 0400 Local Time
Washington, DC

President of the United States Daniel Evans couldn't concentrate on anything. He was exhausted. He had a pounding headache. His blood pressure was up. And he was furious.

He glared at the piles of reports on his desk and catalogued them in his head. The green folder contained information on a failed housing initiative. Those two blue folders were budget disasters. The pile of manila folders dealt with a series of blows to voting rights. And that was just the beginning.

He pulled a newspaper closer and read the lead story, the one that claimed that some of the leading Democrats in the Senate were having trouble gathering support for two of the president's key policy initiatives, both of which had enjoyed wide, bipartisan support less than two months prior.

Evans slammed his fist onto the polished surface of the desk. "Damnit."

"Mr. President?"

Evans looked up and saw his chief of staff watching from the doorway leading to his own office.

"What the hell do you want, Leslie?" Evans snarled. His hand was throbbing and he refused to rub it. Better to suffer, he thought. Goddamn idiot.

Barnes shut his own door behind him and crossed the room to the curved door leading to the secretary's office. He spoke a few words to the Secret Service agent nearby and shut that door as well. Finished, he walked over to the seat next to the president's desk and flopped down into it.

"What the hell is the matter with you?"

Evans blinked. He started to respond, but Barnes held up a hand. "You knew what you were getting into here. No one made you do this. You knew this was a tough damn job at the best of times and you didn't run in the best of times. So, what is it? You've been angry at the world for months. What part of this job is pissing you off so much that you're yelling and snapping at everyone and punching shit like you're some dumbass college kid?"

Evans felt his face flush. "Now wait a goddamn minute—"

"Wait for what?" Barnes shot back. "For you to get your shit together? For you to realize that this isn't a fucking pleasure cruise? Hell, Mr. President. You should already know that. You've done shit like this before. You've commanded ships at sea, and there's no way in hell you can sit there and tell me those cruises were all fun and games. So, let's cut the shit."

"Fuck you, Leslie," Evans growled. "You wouldn't understand."

Barnes pointed to the piles of folders on the desk. "Wouldn't understand what? That this is politics and that you're goddamned lucky if twenty percent of the crap you have to deal with goes as planned? Jesus, Mr. President. A few things don't go your way and you think the world is ending? A few nasty messages pop up on social media, some fake videos go viral, and you're quitting? Seriously? What the hell did you think was gonna happen? You'd get your way on the withdrawal and the simplicity fairy would wave her magic wand and make the rest of your agenda just as easy? Come on. You weren't always this stupid."

Evans shot out of his chair. "Now you listen here, you son of a bitch. You can't talk to me that way—"

Barnes popped out of his chair and stuck his face inches from the president's nose. "Or what? You'll fire me? Send me home? Hit me?" He poked the president in the chest, half-expecting the Secret Service agent to rush the room and hit him like an NFL linebacker. "Listen, damnit. This is fucking politics. You have opposition. That's a fact of life. The withdrawal was a walk in the park because damn near everyone agreed on it. But this shit…" Barnes pointed at the reports on the desk. "This shit here has been a wedge in American politics for decades. You are not the second coming of JFK. This is not gonna be easy. You're gonna take hits. From the opposition and from your own damn party. That's the price you pay for being here."

Barnes let the words hang in the air for a moment, then turned and began walking back to his own door. Partway there, he stopped and turned. He jabbed his finger in the air, pointing it directly at the president. "The way I see it, you've got two choices. You can knock off the pity-party bullshit and get back in the damn fight, or you can take your sorry ass to Jack Burroughs' office and tell him you're the wrong man for the job. Either way, you're gonna stop taking your frustrations out on the staff. They bust their asses for you, Mr. President. And they deserve better."

Evans stood there with his mouth open, watching Barnes disappear through the door to the adjoining room. When the door slammed, he dropped into his chair.

For the next several minutes, Evans sat there stewing and muttering to himself. The rage came first. He could feel the vessels in his temples pulsing again. He knew his face was red as hell and he wanted, more than anything, to cross into the chief of staff's office and tell the man sitting there to go find another fucking job.

But Evans didn't move. He took a breath and eyeballed the files on his desk. He took another breath. He thought about the job. It had looked so easy from afar. From the Senate. From his armchair in Virginia. Hell, he thought, even from the bridge of a warship. Evans smiled. Back then, he'd probably held the same opinions of the president at the time that his junior sailors had had of him. Wasn't that a laugh?

This job was hard. Leslie was right about that.

"Shit," Evans muttered. Leslie was right about damn near everything.

The president took another breath and got to his feet. He'd made it halfway to Barnes' office when the door burst open and Barnes stepped into the room.

"Sit Room, Mr. President. Right now."

♦ ♦ ♦

Russian president Dmitri Mikhailovich Barsukov's face covered three of the larger screens on the situation room's wood-paneled walls, and President of the United States Daniel Evans pointed to a man wearing the uniform of an Army major.

"Major Alexander. Volume, please."

The major obliged and Barsukov's voice reverberated around the room.

"I am pleased to report that the crew of the frigate *Makarov* rescued five American sailors and one civilian who were adrift in the vicinity of the *Neptun Deep* Natural Gas facility. The five sailors are currently on board the *Makarov*. They are reported to be in good health and will be returned to the United States as soon as is practicable."

On the screen, Barsukov looked down and flipped a page of notes before continuing. "Before coming here, I spoke to the *Makarov*'s senior medical officer. He reports that the civilian we rescued suffers from several life-threatening injuries and is in critical condition. According to the ship's doctor, this man's condition is too fragile to risk a medical evacuation. This man is getting the best care we can offer him, and I have ordered my own physician to travel to the *Makarov* to attend this case."

Barsukov paused again. Evans looked around. "A civilian? Can't be from the *Williams*."

SECDEF Franklin Tolchanov shook his head. "No, sir, he's not. *Williams* has two tech reps embarked and both are accounted for. Gotta be a survivor from the rig."

Evans nodded and turned back to the television screens. He

saw Barsukov frown.

"Now," the Russian president said. "You may ask why we would go to such lengths to care for a single man. The simple answer would be that to do otherwise would violate the laws and traditions of the sea. To do otherwise would be an unfriendly act. Our actions are, on that front, simple good manners. A goodwill gesture on our behalf."

Barsukov paused again. He turned another page in his notes. When he looked back at the cameras, his face had changed. Evans leaned forward as his counterpart began speaking.

"There is another reason we are making such a remarkable effort to care for this man, and it is infinitely more complex than extending courtesy to the victim of a tragic event. I recently made public evidence implicating the United States and her allies in the ramming of the *Neptun Deep* rig. This man's presence at the scene is further confirmation of the evidence I have already presented. When I tell you his name and his occupation, the world will be forced to accept that the events that have unfolded in the Black Sea are nothing less than an act of aggression by the United States."

Barsukov took one last pause and Evans found himself scanning the room. Everyone had their eyes locked on the screen.

Barsukov smiled. "This man is Jonathan Evans, nephew to President of the United States Daniel Evans, and he is both an employee of Exxon Mobil and the Central Intelligence Agency."

Evans felt his stomach turn to ice, and he fought a shiver. "Oh, holy Christ."

Against the wall to the president's right, Major Harlan Alexander worked hard to keep his face impassive.

9

Novokuznetskaya Flats
05 December 2022 | 2100 Local Time
Moscow

Two hours after the president's address, Anatoly sat in his tiny apartment on Novokuznetskaya Prospekt, a half-empty bottle of samogon in front of him. He'd come straight home after his appointment and started drinking, an old reaction to stress he'd been denying himself for years, especially during his first bout with cancer.

Went through all that for nothing. The pain. The exhaustion. The hair loss. The nausea. For nothing. Didn't learn a damn thing, did you? Bought everything those kids in lab coats told you. Idiot.

Anatoly turned back to the samogon. The half-bottle of bootleg liquor he'd consumed in the past two hours had done its job. He was filthy drunk and a half-formed idea flitted through his brain. Anatoly eyed the container closely, as though the handwritten label might contain some helpful information about drinking oneself to death.

"What do you think, bottle? Is there enough left in here to kill me?" Anatoly poked at the bottle. "Speak up, little friend. Can you finish me off?"

The bottle and Anatoly sat in strained silence for a few moments before Anatoly laughed. "Shit. I'm talking to my drink."

He picked the bottle up and pressed the cool glass to his lips, guzzling down half of what was left. The liquor burned its way down his throat and warmed him. Anatoly felt his skin begin to flush.

Cheer up, Anatoly. At least you made it this long.

He snorted, a ripping, throaty noise that echoed in his sinuses.

Your brother died after what…four days? Your wife died after two weeks. You've outlived them all. Even collected a pension for your trouble. Pension? No. That wasn't retirement cash. They told you that. After you spoke up. That one time you stepped out of line. That young major from the KGB had been crystal clear.

Anatoly could still hear the major's voice.

"Anatoly…take the money, retire to Moscow, and never speak of what happened. Never question the events leading to the explosion at Chernobyl. It was operator error, Anatoly. Your brother let the reactor get away from him and it killed him. Didn't trust his supervisors. Didn't listen. Didn't believe the Party knew better than him. And your wife, what was she doing at the facility so late? Catching up on paperwork that should have been completed already? And she died for it. Just like your brother. She ignored her daily work quotas and found herself behind. In the wrong place at the wrong time. If she'd only listened, Anatoly. If she'd believed that the Party set those quotas for her own good, she'd be here for you now. They both died because they lacked faith. They didn't trust. Are you going to make the same mistake? Are you going to fail to trust? Take the money, Anatoly. Trust the Party. We know what's best. Take the money, retire, and never speak of this…or we can make you disappear. Happens all the time. Gulags and work camps are terrible places. Accidents happen. Accidents with bullets. Take the pension, Anatoly. Take the pension and keep your mouth shut."

Anatoly had taken the rubles and he'd never again openly questioned how his wife and brother had died. He'd stayed in Moscow, as he'd been told. He'd toed the line and had accepted a steady job where Russia's spies could keep an eye on him. And he'd never uttered another word about the matter. Not one. Of course, it wasn't that Anatoly had developed some newfound trust in communism or the Party or anything like that after the major's warning. It had been simpler than that. The KGB terrified him.

He'd heard the stories and rumors and old wives' tales. He believed every last word.

How could I not believe, after the major's threats?

So, Anatoly had done as he was told. He banked his monthly stipend and kept his mouth shut while his wife was forgotten entirely and his brother was blamed for the "accident."

Accident, my ass.

He barked out another dry laugh. "Piece of shit reactor," he slurred. "Piece of shit design. Everyone knew. They'd been warned. That one prissy bastard. The physicist. He'd testified how the fucking thing could explode. He'd published a paper."

Anatoly grunted. "That bastard had warned everyone. Fucking graphite tips. Fucking unstable reactor." He made an explosion sound with his mouth and cackled. "They fucking knew. And did nothing."

Anatoly played with the bottle, tilting it this way and that. Speaking to it as though it could hear. "And then Chernobyl happened. Followed that bastard's report like a screenplay." Anatoly felt the tears well up in his eyes. "And what did they do? They bought your silence. They blamed the operators. Called them reckless. Irresponsible."

And now here you are, Anatoly. Thirty-six years later. Dying of cancer. Without the balls to say anything. Coward.

Anatoly watched the late afternoon sunlight break against the pale green glass of the bottle.

And what are you going to do about that, Anatoly? What can you do? Nothing. You're going to sit here on your drunk ass and get busy dying.

Wimp.

He took another long pull from the nearly-empty bottle and rose to his feet, clutching it by the neck.

Anatoly began wobbling across the ninety-nine square meters of his apartment towards the small bedroom, using the walls and shoddy furniture to steady himself. His head and stomach were spinning, both angry at the volume of alcohol Anatoly had ingested. He bobbed back and forth like a damaged bumper car while everything in his apartment shifted in and out of focus.

Steady, Anatoly. Steady. Almost there.

He could see his dirty, unmade bed, and a pair of hazy duplicates nearing slowly, each of the three incarnations sliding in and out of his view as he ricocheted across the apartment.

He'd almost made it to the hall when he crashed into a cheap wooden chair. Anatoly tipped over, reaching for the doorjamb and missing. He collapsed in a heap, splashing the last of his alcohol onto the floor.

After a few moments, Anatoly looked up, saw the three beds drifting lazily behind what looked like fragments of a chair, and decided that crawling might be safer. Clutching the now-empty bottle, he pushed himself to his hands and knees and began moving again, shuffling along like an infant over the rough hardwood floor. He tried to keep an eye on the beds as he crept forward, swaying this way and that like a newborn calf, the bottle bumping hollowly as he went.

Just a few meters more. Almost there. He was sweating profusely now, each pore oozing alcohol. *Good God, I stink.*

"Come on Anatoly! Almost there." Anatoly cheered himself on. *Who the fuck are you talking to? Doesn't matter. Keep crawling.*

Anatoly paused, his chest heaving. Sweat dripped from his chin, forming a small puddle on the floor.

Take a rest, Anatoly. Just a minute.

Anatoly slumped to the ground, finally letting go of the bottle and sending it rolling across the floor.

Brookshire Apartments
05 December 2022 | 1730 Local Time
Alexandria, Virginia

Major Harlan Alexander stepped out of his Alexandria apartment in faded jeans, a black t-shirt, and a mock-peacoat he'd purchased at a nearby mall. He shivered in the falling snow as he pulled a gray knit cap down over his hair and ears and climbed into his car, a white, one-year-old Mercedes A220 that he'd started remotely. He sank into the leather seat and felt the warm air flowing from the vents wash over him.

"Fuck, it's cold," he grumped.

As he backed out of his parking space, he thought about everything he could be doing instead of taking an evening drive into southern Maryland. Reading. Watching television. Scrolling through social media. Drinking. Anything beat being out in the cold on a night like this.

It could be worse, he thought. I've got this car and it has a hell of a sound system. Harlan smiled and cranked the volume as he steered towards King Street and the nearby connections to the DC Beltway. By the time he merged onto Maryland 4 South, Harlan's brief irritation was being drowned by the sounds of a nineties rock playlist on his iPod.

He traveled south, weaving smoothly in and out of traffic. In forty minutes, he'd passed through Dunkirk and Prince Frederick and was nearing his destination. Harlan turned off the highway after checking the time. He had forty-five minutes before his appointment and there was a barbecue restaurant less than a mile from the location that he'd been wanting to try. He found the eatery and devoured a pulled pork sandwich, fries, and a beer before driving his car across the highway to a retirement community nestled against the banks of the Patuxent River.

Harlan circled the main building complex to the cottages on the waterfront and found the one he was searching for. He parked in the driveway, walked to the front door, and knocked.

A man in his mid-sixties, with crew-cut salt-and-pepper hair, opened the door. "Harlan, get yer butt in here, boy."

"Hi, Dad." Harlan followed his father inside and found a spot on the couch.

"You want a drink?"

Harlan shook his head. "No. I gotta head back tonight."

Henry Alexander poured himself two fingers of scotch, neat. "Suit yourself." He slurped from the tumbler and found a spot on the couch opposite Harlan. "I'm supposed to pass on some thanks. That report you sent up, the one about the president barking and snapping at folks—that was useful."

Harlan shifted in his seat, uncomfortable with the way his father tended to just blurt out things like that. "Dad, I wish you wouldn't…"

"Wouldn't what? Say shit like that?" Henry took another gulp from his glass and grinned, his yellowed teeth on prominent display behind a pair of paper-thin lips. "What, boy? You don't like spying for Russia?"

"Dad!" Harlan launched to his feet. "What the hell?"

Henry Alexander just sat, sipping his drink and grinning. "Relax, boy. Relax." He waved Harlan back to his seat. "I didn't fall off the turnip truck yesterday."

Harlan eased himself back down. His heart was pounding and he remembered why he hated these meetings. It hadn't always been like this. There was a time when Henry Alexander had been Harlan's hero, when the half-drunk man in front of him had taught him how to play baseball and golf. But that was a past life, before his father's last posting as a CIA chief of station and before his mother had been murdered. Harlan had been in school then, a senior at West Point.

His father, after a series of missteps at other postings, had been assigned COS in Bamako, Mali. The assignment, intended to get Henry Alexander to retirement quickly and quietly and without repeats of incidents that had plagued him in Belarus, Moldova, Iraq, and Estonia, went disastrously wrong when a local group of militants fired more than three hundred rounds into the car Henry normally used. Harlan's mother, who'd been smuggled into the country for a visit against agency regulations, had died at the scene.

"I know, Dad." Harlan acknowledged. "It's just that…"

Henry put his drink down. "Just what?"

"I don't know about all this anymore. Is it worth it?"

Harlan occupied himself with an examination of his shoes. He knew what was coming.

"I see," Henry said. "And your mother? Is she worth it?"

"That's not what I meant, Dad."

Henry stood. Harlan could feel his dad hovering, could almost smell his breath.

"Now you listen here. You know why we do this." Harlan looked up to see his dad pointing off in a random direction. His face was reddening and spittle was collecting at the corners of his mouth. "Your mother. You know what they did. What they fucking knew."

Harlan knew the story. After the incident in Mali, his father had been summoned home for the investigation and eventual early retirement. While staying at a hotel near Dulles, he'd awoken one morning to find an envelope under his door. The package had contained twenty sheets of paper, xeroxed copies of intelligence that claimed the CIA had known of the attack beforehand and had dismissed the information as unreliable.

"I know, Dad. I know. But…"

"But what, damnit? Those sons of bitches knew. They knew about the attack and they didn't say shit. Not one fucking word."

"I know that, damnit," Harlan snapped. "But spying on the president? Jesus, Pop." It occurred to Harlan that referring to his actions as spying was surreal. And vaguely amateurish. Like something from a damn fiction book, he thought.

Henry Alexander sat back down. "You didn't see your mother in that car. You didn't see what those animals did to her. What some punk-ass desk pilot at the agency let them do. We wouldn't know the truth if it wasn't for these people."

Harlan sat there, waiting him out. This was a useless argument. They'd had it before. It always came down to the same thing. His mother. It was a guilt trip that his father had always used effectively. Harlan had loved his mother. She'd been the one who'd always been there, in between the baseball games and golf tournaments. She'd been the one who'd stayed up late with him to study. She'd been the one who'd made him laugh after two tough breakups by using her colorful language to express how she felt about the departing young women.

As much as Harlan hated to admit it, he was a mama's boy. And his mother was dead. And her death had been preventable. And sure, maybe she shouldn't have been in Mali. But that wouldn't have mattered if the threat had been taken seriously. So, he owed her this. His father was right. Again.

Harlan sighed. "All right, Pop. What next?"

They talked for twenty minutes before sharing an awkward hug goodbye. Henry Alexander cupped his son's face with a pair of big, rough hands. "Remember, boy. This is for your mom."

Harlan nodded and climbed back into his car for the drive back to Alexandria. In two hours he was in bed, fighting to shut his brain off and staring at the ceiling.

**USS *Key West*
06 December 2022 | 0045 Local Time
Black Sea**

Commander Reynes ordered the USS *Key West* deep and turned for his stateroom. "Nav, you have the conn. XO, with me."

"I have the conn," the *Key West*'s navigator confirmed.

Reynes and Lieutenant Commander Will Sandler walked the few steps to the captain's stateroom. Reynes took a seat as Sandler slid the door shut.

"Read this, Will." Reynes handed over the message they'd just downloaded. "Tell me what you think."

Sandler took the paper and began scanning, his eyes moving back and forth quickly. When he finished, he looked up. "Jesus Christ, Scott. Is this for real?"

Reynes looked at his XO, one eyebrow raised. Sandler shook his head. "Okay. That was a stupid question. But…it's not really that stupid."

"Maybe not."

Sandler scanned the paper again. "This says that the tanker rammed the rig on purpose."

"And that the Russians are blaming us," Reynes noted. "It doesn't say why we supposedly hired some poor bastard to ram the rig, but I'm sure we'll get that information later. It's not important anyway."

"So, we're supposed to remain on station and monitor events. And keep track of the *Kazan* and the *Makarov* and anyone else we hear." Sandler was reading the missive for the third time. "Doesn't give us a reporting schedule." He paused. "At our own discretion?"

Reynes nodded. "I want to brief the chiefs and officers in the next thirty minutes."

Sandler handed the message back. "Walkdown?"

"As soon as the briefing is over," Reynes confirmed. "I want it so goddamn quiet I can hear all of the angry things Fireman Higgins is thinking about me. How is he, by the way?"

"Still delinquent," Sandler noted. "Getting awfully close to decision time with that kid. Sixteen months on board and no closer to getting his fish than he was on day one."

"Send him home or to the surface fleet?"

"Surface should do nicely. Stick him on a carrier somewhere," Sandler opined. "He's a good mechanic and all. Fits in nicely with the guys in A-Gang. Knowing the whole boat is just beyond him."

"All right. We'll deal with that later. Get the khakis together and set up the walkdown."

"Yes, sir."

USS *James E. Williams*
06 December 2022 | 0100 Local Time
Black Sea

Commander Derrick Allen scowled at the displays in front of him. His eyes flicked back and forth between the various annotations. The *Williams*. The *Makarov*. The rig.

"Shit." He looked down at the messages in his hands and scanned the one on top. He looked up. "Christ, Master Chief. As if I don't have enough fucking problems."

Logan Carrillo shrugged. "At least it's just his leg. Could have been worse."

Allen nodded. The short message in his hands told him that his executive officer, the recently promoted Commander John Polian, would not be returning to the ship. Expected to fleet up and replace Allen as the ship's commander after deployment, Polian had been temporarily detached to complete the Prospective Commanding Officer's course in Norfolk. He'd been riding his Harley home the previous evening—Allen had briefly attempted to get a grasp on the time differences before giving up in favor of other, more serious issues—and had been hit by a car crossing Dam Neck Road. Except for Polian's broken leg—tib, fib, and femur—and a severe case of road rash, there had been no other injuries. The driver of the car—a mid-thirties software engineer—had simply missed the red light and had suffered only a minor concussion and bloodied nose in the accident.

"And just like that," Allen pointed at the second message, "OPS is the new XO." He turned to Carrillo. "This gonna be a problem?"

Carrillo looked around and lowered his voice. "Sir, you have to know how the crew feels about OPS. Hell, we've talked about him a few times."

The operations officer for USS *James E. Williams* was Lieutenant Lance Caldwell, a United States Naval Academy graduate whose air of superiority routinely manifested itself in his dealings with both the enlisted crew and the ship's complement of ensigns and junior-grade lieutenants. He'd gone toe-to-toe with the Chiefs Mess on several occasions, and the most recent incident was barely a week old.

"He needs to learn respect, sir. Plain and simple. And not just for those senior to him. You can't stomp all over junior personnel and expect them to have your back," Carrillo offered. "That thing last week, trying to write up Chief Thompson for disobeying an order. Shit like that does not endear him to the crew."

The captain nodded. The whole incident had been a damn disaster. Caldwell, who was not part of the ship's Damage Control Training Team and, therefore, subject to the team's evaluation of his actions during a planned drill set, had demanded a copy of the drill plan. Thompson had refused twice. Probably, Allen thought, with little in the way of diplomacy. That wasn't the Top Snipe's strong suit. The result was as predictable as it was stupid. The drill had been run. OPS had screwed it up. The drill team had noted the faults. And OPS had placed Chief Thompson on report, blaming the older chief for damn near everything.

"I know that, Master Chief. But that's not what I'm asking."

"I know, sir." Carrillo pointed at the message. "Personal opinions aside, this piece of paper says he's the new XO and that's how it is. The crew doesn't have to like it. But they will support it."

"If it were only that simple, Master Chief." Allen looked down at the message again and shook his head. "Shit. Guess we'd better tell him."

Carrillo nodded. "Yes, sir."

Allen moved to leave the ship's Combat Information Center. He paused and turned back. "Any word on Chief Thompson?"

"He's awake. Senior Martin is keeping an eye on him for a few more hours before he cuts him loose."

"He know about the boat crew yet?"

Carrillo shook his head. "No, sir. Given his reaction to the news about Faulkner, Senior and I figured that news could wait."

"All right. We'll tell him about that before Senior discharges him. Might as well break the news in medical in case he passes out again."

"I'll let Senior know."

"Good." Allen waved the papers in his hand. "I'll brief the wardroom on this after I tell Lieutenant Caldwell. Want me to tell the chiefs too?"

"No, sir," Carrillo said. "I'll get the chiefs together and let 'em know what's up. You want to talk to them afterwards, that's up to you."

Allen nodded. "Set it up. Thanks, Master Chief."

16

Novokuznetskaya Flats
06 December 2022 | 0700 Local Time
Moscow

Anatoly's eyelids blazed orange against the sunlight pouring through his curtain-bereft windows. His first conscious action was to shut them tighter as his central nervous system tried to report in.

His head was pounding, threatening to rattle his eyeballs out of their sockets. His hands moved slowly to cover his head, a reflexive movement intended to dampen the pulsing sensation he felt in his brain.

Mother of God, Anatoly. What did you do?

Anatoly cracked open one eye and tried to look around. His head lolled to one side. An empty liquor bottle rested against the baseboard.

Oh.

He eyed the bottle.

That's a big damn bottle. A big damn empty bottle.

Anatoly closed his eye and tried to breathe, making an empty promise to never drink again. He took a deep breath in and exhaled slowly.

His sockless feet were freezing and his knees felt slightly raw, a reminder of his drunken crawl the night before. His back was stiff. His thighs were…cold?

The hell?

The realization hit him when the smell did.

Lovely. I pissed myself.

The smell of stale urine was cut by another scent, one that Anatoly couldn't quite place. He rolled over and placed his hand on the floor to push himself upright. A soggy mass squeezed between his fingers. Anatoly looked at his hand and gagged.

Some Russian you are. Can't hold your liquor.

He stayed there for a few seconds wiping his hand on his shirt and looking at the acidic puddle with its bits of partially digested black bread and cabbage.

You're a fucking mess, Anatoly. You know that?

He tried to take another deep breath, attempting to ease the pounding in his skull. The scent of urine and bile, mixed with his own sweat and body odor, filled his nostrils. Anatoly felt his stomach heave.

Oh shit.

Anatoly lurched forward towards the lavatory. He emptied the scant contents of his stomach, mostly bile, for several minutes and pushed the little handle on the front of the toilet. He watched the rush of water carry remnants of the previous night away to one of Moscow's sewage plants. He put the lid down and turned, sitting on the toilet and leaning sideways on the sink. He was exhausted again. He closed his eyes and worked to control his breathing. After several minutes, Anatoly opened his eyes. He kept leaning the side of his head on the cool, curved metal edge of the sink and peered out of the bathroom. He could see every room in his flat from here.

Anatoly almost laughed with the realization that his job really did carry more prestige than pay. Who would believe, he thought, that someone in my position would live like this? He almost laughed again when the answer popped into his head. Everyone would believe it. This was Moscow, where the cost of living was lapping the meager pay on an annual basis. Unless you really were one of the elite. One of the faces and names that everyone recognized. And wasn't that a funny thought? The elite. Here. In the heart of a city that had railed against social classes. Anatoly chuckled and his head ached. He looked around.

What a shithole.

The bathroom, just a sink, a small, dripping shower, and the toilet, was so small that, seated as he was on the toilet, Anatoly's knees touched the opposite wall. The white tile on the floor was yellowed with age, hard water stains, and, probably, urine. It was cracked in several places, with sections of grout missing here and there. The wallpaper, crispy and old, was 1970s Soviet-chic, a pretentious design probably copied from some tsarist-era palace.

The bedroom, hardly big enough for a proper bed, consisted of cracked, grayish-white plaster walls and a hardwood floor that looked like it might have been more than a century old. A small chest of drawers, with at least three layers of paint peeling from the dented and scratched surfaces, stood against one wall. The bed, a cheap metal frame with a shitty old mattress, was pressed against the flat's back wall, providing just enough open space for one person to get dressed. A single, bare bulb usually lighted the room, but the wiring had shorted out weeks ago and the building's owner had ignored all of Anatoly's requests for repair.

Beyond the bedroom was the combination kitchen/dining room/living room. It couldn't be considered a proper kitchen, with only one burner, a sink, and a small, waist-high refrigerator with a rattling compressor. Nor was it a proper dining room, with one rickety table and three mismatched chairs, one of which, Anatoly saw, was wrecked from the previous night's stumbling. The room was only a living room in the sense that a living person could exist there, watching television while eating. Anatoly owned a small television, which sat on the kitchen counter opposite the table. There was no room for an armchair, much as Anatoly would have liked one. He probably could have purchased one second-hand, but the prospect of carrying something that bulky up endless flights of stairs and trying to squeeze it into the room had always struck him as preposterous exercise, something the laws of physics simply would not permit.

Everywhere he looked, Anatoly saw squalor. The tile on the kitchen wall, a pale green color that had been a trademark of socialist architecture more than forty years before, was coming apart. The kitchen faucet was leaking, the constant pinging drips of water hitting the metal basin completely out of sync with the pounding in Anatoly's head.

I live in a shithole.

Anatoly blinked.

I hate this place. I've lived in this same shitty flat for twenty years. Twenty damn years! Just wasting away.

He shifted on the toilet so that the back of his neck rested on the cool edge of the sink. He moved his hands to his head, rubbing his temples and trying to calm the demons that were still trying to dislodge his eyeballs.

Cheer up, Anatoly. You only have to live here for four more months. Less than that now. You're going to die here, Comrade.

Anatoly stopped rubbing his temples. He opened his eyes and lifted his head, fighting the heaviness of the hangover. He looked around again. His gaze stopped at the chest of drawers, taking in the two pictures there.

Valentina Ivanova. My poor wife. Dead for, what, thirty-six years now? Vladimir. My brother. Thirty-six years for him, too. Radiation. Both gone.

Anatoly sat up, head aching, and looked around again. He looked at the rotting floorboards of the bedroom and the puddle of vomit drying in the sunlight. He looked back at the pictures of his wife and brother. He looked at the kitchen, with the dripping faucet and broken tiles. He looked around the bathroom, at two roaches in the corner, one alive and one dead, on its back, legs pointing at the ceiling. He looked back at the pictures.

The hell with this. I'm not dying in this roach-infested shithole.

Anatoly stood and moved to the dresser, wondering just how in the hell he'd make good on that idea.

USS *James E. Williams*
06 December 2022 | 0715 Local Time
Black Sea

"For fuck's sake, stop rolling your neck," Senior Chief Martin barked.

Chief Petty Officer Brian Thompson ignored him and reached up again to rub the side of his neck. Pain was radiating from there, a burning and tingling sensation that kept him on edge. Martin batted his hand away.

"Dude."

"Leave your neck alone," Martin ordered. "You're just making it worse." Martin checked Brian's eyes and ran his hands down both sides of Brian's neck. "How's the headache?"

Brian paused for a moment, taking measure. "It's there, but better."

Martin nodded and turned as the door to the medical office opened and shut. "Captain?"

"How is he, Senior Chief?"

"He's a stubborn shit. He'll live. I'd feel better with a scan or two, but…" Martin shrugged and stood, offering his seat to the captain.

Commander Allen nodded and took Martin's offered seat. "Chief, we've got some news you aren't gonna like."

Brian looked around the room. Lieutenant Walker was there, as were Carrillo and Lieutenant Caldwell. "Faulkner?"

Allen shook his head. "No. You know about Faulkner. MA1 Gramble and two of the chiefs are inventorying his things now."

"So, what's this about?" Brian started to roll his neck again and caught a warning look from Martin.

"This is about the boat crew."

Brian thought he saw where this was headed. "Captain, I don't know if you've noticed, but I'm not in the best shape to go riding around on those things."

"*Thing*, Chief. Singular," Caldwell blurted out.

Brian leaned sideways and looked around Commander Allen. "No, sir. Things. Plural. We have two boats."

Allen turned and shot Caldwell a dirty look that Brian caught. "Captain?"

"Chief, when you took that spill down in Steering, we were maneuvering to avoid a collision. We had both choppers up and one boat in the water. When we maneuvered clear…"

Brian felt the pounding in his head grow stronger. "Oh, hell no…"

Allen nodded. "I won't go into details, but our boat crew got picked up by the Russian frigate."

Brian took a deep breath and exhaled. "Which crew?" he asked through clinched teeth.

"Mr. Strater's crew," Caldwell announced.

"I wasn't asking you," Brian growled. He could feel his face flushing red, could sense the heat there.

"Sir," Caldwell said.

Brian looked up. "Excuse me?"

"Sir," Caldwell repeated. "When you talk to me, you call me sir."

Commander Allen turned before Brian could say anything. "XO, why don't you wait outside? Master Chief and I will be out in a second."

Brian watched Caldwell leave. When the door was shut, he turned to Master Chief Carrillo. He started to ask about the boat crew, but a thought got his attention. "Did you just call him XO? Did I fucking hear that right?"

Allen and Carrillo nodded.

"You gotta be shitting me." Brian stood up. He wobbled for a moment and saw Senior Chief Martin reach for him. Brian knocked the hands away. "Get the fuck off me."

"Listen, Chief… About…" Commander Allen started, standing.

"Listen to what?" Brian barked. "I get knocked out and while I'm out, Faulkner hangs himself, a boat crew gets hijacked, and that son of a bitch becomes the XO? Anything else y'all wanna tell me? Any more little fucking surprises?"

Brian saw the anger flare in Commander Allen's eyes. He saw the much larger man stepping forward and saw his mouth open to say something. But nothing came out. Master Chief Carrillo's hand appeared on the captain's chest.

"Captain, wanna let me fix this? Before you both go down this road?"

Brian could see his commanding officer's temper flaring. The man was breathing hard and his jaw was set. But the eyes shifted, away from Brian. Commander Allen looked at Master Chief Carrillo and pointed at Brian. "Fix him, Master Chief. Fix him now."

Commander Allen left the room and Carrillo shut the door.

"Jesus, Logan. What in the…"

"Shut the fuck up." Carrillo turned and advanced on Brian. "What in the flying fuck is your problem?"

"But…"

"What? You think that man just let the boat crew get snatched up? That he doesn't give a shit about Faulkner? That he doesn't have enough problems without having to deal with some disrespectful shit like you?"

Brian's eyes went wide. "Listen, Logan—"

"Master Chief, you dumb bastard. Master Chief. This isn't the fuckin' mess and we aren't on the same page. I'm a fucking master chief." He pointed at the door. "And the men standing outside that goddamn door are your commanding officer and executive officer and you will fucking respect that shit or so help me God I will fucking end your goddamn career. Do you get me, Chief?"

The last word was delivered with a snarl and menace Brian had never heard before, and Brian felt his skin go pale. Senior Chief Martin must have seen it, because he stepped forward.

"Listen, Logan. Brian needs to…"

Carrillo turned on Martin. "I don't give a good goddamn what he needs right now. He's gonna hear this." He turned back to Brian.

"I don't know what kind of shit goes through that thick skull of yours and I don't care. I also don't give a shit how technically proficient you are or how well your damn department is doing. You are entirely too comfortable running your mouth, you don't know shit about diplomacy, and you don't know jack shit about what it takes to do their damn jobs." Carrillo took a deep breath. "If you think that one-man circus you had running the last time we were out gives you the right to talk shit to your chain of command, then you're a whole lot dumber than you look. That crap stops today. You will do your damn job. You will maintain your military bearing at all times. You will impress upon your people the importance of doing the same." Carrillo took a step closer to Brian and jabbed him in the chest. "And you'll start right fucking now. Because the next time I see or hear about you mouthing off to, or about, anyone senior to you, I will drag your ass to mast myself. Do you get me?"

Brian looked down at the deck. Carrillo moved to the door. "Senior. Get him discharged and get him back to work."

Carrillo opened the door and stopped. He turned. "Oh. One more thing."

Brian looked up.

"Chief, you're going to apologize to both of those men. Today." Carrillo stepped into the passageway and slammed the door.

Brian went back to examining the floor.

Warehouse #4, Arbat District
06 December 2022 | 0830 Local Time
Moscow

Anatoly wished he'd stayed home for the day, and it amused him that, for the first time in almost a year, the wish didn't stem from his cancer or the side effects of chemotherapy. He'd almost gotten used to working through all of that, or so he told himself. No, cancer wasn't to blame today. Chemo wasn't to blame. Anatoly could only blame himself. And the empty bottle of samogon. His head ached. His stomach kept turning over. He was tired.

But he was here, at work, despite suffering from the mother of all hangovers, because there was a job to do.

At least, he thought, I'm not in my stuffy office. It is cooler here.

Here, was the operations center for the ongoing cyber war against the United States. In the movies, Anatoly thought, such rooms were always dark. Black walls and stainless-steel workstations and the eternal bluelight glow of hundreds of computer monitors. And cabling. There were always miles of cables and cords in the movies, nearly all of it blue or clear or black.

But that was in the movies. This room was well lit and it was five hundred meters square. The walls were beige. The ceiling white. And the cabling was an assorted rainbow of power supplies and data wiring. The room didn't look Russian. It looked vaguely American, he thought. New. Cheap. Undistinguished. Like one of those mega-churches Americans were fond of.

The First Russian Orthodox Church of Disinformation.

Anatoly grinned at the irony and began walking around. His people were hard at work and he checked in on them as he moved about the room. In that section, ten of his people were creating and uploading deepfake videos. Over there, in the corner, another ten people were busy building botnets. In the center of the room, a full thirty people were busy creating and managing social media accounts, posting and liking and commenting and starting virtual fights.

Anatoly nodded in approval and left the main room. He walked down a short corridor and entered the second conference room on his left. At the table, ten men and women rose and Anatoly waved them back to their seats before taking his own.

"Good morning."

The group responded in unison and Anatoly had to stop himself from rolling his eyes.

"Thank you for being here." Anatoly cleared his throat. "Your section chiefs selected you from your brothers and sisters out there because you are the best at what you do. Your…ah…creations," Anatoly paused when some of the group chuckled, "have the most views and your personas have the highest levels of interactions. In short, what you put into cyberspace is believable. Americans are eating it up. Congratulations and thank you for your hard work."

Anatoly clapped his hands a few times and the people at the table followed suit. When Anatoly stopped, so did the group.

"So, what is next?" Anatoly smiled. "Up to now, you've generated intangible results. Shifted opinion. Moved the political needles, as it were. I am here to give you new direction."

A hand rose halfway down the table on the left. "Excuse me, sir. What do you mean?"

"I'm glad you asked." Anatoly leaned forward. "Using information and scripts that we provide, you are going do what you have been doing, but with a different goal."

"A different goal, sir?"

"I want you to produce a tangible result."

The room went silent for a few moments before a hand went up to Anatoly's right. "Sir, can you clarify what you mean by that?"

"To date, you've created videos and seduced portions of the American public in order to sway public opinion. You are now being authorized to take it one step further. I want you to push people into the streets. I want to see riots in American cities when I turn on the news. I want you to feed both sides and set them against each other using the information and evidence my office will provide."

Ten pairs of eyes blinked at Anatoly and he saw sly grins beginning to form on each face.

Anatoly smiled back. "Your ultimate goal, the purpose of this exercise, is simple. When the opposition to the Evans Administration is at its peak, when you have completely and utterly enraged the American public so that they are at each other's throats, I will have you unleash all of that hatred."

11

**USS *James E. Williams*
06 December 2022 | 0900 Local Time
Black Sea**

Chief Petty Officer Brian Thompson didn't see a soul in the passageways when he left the medical office. The usual noises were there. The vent ducts wheezed and sputtered. The sea swished against the hull. Nearby, a check valve for the ship's masker air system rattled. But there were no voices. No sailors were walking around, going from space to space as they did their jobs and operated the ship. And that was good. Brian didn't want to see or talk to anyone. He turned and headed aft down the portside passageway.

He'd been going over the ass-chewing he'd just received for more than an hour while Senior Chief Martin went through the trouble of conducting one more physical exam, signing off on the paperwork, and making the appropriate entries in the medical records. Brian's brain hadn't stopped working on the problem. What was said. What he should have said. What he wished he had said. He argued with himself, told himself he'd had a right to be pissed. That it was a normal reaction.

Wasn't it?

Brian kept moving aft, bypassing his office and the entrance to CCS on his way to his berthing compartment. He'd planned on changing clothes before going to see the captain, but a sniff at both armpits told him he could stand a shower. Probably a shave too.

Brian stripped out of his uniform, gathered his shower gear, and moved into the head. There was no one there, so Brian set his gear up, hung the towel over the curtain rod, and stepped into the shower. He turned the water on and jumped when the cold water hit him like frozen sandpaper.

"Fuck."

"Brian? You in here?"

It was Logan's voice. Brian hadn't heard the door open. He didn't answer. He didn't want to answer. The water had warmed up and it felt good.

"Brian?"

Brian leaned his head back. "Yeah. I'm here."

"Need you in the captain's cabin in five minutes."

Brian felt the anger rising again, could feel his body heat up despite the near-scalding water. He said nothing.

"You hear me, Brian?"

Brian clenched his jaw, felt the muscles ache. "Yeah. I heard you."

"Five minutes." The door shut.

The White House
06 December 2022 | 0210 Local Time
Washington, DC

President Daniel Evans hung up the phone and put his head in his hands. To his right, through the door to the anteroom where the executive secretaries went about their business, there would be a collection of senior staffers waiting to update him on various things—everything from hourly briefings on the situation in the Black Sea to concerns over inflation and an array of other economic indicators. Those people needed to get in here, to tell him things, to communicate what they knew so that they could move on to other tasks. But Evans didn't press the intercom button, didn't let his secretary know that he was off the latest call.

The man would know anyway, Evans thought. He'd have seen the light for line four go out and he'd have prepped those who were waiting. But the president needed a moment. This call had been difficult, even more so than the one he wanted to have with Dmitri Barsukov. On that call, he'd simply be trying to forestall a crisis—to deter military confrontation in the Black Sea. That, he thought, would be child's play compared to having to sit and listen while his brother had screamed at him and his sister-in-law had cried. That they'd already been awake when he'd called wasn't surprising. They'd been waiting for an update, for information. Anything.

The president took a few deep breaths to calm himself and pressed the button.

"Send them in."

There was a short, courteous reply and the molded door to the president's right opened to admit his staff.

"Mr. President." Barnes nodded his greeting. "How did that go?"

Evans bit off his initial reply and shook his head instead. "Telling them we don't yet know anything about Jonathan other than what was on television? It was just peachy." Evans laid the sarcasm on thick, but he thought that was better than biting the man's head off.

Barnes raised an eyebrow. "I thought we were sticking to the standard line on this. We are looking at the situation and…" Barnes stopped when he saw the president's face change.

"Leslie, the people I just got done talking to are my family. My older brother and his wife. I am not going to, and never will, feed them some line of politically neutral bullshit. Especially not over this. Is that clear?"

Barnes nodded. "Fair enough, sir."

Evans stood and waved everyone to the sitting area. He took a seat in one of the wingback chairs and crossed his right leg over his left. The briefings on economic activity and a slew of other domestic issues took ten minutes. Evans asked the occasional question and assigned two staffers to gather more information on a few items. At the end of the briefing, he looked around the room.

"All right, folks. What else have you got?"

"Mr. President," DNI Adams started, "we've got indications and reports that Barsukov may be planning on ordering reinforcements into the Black Sea. Satellite passes over various naval facilities show heat blooms in approximately sixty vessels and lots of pierside activity."

Evans nodded. "Supply trucks and trains and whatnot?"

"That's correct, Mr. President."

Evans chewed on his lip for a moment. "If Barsukov orders those ships into the Black Sea, they can effectively blockade the rigs. Right?"

"Yes, Mr. President," Adams confirmed. "And not just the ones on the Romanian coast. These drilling platforms dot the coast. Ukraine. Bulgaria. With the vessels we have information on, the Russian Navy can effectively seal off the area and keep it that way."

"To what purpose, though?" Barnes asked. "They don't own the rigs and they don't control the gas fields."

DNI Adams shook her head. "We don't know, and taking Barsukov at face value is a gross miscalculation. Russia isn't doing this to curry favor with the companies or countries who own those facilities. At least, I don't think they are."

"But the Russian people will believe that," Evans noted. "So will people in those countries who support Russia. The people in Russia don't exactly get both sides of the story on any topic, and Russian support outside their own borders tends to be pretty…ah, strong."

"Belligerent might be a better description, Mr. President," Barnes offered.

Evans shrugged. "Well, whatever we call it, it's been growing." He paused. "Hell. It's even growing here. All of that crap on social media. One side saying that Russian intelligence interfered in the election and the other side screaming to stop blaming our internal disagreements on Russia."

"Mr. President," Adams said. "It is possible that this is something else."

Barnes and Evans turned. The president raised an eyebrow. "I'm listening."

Adams cleared her throat. "In 2012, Ukraine announced that it had discovered natural gas reservoirs in its territorial waters. Almost two trillion cubic meters of gas just waiting to be exploited. Ukraine lost most of the original find when Russia annexed Crimea in 2014 and extended the annexation to include most of the territorial waters and the gas fields underneath."

Evans frowned. "A military takeover? I don't buy it, Ophelia." He paused, thinking. "Unless you've got some intel pointing to troop movements preparatory to a land invasion, I don't see the Russian Navy doing anything other than being a general nuisance and driving people off."

"I agree, Mr. President," Adams said. "We have no indications that Russia is putting troops anywhere but the Ukraine border, and that's been going on for a while now." She paused. "There is something else."

"What's that."

"In 2020, Naftogaz, Ukraine's state-owned gas company, lost almost seven hundred million dollars. They fired the CEO and went looking for partners."

"Don't tell me," Barnes said. "Gazprom?"

Adams shook her head. "Not exactly. Naftogaz announced a deal in March of last year with Naphta Israel Petroleum."

"That's not a big deal," Barnes pointed out. "Israel's politicians have no real love for Russia right now."

"That's true," Adams admitted. "But what wasn't announced, at least not trumpeted across the airwaves like the Naphta deal, was a deal signed in February with the Romanian branch of Austrian OMV. That company is one of the primary shareholders in Gazprom's Nord Stream 2 project. That project will allow Russia to bypass Ukraine and cut it out of trillions in transit fees."

"Clever." Evans grunted. "Russia stole most of the gas fields by military force when they annexed Crimea. And what they couldn't steal, they'll bypass with this deal? Right?"

"Yes, Mr. President," Adams said.

Evans frowned again. "And how does this relate to the current activity in the Black Sea?"

Adams shrugged. "Right now, we don't have a link. I only bring it up because the military takeover angle seemed illogical and because the Russians have been very successful with approaches like these in the past."

Evans grinned. "So asymmetrical business instead of asymmetrical warfare?"

Adams shrugged again. "That's one way of putting it."

"And all these ships?" Evans asked. "The ones loading up pierside? If they don't want this to look like a military takeover, why send them out?"

"You heard Barsukov. For security," Adams said. "Maybe they're not heading for the rigs."

"The blockade claim?" Evans asked. "Any proof, or are you just spit-balling here?"

"Just spit-balling, Mr. President," Adams admitted. "But it makes more sense than thinking they're just going to roll the entire Black Sea Fleet out to each rig."

"Fair enough. Put a team together to brainstorm ideas, reasons other than the crap Barsukov stated on television," Evans said.

"Already on it, Mr. President."

"Good. " Evans looked down at the printed schedule. "I want an update later today in the situation room."

USS *James E. Williams*
06 December 2022 | 0915 Local Time
Black Sea

Brian knocked on the door to the captain's stateroom and entered when he was ordered to do so. He saw most of the seating in the room occupied by the captain, Lieutenant Caldwell—Brian couldn't bring himself to acknowledge the man's new job title—Logan Carrillo, MA1 Gramble, and two of the ship's other chiefs.

Brian shut the door and stood next to it. Commander Allen and Master Chief Carrillo finished their whispered conversation and the captain turned to Brian.

"When Faulkner came to see you and Lieutenant Walker, what did he say?"

Brian thought for a minute. He was temporarily relieved that he wasn't here for another ass-chewing. He wasn't sure he had enough ass left for another round. "Well, sir. He just said he had a problem. Something CHENG and I might be able to help with."

"Did he say what it was?" Lieutenant Caldwell asked.

"No. We just asked if it was something at home and then the

ship went to GQ," Brian said. He searched his brain. "I think that was it."

Lieutenant Caldwell stiffened. "Sir. I think that was it, sir. I am an officer."

Brian started to respond and caught the look on Carrillo's face. He bit his tongue.

"He didn't say anything else?" Allen asked. "Nothing at all?"

Brian shook his head. "No, sir." Brian's eyes shifted to Lieutenant Caldwell and he saw the man's jaw clench.

Allen nodded at the ship's master-at-arms.

"Chief, when we went to inventory Faulkner's things, we found this tucked under the pillow on his rack." Gramble handed over an envelope and a few sheets paper, each of which was tucked into a sealed plastic bag. The papers, by themselves, would have made Brian uneasy. In plastic sleeves, presented as though they were evidence, the papers made warning lights and sirens go off in Brian's head.

"What is this?" Brian asked, afraid to start reading but not quite understanding why.

Carrillo took a deep breath. "Chief, that's a suicide note in which Petty Officer Faulkner alleges harassment and abuse by several junior sailors, three chiefs, and two officers."

**Frigate *Admiral Makarov*
06 December 2022 | 1000 Local Time
Black Sea**

Captain Yuri Nikolayevich Dashkov folded the message into his pocket and lifted the phone bolted to his desk. He spoke for a few moments, giving clear and concise orders that were repeated back to him verbatim. Satisfied, Dashkov hung up the phone and walked five steps to his private head. He used the toilet, washed his hands, and was splashing some cool water on his face when the ship's announcing system relayed his messages.

Three minutes after rehanging an impossibly white hand towel in its proper place, there was a knock at his stateroom door.

"Enter."

The door opened to admit Lieutenant Gorshkov—who looked less pale than usual, Dashkov noted—and Colonel Ilya Gregorovitch Chernitsky. Dashkov motioned for both men to sit. He took the message form from his pocket, handed it to Chernitsky, and sat back against the edge of his steel desk.

"Green lights for the next phase of operations," Dashkov said, pointing at the note as Chernitsky passed it to Gorshkov. "The *Williams* is remaining close and we are to begin harassing it. Helicopter flights. Close proximity. Weapons radars."

Gorshkov nodded. At Dashkov's direction, he'd spent the past day reviewing tactics and strategy. "Easy, Captain."

Dashkov raised an eyebrow at that remark, but said nothing. It pleased him that Gorshkov was getting comfortable with his duties. He turned to Chernitsky. "Colonel, according to the operational orders we received before sailing, your next objective is the EX-30 *Trident* Drilling Platform."

Chernitsky nodded. "Yes, Captain."

"I'm sure you know that our portion of the orders do not contain specifics of your operations. We are only logistics support for that end of the mission. Do we need to know anything?"

Chernitsky thought for a moment. "For this task, the biggest danger is in the logistics." He explained for a few moments, paused, then smiled broadly. "The primary risk is an accident on the flight or while we deploy from the helicopter."

Dashkov smiled as he reviewed the information he'd just received. It was, in a way, brilliant. Low risk. High probability for success. Little in the way of legitimate danger to the troops involved. And it didn't involve destroying another expensive drilling facility.

"Excellent." He turned to Gorshkov. "Anything to add?"

The young man thought for a second and looked at Chernitsky. "Colonel, when the distress call comes, won't the *Williams* also attempt to deploy a rescue team?"

"It's possible, but unlikely," Chernitsky said. "Intelligence reports that they do not carry an assault team like ours. They do have more than one small boat team and they could deploy that team in one of their own helicopters. But that is risky."

Dashkov took the message back from Gorshkov. "Why is that,

Colonel?"

"Their boat teams, the boarding teams, are not trained to deploy from helicopters. They have little or no fast-rope training. That is a dangerous evolution, even for my men. For the American boat team, like the one we captured, it could be disastrous."

Dashkov nodded and folded the message back into his pocket. "Well, Colonel, when the time comes, we will make every effort to keep the *Williams* busy. Just in case."

"Yes, sir," Chernitsky said.

Dashkov stood. "Gorshkov, get the ship ready for our part. You have one hour." He turned to Chernitsky. "Colonel, if you need anything, contact me directly."

Both men nodded as Dashkov opened the door. He smiled. "Now, if you will excuse me, I must visit our American guests."

After Gorshkov and Chernitsky departed, Dashkov lifted a second message form from his desk and read it for the third time. He tucked that message into his pocket with the first, opened a desk drawer, and removed a small digital camera. Dashkov turned the camera on and ensured the battery life was sufficient before collecting the license belonging to Jonathan Evans from his safe. He stuffed these items into another pocket and began the short trip to the *Makarov*'s medical ward.

TE

The Kremlin
06 December 2022 | 1030 Local Time
Moscow

Anatoly Mikhailovich Shablikov looked at his watch. It was time. He lifted one of the two phones on his desk and gave the order. After his direction was confirmed, Anatoly replaced the phone in its cradle and settled back in his chair. The group, his task force of ten, would proceed on autopilot until the next…

"Waypoint?" Anatoly wondered. Was that the word for it? Was that the word we used back in Pripyat?

Anatoly's mind wandered and he closed his eyes. He could still see it all. He'd arrived on scene two days after the explosion, his unit ordered into action when it had become clear that Chernobyl was not just a simple fire. He'd seen hell on earth there. The wrecked remains of what had been the largest nuclear power station in the world had been alive with bright yellow and orange flames, and a shimmering violet light had been reaching up to the heavens. Ionizing radiation shooting skyward to bring down God himself.

Anatoly chuckled to himself. He'd thought that then. That—contrary to everything he'd been taught—there might actually be a God. But what he'd seen in Ukraine, what had happened to his brother and wife, had convinced him otherwise. No, he'd thought, no loving and merciful being could inflict such pain and suffering.

No, there was only man in this world. Man and his—or her,

Anatoly was now forced to admit—insatiable greed. Money and power.

Anatoly's intercom buzzed.

"Yes?"

"Your driver is here."

Anatoly had to think for a moment. Why did he have a driver here? He checked his personal calendar and saw the answer. Chemotherapy. His stomach turned at the very appearance of the word and he considered making some excuse. Surely there was something here he could do instead. But there wasn't. He thought back to the leave request and the insurance rejection. "Indispensable, my ass."

The intercom buzzed again.

"Sir?"

Anatoly stood and pushed the button. "I'll be right down."

Warehouse #4, Arbat District
06 December 2022 | 1035 Local Time
Moscow

Anatoly's task force was already hard at work. Two were busy uploading deepfake videos of various American politicians and forged, official-looking documents—mostly printed correspondence, email conversations, and items purporting to be official government studies and reports—to the team's servers for use by the rest of the group. Six members of the group sat at their desks in front of banks of monitors and began pushing out the material prepared for them.

One video showed a leading member of the Senate, a democrat, in a strip club getting lap dances from a variety of young women. Another showed one of that man's cohorts doing grip-and-grins with two members of a far-right extremist group based in Oregon. There were emailed conversations between prominent Democrats about siding with the Right to Life crowd in order to shore up support for re-election in purple states. Videos of both sides hanging out with neo-Nazis were posted with 'private' conversations between Democrats reneging on promises to curtail drilling and fracking in favor of sizable campaign contributions. Documents were 'leaked' showing payments and contributions from fringe groups that neither side approved of, and in each of those cases further 'leaks' would seem to indicate that foreign business and government interests were held in higher regard than the needs and opinions of the American taxpayers.

The team worked hard for the first hour, posting with one account, usually one with followership numbering in the seven-digit range, and sharing with other accounts by using a variety of created botnets. Likes and favorites came rolling in. The information shared was commented on by real American citizens, while Anatoly's team monitored the situation and provided the appropriate nudge or spark when necessary.

Arguments erupted and more than one of the team members was both shocked and amused when actual Americans began fighting with and, eventually, threatening each other.

After ninety minutes, each of the first eight members of the team was able to push back from his or her station and take a break. In all, they had rolled more than fifty snowballs down this particular mountain and now they could, almost, sit back and watch as each snowball morphed into an avalanche that they would continue to feed on a more regimented basis. Eventually, they knew from the briefing, they'd begin marshaling troops, as it were. Coordinating protests and counter-protests where local agents would attempt to create chaos by inciting violence before melting into the shadows.

The last two members of Anatoly's team moved up to their consoles. While the rest of the team was responsible for targeting the American public at large, these two had a much more specific task. Each had a short list of specific targets, individual people in the American government with secrets to hide. Secrets that would destroy them. Secrets that would see them sent to prison. Secrets that the SVR had troubled itself to learn.

Frigate *Admiral Makarov*
06 December 2022 | 1100 Local Time
Black Sea

Captain Yuri Nikolayevich Dashkov stepped into the *Makarov*'s Combat Information Center and looked around before taking his seat. It had been an infuriating hour.

Getting video of the six Americans hadn't been difficult. The five sailors had cooperated to the extent allowed by their officer and the Geneva Conventions, providing their names, ranks, and serial numbers for the video camera. Dashkov had required the doctor's assistance to get good images of Jonathan Evans. Satisfied that Evans could be positively identified in the video, Dashkov had then placed the doctor in front of the camera to outline the medical condition of each American. The physician on the video was supposed to have been President Barsukov's personal doctor, but mechanical difficulties had prevented the helicopter flight.

The smooth sailing had ended when Dashkov and two of his information systems technicians had been attempting to encrypt and upload the video files. Two power shifts, a server crash, and an unbelievably slow connection had sent Dashkov's blood pressure through the roof. Well, he thought, that and four messages from fleet headquarters demanding to know why it was taking so long to deliver the video files.

"Gorshkov?"

"The ship is at battle stations, Captain."

Dashkov nodded. "And the *Williams*?"

"Holding position. Same as before."

Dashkov glanced around again. It was time. "Good." A pause. A smile. Dashkov stood and put a hand on Gorshkov's shoulder. "Are you ready, Lieutenant?"

Gorshkov stood up straight. "Yes, Captain."

"Good. Make it happen."

USS *James E. Williams*
06 December 2022 | 1105 Local Time
Black Sea

Chief Petty Officer Brian Thompson looked at the people around him and again at the letters in his hand. They'd been sitting in the captain's stateroom for nearly two hours discussing the letter, and he'd just denied knowing any of the letter's details for the fifth time.

"I just don't get it. This seems so…"

"Out of character?" Carrillo offered.

Brian thought about that and nodded. It did seem out of character. He'd been racking his brain and couldn't come up with any indication that something like this was possible. He scanned through the letter again and became aware that Lieutenant Caldwell, the *Williams*' new XO, was talking.

"It's just the way some people are wired."

Brian's head came up slowly. "What?"

The XO leaned back. "Everything I've read says that. Some people just internalize everything. They take everything negative and stuff it deep inside. Years and years of memories and life experience packed away until one day they can't hack it anymore." The XO turned to Brian. "I'm willing to bet Faulkner had some discipline problems, right, Chief?"

Brian glanced at Carrillo and caught a small shake of the head. He looked at the papers in his hands. "No, sir. No discipline problems."

"You sure, Chief?" the XO said. "Seems to me an enlisted sailor with all those run-ins with chiefs and officers likely had some discipline issues. Maybe unresolved ones."

Brian's head snapped up, but Commander Allen spoke first. "Tread lightly, XO. We're talking about a sailor who appears to have taken his own life."

"Yes, sir. That we are," the XO replied. "I'm just saying maybe there's two sides to this story. I don't know about how things are run in down there in the mess, but this claim that my officers were somehow being abusive without cause is almost insubordinate."

"XO," Allen cautioned.

Brian dropped the papers and stood suddenly. The XO flinched. Carrillo started to move, but stopped when Brian stepped to the door, opened it, and stormed out.

Brian had just walked into the hangar bay when the ship's 1MC boomed to life.

"General quarters. General quarters. All hands man your battle stations."

Brian leaned his head back and looked at the white overhead lights.

"Christ, what now?"

**Frigate *Admiral Makarov*
06 December 2022 | 1110 Local Time
Black Sea**

"Is the helicopter ready?" Dashkov asked.

"Yes, Captain," Gorshkov answered. "And the colonel reports that his men are prepared and standing by."

Dashkov nodded, a gesture unseen by the man on the other end of the phone line. "Very good, Gorshkov. And everything else?"

"Everything else is ready, Captain. The consoles are manned and the operators have been properly briefed."

"Good. There can be no accidents. It is not our intention to start a shooting war. Just to irritate and annoy. Understood?"

"Yes, Captain," Gorshkov confirmed. "And to keep them from responding to the colonel's next incident. I understand."

Dashkov paused for a moment. So many things could go wrong. A twitchy operator was less of an issue than it had been in the past—there were plenty of safeties in place for that. But a glitch in the software or some other unforeseen malfunction could result in an inadvertent weapons release. Dashkov knew that. He'd seen it happen.

"Let them know we are here, Gorshkov," Dashkov commanded. He hung up the phone and turned back to the array of windows overlooking the *Makarov*'s bow. What he'd said was borderline absurd. The *Williams* already knew where they were—neither ship had strayed far from the remains of *Neptun Deep*, and the *Makarov*'s sensors had detected the American destroyer's surface search radar.

But this was different. They were charging at the *Williams* and, in a few seconds, Gorshkov would order the *Makarov*'s fire control radars to begin sweeping the American ship. The PUMA, 3R14N, and MR-90 Orekh Fire Control Systems were powerful systems that the *Williams* would certainly notice and react to. It was, technically, an overtly hostile act. Like pointing a rifle at someone. But the finger was still off the trigger. And the safety was still on.

And if the Americans responded in kind? Dashkov grinned into the gathering darkness and watched the rolling sea. Then, he thought, I turn everything off and head back to the rig, and Moscow will announce that we were provoked.

**USS *James E. Williams*
06 December 2022 | 1115 Local Time
Black Sea**

Commander Allen stormed into the bridge. "OOD, report."

"Sir," the OOD began. "Approximately two minutes ago, the contact turned toward us and increased speed. Distance to contact is fourteen thousand yards."

"No other contacts?"

"Combat hasn't reported any, sir."

Allen picked up a pair of binoculars and tossed the strap over his head. A nearby speaker blared.

"Bridge, Combat. Contact lit off fire control radars."

Allen turned to the bulkhead-mounted speaker and flipped the transmit button. "Bridge, aye. They have us?"

"Safe bet, sir. We've not been off their surface search systems since the near-collision."

Allen's mind raced through his options. He turned to the OOD. "Start warning them off. Increase speed to two-thirds and maneuver to keep ten thousand yards' separation."

"Aye, aye, sir." The OOD turned to execute the orders and Allen depressed the transmit button on the speaker.

"Combat, Captain. Get a message off to Fleet Forces and let me know if the fire control systems lock us up. Got it?"

"Yes, sir."

Allen released the button and turned forward. A voice to his right got his attention. "Shouldn't we light off our own fire control systems?"

Allen turned and saw Lieutenant Caldwell standing in the dark. "XO, what the hell are you doing up here?"

"What do you mean?"

"Get back down to combat."

"But Captain—" the XO started to protest.

Allen turned away. "Now, XO." He heard the hatch open and shut behind him as he lifted the binoculars. Beneath his feet, the ship surged forward and heeled over to port.

◆ ◆ ◆

In CCS, Brian settled into the EOOW chair and began scanning gauges and readings. On the EOOW console, he began typing in a series of number groups and scrolling through the engine readouts that weren't displayed by the large red, digital numbers on the propulsion or electric plant consoles. He saw something on two of the gas turbine mains that was disconcerting.

"How long have the temps been this high?"

"Since start-up, Chief," Petty Officer Cruz responded. "As soon as we placed the extra engines online, the T5.4 shot right up to warning levels and stayed there. Vibe levels rising too."

Brian turned to the PACC and craned his neck. "Two-thirds bell?"

"Yes, Chief."

Brian made a note in grease pencil on his station's plexiglass desktop. He searched his brain for information for a few moments but was interrupted when a buzzer sounded on the PACC.

"Coming up, Chief. Full bell."

Everyone felt the ship squat at the stern as it surged forward. Brian watched Cruz at his console and waited for the ship to come to the ordered speed. As Brian watched, warning lights began flashing on three engines.

Cruz acknowledged and announced each alarm. "Chief, we got high vibes on 1A and 2A GTMs. T5.4 warning on 1A. Torque limiting on both shafts."

"Aye. Keep an eye on it, Cruz." Brian picked up a phone and dialed the bridge.

"Bridge, JOOD speaking." It was Chief Roberts.

"Jason, Brian here. Having some engine troubles. Vibe warnings on 1A and 2A. Hot exhaust on 1A. Torque limiting on both shafts."

Roberts read the list of issues back. "I'll let the captain know. Limits?"

Brian turned to his own screen and dialed up the readings again. "Another bump in speed and we're gonna lose two engines. You gonna need 'em?"

"Probably. Got some damn Russkie frigate trying to chase us off again. Best available speed for split plant?"

Brian told him. "Russian frigate? The same one that—"

Roberts cut him off. "Not the time, man. Gotta relay this to the captain. Anything else?"

"No. That's it. Remind him about battle override and tell him we might do some damage since we don't know what's causing all of this."

"Will do." Roberts hung up and Brian replaced his own handset. He turned and watched the readings fluctuate and thought about the Russian ship. *The ship with my sailors on it. Brooks. Strater. Everyone else.*

"Fuckers."

13

The White House
06 December 2022 | 0430 Local Time
Black Sea

Major Harlan Alexander risked a glance at his watch. Two hours. And then some. The president and his staff had been at this for just over two hours. They'd discussed the Russian president's recent statements and allegations, the recent uptick in allegations on social media against various politicians, and the confirmation that the president's nephew was indeed in the ICU on board the Russian frigate. There had been several mentions of sources and the detailed description of more than a few methods and capabilities, information that Harlan knew he'd have to report.

Bringing in a recording device was something he knew to be too risky—hell, he thought, I can't even bring a cell phone down here. Accessing the recordings made of the meetings in the Situation Rooms was theoretically possible, but not something a major in the United States Army could do without raising a lot of eyebrows and suspicion. No, Harlan thought, I have to remember all of this. No notes. No recordings. Just me and my brain.

"Shit," he muttered. For that, he received an elbow in the side from the Air Force major standing by his side. He looked over at the man, saw the reproachful look, and returned to his imitation of a statue, albeit one with ears and a memory.

Frigate *Admiral Makarov*
06 December 2022 | 1135 Local Time
Black Sea

Dashkov watched the *Makarov*'s lone Kamov KA-27 helicopter circle to port. Normally an anti-submarine platform, it would serve its purpose in this exercise. Satisfied with the launch, Dashkov evaluated the recent changes in course and speed made by the American destroyer and issued his next set of orders, working constantly to keep the *Williams* moving. He had just returned his attention to the bridge windows and the world beyond them when he felt the *Makarov* heel over to starboard and increase speed.

Good, he thought. Let's see what they do next.

Dashkov looked at his watch and began counting down the minutes.

USS *James E. Williams*
06 December 2022 | 1136 Local Time
Black Sea

"Shit, Captain. Contact shifted course and speed."

"Very well," Commander Allen snapped. He rippled off a series of orders, trying to ride the line between speed, maneuverability, and the possibility of damaging two of his main engines. He'd briefly considered ordering the struggling engines placed into battle override, but he wasn't convinced that the *Williams* was in any real danger. No, he thought. They're just trying to piss me off.

The *Williams* turned hard, actually shuddering slightly as the bow bounced through a trough and smashed into the next oncoming wave.

A detached portion of his brain kept reviewing options as the *Williams*' bow kept coming around. Allen thumbed the transmit button on the speaker.

"Combat, Captain. We get that message off to Fleet Forces?"

"Affirmative, sir."

Frigate *Admiral Makarov*

06 December 2022 | 1140 Local Time
Black Sea

"Reverse course. Now," Dashkov ordered, his voice calm and measured. This task had been easier than expected. The American captain was not using all the speed available to him. That, he thought, was both wise and foolish. Holding performance in reserve was always a smart move, but only when your true capabilities were unknown to your enemy. That, Dashkov thought, did not apply in this case. The Burke-class destroyers had been around since the early nineties and their engine performance wasn't exactly a secret. Dashkov wondered briefly if there might not be some sort of technical problem on the *Williams*.

As the *Makarov* swung around to a reciprocal course, the speaker next to the captain crackled to life.

"Captain, we are receiving a distress signal from the EX-30 *Trident*. Reports of a hostage situation."

Dashkov resisted the urge to smile. He stepped to the nearest radio and jabbed the transmit button. "Understood. Put me through to the helicopter."

"Yes, Captain." There were a few moments of silence. "Go ahead, Captain."

Dashkov pressed the transmit button again. "Colonel, you have a green light to assault EX-30 *Trident*."

Colonel Chernitsky's voice crackled across the line. "Understood, Captain."

The line went dead.

USS *James E. Williams*
06 December 2022 | 1141 Local Time
Black Sea

"Captain, Combat."

Commander Allen growled at the chart and turned to the speaker. He stabbed the transmit button. "Captain."

"Sir, Radio reports a distress signal from one of the rigs. North of our position. EX-30 *Trident*."

"Forward it to Fleet Forces for action." Allen released the button and swore. Whatever the issue was on the *Trident* rig, there wasn't a damn thing he could do about it.

"Rescue and assistance, Captain?" Chief Roberts asked.

"With this guy tailgating us like rush hour in Hampton Roads?" Allen shook his head. "Wouldn't be much help."

"Think he'd follow us all the way there, Captain."

Allen considered that. There couldn't be anything relating to the *Neptun Deep* rig tying the *Makarov* to this location. So that meant…

Allen nodded. "Yeah, Chief. I do."

"Captain, contact is reversing course," the OOD reported.

Allen issued orders to the OOD, got confirmation, and turned back to Chief Roberts. "What the hell is this guy's deal?"

It was Roberts' turn to shake his head. "No clue, sir. Never seen them like this."

Allen bent over a nearby chart table. "What do you mean?"

"Been in the same waters as Russian boats before. Usually, it's just one or two passes, just to let us know who's boss and how big their dicks are. But this clown is different. He's relentless."

"Opinion?"

Roberts glanced at the charts. "Something else going on that we don't know about yet?"

Allen stood up straight and rubbed his back. "Your guess is as good as mine."

**USS *Key West*
06 December 2022 | 1142 Local Time
Black Sea**

USS *Key West* drifted silently through the waters two miles south of the USS *James E. Williams*. Commander Scott Reynes stood behind his sonar chief, eyeballing the monitor and listening to the commentary.

"Hell, sir. Maybe they're playin' tag." Chief Hughley leaned back. He eased the headphones off and rubbed his ears. "They sure as hell ain't being quiet. You could put a cup against the hull and hear these two."

"Nobody else?"

"Aside from that helo that took off north a few minutes ago and the *Kazan*? Nope. No other targets on the roof."

Reynes smiled. "One of those targets is an American destroyer."

Hughley grinned. "You know what they say, sir."

Reynes grinned back. All submariners believed the same thing. There were only two types of ships. Submarines and targets. "Well, let's not shoot our own target." He patted the man on the back. "Where's the *Kazan*?"

"Still a ways out. Just drifting back and forth like us." Hughley tapped one of the screens. "Quiet bastard. Keeps fading out on us."

Reynes took in the data and patted the man on his shoulder. "Thanks, Chief. Keep an ear open."

USS *James E. Williams*
06 December 2022 | 1144 Local Time
Black Sea

Brian held on as the *Williams* leaned through another radical turn. He checked the clinometer and saw the bubble slide to port, clearly visible in the plastic tube with its pink backing plate. Fourteen degrees. The bubble began easing back to top dead center as the ship steadied on course and came back up to full speed.

"Chief. We're getting awfully close to losing 1A."

Brian looked. "What about 2A?"

"Close too, Chief. Anyone sneezes near the modules and they'll shut down."

Brian picked up the phone to call the bridge. "Thanks, Cruz."

♦ ♦ ♦

Commander Allen scowled. "How close to losing the engines?" He waited for the answer, thanked Chief Thompson, and hung up. Allen turned his attention to the paper in his hands. He'd read the message four times and still couldn't believe it. Behind him, a phone rang and one of the *Williams*' undesignated sailors answered.

"Sir, it's the XO for you."

Allen turned and grabbed the phone. "You read it, XO?"

"Yes, sir."

"Any inputs?"

There was a lengthy pause. "If it's true…"

"XO, we have to take this at face value. We assume it's true."

"But Captain—the president's nephew? I don't know what to make of that."

Allen was disappointed, but didn't say so. Now wasn't the time. "What to make of it, XO, is that we can't shoot. We have to keep running around the chessboard until the folks in Washington get our folks, and Mr. Evans, returned. To us or to a shore facility."

"But what if they shoot? Their fire control system has been up and sweeping this whole time."

Allen didn't say that that thought had been bouncing around in his head for hours. Ricocheting back and forth with no clear answer. Well, until now.

"If they shoot, we use countermeasures and get the hell out of Dodge."

"But sir—"

"But nothing. You do not have permission to engage the *Makarov*." Allen thought for a moment. "Or any other target that may present a threat. Those are our orders. You will hold fire. Understood?"

The pause that followed was longer than Allen was comfortable with.

"XO?"

"Understood, sir."

Frigate *Admiral Makarov*
06 December 2022 | 1148 Local Time
Black Sea

Dashkov read the message in his hands. Good, he thought. Very good. The video files identifying his American guests, including the one of Jonathan Evans, had been delivered to the American government. That meant that there was a better than average chance that the captain of the *Williams* would be aware of the information and would not turn this incident into a shoot-out. The Americans prided themselves on that, on not shooting first in situations like these. And though he personally found such reservations to be an odd tactic, he understood and appreciated the restraint in this case. After all, it made what he was about to do easier and marginally less risky. Dashkov picked up the phone next to his chair on the bridge and dialed.

Gorshkov answered on the first ring. "Yes, Captain?"

"You know what comes next, yes?"

"Affirmative, Captain. Target them for thirty seconds. No more. No less."

"And you are ready?"

"Yes, Captain."

"Very well. You may begin as soon as I order the next course and speed change."

"Very good, Captain."

Dashkov hung up and frowned. Even with the information he had, this next step wasn't risk free. It was aggressive. Belligerent, even. He took a breath. He'd been wrong before. Lighting off the fire control systems and sweeping the American was simply the act of displaying the weapon. What was it they called it in the United States? Open carry? This was different. This would be a half-minute of running directly at the Americans while pointing a loaded weapon at them.

Dashkov turned and gave the orders. They were confirmed and relayed and, after no more than ten seconds, the captain felt his ship accelerate through a hard turn.

USS *Key West*
06 December 2022 | 1151 Local Time
Black Sea

On the *Key West*, Chief Jerome Hughley slipped one side of his headphones off. "Jesus, sir. Contact just stomped on the damn gas."

Commander Reynes turned slightly. "Which contact, Chief?"

"Shit. The *Makarov*, sir. Sorry. Aspect change and increased engine noises." Hughley paused, eyeing his screens. "She's heading right for the *Williams*. Gotta be a flank bell, sir."

"What's the *Williams* doing?"

USS *James E. Williams*
06 December 2022 | 1152 Local Time
Black Sea

"Fucking hell," Allen barked. "OOD, best available speed. Right full rudder. Now!"

The helmsman didn't wait for the order to be relayed. One hand began spinning the wheel, sending the necessary signals to the HPUs in Steering. The helmsman's other hand moved of its own accord. He grabbed the linked throttles and shoved them forward to the stops. It was an automatic reaction to an emergency, a conditioned response to the situation.

◆ ◆ ◆

The steering signals were received, processed, and dispatched aft to the steering gear room where two of the units began pumping hydraulic fluid into their respective ram assemblies. Forced by thousands of pounds of hydraulic pressure, the rams began moving, pushing their linkages to the rudder posts and rudders and turning the ship over hard. On the ship's 2B HPU, a flexible hose assembly normally rated for more than ten thousand pounds per square inch of pressure had been rubbing against a nearby angle iron for more than a year. At the center of the rub mark, the hose failed. A pinhole leak atomized the hydraulic fluid, spraying a misty cloud of liquid into the space with more than three thousand pounds of pressure behind it. As the HPU continued pumping, the pinhole leak widened and the mist changed to a massive spray of hot, golden hydraulic oil that shot forward dousing three sailors and the ship's 2A HPU.

Warning alarms sounded in the space and at the control console on the bridge. The watch on the bridge did not know what had failed or why. Reacting as trained, the *Williams'* helmsman punched the button to shift from the failed unit to the offline 2A unit. The signal traveled aft through the same data multiplexing system that had transmitted the steering information seconds before. The 2A unit started. The motor windings, covered in hydraulic fluid, began smoking almost as soon as the four hundred and forty volts of power hit. The sailors in the space, still reacting to getting sprayed with the same hydraulic fluid that was now cooking off 2A's motor, did not notice the first wisps of smoke. It wasn't until a call came from the bridge informing them of the shift in units that one of sailors in Steering turned around and saw the first flickers of yellow-orange flame licking up the side of the 2A HPU motor casing. One sailor lunged for a nearby fire extinguisher as another used his radio to call the casualty away. Because the flames came from a motor, he reported a class C fire.

◆ ◆ ◆

Brian's attention had just been jerked in multiple directions. He'd been staring at the screen with the GTM readings when the helmsman on the bridge had shoved the throttles forward. He'd actually seen the vibration reading for 1A GTM spike, rising far above what the engine's software permitted.

"High vibe shutdown on 1A, 2A GTMs!" Cruz yelled.

Brian acknowledged the report, barked instructions that Cruz was already carrying out, and was reaching for the 1MC microphone to call the casualty away when the speaker above his head blared to life.

"Loss of steering. Loss of steering." The speaker continued with the standard announcement as Brian spun towards Lieutenant Hunter, the ship's DCA. He started to speak, to request two of the ship's machinist mates from Repair Five to lay to the steering gear room to assist, when a new announcement from the loudspeaker got his attention.

"Fire. Fire. Fire. Class Charlie fire in Aft Steering."

Brian shot a look at the DCA. She turned to her team and began shouting orders. The phone talkers for two of the repair lockers relayed her instructions to deploy attack teams to the location as she picked up the 1MC.

"This is the DCA from CCS. We have a report of a class Charlie fire in Aft Steering. Away the repair electricians, away. Provide from Repair Five."

As the DCA continued ordering the establishment of smoke boundaries and directing the relocation of the ship's Repair Three personnel to a space outside the secondary boundary, Brian turned his attention back to the propulsion plant and the 1MC microphone in his hand. He set it in its holder and picked up the one that went only to the bridge and combat. Brian relayed what information he had about the casualties to 1A and 2A GTMs. After a short hold, he was directed to place the remaining engines in their battle override condition. He replaced the handset and turned to give the order to Cruz when the 1MC above his head stopped him cold.

"Fire. Fire. Fire. Class Bravo fire reported in Aft Steering."

14

Frigate *Admiral Makarov*
06 December 2022 | 1154 Local Time
Black Sea

Captain Yuri Nikolayevich Dashkov went pale and began barking engine and steering orders to his bridge crew. Behind him, one of his sailors pulled on the lever that activated the ship's collision alarm. Klaxons erupted and it seemed as if the entire bridge crew began yelling at once. The *Makarov* began leaning away from the turn. Dashkov's brain raced, trying to figure out what had gone wrong.

He had practiced this maneuver hundreds of times. In simulations. In real life. He'd executed it perfectly just days prior, and he'd made several additional passes—though not as aggressive—in the intervening days. But something had gone horribly wrong this time. He'd driven in close and fast, harassing the *Williams* and working, again, to force the American ship farther away from the drilling fields to their north and east. He'd seen the American begin to turn away, just as before. Just as it had always been. He'd given his own orders to hold course, intending to pass close aboard and secure in his estimation of the *Williams*' ability to evade safely.

But the *Williams* hadn't evaded. She'd stopped turning. She'd slowed. Dashkov had watched in horror as the rooster tail of foam at the American's stern disappeared and the *Williams* settled, drifting right into the *Makarov*'s intended path.

The call to brace for collision came and Dashkov latched onto his chair, watching as the bow of his ship raced towards the starboard side of the American destroyer. The geometry of the approach flashed through his mind and he prayed that he was wrong.

USS *James E. Williams*
06 December 2022 | 1155 Local Time
Black Sea

The collision alarms on USS *James E. Williams* were deafening. Brian turned to the speaker in disbelief and latched onto his chair in CCS. Around him, everyone in the space did the same thing, bracing against anything solid to prepare for the impending collision.

He counted off the seconds in his head, wondering what in the hell was going on. A remote portion of his brain was still tracking a fire back in Steering. Possibly two. Neither of which was being dealt with while everyone held on for the moment when the nine-thousand-ton destroyer came into physical contact with the four-thousand-ton Russian frigate. Brian had no idea how it was possible or what had gone wrong. But it was happening. Would happen in just a few moments. With only two engines up and running. At least, his mind rationalized, the engines were on separate shafts.

Brian felt his muscles tensing as the collision alarm kept sounding.

Frigate *Admiral Makarov*
06 December 2022 | 1156 Local Time
Black Sea

The *Makarov*, moving at twenty-four knots, struck a glancing blow to the *Williams'* starboard side, the bow making contact with the American destroyer's hull just aft and slightly below where the larger ship's lone remaining RHIB rested in its deck-mounted cradle. Dashkov was thrown forward and caught himself by flinging his hands out in front of him. His right hand caught on the side of a chart table and his left smashed into a bracket welded nearby. A fiery tingling shot all the way to his elbow as the captain struggled to hold on.

His head came up, taking in everything around him. A terrific screeching, the unmistakable sound of two steel hulls pressing and tearing at each other, filled his ears and made his brain ache. To his left, two sailors were down, one on his hands and knees trying to grab onto anything and the other bleeding from what looked like a laceration on the side of his face. It was, Dashkov thought, hard to tell. The entire ship was shuddering as it raced down the side of the *Williams'* hull, a metal-to-metal pair of shifting tectonic plates.

Dashkov looked forward and saw a crumpled portion of his bow pressing into the side of the American ship, and his brain reasoned that that couldn't be. The ships should be separating by now, driven apart by the orders he'd issued before contact.

He barked a set of orders again and turned to see that they were followed. At the *Makarov*'s helm, he saw…no one.

"Goddamnit." Dashkov began pulling himself across the room, one piece of gear at a time, the ship trying to shake him loose with each move. After what felt like forever, Dashkov was able reach over the console, his back to the ship's bow. He checked the rudder angle indicator—no small task given how violently the ship was shaking—and grasped the helm. He eased it over and turned to look forward. He saw the bow pull away from the *Williams'* side and slam back into the larger hull. Dashkov almost lost control of the helm, hanging on by only his index finger. He checked forward again and eased the rudder over, a little more this time.

The *Makarov*'s bow pulled away from the *Williams'* starboard side and hung in space, wavering back and forth like a sailor on shore leave. Dashkov thought he could feel the rudder fighting him, imagined the forces of the Venturi effect as the ocean raced between the two wrinkled hulls.

Little by little, the screeching and shaking eased. A single meter of separation became two. Then five, then ten. Dashkov maintained course, checking over his shoulder every few seconds. When the separation between the *Makarov* and the *Williams* looked to be approximately fifty meters, Dashkov looked around. He motioned to one sailor, a young man who looked the least shaken, to take over the helm.

The sailor put his hands on the wheel. "I am not qualified,

Captain."

"Can you read? Can you follow my instructions exactly?"

"Yes, Captain."

"See these?" Dashkov pointed to the instruments for the rudder angle and course.

"Yes, Captain."

"Then you're qualified. Do exactly as I say and keep your eye on these. Understand?"

"Yes, Captain."

Dashkov turned and selected a phone.

"Engineering."

"This is the captain. Get me a damage report."

"In progress, Captain." The voice on the other end sounded shaky.

"Very good." Dashkov hung up and looked around. Several more sailors were back on their feet and the orders began to flow from Dashkov's mouth. "Steady on course. All ahead one-third." He pointed at two sailors. "I need medics and the communications officer to the bridge."

Dashkov saw everyone respond. Good, he thought. Give them a purpose. Keep them busy.

USS *James E. Williams*
06 December 2022 | 1200 Local Time
Black Sea

Brian stood back up and felt his forehead. There was blood there. The initial collision had thrown him into the EOOW console and the panel's sharp edge had done more damage to his aching skull. His hearing was fuzzy, but the sounds of alarms and shouting were there. He began to look around. The lights were still on and every console was a mess of flashing red lights and blinking screens, all of which were slightly out of focus. Especially the lights, he thought. Small halos ringed every light source in front of him. He eased himself into his usual seat.

"Chief, lost both Bravo engines," Cruz yelled. "High vibes on both."

Brian nodded and searched his mind for the right response. Nothing came. Brian wanted to shake his head but was afraid to, thinking it might make the headache worse.

The DCA's voice broke through Brian's haze, ordering every repair locker on the ship to dispatch investigators to check for damage. That made sense, he thought. Brian picked up the microphone for the engineering spaces.

"All spaces, EOOW. Check for damage."

Brian listened in as his sailors responded without really hearing anything. To his right, the DCA was receiving reports of damage to the ship's starboard side, and it took Brian a few moments to realize that the most of the announcements—flooding, a tear in the hull, and two small electrical fires—affected the passageway immediately outboard of CCS and the engineering log room.

"Central, Bridge."

Brian looked around for a moment before finding the right handset. "Central."

"Central, we have no propulsion or steering control. We show all steering units down."

Brian blinked. Everything around him was moving at warp speed and he seemed to be stuck in neutral.

"Central? Did you copy my last?"

Brian thumbed the transmit button.

"Central copies all." He paused. "Investigating now."

Brian looked at his status chart, vaguely aware that it was wrong and that his watch standers were speaking to him. He looked at the electric plant operator, Petty Officer Becker, and forced himself to concentrate on what she was saying.

"Chief, the plant is stable." She was running through a list of equipment failures.

Brian held a hand up. "Write it down for me?"

A funny look crossed Becker's face, but she nodded and began marking up her own status chart with black and red grease pencils. She also picked up a phone. Brian turned to Cruz.

"PACC?"

"The hit knocked out both online GTMs before I could put them in battle override. I've got both Engine Room Operators resetting the mains. Fuel system is still up. Main lube oil is still up. Same for prop hydraulics," Cruz reported. "Try for a restart in two minutes. Maybe three."

Brian nodded at that, then tried to pull the red binders with the start-up and casualty response procedures out of a nearby holder and fumbled them. He snagged both on the second attempt, snaking a finger through the small, red wire loops that served as binding. He tossed the casualty control book on the desk in front of him and began thumbing through the binder containing operational procedures.

The words on every page were out of focus. Not enough to be illegible, but enough to cause Brian to squint and pull the books in close. Brian struggled to think, to focus amid the chaos around him. His brain was screaming, nagging. There was something he was forgetting. He couldn't think what.

Brian stopped searching and forced himself to think through the previous few minutes. They'd prepared for a collision. They'd sped up. Two engines had shut down. Vibes? But before that. Something had happened before that. What?

Brian rubbed his temples and his eyes. His head felt like it was about to explode, like his eyeballs were going to rupture.

Brian blinked. His vision was still blurry. Organized chaos whirled around him.

Rupture.

Something had ruptured. He was sure of it. But…

"Central, Bridge. Status on propulsion and steering?"

That was it. Steering. Hydraulic leak. Fire. Brian turned to the DCA, certain that Steering had been forgotten.

"DCA!" Brian made it to his feet. Everything went hazy. Then gray. Then black.

EX-30 *Trident* Natural Gas Platform
06 December 2022 | 1212 Local Time
Black Sea

Colonel Ilya Gregorovitch Chernitsky and his team, nine men in all, had—after several reconnaissance passes and three attempts to establish radio contact with the EX-30 *Trident* natural gas rig—fast-roped onto the massive drilling platform. His men had divided into three teams to sweep and clear the rig, working their way from top to bottom with mechanistic precision.

Chernitsky, with Sergeant Vorobyov and one other operator, had led Team Alpha. They'd taken several minutes to clear the rig's centerline catwalks, passages, and spaces and were now stacked up outside the rig's main control room. They'd engaged one member of the OPFOR, a man Vorobyov had dropped with two rounds center mass.

Chernitsky spoke into his waterproof microphone. "Bravo and Delta Teams, report."

"Bravo on station. Southwest entrance to main control. Two tangos down."

"Delta on station. Overwatch on Alpha and Bravo positions."

"Opposition?" Chernitsky asked.

"None, sir."

Chernitsky nodded and reviewed the situation. He had three teams on station. Bravo had taken two of the OPFOR down. His team had dealt with one tango. That left, according to his information, five armed men inside this control room guarding a roomful of hostages. His team had three shooters stacked up outside the only two entrances to the room. Good.

Chernitsky thumbed his mic. "Get me video feeds."

A series of clicks answered him. Chernitsky kept his focus on the door in front of him, but caught Vorobyov moving out of his peripheral vision. The man stayed low, crab-walking to the end of the catwalk and around the corner. He was out of sight for no more than thirty seconds before returning. He handed Chernitsky a small, handheld device.

Chernitsky looked at the screen and smiled. The video, fed from a wireless camera Vorobyov had just placed on one of the control room's large windows, showed fifteen hostages, all seated on the floor facing the room's rear wall—a place where they were easily guarded and from where they could create little in the way of mischief. Each of the hostages had a thick, black canvas bag over his or her head. The OPFOR were all standing, each one holding a rifle at low ready and presenting himself as a damn near unmissable target. Chernitsky was pleased to see that each of his opponents was dressed in a way that clearly marked them as Americans, possibly even American military. All, he noted, carried M4 rifles, and two of the targets were standing near the hostages. Chernitsky assigned both of them to Bravo Team and designated the nearer three men to his own team.

Chernitsky pulled out an older cellular phone and activated the video camera feature before he thumbed his mic again. "Breach in five, four, three, two…"

On his count, both control room doors were blown open by small explosive charges. Chernitsky's team rushed in, each man peeling off to cover his sector and engaging whatever targets were there. Chernitsky's sector had no targets and he lowered his rifle to watch the scene unfold.

To his immediate front, Vorobyov engaged the first of two men. He double-tapped his target in the chest before shifting fire to drop the second man. Alpha Team's third member, a corporal, engaged the last of the targets on this side of the space, planting two shots in the man's chest and one to the helmeted head. All three targets stumbled against the impacts of the rounds and dropped their rifles to the ground.

Chernitsky continued watching as the rest of the act played out in front of him. Each of the "dead" men collapsed, lifting a pint-sized bag of blood and squeezing for all they were worth. On the other end of the room, Bravo Team's "victims" performed the same act. As the rounds impacted, each dropped his weapon and fell to the deck spraying blood from a small bag they held in one hand. In these two cases, the "dead men" made sure to splash a little on the nearest hostages.

When all five targets were down, Chernitsky issued the order—he took care to make it audible to the hostages wearing blackout hoods—for his team to remove the bodies and prepare to egress. Each man from his team hefted a "body" and carried it up to where the *Makarov*'s helicopter had just touched down. Chernitsky followed his team to the pad.

Chernitsky boarded the helicopter with the bodies, the prisoners, and two-thirds of his team and spoke into his microphone.

"Delta Team. Helo will return for pickup in one hour."

A pair of clicks answered his order and Chernitsky turned his attention to the bodies at his feet. As the helo lifted off, he kicked the nearest body. The man stirred and sat upright, one hand rubbing his chest. Next to him, the remaining "dead" men did the same. The senior man, a major, looked around, rolled his neck, and glanced at Chernitsky.

"Mother of God, Colonel. Those damn Simunition rounds fucking hurt."

Chernitsky smiled. "Good to see you too, Major. Nice touch with the blood. Whose idea?"

The major jerked a thumb over his shoulder. "The new private. He was a theater major at university!" The major poked Chernitsky in the leg. "You believe that? A theater major."

Chernitsky laughed over the roar of the helo's engines. "Whatever is the world coming to?"

15

Warehouse #4, Arbat District
06 December 2022 | 1300 Local Time
Moscow

Anatoly answered his phone on the first ring, his eyes tracking across the various displays and screens and taking in the actions of his cyber-espionage team. "Yes, sir?"

"Anatoly. How are you feeling?" Director Tolstov sounded cheerful, happy even.

Anatoly blinked at that. He felt like hell. He'd felt like hell the first time he'd gone through chemo and he'd not expected it to be different this time. Worse, probably. Anatoly knew little of human biology, but it didn't take a genius to figure out that the body wasn't designed to handle the kinds of poisons the doctors were pumping into him. "It's chemotherapy, sir. It's not something I would recommend."

"Wonderful," Tolstov said. "I have something for you and your team."

Wonderful? Anatoly briefly considered telling his boss just how wonderful chemo was. He felt his face flush as he bit his tongue and fought back a wave of nausea.

"Anatoly, are you there?"

"Yes, sir. What do you have?"

"Admiral Borshevsky just sent these files from the *Makarov*. I'm uploading them to you now. You should have them in a few moments."

"What are they?"

Tolstov explained briefly. When he finished, Anatoly nodded to himself. "And you want us to edit the footage? To show the American destroyer was the aggressor and is at fault?"

"That's it exactly, Anatoly. How long?"

"Depends on the files." Anatoly asked a few questions about the video specs and a few more about the system that had recorded the footage. Tolstov passed on what he knew.

"So how long, Anatoly?"

"No more than an hour, Director. Maybe less. What you ask for is child's play for these people."

"Very good, Anatoly. Send me the finished product." Tolstov paused for a moment. "It's good to hear that you are feeling better."

The Director of the SVR hung up and Anatoly was left staring at his phone.

"Asshole," he mumbled.

The White House
06 December 2022 | 0618 Local Time
Washington, DC

President of the United States Daniel Evans walked into the situation room and took his seat, motioning for everyone else to do the same. He scanned the room, taking in the odd mixture of wood paneling and high-tech gadgetry before his gaze settled on the Director of National Intelligence. He nodded in her direction.

DNI Adams cleared her throat and stood.

"Mr. President, there were two incidents in the last few hours that have escalated tensions in the Black Sea." Adams pointed to a map display that zoomed in on the geographic area surrounding the *Neptun Deep* rig. The positions of the USS *James E. Williams* and the Russian frigate *Makarov* were clearly marked. Each was just south of the rig's debris field, with the *Makarov* in close and the *Williams* further afield. There was a red circle well north of everything else.

"What's that marker to the north?" Evans asked.

"That's the EX-30 *Trident* rig. It's the same as the *Neptun Deep* platform. Slightly older. It has been in production for a few years at this point."

"Fair enough," Evans said. "Why is it marked?"

Adams pointed to Major Alexander and a video began on one of the large-screen televisions. It wasn't the greatest or clearest footage, but it got the point across. "Approximately two hours ago, the *Trident* platform initiated a distress call, for what they called a terrorist event. Several armed individuals assaulted the platform and took possession of the control room. They also took the rig's operating crew hostage. There are about four minutes of footage during the initial assault, and we counted at least six different individuals."

Evans nodded. "Do we have assets in place to deal with this? Or nearby?"

DNI Adams shook her head. "The *Williams* does not have assets to conduct a hostage rescue, and the nearest available group is a JSOC team on station in Ukraine." Adams took a breath. "Plus, it isn't necessary."

Evans let his temper flare for a moment. "Then why in the hell are we talking about it, Ophelia?"

Adams ignored the attitude and used her remote to play a second video. "Because, Mr. President, we just picked up this footage in the last few minutes. Someone else assaulted the rig, executed a takedown, and freed the hostages. The video is shaky. It's from a cell phone. The terrorists who took the rig destroyed every camera on the platform."

"Any casualties?" Evans asked. He could feel the frustration building. He knew Adams wouldn't bring this up for shits and giggles. But Christ, he thought. Get to the point.

The video stopped. "No, Mr. President. No civilian casualties. From the video it looks like several of the terrorists who initially took the rig were either killed or wounded during the raid." She glanced at the video. "And the raiders removed every OPFOR body, living or dead."

Evans took a breath and told himself not to lash out. This had to be going somewhere. "Okay, Ophelia. I'll bite. Who conducted the raid—rescue?"

Adams slid a sheet of paper down the table. "Russia. This is a statement from President Barsukov detailing the rescue. It says that the raiding team launched from the *Makarov*."

Evans picked up the paper and scanned. He got to the second paragraph and looked up. "Wait. He's blaming us for the act?"

"Yes, Mr. President," Adams confirmed. "Russia is claiming that we, the CIA specifically, undertook an operation to hijack a rig."

"How? And what the hell for?"

"Unknown, Mr. President. We'll need more time on that. It's worth noting that the evidence he's basing this on is shaky."

Evans looked back at the paper. "Western clothing and M4 rifles?"

Adams nodded. "Yes, Mr. President. The video does show the terrorists wearing clothing that one might be more apt to see here. That's really irrelevant. The internet means that just about anyone with a connection and a credit card can get American clothes shipped right to their door. And the rifles certainly look like M4s. Again, it wouldn't be difficult for the Russian government to obtain some to stage an incident."

Suddenly, Evans got it. That's why she'd drawn this out. "And you believe that this is a false flag operation? Russian troops posing as Americans stage a hostage situation and Russia comes to the rescue?"

"I'm saying it's possible, Mr. President. I have no hard data to support the accusation, and, unless Barsukov parades a group of dead Americans with DNA tests and social security cards, neither does Russia."

"DNA?" Evans asked. He pointed to the second video. "There's blood at the scene. Can we get an ID that way?"

"Waste of time, sir," Adams noted. "It's likely that cleanup has already started. Even if it hasn't, whoever the blood belonged to would have to be in the database you were using in order to make a match. It's more complicated than that, but you get the idea."

"Shit," Evans said. "All right. Anything we can do with this?"

"Not right now. Just keep it in mind. It's going to make the rounds with all the rest of the disinformation coming out. There has been an uptick on that score. The material flooding social media and fringe news groups has increased exponentially over the past few hours. Expect that something this sensational will get playtime. People will see this and take Russia's word for it."

Evans began to say something, but a voice to his right interrupted. It was the young major. Alexander, Evans reminded himself.

"Um. Excuse me, Mr. President," Major Alexander said. "There's a breaking news alert. A press conference out of Russia."

Evans turned. "Barsukov?"

"No, Mr. President." Alexander looked up from a computer screen and pointed a remote, changing one of the TV screens to a Russian news station. "Admiral Fyodor Kirilovich Borshevsky. He's the head of the Russian Navy. Like our Chief of Naval Operations."

Evans turned to the screen. "Volume, Major?"

"Yes, sir." Alexander clicked the remote and Borshevsky's voice broadcast into the room.

"Shit. It's in Russian," Evans said. "We recording this so the interpreters can tell me what he's saying?"

Adams nodded. "Yes, Mr. President."

"Um. Sir? I speak a little Russian," Alexander said.

Evans turned. "Well, hell, Major. What's the admiral got to say?"

Everyone watched the screen. Borshevsky wasn't an animated speaker. His hands remained on the podium and there was very little in his delivery that screamed excitement.

Evans turned to see Major Alexander staring intently at the screen and listened as the young officer began to speak.

"He's saying that an American warship tried to ram a Russian vessel in the Black Sea." Alexander listened some more. "And he is saying that Russia abhors the incident…calls it an act…an irresponsible act of anger…sorry, aggression, by the United States Navy."

Evans kept staring at the screen. "Anything else, Major?"

"Uh, he says they have proof, Mr. President. A video that will be released after…after a security review."

Evans looked at Alexander. "And you're sure of your translation?"

"Ninety percent, Mr. President," Alexander said. "It's been a while since college."

Evans turned to the DNI. "Ophelia?"

"When he's done, we'll have it translated," Adams said.

Evans stood and glanced at his watch. "I've got a meeting in ten minutes with Senate Oversight. Have we heard anything from the *Williams* about this?"

No one in the room answered. Evans nodded. "So, this could be bullshit too? Like the hostage video?"

DNI Adams began to answer, but the phone in front of the president began ringing. Evans leaned over and punched the button to place the call on speaker.

"Situation Room. This is the president."

"Mr. President, this is Rear Admiral Gomez at the NMCC. We have an OPREP NAVY BLUE message from USS *James E. Williams*. She is dead in the water and adrift after a ramming incident in the Black Sea."

USS *James E. Williams*
06 December 2022 | 1800 Local Time
Black Sea

Chief Petty Officer Brian Thompson was sitting upright in his bed in the *Williams*' medical ward. The room was dim and, he noticed, quiet. He was trying to imagine why when the door to the ward opened and Senior Chief Martin entered the room.

"Why's it so quiet?"

"Not sure," Martin said. "How are you feeling?"

"I'm fine," Brian lied without thinking. He wasn't. His head ached. His whole body was sore as hell. And there was a faint wave of nausea lapping at the edge of his consciousness. Nothing imminent, but strong enough to get his attention. "Why's it so quiet?"

Martin looked at Brian and cocked an eyebrow up. After a few moments, he apparently had made a decision. "We're dead in the water."

Brian started to get up, but a tugging sensation at his right elbow stopped him. Brian looked at his elbow in the dim light. There was an IV there. "Dude, what the hell?"

"IV drip."

"I know that. Why's it there?"

Martin's voice remained calm. "Because you got knocked out. Again. And you were out for a while this time."

Brian tried to get up again. "Well, I'm awake now. I need to get to CCS."

Martin extended a long arm and gently pushed Brian back.

"No. You need to stay in the bed."

"But—" Brian protested.

"But nothing, Brian," Martin said. "You've got one hell of a concussion and you aren't leaving until I say you're leaving. Got it?"

Brian began to stand again. Martin didn't try to stop him this time. "Listen, if we're DIW, like you say..." Brian began, then stopped talking. The room went out of focus and his vision alternated from black to flashes of light. He felt his knees weaken and he leaned back towards the bed. "Shit," he mumbled. He took a few deep breaths and looked up. His vision was clearing and he could see Martin smiling. "What?"

"I'm not here to prevent you leaving. In your condition, you couldn't make it four steps past that door." He jerked a thumb over a shoulder. "I'm here to make sure you don't injure yourself trying."

"But the plant..." Brian said. His head was pounding with the rise in blood pressure.

"The plant hell, Brian," Martin said. "For God's sake, man. Give me a break here. I signed you out after you took that first whack to the skull before fully checking you out. Ain't happening again. It's my ass if you keel over out there."

Brian lay back down, propped up against the bulkhead. "Fine. How long am I stuck here?"

"Until the symptoms subside," Martin said. "XO doesn't want you out and about and making it worse."

"Since when does that sonofabitch give a shit about anything but himself?" The words raced out of Brian's mouth before he could think about them.

Martin took a deep breath. "Listen, Brian. What Logan told you was right. I know we've had problems with XO in the past, but nothing gives you the right to spout off like this."

Brian started to argue, but Martin's raised hand stopped him. "I know. He's an asshole. But he's part of the chain of command and if you ignore that, ain't shit gonna go right for you."

Brian sulked for a few moments, then changed the subject. "So, what's wrong with the plant?"

Martin shrugged. "Shit's turning, but nothing's burning. Something like that. Power's on at least."

"That's not really helpful."

Martin picked up a clipboard and made a few notes. "Hell,

dude. I'm a corpsman. What the hell would I know? I spent most of my career out doing young-guy shit with the Marines."

Brian thought about that. "Can we get CHENG or Tim in here?"

Martin set the clipboard down and eyed Brian appraisingly. "Tell you what. Let's try to get a meal in you first and then I'll get them down here."

"Works for me," Brian agreed.

Martin stood and moved to the door, then turned back to Brian. "Deal only stands if you stay here, in that bed. You try to leave and I'll have the deck apes tie your ass to that bunk while XO sets up your mast case. Got it?"

Brian mumbled.

"I didn't hear you, Brian."

"I got it."

"Good. 'Cause I ain't joking."

With that, Martin left Brian alone to think in the dark.

Novokuznetskaya Flats
06 December 2022 | Local Time
Moscow

Anatoly was drinking again and he was sure that his physician wouldn't approve. He thought about the man, the prim doctor with his absolute belief in his government. Anatoly laughed at that. The kid was so certain of himself, of the righteousness of what he'd been taught.

"Hell, child," Anatoly mused, staring at the bottle. "The things I could tell you about your government. About what your government did today."

Anatoly laughed again. That boy wouldn't believe it. Because he was a doctor? Anatoly wondered. That was part of it. Doctors were supremely confident people. Anatoly had to admit that. No one wanted a doctor slicing into them who constantly second-guessed himself. Or herself.

There was something else there, though.

Anatoly took a long pull on the bottle, swallowed, and blew out his breath with an explosive "Pah!"

It was vodka tonight. Shit vodka. But beggars couldn't be

choosers. That was the American saying. Right?

Anatoly giggled to himself and returned his thoughts to the doctor.

"Why are you so confident, Doctor?" Another drink. "Because you have to believe in the system? Because you have to believe your government is just?"

Shit, Anatoly thought. You have to be young to think such rubbish. He took another drink and held the bottle up, putting it between his eyes and the lone, bare bulb hanging from the ceiling.

"What about you, little bottle? Do you agree with the good doctor?" Anatoly asked. He gave the bottle a shake and watched the contents splash back and forth, the clear liquid a miniature, angry sea. "What, bottle? Are you afraid?"

Anatoly took another long pull and exhaled.

You *should* be afraid, he thought. He set the bottle on the table and pointed at it. You, he thought. And the doctor.

Such belief. The state is always right. Absurd.

But the state was not always right, he knew. They hadn't been right when that damned reactor had killed his wife and brother. And when they'd bought his silence with a pension and a comfortable job—had that been right?

Anatoly paused, thinking. There was a thought out there and his last tendrils of sobriety were reaching out to it. Nearly in contact with it.

Right?

Are we right now? Anatoly pondered that. What we are doing—the fake videos and bribes and bullshit claims backed by bullshit evidence? Is that right? Is that something a righteous government does? Is it something a righteous government finds necessary?

Anatoly took another swig from the bottle. It was almost empty.

"Finish it off, Anatoly," he muttered. "And get some sleep. Busy day tomorrow."

He laughed. And coughed. And spat on the floor.

"Shit."

16

The White House
06 December 2022 | 1900 Local Time
Washington, DC

Major Harlan Alexander left the White House after showering and changing in the gym set aside for staff use. He bundled himself up against the icy wind and walked through the gates to a nearby parking lot—he wasn't senior enough to rate a spot on West Executive Drive—found his car, and climbed in. He pressed the start button and sat, waiting for the engine to warm up.

He debated making the drive. Thought about ignoring what his dad wanted. Just drive home, have a drink, and go to bed. How hard was that? It wasn't as if his dad would know. The old man couldn't possibly know whether or not something had happened that would have sent the president to the situation room. Could he?

Harlan closed his eyes.

Dad always knew. Always. Harlan could run through the times he'd not made the drive after overhearing valuable information, and his father had known every single time. There'd been a phone call each time. Precisely at five the next morning, usually with some semi-apologetic request for Harlan to get his butt down to the retirement community.

And Harlan always went. Not because his father demanded it. But because of his mother. Because of her death. Harlan did what he was told to do because he knew no other way to exact revenge for the loss of his mother.

If we ever get found out, it won't be Dad I'll have to answer to.

It'll be a team of FBI agents who specialize in counterintelligence. Pros. Guys with no agenda other than a near-insatiable desire to root out spies. And that, Harlan thought, was a problem.

Henry Alexander would stand up to such an interrogation well. He knew the tricks and tactics and would be able to fence with the average FBI agent.

Me, Harlan thought, not so much.

As the engine temperature crept up, Harlan considered that.

Harlan knew he had a few narcissistic tendencies. The car. The civilian clothing. Hell, he thought, even some choices in food and drink—especially on dates. He knew he possessed roguish good looks and probably spent too much time in front of a mirror. He was, he believed, physically gifted and possessed of above-average intelligence.

And none of it mattered a damn because Harlan knew something else.

He was deathly afraid of getting into trouble. He didn't know why and he didn't understand the cause, but the threat of punishment made him physically ill. It always had. All the way back to the time when he and two other boys had stolen another kid's gym shorts out of the boys' locker room in fifth grade. No one else had said a word to the vice principal, but when she'd threatened suspension, Harlan had vomited all over her pants, shoes, and carpet. And then he'd produced the missing shorts.

He just didn't process guilt well. Not then. Not now. And for that reason, he couldn't get caught. If he didn't do anything else, he couldn't get caught. He could just stop now. *Refuse to do anything else. Right?*

"If you could stop, why are you making this drive?" Harlan grumbled. He put the car in gear, left his parking space, and began picking his way towards Maryland 4 South.

Almost ninety minutes later he was sitting on his father's couch.

"So, my boy. What have you got?"

Harlan spent ten minutes outlining the information he'd heard in the situation room that day. His father asked a few questions and Harlan answered as best he could. Finally, Henry Alexander leaned back in his chair.

"It's late." He rolled ice cubes around in a nearly-empty tumbler. "You were gonna skip tonight, weren't you?"

Of course, he knew. "No, Pop. Just needed a shower first."

"Uh huh." Henry leaned forward. "Do I need to remind you why we do this? What they did?"

Harlan could feel his stomach churn. "No, Pop."

"Then what took you so long?"

Harlan eyeballed the floor. "I told you. Needed a shower. It was hot as hell in there today."

"Maybe," Henry said. "Or maybe you're sweating all of this."

Harlan looked up. "Dad, I always sweat this. But I did it." Again, he didn't say.

"This time. What about next time? And the time after that?"

Harlan fought a wave of nausea. Here it comes, he thought. The guilt trip. "How long are we supposed to do this?"

"Till we're done." The statement was delivered matter-of-factly, as if there was a clearly published timeline.

"Till we're done?" Harlan asked. "And when is that? When will that be?" Harlan wanted to add to that, to know what happened after they were done. Did it just stop? Did everyone just go their separate ways and pretend none of this had ever happened? Like some damned one-night stand that you prayed you'd never see again. "Jesus, Pop. When's enough, enough?"

Harlan expected his dad to tell him that it was over when they'd gotten payback. It sounded too much like something out of a movie, but that was the kind of thing that popped into his head. When's it enough, Dad? When the bastards have paid for what they did, son. When we get even, Harlan.

But that was not what Henry Alexander said. Harlan watched his dad take a last sip of bourbon and lean forward. He grinned.

"We're done, Harlan, when they say we're done."

For the first time, it occurred to Harlan that this might not be about his mother at all.

USS *James E. Williams*
07 December 2022 | 0430 Local Time
Black Sea

Chief Petty Officer Brian Thompson couldn't sleep anymore, and that would have brought a smile to his face had it not been for the circumstances. He remembered his first few months on board, a time when he'd gotten maybe two or three hours of sleep per day and would have killed for this kind of rack time.

But not now. His team was out and about, working to repair damage to the ship—some caused by the ramming and some just pure coincidence—and he was here, in the medical ward, complaining about too much sleep.

Brian rolled and popped his neck and began reviewing the list of damage for the hundredth time since CHENG and Chief Tim Guillory had briefed him in.

None of the ship's gas turbine main engines would start—the power-generating ones were apparently still operational—and troubleshooting was still ongoing. No one knew exactly why yet—the auxiliary systems like fuel and lube oil seemed to be functioning as designed—and the inability to fix the engines meant that USS *James E. Williams* had no ability to propel herself through the water.

One of the steering HPUs—the one that had been sprayed with fluid and had caught fire—was a total loss. The unit with the rupture had no physical damage other than the hole in the flexible hose, and that could be replaced if Supply Department found a spare in one of the ship's many storerooms. There'd been some other, minor damage caused by the fire—melted wiring and destroyed lighting fixtures—but nothing that couldn't be fixed in a few days.

There was a twenty-foot-long tear—how it wasn't any bigger, no one knew—in the starboard side of the ship that started just forward of the CCS passage and stopped just after the entrance to the log room. Pretty much everything lining that outboard bulkhead had been wrecked. Two potable water lines had ruptured. A portion of the chilled-water main had been torn loose and was now isolated upstream and downstream. Electrical cables had been ripped to shreds, and two distribution panels had been dislodged and thrown inboard and forward by the initial collision.

Brian flipped through the notes he'd been given and swore. In addition to the major problems, there were now hundreds of little issues. Breakers that wouldn't reset. Computer systems that wouldn't boot up. Gear foundations snapped. Brian went through that list and shook his head. The ship was shock tested against events like this—bigger than this, actually. Equipment could, and should, have withstood the ramming. But it hadn't.

There was enough here to keep three whole yard teams and the ship's crew busy for months. But they didn't have yard crews. And they didn't have months. Whatever was going on—Brian didn't know and neither, it seemed, did anyone else—there was still a Russian ship out there that didn't seem averse to hostile acts.

A ship we can't shoot at. Because there are American sailors on board. The Williams' *sailors. My sailors.*

"Goddamnit," Brian grumbled.

He went through the list again because he didn't have anything else to do.

Patuxent Shores Retirement Community
06 December 2022 | 2200 Local Time
Solomons, MD

Harlan ate dinner with his dad, food ordered from the main building's expansive, twenty-four-hour-a-day kitchen. They talked little. Henry seemed content to work his way through a Reuben sandwich and watch some television show Harlan had never heard of. Harlan, for his part, was happy to be left alone with a grilled chicken Caesar and his thoughts.

Shortly before eleven, Harlan picked up the remnants of both meals and tossed them in the garbage before heading for the door. As he slipped on his coat and checked his pockets for his keys, wallet, and phone, he looked at his dad.

It crossed his mind that Henry Alexander didn't appear to have a care in the world. He just sat there, in jeans and an old crew-neck sweatshirt, chuckling at the television.

"I'm out of here, Pop. Early day tomorrow."

Henry didn't even turn away from his show. "You don't forget what I said. This is over when we're done. Not before."

Harlan began to say something, but Henry began laughing at the television. Harlan watched him for a moment and then slipped out into the night. He spent the entire drive to his home in Alexandria going over all the things he could have said. Should have said. Wished he had the guts to say.

17

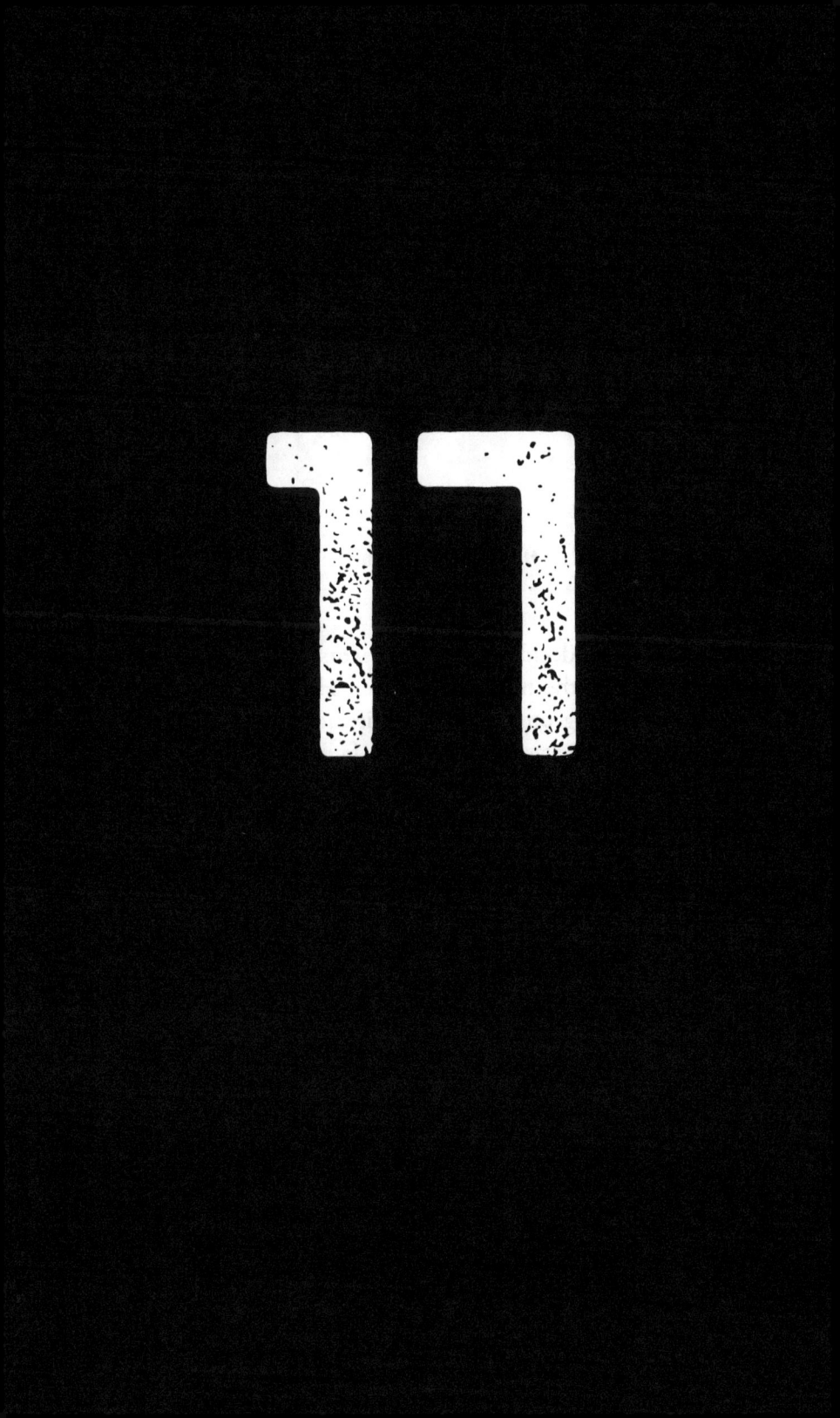

The Kremlin
07 December 2022 | 0700 Local Time
Moscow

Anatoly couldn't decide which was worse—the side effects of chemotherapy or the massive hangover. He was leaning towards blaming everything on the former this morning, if only because the chemotherapy wasn't entirely his fault. Sure, he thought, I elected to go through this again, but there was plenty of blame to go around. The idiots who'd built Chernobyl. The dumb bastards who'd rushed the testing that fateful night. Anatoly wasn't even beyond laying some of the blame on the geniuses who'd thought up chemo in the first place.

But the hangover. That, you dumb bastard. That was all you.

Anatoly would have grunted at that, but the effort to do so required more strength than he had at the moment.

He was rubbing his temples when the buzzer on his intercom went off.

"Anatoly, come in here."

Anatoly stood, wobbling a little, and took a few deep breaths, hoping to ward off the waves of nausea. He walked to the director's office door, grateful for having skipped breakfast. Nothing in there to vomit.

Anatoly knocked on the door, opened it, and stepped into the room. The director was on the phone and waved Anatoly to a seat.

"Twenty minutes? Excellent. I'll be waiting." Tolstov hung up the phone and looked at Anatoly. The smile that had been on his face vanished and was replaced by shock. "Mother of God, Anatoly. I thought you said you were feeling better."

Anatoly felt a surge of anger. He'd said nothing of the kind. This was why he'd asked for time off. He knew what he looked like. Knew that his skin had a papery-thin look to it. Knew that the ruddiness he'd previously enjoyed was gone, replaced, probably permanently, by skin that was sallow and slack. And it would only get worse. His appearance and health were rotting away in real time and there wasn't a damn thing he could do about it.

Hell, he thought, I'm paying for it to happen. Out of my own pocket.

Anatoly wondered briefly how to explain that to the man in front of him. How to tell the man who enjoyed the benefits of great wealth and good health that this was what real life looked like.

Well, Anatoly considered. Maybe not that. Not what life looked like. Death. This was what dying looked like. Would he understand? Would he care?

No, Anatoly decided. He would not. That thought made his skin flush and his stomach heave. Tolstov must have seen it, because his face changed again. There was alarm there now.

"Anatoly, are you okay?"

What, Director? Afraid I might die in one of your expensive chairs? Anatoly coughed. "I'm fine, Director. You wanted to see me?"

"Yes." Tolstov tossed a paper across the desk. "Read that."

Anatoly reached for the paper. He saw Tolstov flinch at the sight of his withered hand grabbing it off the desk, and he would have bet money that Tolstov was already thinking about disinfecting the entire desktop.

Relax. It's not contagious, you ignorant bastard.

Anatoly began reading. It was another intelligence report, purporting to assess the American president's reaction to recent events. Most notably, it covered the collision between the *Makarov* and the American destroyer.

When Anatoly finished, he looked up. "Is this confirmed?" He placed the report on the edge of Tolstov's desk and saw the man flinch again.

Tolstov's eyes lingered on the report. "No. The placement of the source is such that independent confirmation is difficult."

Anatoly jabbed the cover of the report twice. Again, Tolstov flinched. "So, this could be disinformation?"

"It is possible, but unlikely," Tolstov said. "The information from this particular source has always been accurate. There is no reason to suspect that this is false."

Anatoly leaned forward and put a hand on the report, slightly off-center so that his thumb touched the bare desktop. He saw Tolstov eyeball his thumb. "Director, there are plenty of reasons to suspect that this is false." He took a breath. "We're doing it to them. Giving them false data. Turnabout is fair play."

"You're forgetting one thing, Anatoly." Tolstov seemed to recover, but Anatoly was certain that his boss was thinking about having the entire desk burned by now. "For this to be false, for the Americans to fake this, they would need to suspect that there is someone in that room listening."

Anatoly cocked his head to one side. "What room?"

Tolstov froze for a moment. He didn't attempt to cover the mistake, just ordered Anatoly to ignore it. "That is not something you need to worry about."

Anatoly shrugged but filed the information away. "I believe you are mistaken about the Americans, Director."

"How so?"

"Is it possible that your source is just feeding you information that he thinks you want to hear?"

Tolstov considered this. "It is possible, but to what purpose? We don't pay this man."

"I don't know, Director. I'm not an intelligence officer."

Tolstov smiled at that. "No, Anatoly, you're not. And this isn't the reason I'm showing you this."

"Okay," Anatoly said. "Why, then?"

"Because your part of this operation will directly impact the American president's mental state. This…" He pointed to the report without touching it. "This will be our indication that your campaign is working."

Anatoly sat silent for a few seconds. "Can't President Barsukov tell? During his conversations with the American president?"

"If they were talking, yes." Tolstov leaned back. "But they haven't spoken yet, Anatoly."

Anatoly turned that revelation over in his mind. "Isn't that unusual?"

"It is. But in this case, they have not talked because Barsukov has refused to pick up the phone."

"Jesus." Anatoly's mind was churning now. "But we've got American sailors of his on our ship. We've got his nephew. The incidents with both rigs have to be raising questions. Not to mention the collision between their ship and ours."

"It's the opinion of the Foreign Ministry that Evans's staff are advising him against such a call, that they wish to handle this at the ministerial level, and that Evans is ignoring that advice," Tolstov pointed out. "Barsukov is giving Evans's staff what they want."

Anatoly shook his head. "I'm no politician, but that seems wrong to me. This is out of character for them."

"What do you mean?"

"He's a military man. America is, at his level, a military culture. One of their tenets is to bring everyone home. They put a great deal of importance on that idea. And you tell me that he's not called Barsukov yet to demand that his family and his sailors be returned? That's unbelievable."

Tolstov checked his watch. "I didn't say Evans hasn't called, Anatoly. He has tried. As I said, the lack of communication is being considered strategically. To benefit the entire operation." Tolstov paused. "You said it yourself, Anatoly. You aren't an intelligence officer, a politician, or a diplomat. Stick to what you know and..." He pointed to the report without touching it again. "Keep up the good work."

Anatoly sat in silence for a moment before standing. "Anything else, Director?"

"Yes. The next phase, with the politicians. When?"

"We've initiated file delivery to our agents. Contact will occur tonight. My deputy will oversee that process and I will have confirmation to you by noon tomorrow."

Tolstov frowned. "No. You oversee the process and get me the report."

Anatoly froze. "Director, that last session... Chemotherapy." He saw Tolstov flinch at the very word. "I'm still not recovered. I need to rest." He didn't mention the recent binge drinking.

"I understand, Anatoly," Tolstov said. "But this will require your full attention. It demands it. You can rest when this is over. Yes?"

Anatoly nodded and moved to the door. As he returned to his desk, he felt his face flush again and felt his stomach heave. He rushed to the trash can next to his desk and made it just in time. His stomach contracted and his abdominal muscles tightened. Bile and spit dribbled into the trash can for two full minutes before the dry heaving subsided.

Anatoly pulled himself into his desk chair, still hugging the trash can. He was sweating and his core ached. His head was pounding and his hearing was fuzzy and vague.

I can rest when this is over.
Of course, Director, I'll be dead by then.

Frigate *Admiral Makarov*
07 December 2022 | 0715 Local Time
Black Sea

Captain Yuri Nikolayevich Dashkov was in the medical ward biting his lip as the ship's doctor poked at his arm.

"You'll need X-rays, Captain. I am certain there are fractures, but without pictures..." The doctor shrugged.

"Can you wrap it?" Dashkov asked. There was a knock at the door and he gave permission for whoever it was to enter.

"We have air casts," the doctor said. "That should help. I will give you a sling as well, even though I know you won't use it."

"Save the sling. Give me the cast." Dashkov grimaced as the doctor set his arm on the table between them. He looked up as the doctor moved off to gather the cast and some aspirin. Gorshkov was standing by patiently. "Lieutenant?"

"How is your arm, Captain?" Gorshkov asked.

"It's just an arm. The doctor says it is broken—" Dashkov started.

"Not broken. Fractured," the doctor called from the next room.

"Broken. Fractured. Whatever." Dashkov grinned. "Tell me about the damage."

"First, I have the ship patrolling in our original position. No more than five knots. Nothing aggressive. The American is just sitting there. Not moving. Not turning."

"Licking her own wounds," Dashkov said.

"Likely," Gorshkov agreed. "No major injuries to the crew. Your arm is the most severe injury reported. We had some minor flooding, dislodged equipment, and sprung piping. Some wiring issues. Those are the simple problems, and I've assigned teams to each one."

"What about the gun?" Dashkov asked. The *Makarov*'s 100mm A-190 Arsenal deck gun had been sitting askew when he'd left the bridge.

Gorshkov shook his head. "A large portion of the port side was crushed in the accident and there is extensive damage to the support systems feeding the gun. The portion of the deck supporting the gun was shoved to starboard and severed hydraulics, compressed air, data cables, power cables…"

"That will take a shipyard to repair," Dashkov noted. "What else?"

"There is some damage to our VLS capabilities. CIWS appears to be functional. Same for the torpedo systems and rocket systems. The radars don't appear to have been damaged, though we lost two when a portion of the chilled-water cooling system was punctured. That has been repaired and the systems have been restored. We've also lost the sonar dome. I have to assume that it was destroyed in the incident. Nothing we can do about that."

Dashkov nodded. "What of the Spetsnaz team?"

"We were able to recover them easily. Two flights. No issues reported. Some of the team are assisting with repairs to the ship. Helping to run cabling and weld piping."

"Really?" Dashkov asked, surprised.

"Yes, Captain," Gorshkov said. "The ones who aren't skilled in such things are assisting with guarding the American boat team, and both team medics have been aiding the doctor here."

I'll be damned, Dashkov thought. "Very good, Pavel

Stefanovich. Very good." He smiled through the pain as the doctor returned and began fitting the air cast to his arm. "Any word from Moscow?"

"Yes, sir," Gorshkov said. He pulled a message from his pants pocket and handed it over.

Dashkov read it and grunted. He turned to the doctor. "How is our celebrity patient?"

The doctor looked up. "What?"

"Our patient. Mr. Evans. How is he?" Dashkov waved the message with his free hand. "Moscow wants to know. Nothing for us, you'll note. Not an order to remain on station or head in for repair. Just an inquiry about the health of our illustrious guest."

The doctor returned to fitting the air cast and gave a brief update on the condition of Jonathan Evans. "In all, his condition is really unchanged from the last report. He's in critical condition. He needs more than we can provide here. Moving him may still kill him."

Dashkov turned to see Gorshkov taking notes. He nodded approvingly. "Got that?"

Gorshkov finished writing. "Yes, Captain."

"Good. Get the message ready for my signature. I'll be done here shortly."

"Yes, Captain."

Dashkov watched his operations officer leave the room and turned back to the doctor. He watched the man adjusting the cast and felt the pressure on the breaks. He winced and forced his mind to think of something else.

Like my broken ship. Damnit.

The Kremlin
07 December 2022 | 0800 Local Time
Moscow

Russian president Dmitri Mikhailovich Barsukov swore at the report in his hands and began reading through it again. Finished, he looked up.

"And how did this happen? How is it that this idiot wrecked

one of our ships?" He was fuming and tried to tell himself to calm down.

Admiral Borshevsky cleared his throat. "This was an accident, sir. Nothing more. Captain Dashkov did exactly as ordered. He employed and executed the techniques exactly as specified."

"Then what happened, Admiral? What?"

"It's impossible to know, sir." Borshevsky pointed at his copy of the report from the *Makarov*. "From what this says, I would guess that the American destroyer suffered some sort of casualty to its propulsion and steering systems. Something that made it impossible for her to maneuver clear."

Barsukov glared at his report again. "Two separate systems? Like ours?"

"Yes, sir."

Barsukov looked up. "So, at the exact moment the *Makarov* is making his run, this ship just happens to have two separate problems to two critical systems and blunders directly into the path of a ship half its size? Does that sound reasonable to you, Admiral?"

Borshevsky blinked and stiffened. "Yes, sir. It does. The American Navy does not usually allow its ships to be rammed."

Barsukov nearly rolled his eyes at that remark, but he let it go. He tossed the report on his desk and turned to the other man in the room. "Director Tolstov. How does this affect your part of the operation?"

Tolstov looked at Borshevsky. "Actually, this helps us."

Borshevsky turned his head and Barsukov leaned forward behind his desk.

"I don't see it that way, Director," Barsukov said. "This whole situation depends on our ability to get the Americans to be aggressive. To shoot first, so to speak."

"No, sir," Tolstov said. "With respect, it does not. This operation depends on our ability to convince the world that the Americans are troublemakers. They don't need to be aggressive or shoot first. We just need to be able to convince people that they did."

"By ramming one of their ships and saying they are somehow responsible?" Barsukov shook his head.

"But that's not what happened." Tolstov smiled.

Barsukov rubbed his eyes. "Of course that's what happened."

"But that's not what he told the cameras." Tolstov pointed at Borshevsky. "That's not what our edited footage shows."

"And when they come out with their own footage? What then?"

Tolstov shrugged. "What of it, sir? Then it's their word against ours, and the world doesn't exactly trust them anymore."

"Explain," Barsukov snapped.

"Simple, sir. Even without our operation—my portion, that is—the world does not take what the United States does or says as absolute fact anymore. They've abused that trust for too long. They've caused too many incidents and deaths, and frankly, sir, their list of true friends is extremely short."

Barsukov sat still, thinking. "And assuming this is all true…"

"Then we keep going," Tolstov said smoothly. "Our truth is that the American destroyer hit us. At the very least, it violated right of way and caused a collision. Like one of those sorry bastards that flops on the ground in football. We stick to that story and keep pushing."

"Will it still work?" Barsukov asked.

"The end goal is to keep everyone out of the Black Sea, correct? To drive away buyers until Russian companies and subsidiaries are the only remaining interested parties."

"Yes," Barsukov confirmed.

Tolstov opened a folder and withdrew a sheet of paper. He handed it across the desk. "Then it is already working, sir."

"What is this?" Barsukov asked, looking at the paper.

"That is a list of the companies who have withdrawn bids for rig purchases in the last forty-eight hours," Tolstov noted. "Four rigs. Seven corporations or government agencies, depending on the rig's location. In each case the originator cites the increased tension in the region and an assortment of additional issues that no longer make it in their interest to purchase the various platforms."

Barsukov scanned the document. "Insurance?"

Tolstov smiled. "When the British tanker rammed the *Neptun Deep* platform, the costs to insure each facility skyrocketed."

Barsukov stared at the list in his hands for several more seconds before placing it to the side. "Okay. What about the domestic side of this? The plan to keep Evans unable to interfere politically with the purchasing of the wells?"

"That is progressing, sir," Tolstov reported. "The work by my deputy and his team is having the desired effect. Tensions are high within the American public. This team has been extremely successful in locating fissures and exploiting them. With proper direction and motivation, we can generate riots in the next few days. They've already had a few incidents. Minor ones. Small groups of people fighting against each other at protests. We've had larger riots after FC Spartak loses."

Football hooligans. Barsukov shook his head. "And the other part? The politicians?"

"Those contacts will be made tonight. That part is simple. They will either do as they're told and pressure the American president to withdraw from the Black Sea or we will destroy them publicly." Tolstov paused. "That, I recommend, should be the determining factor in unleashing full-scale riots. It is a risky step that should be necessary only if the American politicians refuse to play along."

Barsukov considered that. He understood this part of the operation better than most. With what Tolstov and the SVR had on some high-ranking politicians, this was child's play. Most would play along. Some would resist. And the information the SVR had on those individuals would kill any chance at re-election. A few would face criminal investigation and likely prosecution. And if none of them played along, well… America would find itself busy trying to quell whatever riots the SVR could initiate. Those, Barsukov suspected, would be on a scale unprecedented in American history.

Though not in our own history, Barsukov remembered. He barely repressed a shudder and nodded. "Very well. Report to me when contacts are made."

"Yes, sir," Tolstov said.

"Good," Barsukov said. "Anything else?"

"With your permission, sir…" Borshevsky said. "I would like to order the *Kazan* in closer, to keep an eye on things."

"Why?" Barsukov asked.

"Call it precaution, sir," Borshevsky said. "On the off chance the Americans start shooting. On the chance that the damage to

Makarov is worse than reported or something else breaks."

Barsukov considered that for a few moments. "Are there American submarines in the area?"

Borshevsky shook his head. "None, sir."

"Isn't that strange, Admiral?"

"Not really, sir," Borshevsky said. "We blockaded the entrance to the Black Sea when this began, and the *Williams* was the only American ship to transit the Bosporus in some time."

"And they couldn't have snuck a submarine past you?"

"No, sir." Borshevsky bristled. "We shifted fleet assignments around to bring in our most technologically advanced platforms in the weeks prior to the incident with the *Brixton*. Anyone going through the Bosporus would have had to sneak past three of our best attack submarines."

Barsukov thought for a moment more and nodded. "Permission granted. Move the *Kazan* closer."

16

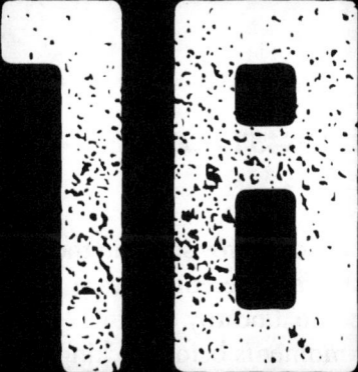

K-561 *Kazan*
07 December 2022 | 0845 Local Time
Black Sea

Captain Ivan Sergeyevich Korov stood in the dim light of the attack center and folded the most recent message form into a pocket. He walked the few paces to a nearby chart table and let his eyes dance around it for a few moments before picking up a handset.

"Sonar. Report contacts," Korov ordered.

"No subsurface or air contacts, Captain," Lieutenant Belyaev announced. "Tracking five surface contacts. Three commercial tankers to the east. *Makarov* to the west. The American destroyer is also there, but faint. It is not moving and has decreased plant and propulsion noises."

"Last known location for the *Makarov* and the American?"

Belyaev provided the information and Korov's eyes found the approximate spots on the chart. "Nothing else, Belyaev?"

"No, Captain."

Korov hung up the handset and turned to the *Kazan*'s navigator. "Dima, we are to take up station…" Korov ran his finger along the chart. "Here. Close to both, but not in the way."

"Yes, Captain." Lieutenant Dima Igorovich Antonov began plotting the course. After a few moments he lifted his head. "Something change, Captain?"

Korov smiled grimly and pulled the message from his pocket. "Remember that mechanical transient Sonar reported. It would seem that our brothers on the *Makarov* got themselves run over by the American."

Dima shuddered. "What's the size difference?"

Korov thought for a moment, trying to recall the specifications for American destroyers. "Four and a half thousand tons. Plus or minus."

Dima nodded and finished his plot. "And we're the bodyguard now?"

"It would seem so," Korov agreed. He didn't particularly relish being in the general area on the off chance that the two surface ships began shooting. With that thought, he checked the navigator's work, suggested a minor change, and gave the order to execute the move. "Notify me when we are on station, Dima."

"Yes, Captain."

"Captain," a voice said, the tone almost an admonishment. "You disagree with our orders?"

Korov closed his eyes briefly. The voice was easily recognizable.

No, you arrogant pig. They're just fine. Using a cruise missile submarine as a bodyguard is exactly what we should be doing.

Korov forced a smile and turned. "No, Mikhail Gregorovich. I do not disagree with our orders. I am merely concerned about the capabilities of this ship against the possibility of an American hunter submarine. They have advantages in speed and maneuverability."

"Rubbish." Alexandrov waved his hand around. "Look at these fine boys. In their hands, the Americans are no match for us."

"As you say." Korov bit off his honest response and picked up the handset again. "Sonar, Captain. No submerged contacts? You are certain?" Korov said.

"Yes, Captain."

"Very well." Korov hung up and turned back to the navigator while Alexandrov looked on with a smug smile. "Get us on station quietly, Dima."

USS *Key West*
07 December 2022 | 0848 Local Time
Black Sea

"Conn, Sonar. Submerged contact. Bearing zero-three-two."

"Conn, aye," Commander Reynes answered. He replaced the mic and walked forward to Sonar. "What have you got, Chief?"

"The *Kazan*, Skipper. We lost him for a bit when he went up near the surface. Probably getting message traffic." Hughley pointed at the screen. "Got some hull creaking when he came back down."

Reynes eyeballed the screen. "Speed?"

"Maybe eight or ten, sir," Hughley pronounced. "Sneaking off to the west, looks like."

The sonar chief paused, one hand on his headset. He poked the seaman sitting next to him, pointed at the sailor's screen, and turned back to the captain. "Aspect change, sounds like. Definitely west. Heading over by the rigs and all that ruckus." Hughley pulled one earpiece off. "Any idea what's going on?"

Reynes shook his head and pulled the phone handset off the console. "XO, come to Sonar."

Lieutenant Commander Will Sandler poked his head into the space sixty seconds later. "You rang?"

"*Kazan* is moving over by our boy and the Russian frigate," Reynes said. "I want to follow. Keep an eye on things. Not too close, XO. I don't want him counter-detecting."

Sandler looked at the displays, asked a few questions, and disappeared for two minutes. When he came back, he was carrying a paper chart with his proposal. Reynes scanned it and approved.

"Make it happen, XO," Reynes noted. "But let's go up first and call this in."

NMCC, The Pentagon
07 December 2022 | 0200 Local Time
Arlington, VA

Rear Admiral Hector Gomez had been on watch for his shift in the Pentagon's NMCC for exactly twenty-three minutes when the message transmitted from USS *Key West* hit his desk. He scanned it, ordered the appropriate notifications to various fleet, type, and operational commands, and went back to reviewing the damage assessments from the USS *James E. Williams*. He thought back to the ship's previous deployment and tried to remember all of the damaged sustained when the *Williams* had been sent to interdict a cargo vessel transporting a stolen nuclear warhead.

Christ, he thought. Bad luck ship.

Gomez reproached himself for that. He knew there was no

such thing as a bad luck ship. He understood that everything that had happened to the *Williams*, more or less, was the direct result of people and the actions they took. If a combatant ship took fire, that was because she had been ordered into the fray. It had nothing to do with luck.

Right?

Gomez reviewed the reports in front of him and shook his head. On the technical side, the ship was a mess. Busted engines—though the prognosis for one was looking better—and damaged steering systems were big problems for a ship sitting in the middle of a crisis. Add the damage to the firefighting, chilled water, electrical cabling and distribution, weapons systems, and a myriad of other nickel-and-dime issues and the ship was in deep shit.

Things weren't much better on the personnel side. Five sailors picked up and being held on the *Makarov*. An apparent suicide under questionable circumstances that demanded an investigation. The ship's OPS had been promoted to executive officer after the original XO had been nearly killed by some jackass who'd run a red light.

Gomez's brain began summarizing every known piece of data. He had a disabled ship floating in the Black Sea. She was being hounded by a Russian frigate that might or might not have been similarly damaged in the recent collision. A Russian cruise missile sub was headed to the area, probably stalking the wounded destroyer.

"Shit." Gomez began rubbing his temples. His first instinct was to recall the *Williams* and send in some help to keep the Russians at bay. But he couldn't do that. For one, the Russians had blockaded the damn strait. For two, the repairs to one of the destroyer's engines weren't a sure thing yet. It was still likely she'd need a tow to the nearest friendly port.

Gomez lifted his eyes and examined the electronic chart display on the near wall. He saw the updated position for the USS *Key West*. As he dialed the number for the SECDEF, he thanked providence for the ability to pass on some good news. *Williams* could probably not maneuver, but at least she had a guardian angel lurking nearby.

The White House
07 December 2022 | 0245 Local Time
Washington, DC

President Daniel Evans walked into the situation room, nodded at Major Alexander, who was standing in his usual place, and took his seat. He pointed at DNI Adams and SECDEF Tolchanov and started to tell them to begin their briefings, but stopped in mid-sentence.

"What the hell is that smell?"

Noses turned up, sniffing the air. It was a full ten seconds before one of the Air Force officers in the opposite end of the room yelled.

"Fire!"

Evans saw the scramble of activity at the far end of the room. He saw Major Alexander move to assist as the various screens and displays blinked off. The lights went next, flickering off and on before finally staying off. The acrid stench of burning electrical reached the president's nostrils as he was escorted from the room.

The meeting's attendees—just Evans, his chief of staff, DNI Adams, and SECDEF Tolchanov this time—reconvened ten minutes later in the Oval Office.

"Any update on the fire?" Evans asked as he took a seat on one of the room's two couches.

"Wiring issues," said Barnes, the chief of staff. "A portion of the situation room wiring dates back to the seventies. Should have been updated when all the new displays went in a few years back, but it wasn't."

"Any major damage?" Evans asked.

Barnes shook his head. "Nope. Electricians are already in there pulling the old wiring and running new lines."

Evans nodded and filed the information away. "Fair enough." He inclined his head towards Tolchanov. "Frank, what do you have for me?"

Tolchanov shuffled through some papers and handed three sheets over. "Admiral Gomez at NMCC brought this to my attention. The last page is information you already know about. Damage assessments and current capabilities for the *Williams*. Second page outlines some personnel issues. Right when all of this started, the *Williams* reported that a sailor had died as a result of an apparent suicide."

Evans looked at the second page of notes and searched his memory. "Did I know about this?"

Tolchanov shook his head. "No, sir. Generally, stuff like this—horrible as it is—doesn't make it this far. But this one was pushed up the chain because the deceased left a note in which he claimed that members of the *Williams* crew and chain of command were harassing him."

"Harassing him how, exactly?"

"We don't know yet," Tolchanov admitted. "And it would be unwise to speculate. The Navy got this first and will be arranging for an investigation as soon as is practicable."

"Fine," Evans said. He began to scan the first page of notes and saw it was a report from one of the Atlantic Fleet's submarines. "Interesting."

"That's an understatement, Mr. President," Tolchanov said.

Evans looked to DNI Adams. "Ophelia, this says that the *Key West* is tracking a Russian boat that's lurking near the *Williams*. Any indication that the Russians know she's there?"

"We don't have anything other than that report, Mr. President," Adams said. "If I were them, I'd assume there's a submarine of ours in the Black Sea somewhere. That would be prudent, but they're behaving as if they're in the clear, and *Key West*'s commander does not believe he has been detected."

Evans searched his memory again, trying to pull information from his time in the Navy that was more than two decades old. "Would the *Key West* absolutely know if they'd been detected?"

Tolchanov shook his head. "Not necessarily, Mr. President. Without concrete evidence to that point, the commander of the *Key West* is likely basing his belief on a combination of things. Knowledge of his capabilities. Existing data on the Russian boat..."

"And the behavior of the Russian," Evans finished. "Yeah. It says that here. The sub—identified as the *Kazan*—isn't behaving in any way that indicates a suspicion that he's being followed." Evans paused. "That leaves three options. He knows he's in the clear. He knows he's being followed and is playing ignorant. Or he knows and just doesn't give a rat's ass."

Tolchanov nodded in agreement. "That's what the Navy is saying. COMSUBLANT has directed the *Key West* to stay close and quiet and keep an eye on things."

Evans handed the pages back. "We need to talk rules of engagement for the *Williams* and the *Key West* yet?"

"Not yet, Mr. President," said Tolchanov. "But be thinking about it. Navy will ask soon and their recommendation is going to be the obvious one."

"*Williams* can fire in defense of herself and *Key West* can shoot to protect herself and the *Williams*?"

"Yes, Mr. President."

"Any info either way on whether this will turn into a shooting match?"

Both Adams and Tolchanov shook their heads.

"Given what's already happened, it's not outside the realm of possibility," Adams said.

Evans's head was starting to ache and he was reminded of the times he'd had to wargame every possible scenario. You could, he admitted, drive yourself mad what-iffing everything. He opened his mouth to tell SECDEF that his ships could fire in the defense of self and the defense of others, but froze.

"The *Makarov* still has five American sailors and my nephew." He said this to no one in particular, but received nods from everyone in the room. "If I set the ROE as we've discussed and the *Makarov* fires first, or attempts a ramming, I'm virtually guaranteeing six American deaths."

He didn't add that the resulting melee would endanger the three hundred sailors on the *Williams* and another one hundred or so on the *Key West*. His brain raced, ran the scenarios from every possible angle. If the *Williams* or the *Key West* returned fire on the *Makarov*, he was condemning Americans to a fiery death. He was condemning a member of his family—a child he'd known and had sent birthday presents to—to death.

Needs of the many, he thought. He cursed himself for that and wondered just how he'd gotten himself into this mess. If the American vessels did not have permission to return fire, he'd lose three or four hundred American sailors instead of five sailors and one civilian.

But it's not just any civilian. It's Jonathan. He's stayed at your house. He dressed up as whatever Daniel Junior's favorite superhero was for three birthday parties in a row.

"Damnit."

"Sir?" It was Tolchanov. "We don't need an ROE decision right now. We all know Jonathan. Take an hour or two. Call your family…"

Evans shook his head. "Not necessary. The ROEs are approved. Self-defense and defense of others." Evans felt his stomach squeeze into a tiny, acid-filled ball. He took a breath and swallowed and swore one more time. "Now tell me what SECSTATE Burroughs is doing to get those kids back since Barsukov won't take my calls."

Hyatt Regency Hotel
07 December 2022 | 0930 Local Time
Indianapolis, IN

Senate Majority Leader Mark David Bridges left his coat in his car and headed into the lobby of the Hyatt Regency in downtown Indianapolis. He paused upon entering to orient himself with the layout and headed to his left towards the bank of glass elevators. Once inside the car, the democratic senator from Ohio ignored the view from the elevator and spent the two interminable minutes it took to reach the hotel's top floor and the rotating restaurant there thinking and fuming.

When the doors opened, Bridges stormed into the restaurant. He ignored the maître d' and glanced around the mostly empty dining room. He located his party and headed in that direction with a waiter in tow.

The men and women already seated rose as he approached. Everyone settled back into their chairs as greetings and handshakes were exchanged.

"Sir, may I get you something to drink?" The waiter was still there, lingering hopefully.

Bridges waved the young man away. "I'm fine with the water."

"Yes, sir," the waiter said, ignoring the brush-off. "Would you like to know the specials for—"

Bridges cut him off, looking around the table. "House salad. Just like they're having." He watched until the young man was out of earshot and turned back to the table. "Now, what the hell is this all about?"

The man two seats to Bridges' left cleared his throat. He was the junior senator from New Jersey. "Uh, Mark, did you get a phone call last night?"

Bridges glared at him silently. He had indeed gotten a phone call the previous night. An unlisted number. He'd ignored the call, sent it to voicemail and blocked it, as was his normal routine when such calls showed on his phones.

But the caller hadn't stopped. The phone had sounded every few minutes for an hour before he'd hit the green answer button out of sheer frustration.

"Listen, Mark," New Jersey said. "We know you got a phone call. We've been talking. We all got one. The same one."

Bridges raised an eyebrow. "And what did this supposed phone call say?"

"Christ, Mark." It was the senior woman from California. "Stop playing games. We know you got the same call. The same threat. The same list." She gestured around the table. "What are we going to do about this?"

Bridges leaned back as a salad was placed in front of him and waited for the server to leave again. He unrolled the cloth napkin at his place and laid it across his lap. "Do about what?"

He was met with incredulous stares. It was the junior man from Nebraska who broke the silence. "Listen, Mark. I didn't know about any of this shit until last night. None of it. But I had my people pull records. Said I was curious and all. And what those fuckers told me on the phone was right. It's all there for anyone to find. More than two million, in my case. Two million dollars in campaign contributions that can be traced all the way back to fucking Gazprom."

Bridges nodded. He'd pulled his own records. Only, in his case, with more than two decades in the Senate, the amount was nine times higher. He took a bite of his salad, just to stall for time.

"You've got nothing to say?" New Jersey again. "Nothing at all? What do they have you for, Mark? Fifteen? Twenty? You've been in the job for a hell of a long time."

Bridges swallowed. He sipped his water and placed the glass back on the table. "Okay. I got the call too. What did they want?"

"Same thing they told you," California said. "Tank it all."

Bridges had been told the same thing. Subvert the president's agenda. Erode support. Do that, and the money trail goes away. Refuse and, well, use your imagination. "All of it?"

Nebraska nodded. "All of it. Voting rights reform. Environmental protections. Hate crimes legislation. Criminal justice reform. We change our positions on everything and they make all of this go away. We refuse and they shove it up our asses. Legally and in the court of public opinion."

Bridges nodded and looked around the table. "And whoever made the calls…"

New Jersey interrupted. "Who made the calls? Are you serious? The Kremlin made the damn calls."

Bridges ignored the interruption. "Whoever this is, how do we know they will keep their word? If we tank the president's legislative agenda and they decide to out us anyway? What then?"

"Does it matter?" California asked. "I thought about calling the FBI, but that won't work. I'd still have to explain how Russian oil and gas money fueled my last three campaigns. No one, and I mean no one, is going to buy the idea that I didn't know."

"How'd they do it?" Nebraska asked. "How'd they hide it upfront?"

"Who gives a shit?" New Jersey said. "It doesn't matter."

"I was just asking…" started Nebraska.

"I know. Sorry," New Jersey apologized. "But it really doesn't matter. Not legally and not in public opinion. Courts and constituents will expect us to know. It doesn't matter whether the check was signed by a shell company, or the shell company for a shell company, or by Barsukov himself. We're screwed."

Bridges tossed his napkin on the plate and looked at each of his fellow diners in turn. The men and women at the table, himself included, really didn't have a choice.

Resigning wouldn't really help. The optics alone would cause problems. This many senators could not resign at the same time without people digging into the causes. And that, as the caller had said the previous evening, would certainly result in criminal investigations. Each of the men and women sitting at the table would be crucified, first by the voters and then by a jury.

There was another reason resigning wouldn't work. With the exception of California, every senator at this table was from a state with a Republican governor who would, given the chance, appoint a Republican replacement to fill the vacated seat. That, Bridges knew, would give control of the Senate to the Republican Party, and the president's agendas would die just the same.

The group discussed their options for another half hour. When it became clear that they would have to acquiesce to the callers' demands, they discussed how each person should handle their legislative change of heart. That discussion took another forty minutes, after which the meeting broke up and the senior senator from Indiana, who'd had little to offer the discussion, paid the bill.

15

The Kremlin
07 December 2022 | 1830 Local Time
Moscow

Russian President Barsukov glared at the map covering his conference table. There were various markers spread across the table. A great many represented various oil and natural gas platforms, some he had interest in and some he did not. There were several markers for commercial vessels, all of which appeared to be steering clear of the areas around *Neptun Deep* and *Trident*. The *Makarov* was clearly marked, as was the *Kazan*. A small marker, Barsukov saw, denoted the position of the American destroyer, *Williams*.

"You're telling me the Americans have no other ships in the Black Sea. None at all?" Barsukov asked.

"We have no indication that the Americans have any additional assets in the Black Sea, sir," Admiral Borshevsky said. "No intelligence at all. Not even from the *Kazan*. That ship," he pointed at the gray block of wood denoting the *Williams*' position, "is all they appear to have in the area."

Barsukov continued staring at the table, his eyes twitching back and forth between the various markers. "And what instructions do you believe the Americans will now have?"

"They won't shoot first, if that's what you're asking. Their president would not authorize or condone such action," Borshevsky stated.

"Will they leave willingly?" Barsukov asked.

Borshevsky shook his head. "They won't leave unless they have to. We do have their sailors on board the *Makarov*. The idea of sailing away from those men would be unpalatable to them." The admiral paused for a moment. "That's if they *can* leave. Reports indicate that they are just sitting in the water, not moving. They could have suffered a significant amount of damage in the collision, but we don't know. We don't have any information about damage to the *Williams*."

Barsukov turned away from the map and Borshevsky and arched an eyebrow at his SVR director. "Igor Romanovich?"

"We've heard nothing, Mr. President," Tolstov said. "Nothing about the *Williams*. Nothing about additional American warships in the area. Nothing."

"What of your man in the White House?" Barsukov asked. "Surely Evans has been getting routine briefings. Your source has heard nothing?"

Tolstov shook his head. "We have nothing new to report. Our man was not present during the most recent briefing."

Barsukov nodded, thinking. "Have we ever directed this man to obtain specific information?"

"No, Mr. President," Tolstov said. "Information flow has always been one way from this source." The SVR director paused, then added, "Getting him a specific assignment can be done, but there is the risk of discovery."

Barsukov walked behind his desk and sat down, motioning Tolstov and Borshevsky to a pair of chairs on the opposite side. "Explain."

Tolstov cleared his throat. "How much do you want to know?"

Barsukov considered the question. "Do I want specifics?"

Tolstov nodded. "That is my question, Mr. President."

Barsukov took a deep breath and exhaled. He weighed the risks. Did he need the details? Did he need to know how information flowed from the source? Did he need to know, exactly, how intelligence from this individual had got to his desk?

It was, he knew, not outside the realm of possibility that he could let something slip inadvertently during a phone call or a press conference. Or even just in passing. He liked to think that he had more control than that, that he was above such errors. But that was naïve. No one was above such errors. It was the simplest thing, to let the wrong piece of information slip past one's own lips. Many things contributed to such slips. Exhaustion. Stress. Ignorance. Carelessness. Ego.

The president spoke slowly, measuring his words and thinking through the situation. He gestured behind Tolstov and Borshevsky, to the map still resting on the table. "The goal here is the outright ownership of those wells. Not a military takeover. The world would condemn that as nothing more than theft. The resulting sanctions would cripple us and make ownership of those platforms irrelevant. The impact would be felt in every segment of the energy industry and then throughout the rest of the Russian economy. Yes?"

The men in front of him nodded and he continued. "So, we've been covertly causing problems in the hope that insecurity in the Black Sea would cause prospective buyers of the physical wells to second-guess themselves. The incident at *Neptun Deep* and the staged attack on the *Trident* rig both served their purpose. Buyers are recanting. Pulling their proposals and offers and leaving our state-owned corporations as the most attractive client. Except for this American destroyer, everything is working."

Barsukov paused for a moment before continuing. "And the American side of the plan goes well too. Yes?" He looked at Tolstov.

"It does, Mr. President," Tolstov said. "Civil unrest in the United States is boiling over into protests. In the last week alone, we have been able to foment several violent incidents. Again, these are small incidents. Large enough to be noted, but not large enough to garner an in-depth investigation. The cyber campaign is having the desired effect, and that is something that President Evans must focus on."

"And the pressure from his Congress?" Barsukov asked.

"As you know, contacts have been made. A portion of the American Congress will begin turning on Evans and his policies in the next few hours."

Barsukov nodded. "And none of this can be traced to us?"

Tolstov shrugged. "To us specifically? No. To Russia or Russian interests? That is possible."

"Explain."

The SVR director shifted in his seat. "Mr. President, it would not take a smart man to see that Russia is going to benefit from the past few days of apparent good fortune. People will be suspicious. This is especially true of the American left. Some connections might be made, but those connections cannot lead to us here."

Barsukov raised an eyebrow. "You are certain?"

Tolstov nodded. "On my side of this operation, we are using no government hardware, software, or personnel. I, myself, have not set foot in the facility where the operators work. My assistant, Anatoly Mikhailovich, is handling that personally."

"Why him?"

Tolstov smiled. "Because he is already a dead man."

Barsukov cocked his head at the statement and motioned for Tolstov to explain himself.

"Anatoly is a survivor of the accident and cleanup at Chernobyl. He suffers from late-stage thyroid cancer, something he has already battled once before. When this operation was originally proposed, I had planned on using a third party, probably some poor bastard we've had locked up somewhere. Anatoly was too close to me and he was, supposedly, cancer-free. He became a natural choice for the job when his cancer returned and the physicians told him it was terminal. He became angry after that. Despondent. He's furious with the system. With Russian medicine. With us."

The president frowned at that. "I am sorry. Please extend my…" He stopped talking when he realized Tolstov was still grinning.

"Mr. President, Anatoly is not dying. His cancer has not returned. I simply had his physician tell him it had. Because of the way our healthcare system works, I can control the doctor. In this case, I selected Anatoly's doctor for him. We compromised the doctor and forced him to play along. The rest has been child's play. It was a simple matter of faking scans and test results. Anatoly is going through another course of chemotherapy and that has helped convince him that this is real."

"Mother of God," Borshevsky said.

Tolstov shrugged. "A dying man, angry at the world, running his own, deniable operation is perfect for us."

Barsukov swallowed hard. "Wouldn't chemotherapy…"

"Kill him?" Tolstov asked. A shrug. "Probably. The process cannot tell the difference between healthy and cancerous cells. And if it doesn't, and someone makes the link between the cyber operations and Anatoly, we throw him in jail and execute him to further distance the Russian government from the act. It's all nice and neat."

Barsukov forced the conversation away from Tolstov's revelation, resisting the urge to shudder. "What about the Navy's side of the operation? You also believe that is both convincing and secure?"

"Yes, Mr. President," Tolstov said. "On the admiral's side of the operation, we have limited involvement of Russian military forces. No one could really say that our Navy is in the Black Sea for any reason other than the provision of maritime security. That is, after all, the purpose of the Black Sea Fleet. Is it not, Admiral?"

Borshevsky cleared his throat. "Director Tolstov is correct, Mr. President, and the decision to blockade the Bosporus for the purposes of conducting maritime safety and background inspections on the ships and crews wishing to enter the Black Sea helps to sell the idea that this is not an aggressive act, but rather a means of ensuring the safety of sea-bound traffic in the region."

"And the sudden withdrawal of purchase proposals for these wells is not something that would be considered contradictory?" Barsukov asked. Borshevsky began to respond, but the president raised a hand. "Hear me out, Admiral."

Borshevsky nodded and Barsukov continued. "We have incidents, catastrophic and tragic ones, in the Black Sea. We have unilaterally declared that we alone can maintain peace and security in the sea. And corporations still withdraw their proposals to purchase the very wells we are interested in. The ones we have already made several offers for. That is not suspicious or contradictory? If we are trying to ensure the safety of traffic and industry in the Black Sea and events keep happening, does it not make us look incapable?"

Tolstov shook his head. "It shouldn't, Mr. President. Not if you handle it the right way." The SVR director paused and smiled. "We will continue to tie each successive incident to Western intelligence operations. As long as you continue the rhetoric, there is little to worry about on that front. It's our word against theirs, and the nature of such operations, especially failed ones, benefits us. Not them." Tolstov grinned. "As far as the proposals are concerned, we've never officially withdrawn our proposals. Whether planned or not, it was fortunate. Within hours of the incidents, insurance costs to operate the wells skyrocketed. In the wake of such financial implications, it would be perfectly natural for a company to rethink such investments. Yes?"

"That is true, Igor Romanovich," Barsukov said. "And our response is simply spin control. In the wake of these events, we are willing to assume risks to operate these wells to ensure energy and economic security of the nations who depend on these resources. Something like that."

"Yes, Mr. President," Tolstov agreed.

"So, the only issue remaining is the American destroyer." Barsukov turned to the admiral. "Why won't they leave?"

"We have their sailors, Mr. President," Borshevsky said. "They will not wish to leave them behind."

"And if I transferred these sailors to the American destroyer?" Barsukov asked.

Tolstov shook his head. "You can't do that. You would have to turn over President Evans's nephew as well. Or at least provide access to him by American or neutral physicians."

The president nodded. "True. And we cannot allow that. Finding Mr. Evans wasn't part of the plan, but having him fall into our laps was extremely beneficial. Especially with the information that he was offered work at the Central Intelligence Agency. Who found that?"

"One of our analysts," Tolstov said. "After college, Jonathan Evans was recruited by the CIA. His uncle was already in politics then, so he turned the offer down and went to work as a systems engineer for Exxon. Claiming he works for the CIA's Clandestine Service was a logical extension of his public refusal of the CIA's initial offer. The general public, even in America, puts too much faith in movies and fictional books. We played that angle and said that Exxon was Mr. Evans's cover job."

Barsukov nodded. "And that brings us back to the only sticking point. The American destroyer." He turned to Borshevsky. "Would you sink it?"

Borshevsky sat bolt upright in his seat. "Sink it? Sink an American warship?"

"It does still pose a risk," Tolstov pointed out. "Even wounded as it is, the ship's signals intelligence capabilities might not be crippled. Correct, Admiral?"

Borshevsky nodded. "That's correct." He described what he knew about the ship's capabilities and electrical systems, pointing out that communications and intelligence gathering would be two systems that the American crew would attempt to maintain at all costs.

"Is it possible to prevent the Americans from collecting or gathering signals from the *Makarov*?"

Borshevsky shook his head. "No, Mr. President. The Americans are extremely good at intercepting and breaking into our signals. They've made it almost impossible for our SIGINT vessels like the *Yantar* to perform missions along the eastern seaboard and the *Makarov*'s communications suite is not nearly as secure as the systems on the *Yantar*. If we broadcast operational orders to or from the *Makarov*, we have to assume that the Americans will know."

Barsukov sat quietly for a moment. He rubbed his temples and stretched. "Is it possible to send the information through the *Kazan*?"

Borshevsky nodded. "It is possible, Mr. President. Again, it is likely that the Americans will intercept anything within range. Even underwater communications." The admiral thought for a moment. "If I may, Mr. President..."

Barsukov nodded.

"We can communicate with the *Makarov* if we word the message carefully. Make it innocuous. Given what has happened, they will continue to report the status of damage and repairs. Captain Dashkov has operational orders in hand with the timetables for each of the next four staged incidents. We can simply acknowledge his next report and order him to remain on station and continue as before."

"And Dashkov will understand the meaning of such a message?"

Borshevsky nodded. "Yes, Mr. President."

"So, we can communicate orders to the *Makarov*, but that does not solve all our problems," Tolstov said. "The *Williams*'s ability to see and hear is a danger to us. Correct, Admiral?"

"Well, technically," Borshevsky started, "but she could have been intercepting signal traffic the whole time, and we have no indication that the *Williams* has done so."

"We've been lucky, Admiral," Tolstov said. "We cannot trust the remainder of the operation to continued good fortune."

"But sinking an American warship?" Borshevsky argued. "There's almost no way to conceal such action."

"Almost?" Barsukov asked. "So, if it was necessary, it could be done? Yes?"

"Well, yes, Mr. President. It could be done. The *Kazan* could do it, but only if we are absolutely certain no one else is in the area."

"By which you mean?" Tolstov asked, knowing the answer.

"Sound travels a long way under water, Director. We would need to be absolutely certain that there are no additional American vessels in the area. Particularly submarines. Given the right conditions, they would hear the launch and track the weapon."

"And how long would it take to search?" Tolstov asked.

Borshevsky paused for a moment. "Longer than we have. Deployment of the Spetsnaz team for the next incident is scheduled for this evening."

The room remained silent as Barsukov leaned back in his chair. When he finally spoke again, he talked to the ceiling. "We have to know who else is out there. The American ship poses the most significant risk to the remainder of the operation. One intercept could bring this whole operation to our doorstep. And the most expeditious way to get the information we need is to task a source directly who has not been trained to gather intelligence in this manner."

Barsukov paused again, cursed silently, and made his decision. "Tell me all of it, Igor Romanovich."

The SVR director nodded, frowned, and cast a sideways glance at Admiral Borshevsky. The aging naval officer took the hint. "Gentlemen, I will excuse myself for the time being. I await your orders, Mr. President."

Borshevsky stood to leave, but the president directed him back to his seat. Tolstov frowned at this, but cleared his throat and began. "Mr. President, I must remind you that disclosure of this information…"

Barsukov stopped his intelligence director with a raised hand. "Yes. I know. If you tell me details and I screw up, we lose the source. The same goes for the admiral."

"Pardon me, Mr. President," Tolstov said. "It's my job to say these things."

"I understand, Igor Romanovich." Barsukov waved the apology away. "At least the Americans do not shoot such people." He leaned forward over his desk. "Now. Tell me about this source and his process."

Tolstov outlined the details of the information chain in a few minutes. Barsukov interrupted twice, asking for clarification on some specifics. When the briefing was completed, the Russian president shook his head.

"And we had nothing to do with the death of this Alexander woman? Not even through intermediaries?"

"No, sir." Tolstov shook his head. "Nothing at all. Henry Alexander seems to have been a proud man who made a mistake. He let his ego drive a decision and his wife paid the price for it. That same ego would not permit him to shoulder the blame, so he went looking for a culprit and payback. We offered him both."

"And his son?" Barsukov asked. "This Major Alexander. Can he do what we want? Get the information we need?"

"He is very junior, Mr. President," Tolstov cautioned. "But with proper direction, it is possible. Sixty to seventy percent chance of success."

Barsukov thought that over. "Do it, Igor Romanovich." The president turned to Borshevsky. "Admiral, get the *Kazan* hunting. Maybe he gets lucky."

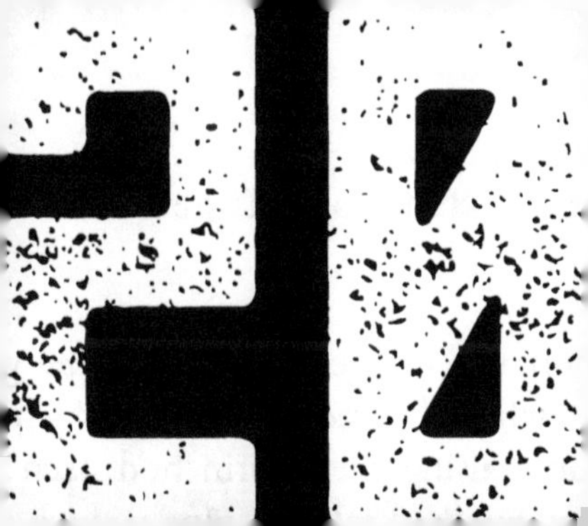

**Frigate *Admiral Makarov*
07 December 2022 | 2030 Local Time
Black Sea**

Dashkov stood on the bridge of the *Makarov* glaring into the distance. He felt awful. His fractured arm was aching because he'd gone hours without using the aspirin he'd been prescribed. His head felt like someone had taken a pipe wrench to it; the sharp, stabbing pain seemingly pulsed with every beat of his heart.

And the body aches, he mused. Dashkov could not believe it was possible for every muscle in his body to be this sore. He'd been in a car accident once, when he was much younger, and it hadn't been this bad.

You're getting old, Yuri.

He smiled.

Well, that, and this ship is a hell of a lot bigger than any car.

Dashkov looked down at the paper in his hand and his wry grin vanished. He took a deep breath and turned.

"Pavel Stefanovich."

The young man appeared quickly, stepping into the bridge from the starboard wing. "Yes, Captain."

"Where do we stand?"

Dashkov listened quietly as Gorshkov outlined the various damage control and repair efforts occurring throughout the ship. He interrupted twice to ask questions about specific troubleshooting processes and impacts to capability.

"So, we will not sink."

"Not today, Captain." Gorshkov paused. "The chief engineer and senior combat officer will be up shortly to provide additional detail." Another pause. "And I have taken the liberty of having both food and the doctor brought here."

Dashkov began to protest, but the junior officer cut him off. "If you will pardon me for saying so, Captain, you look awful. You need food and something to take the edge off. Especially," Gorshkov pointed at the message form in Dashkov's hand, "if that message says that we are to remain here."

Dashkov looked from the young man to the message and back. "How did you know?"

"I didn't, Captain. I just assumed that we are to remain on station, even crippled as we are."

Dashkov eyed his operations officer as the ship's chief engineer and senior combat officer joined them and began their reports.

The Chief Engineer had little new information to offer. One of the ship's twin screws had been damaged in the collision, as had the associated shaft and one of the attached DS-71 cruising gas turbines. Shoring up tears in the hull was almost complete. Piping on critical systems had been patched where possible or cut out and replaced when necessary. Two of the ship's air conditioning plants were damaged beyond repair. One had been torn off its mounts by the force of the collision, and the other had been destroyed by the combination of a fire that had started and spread from a nearby switchboard and the seawater used to extinguish it.

Dashkov acknowledged the update and forced his brain to recall the specifications for his ship. "One shaft. Two usable engines. Eighteen knots? Nineteen?"

"Yes, Captain. Depending on the seas," the chief engineer said. "If you'll excuse me, sir, I need to get back to control."

Dashkov nodded and turned to the combat officer. "Well?"

The man cleared his throat. "We finished assessing damage to the combat systems and the results are not good, Captain."

"Meaning what, exactly?"

"We lost the Fregat air search radar, the Garpun-B and Nucleus-2 surface search systems, and the Puma and Orekh fire control systems. None are repairable. There is just too much physical damage."

Dashkov nodded. He'd suspected as much. A collision generating forces sufficient to rip a one-hundred-ton air conditioning plant off its foundations would exceed any specifications that the builders of the radar systems would consider survivable. "What of the underwater systems?"

"A near complete loss, Captain. Based on my indications, the sonar dome was either completely crushed or it has been torn away from the hull."

"And the tail?" Dashkov asked, hoping. The sonar tail was a retrofit, less than two years old and designed to listen to the area behind and under the ship. It wasn't his preference to drive around with only the rearview mirror functioning, but he didn't have much choice in the matter. It wouldn't be much, but it was better than nothing.

"It is partially deployed and jammed, Captain," the combat officer said. "The collision damaged the coupling between the motor and the spool. We are trying to effect repairs, but…"

Dashkov nodded and looked at the message still clutched in his fist. He waved it at Gorshkov. "So, we will remain here, half blind at half speed." He took a breath and exhaled. "But at least Moscow is having the *Kazan* babysit. That's something, I suppose."

"But Captain," Gorshkov said, "what if the Americans shoot?"

"They won't," Dashkov said. "I'm not even sure they can."

"But what if they do?" the combat officer asked. "We won't have much warning, and our ability to defend—"

Dashkov held up a hand. "Gentlemen, if the Americans shoot, the *Kazan* will sink them for us."

And listen as we drift to the bottom of the damn ocean.

USS *James E. Williams*
07 December 2022 | 2100 Local Time
Black Sea

Brian Thompson walked into Central Control and took a seat in the large leather captain's chair that dominated the center of the space. He glanced around at the various panels and displays and noted the four red magnetic placards above the GTM controls that stated each engine was tagged out for repair. Two similar placards above the shaft controls told him the shafts were locked in place, unable to turn or provide propulsion.

He turned to the starboard side of the space and saw the massive, laminated damage control boards. The covers sat locked open, and, from his position, Brian could see hundreds of marks in black grease pencil, each one denoting the discovery of, or battle to control, damage. Flooding. Collapsed bulkheads. Fire. Smoke. Ruptured tanks. Toxic gas.

Brian turned further, almost directly aft, to look at the displays for auxiliary and damage control systems. On one screen he saw that only one of the ship's air conditioning plants was still operating. On the other, he noted that the ship had four of the pumps that supplied firefighting water tagged out for repair.

Everywhere he turned, there was evidence that the ship was severely crippled. Brian had known all of this. He'd read the reports while he'd been stuck in medical, waiting for Doc to clear him from concussion protocols. But seeing it in person, taking the watch as EOOW for a ship that was on life support…

"Jesus," Brian muttered.

"What's that?"

Brian turned to see Commander Allen and Lieutenant Caldwell walk into the space. He reached back and pulled a microphone from its bracket to announce the captain's location, but one of the junior sailors stopped him.

"Mike's broke, Chief."

Brian looked at the handset and put it back. "Thanks, Cruz."

"No prob, Chief."

Cruz turned back to his work and Brian turned to the captain and executive officer.

"Gentlemen, what can I do for you?"

"Just stopping by for an update," Commander Allen said. "With the interior comms down for repair, it's easier to walk than to find someone to run messages back and forth."

Brian nodded and glanced at his watch. "Well, Captain, doesn't look like much has changed. No major repair updates for another thirty minutes or so. Guillory said that his folks might be able to get us a working main propulsion gas turbine by midnight or so. MPA and CHENG are inspecting the starboard reduction gears, shaft, and bearings." Brian stopped to look at his notes. "And the repair division bubbas think they can get another one of the firefighting pumps working by midnight or so."

"Any luck with the air conditioning plants?" Caldwell asked. "We're going to need chilled water when the radars get up and running."

Brian shook his head. "AUXO was in medical right before Doc cut me loose. He said that they might have a good line on number one AC and that they might be able to fix it. I think he's up trying to get one of the ETs to take a look at damage to one of the control boards."

"Nothing on the rest of them?" Allen asked.

"Nothing," Brian said. "I'll head down there after I get off watch and lend a hand." Brian flipped through his notes. "According to everything I've seen, there's no physical damage to any of the units. Leaks and misalignments, I mean. Maybe the control systems just couldn't handle the shock. We hit pretty damn hard."

Brian saw both officers nod and a question popped into his head.

"Captain, can we defend ourselves?"

"Not very well, Chief. Why?"

"No reason. Just thinking about all the gear that's down. Seemed logical to ask that."

"It's a fair question," Allen noted. "Bottom line is simple. If that ship, or anyone else, flips a missile or torp at us, we're in deep shit right now. So, maybe try to get me that engine, a shaft to turn, and the AC unit?"

"Will do, Captain," Brian said.

"Oh. And Steering. Any word on repairs?" Commander Allen asked.

Brian shook his head. "Not yet. Between the fire and the collision…" His voice trailed off.

Commander Allen nodded, took a long moment to look around, told everyone present to keep at it, and departed the space. Brian started to reach for the microphone again before he remembered that it did not work. He pulled his hand back and looked at Caldwell.

"Sir?"

"That pair of concussions knock some sense into you?" the XO said.

Brian watched Petty Officer Becker walk into the space behind Caldwell. "This a conversation you want to have right here, sir?"

Caldwell shrugged. "I'm just saying. You were all fired up about the boat crew and Faulkner before. Now you're just passive as can be. You need to stay that way."

Brian bit off his initial retort. Barely. "I have work to do, sir."

"Fine," Caldwell said. "Do your work. But you stay passive and respectful."

"Roger that, sir."

"Roger that? That's all you've got to say?" Caldwell's face flushed a dangerous red.

Brian turned away to scan the displays again. "Something else I should say, sir?"

Cruz handed over a tag out form on a clipboard that Brian began reviewing.

Caldwell walked around to put himself between Brian and Petty Officer Cruz. He snatched the clipboard with the tag out forms out of Brian's hands. "You'll show me some damn respect. I'm the XO here." He tossed the clipboard on a nearby desk. "You don't ever say 'Roger that' to me. You hear me, shipmate?"

"And why is that, sir?"

"Don't give me that. I know what 'Roger that' means."

Brian rubbed his temples and reached over to pick up the clipboard. "It means I understand, sir. Nothing else."

"Horseshit. It means 'Fuck you.' I know it, and so do you. You just said 'Fuck you' to me."

Brian stared at Caldwell for a long moment, watching him seethe. "Sir, I think I made it pretty clear that, were I inclined to tell you to fuck off, I'd do it in public, in full view of witnesses, and I sure as hell wouldn't do it in code."

Caldwell snatched the clipboard out of Brian's hands again and tossed it to the side. "You think you're so fucking clever, don't you? You and all your little engineers saved the ship once and you think you're all fucking bulletproof."

"Now wait a minute—" Cruz bellowed. He stopped when Brian held up his hand and stepped out of the chair.

"Lieutenant Caldwell, this is a controlling watch station and you are interfering with the performance of my duties and the duties of other personnel. As the EOOW, designated by the commanding officer, I have positional authority in this space and I am telling you to leave or I will have you removed."

Caldwell's index finger flew into Brian's face. "You can't do that. I'm the XO."

Brian picked up the clipboard. "I can do it, and I will. If you have a problem with it, go talk to the man who signed my qualification. He lives in the captain's cabin."

Caldwell stood still for a moment before turning and leaving the space, slamming the door behind him. Brian, Becker, and Cruz watched as the door rebounded against its orange rubber seal and crashed into a nearby file cabinet and coffee machine.

After a few moments, Cruz got up and shut the door, rotating the locking lever down.

"What the hell was that about, Chief?" Cruz asked.

Brian ignored the question. He looked over the red danger tags and the tag out form, and checked the system diagram. Then he read the purpose of the tag out.

"What's this for?"

"Helping out the electricians and combat peeps, Chief," Cruz said. "Our portion of power to the weapons system. Torps, I think."

Brian looked and saw initials from the combat systems officer of the watch and glanced through the tags again. He saw two mistakes on the tags themselves and pointed them out to Cruz.

"Shit," Cruz said. "This was easier with the computer tag outs. Writing by hand sucks."

Brian shrugged. "The computer system spoiled you guys."

"Work smarter, Chief," Cruz said. He walked to one of the file cabinets, rooted around, and closed the cabinet. "I gotta run to the space. We're out of tags."

After a nod from Brian, Cruz stepped out into the passageway and walked off. Petty Officer Becker leaned back from the electric plant console and stretched.

"You pissed off the XO, Chief."

"I know," Brian said. "My problem. Not yours."

"How?"

Brian turned to look at the damage control boards again. "How?"

"Yeah. How'd you set him off?"

"Long story."

Becker waved a hand around at the various consoles and status boards. "We're not going anywhere."

"Not the time, Becker." Brian closed his eyes and took a breath. He could still feel the adrenaline raging through his system. Could feel his hands shaking.

"It's the Faulkner thing."

Brian's eyes snapped open. Becker was staring at him. She nodded.

"Thought so."

"What?" Brian said. The word barely came out. A croak more than anything.

"Faulkner," Becker said. "OPS. XO…Lieutenant Caldwell hated him."

"How do you know that?"

"Faulkner told me," Becker pointed out. "He stopped by after battle stations. Back when we first got on station for the rescue. He was looking for you and no one knew where you were. He looked upset and I'm his mentor, so I started digging."

"And?"

"And XO hated Faulkner's guts. Did little things to fuck with him. Extra assignments on duty days. Failing him on every maintenance spot-check and space inspection. Failing him during berthing inspections. Extra duty assignments."

Brian could feel his heart race. "Why didn't he say something?"

"Hell, Chief," Becker said. "I don't know. Probably thought it was normal at first. Didn't you ever have some random khaki up your ass for everything?"

Still do, Brian thought. "Okay, but he said something to you?"

"Yeah. Told me about some interactions with XO. Talked about getting yelled at and how tired he was of getting written up all the time."

"And no one said a damn thing to me?" Brian said, his teeth clenched.

"Hell, Chief. I just found out. He told me this stuff, disappeared, and then…"

"Yeah. I know. Sorry," Brian said as his stomach clenched tight. "Did he say anything else?"

"Said he was thinking about reaching out to someone off ship. I don't know who."

"Becker!" Brian snapped. "You have to tell me shit like this."

Becker held both hands up. "I know, Chief, but when was I supposed to do that? Ever since that GQ it's been one casualty after another, and you were locked up in medical." She turned back to her console and dialed up a series of readings, which she wrote down in a small notebook.

Brian tried to breathe and wondered if his face was as red as Caldwell's had been. "Okay. Sorry. Any idea why XO hated Faulkner's guts?"

Becker turned back to Brian. "You haven't guessed?"

"Guessed what?"

"Faulkner was gay. XO hates gays. The male ones, at least. Seems okay with lesbians."

Brian felt his heart stop. "Becker, are you saying…?"

"Am I saying that Faulkner was harassed by XO because he was gay? Yes, probably. I'm fairly sure that's what Faulkner thought."

"Do you have proof?"

"Hell, no," Becker said. "XO isn't that stupid. But Faulkner isn't the only person he's fucked with."

"What do you mean?"

"I live in a berthing. I eat on the mess decks. I hear things."

Brian sat perfectly still, dumbfounded, and angry and wondering just who in the hell would believe this.

Frigate *Admiral Makarov*
07 December 2022 | 2200 Local Time
Black Sea

"You understand your orders, Ilya?" Dashkov asked the Spetsnaz officer.

"Perfectly." Chernitsky grinned and clapped Dashkov on the shoulder. "This one is a piece of cake."

Dashkov considered that and nodded. "Yes. After the last two, I have to agree. No fire fights. No ships involved."

Chernitsky nodded. "Just a rescue on rig EX-29. The *Rapsodia*. We deploy, corral the personnel, and locate and disable the devices. A little showmanship on the back end. Some interrogations, maybe. Just to really sell it. As I said. Piece of cake."

"And the devices?"

"Four disabled limpet mines," Chernitsky said. "Training devices. The two kilos of explosives have been replaced with lead weights. They will appear to be the real thing, especially with an armed Spetsnaz team seen to be disposing of them."

"Very well." Dashkov turned to the officer of the deck. "Are we in position for flight operations?"

"Two minutes more, Captain. Handling on one engine in this wind is…"

"Tricky. Yes. I know." Dashkov nodded and turned back to Chernitsky. "Let's get this over with."

The Spetsnaz colonel saluted and walked off the *Makarov*'s

bridge, leaving Dashkov to stare off into the night. There was very little light and the wind was howling. Visibility, the captain estimated, was two kilometers. Maybe three. The ship heaved on a rolling sea, with lines of barely visible white foam crests offering the only delineation between the black water and the pitch-colored sky. An exchange over the radios behind him caught his attention. Dashkov turned to see Gorshkov holding one of the portable handsets.

"Captain, we are in position. The colonel and his team are on board and the pilot is requesting permission to depart."

Dashkov acknowledged the report. "Pavel Stefanovich, launch the helo."

♦ ♦ ♦

Colonel Ilya Gregorovitch Chernitsky finished strapping himself in as the pilot relayed the launch order and advised everyone to strap down tight. He acknowledged the warning and turned back to his team just in time to see Sergeant Vorobyov vomit through the helicopter's portside hatch. Through the hatch, Chernitsky could just make out the form of the sailor assigned to remove one set of the tie-down chains keeping the helo firmly on the *Makarov*'s flight deck.

"Did you get him, Sasha?"

Vorobyov wiped his mouth with the sleeve of his tunic and peered through the hatch. He nodded and moved his helmet-mounted microphone back into place. "Poor bastard."

"That's no way to treat our hosts," Chernitsky admonished.

Vorobyov grunted. "The only thing I hate more than boats, Colonel, is flying off them."

Chernitsky smiled and leaned back. He felt the aircraft rocking with the ship. Port. Starboard. Up. Down. Back to port. He closed his eyes and waited for the moment when the rocking would cease and he'd feel the pull of gravity as the pilot pulled up and away from the heaving ship.

Port. Starboard. Up. Down.

Any moment now, he thought.

Chernitsky's eyes opened when he felt it. The rhythmic rocking stopped. The craft lurched skyward, just fast enough to push him down into the molded metal seat. He heard the engine scream as the pilot added power and felt the craft lean over, climb, and begin racing off to the northeast.

Except for the weather, he thought, this op should be a walk in the park.

"Colonel?" Vorobyov's voice sounded through the headset. "What happens if one of the engineers decides we're the bad guys?"

Chernitsky smiled inwardly at that. They had orders for such a contingency.

"You shoot the bastard, Sasha," Chernitsky said. "You shoot the bastard and the SVR will hang him out to dry as a Western spy."

In the noisy dark of the helicopter's cabin, Chernitsky saw Vorobyov shrug and turn to look outside.

K-561 *Kazan*
07 December 2022 | 2215 Local Time
Black Sea

Captain Ivan Sergeyevich Korov stepped away from the scope and ordered its retraction before turning to the man beside him.

"What does Moscow say, Dima Igorovich?"

"A slight modification to our current assignment, Captain," the *Kazan*'s navigator said. He handed over the message form. "Apparently Moscow is having trouble believing that we are alone out here."

Korov took the message and scanned it. He looked up. "They want us to search the area for American submarines."

"Yes, Captain."

Korov shook his head and waved the message around. "This, Dima, is what happens when you have surface sailors dictating operations to submarines." He looked back at the message. "Don't they know that this is almost all we do? Searching and clearing endless sections of ocean?"

"I'm sure they know that, Captain."

Korov thought for a moment, remembering two decades of such orders. "Don't be so sure, Dima. Don't be so sure."

"Does this mean that they think there might be an American

lurking out here?"

Korov's eyes traced the words on the page for a third time. Did Moscow suspect that he had company? He asked himself that question over and over, then shook his head and pocketed the form. "No, Dima. It doesn't read that way. Just an admonition to keep our ears open and keep the *Makarov* safe."

The younger officer thought for a few seconds, nodded, and stiffened. "Your orders, then, Captain?"

"Continue as before. Keep searching the area. Keep me informed."

The navigator walked back to his chart table, leaned over it, and looked back at the captain. "Do you think there is an American out here, Captain?"

"There should be, and we should have found him by now," Korov said.

"Maybe we got lucky, Captain," Antonov said.

"Maybe," Korov said. "Trusting to luck is a poor habit for a sailor."

USS *Key West*
07 December 2022 | 2218 Local Time
Black Sea

"Captain, ESM mast is picking up signals from an airborne radar. Likely that helo from the *Makarov*. Heading out of the area."

Commander Scott Reynes turned his head away from the chart table and looked towards the sailor who'd made the report. "Got it. Anything else?"

"No, sir. Nothing else we've not already tracked."

Reynes nodded and took the few steps necessary to get to the *Key West*'s sonar room. In the cramped space, he found Chief Hughley and the XO with headsets on. "Gents?"

The XO turned and pushed the set off one ear. "Skipper?"

"Where's our friend?"

"The *Kazan*?" Lieutenant Commander Sandler asked.

Reynes nodded.

"Moving off some, looks like. Chief here can give you more detail." Sandler poked at the *Key West*'s sonar chief. "Chief?"

The man pushed one side of the headset back without looking

away from his screens. "Our buddy just went deep again and moved off. Before he went deep, he'd settled into a pretty regular pattern. Ladder search." Hughley shrugged. "Looks like he's starting over, maybe."

"Looking for us?" Reynes asked. It was an obvious question.

"Probably," Hughley said. "Safe bet he knows where all the surface tracks are. They ain't exactly quiet."

Reynes thought for a moment. "XO, is this a directed search, like he knows something is out here? Or is he just poking holes in the water?"

"Probably the latter," Sandler said. "Could he have already gotten a whiff of us? Sure. But, he's still acting like he thinks he's alone and wants to make sure."

"Is he approaching the *Williams*?"

"No, sir," Sandler said. "He's staying well clear of her. He's behaving like the bodyguard he's supposed to be. Sticking around the *Makarov* and playing defense. Like he knows approaching the *Williams* would cause trouble."

"And how much noise is *Williams* putting out?" Reynes asked.

"Not much, Cap'n," Hughley said. "Don't hear prop noises. Faint plant noises. She's still blowing bubbles. Prairie and masker and what not. Lots of grinding and banging noises. Probably repairs and shit."

Reynes nodded. "XO. Wait for *Kazan* to make a turn away and get us on the other side of *Williams*. Hide behind the noises she's making. No sense letting the *Kazan* find us by accident."

Sandler took the headset off, stowed it, stood, and stretched. "Sounds good, Skipper."

The White House
07 December 2022 | 1645 Local Time
Washington, DC

President Daniel Evans slammed the remote down on the polished surface of the Resolute Desk as Leslie Barnes entered the Oval Office.

"What in the hell just happened?" he barked.

"We just lost the majority leader and a portion of key support in the Senate," White House Chief of Staff Leslie Barnes said. He held a hand up. "And no, we didn't see this coming."

Evans stood from his chair. "How? How in the hell did we not see this coming?" He pointed to the cart-mounted television screen, where Senator Mark Bridges was busy taking questions in the Capitol Rotunda. "This man, and the group standing behind him, just woke up today and decided to turn their backs on me? On the whole damn party? Without even a hint of dissension before now? That's horseshit, Leslie. And you know it."

Barnes shook his head. "Mr. President, the why doesn't really matter right now. Those five folks have more power right now than we do. Committees. Subcommittees. Whatever. Never mind that Bridges can just refuse to call a vote on any issue he damn well pleases."

Evans shot his chief of staff a poisonous look. Barnes raised his hands. "What is it you want me to say? You heard the man. He said this is something that's been pulling at his conscience for a long time. It might be bullshit. It might not. But there isn't a damn thing you can really do about it. Not to them and not on the issues you just lost support for."

"These aren't just any issues." Evans waved at the television. "Bridges just unilaterally tanked environmental protections, hate crimes legislation, criminal justice reform, and voting rights in one three-minute speech."

Barnes took a deep breath. "Mr. President, this is politics. Plain and simple. Bridges doesn't want to kill these issues off. Hell, he's spent half his career pushing for the voting rights bill and the climate control regulations. He's not tossing that in the trash because he had a bad day at the office or because someone flipped him the bird on his way to work. He wants something. We just need to figure out what that is. Simple as that."

"No, Leslie. It's not," Evans said. "This is a group of folks who have led the charge on some of these issues. They've been working to garner support in the House and from across the aisle. Anything he wants should have, would have, come up by now. Something else is going on."

"What, Mr. President?" Barnes said. "What is it you think

happened here?"

"How the hell should I know?" Evans threw his hands up. "All I know is that I had the full-throated support of each one of them yesterday and today…" Evans pointed at the television again. "I get this bullshit. Something happened. Someone got to them and changed their positions for them. The whole 'This has been pulling on my conscience' thing is utter crap."

Barnes stuck his hands in his pockets and cocked his head. "What is it you want me to do? Conduct an inquisition? Haul his ass into my office, lock him up, and play the damn dinosaur song until he tells me what's really going on? You can't do that, Mr. President."

Evans smiled. "No, Leslie, I can't. But I can haul him in here."

"What?"

"I want Senator Bridges in here. Today."

"Mr. President, that's going to look like—"

Evans raised a hand. "Leslie, I have a plateful of shit going on right now. I have the Russian Navy playing stupid games in the Black Sea. They've crippled one of my ships. I've got attacks on rigs out there. My nephew and several American sailors are being held captive. And now this. I've had no damn success getting anything settled in the Black Sea and for whatever goddamn reason, I've had even less luck getting my people back. This is a political issue between me and the democratically elected leader of the United States Senate." Evans sat down behind his desk. "I am expected to haul that man in here and hear him out. I can do it. So that's what's going to happen. I don't care if it looks like retaliation or like he's being called to the principal's office. I want Mark Bridges in this office by the end of the day. Make it happen."

Patuxent Shores Retirement Community
07 December 2022 | 1930 Local Time
Solomons, MD

Major Harlan Alexander sat on his father's couch and sipped at an iced tea he'd purchased on his way down from Washington.

"Want a sandwich, Harlan?" Henry Alexander's voice drifted in to him from the small kitchen.

"What?"

"A sandwich. Want one?"

"No," Harlan said. He stood up and walked into the kitchen, where his father had a wide array of bread, condiments, sandwich meats, and toppings spread across the marble counter. "Dad?"

Henry selected some ham and threw it onto a slice of potato bread. "Yeah?"

"What is it you wanted?"

A slice of baby Swiss went on the stack of ham. "What's that?"

"You called and said there was a plumbing emergency, so I said I'd drive down. Since the plumbing seems fine, I know that's not why you called."

"Oh. Right." Henry added some mustard to the sandwich and covered it with a second slice of bread. He picked up his plate and headed for a small kitchen table. "Have a seat."

Harlan sat. "What is it?"

Henry took a bite. He chewed thoughtfully for a moment and swallowed. "Baby Swiss at the Giant always tastes funny. Ever notice that?"

"Dad."

Henry put the sandwich down and wiped his hands on a napkin he pulled from a wooden holder in the center of the table. "Got an assignment for you, boy."

Harlan felt his pulse skyrocket. "An assignment?"

"Relax. Ain't nothing big. Just some specific information they want. Hell, you might already know the answer."

"What?" Harlan heard his voice crack.

"Is there an American boat in the Black Sea?"

Harlan relaxed slightly. Hadn't he reported this already? Hadn't it been in the news? The collision? "The *Williams*. A Burke-class destroyer. Aegis ship."

Henry laughed. "No, boy. Not a ship. A boat. You know. A submarine."

"I don't think so," Harlan said.

"Don't think or don't know? Big difference, Harlan."

Harlan had to sit quietly for a minute and search his memory.

He was fairly certain that he'd not heard any mention of an American submarine in the Black Sea. But did that mean that there wasn't one, or simply that it hadn't been brought up? He didn't know, and he said as much.

"Then you're gonna have to find out."

"Find out?" Harlan stammered. He felt his pulse quicken again. "How? I'm not a spy. I don't know how to—"

Henry's hands came up. "Whoa there, Mr. Bond. Not asking you to break into computer systems or infiltrate the office of the Chief of Naval Operations. Just keep your ears open and maybe ask an innocent question or two."

"But—"

"Listen, boy. This is simple. If you don't hear or say anything, you find a way to bring it up. You're allowed to speak during these briefings. Play the part of the dumb Army major and ask about undersea protection for the *Williams*. Couch it as a suggestion, even. Then tell me how they respond. Simple. No risk."

"Dad," Harlan said. "I'm not normally the speaker in there."

"But you were a few days ago. Right?"

"Well, yes."

"And did anyone shut you down?"

Harlan shook his head.

"Good. Then it's settled. Get the info and get it back to me. Soonest, boy." Henry picked up his sandwich and took another bite. "The cheese really is awful."

22

Admiralty Apartments
08 December 2022 | 0300 Local Time
St. Petersburg

Admiral Fyodor Kirilovich Borshevsky sat on the edge of his bed in the darkness. His head and shoulders sagged, a raging headache dominating one and a dull soreness penetrating the other. His eyes felt dry and itchy, and he longed to close them.

But they won't close, he thought. In every quiet moment he'd had since returning from Moscow and the president's office, his brain had been screwing with him. It was replaying the conversations there and memories of his father's battle with cancer—a stop-motion picture show of the aftermath of chemotherapy.

But this Shablikov fellow had had cancer, he reasoned. And now?

Now he doesn't. But what does it matter? One man against the financial security of Russia?

"Shit."

Borshevsky's hand fumbled for the watch he knew to be on his nightstand, a venerable Citizen he'd purchased on board one of the American Navy's aircraft carriers.

The USS *George Washington*, he remembered. What had that been? Twenty years ago? More? Back when the spirit of friendship between America and Russia had been... what? Not true friendship. Not quite. But less acrimonious than during the Cold War. Better than it was now.

Borshevsky's hand found the watch and he glanced at it. Three in the morning according to the luminescent markings.

"Shit."

Behind him, under the covers, his wife murmured and stirred, her feet and arms adjusting the blankets as she rolled away from him. He glanced over his shoulder, offered the sleeping form a tired smile, and stood up, ambling off to the bathroom. Five minutes later he found himself in the kitchen and punched the button to start the coffee machine. Three minutes after that he situated himself at the dining room table with a full mug and wondered what it was about his upbringing that made him prefer coffee to the traditional morning tea.

"You're up early." His wife, Katya, shuffled into the dining room, tying her bathrobe and yawning. "Something the matter?"

Borshevsky took a sip and nearly burned his tongue. "Can't sleep."

"Work?" Katya yawned again.

"Something like that." Borshevsky put the mug down.

"Can you talk about it?"

He shook his head. "No. Not really. Just something bothering me." He waved his hand in the air. "It's minor."

Katya raised an eyebrow. "You're a horrible liar, Fyodor. You know that?"

"What?"

"Something so minor that it's keeping you awake at night? You? A man who can sleep through anything?"

Borshevsky grunted. "I'm fine. I promise."

She stood, walked around the table, and wrapped her arms around his shoulders from behind. She gave him a kiss on his scruffy cheek. "Well, I'm going back to bed, Fyodor. Whatever is bothering you, you'll do the right thing. You're a good man."

Katya walked away from the table. She was almost to the hall when Borshevsky called out. "Why'd you say that?"

Katya stopped and turned. "Say what?"

"That I'll do the right thing because I'm a good man."

She gave him a tired smile. "Because you are and you will."

Borshevsky nodded. "Good night, Katya."

"Good night. I'll see you when you get home."

It took Borshevsky forty minutes to shower, shave, dress, and walk to the office. It was a routine that he could normally execute in less than thirty, but a pair of nicks while shaving and a broken shoelace pushed back at what was normally a precise schedule.

After the usual array of security checks, the admiral found himself seated at his desk with little to occupy his time. He flipped on the desk lamp, choosing its soft, green glass–shaded glow over the buzzing intensity of the installed fluorescent lighting above his head. He tried reading the newspapers he'd picked up from his front steps and the main lobby of the Admiralty Building, a nineteenth-century palace with golden spires on the River Neva in Saint Petersburg.

When nothing in the papers captured his attention, Borshevsky opened a folder resting in his inbox. He saw the usual array of briefings and status reports and a few sheets of paper that contained his daily, weekly, and monthly calendar appointments. He tried reading through some of the briefing material first and soon found, as with the newspapers, that his mind couldn't quite fix itself on the task at hand. He pulled the calendars from the docket and looked through them, noting that two more meetings in Moscow had been added for the following week.

He grunted, muttering to himself in the nearly dark space. "Should just move there."

He grunted again, this time with a smirk on his face. It wasn't the first time he'd considered that idea. Of late—the past two years, to be exact—he'd been making several hops to Moscow per week. It wasn't far—only ninety minutes each way by air—but it was time that could be better spent at his desk. Or out at the fleet concentration areas. But the move would never happen. Moscow wouldn't pay for it, and, truth be told, he didn't care much for the capital city. Borshevsky liked Saint Petersburg. He'd grown up here. He liked it here. He just hated the time wasted traveling back and forth to say things he could just as easily put in a memo.

That thought stopped him, and he put the calendars back in the folder.

"Most things," he muttered.

Not everything, he knew, could be committed to paper. Some information needed to remain intangible. To exist only in whatever form it was that allowed men to have ideas and memory.

Borshevsky looked at the ceiling and swore.

"That's what's bothering you Fyodor Kirilovich? The thing with the Shablikov fellow? But why?"

Because, his mind raged, you've seen what chemo does to a sick person, and Shablikov is not sick.

"Why do I care?" Borshevsky asked the ceiling.

His mind began replaying the last months of his father's life. The weight loss that had robbed the old man of his size and strength and left him looking like a wraith. The way his skin had gone from robust and healthy to a baggy, graying, papery sackcloth. The hair loss. The nausea and vomiting.

Chemo for a sick man was one thing. It was, what? The lesser of two evils? Something like that.

But Shablikov wasn't sick.

And he thinks he is. This man has been convinced that he's dying. He's a healthy man submitting to chemotherapy not because he needs it, but because of someone's political agenda.

Borshevsky swallowed hard and picked up the phone on his desk.

"I want a flight to Moscow in the next two hours."

Novokuznetskaya Flats
08 December 2022 | 0700 Local Time
Moscow

The knocking on the door nearly split Anatoly's head in two. He moaned piteously and half-rolled, half-fell out of his soiled bed. On all fours, Anatoly felt his stomach heave. He forced himself upright as he stumbled to the bathroom. He nearly made it.

Vomit and bile exploded from his mouth two full steps from the toilet and covered the already stained floor and ceramic bowl in a layer of watery, acidic waste. Anatoly stopped in his tracks and waited, choking, until the heaving subsided. It took nearly two minutes before Anatoly's body calmed down enough that he could stand back up.

As he drew himself upright, his dirty t-shirt and boxers stained with the same bits and drips that now covered the floor, he became aware that the knocking on the door hadn't subsided. Each bang of someone's heavy hand seemed to drive fiery spikes deep into his brain. Again, as on many recent mornings, Anatoly had difficulty deciding whether his aches and pains were related to the chemotherapy or to the half-liter of vodka he'd drunk the night before.

Does it really matter? he thought as the banging on his door continued. *Not especially.*

The pounding grew heavier and more urgent, and Anatoly wondered just how long it would be until whoever it was knocked the flimsy door right off its hinges.

"All right," he shouted. "I'm coming!"

Anatoly stumbled into the kitchen, ran some water over his face, and wiped it with a towel. He walked to the door and looked down at his stained underwear.

"The hell with it," he muttered.

Anatoly opened the door and stood there with his mouth open. He'd been prepared to tell whoever it was to get the hell away from his home, but nothing came out. He recognized both men. One was his doctor. The other was Admiral Fyodor Kirilovich Borshevsky, Commander of Russian Naval Forces.

"Christ, Anatoly," Borshevsky said. "What the hell have you done to yourself?"

Anatoly said nothing. He just stood there, holding the door open and staring at the two men.

The admiral entered unbidden, shoving the doctor in front of him. "Get him cleaned up. I'll get him something to drink."

Anatoly was watching the admiral as the doctor grabbed him by the arm and led him off in search of the bathroom. Only when they entered the decrepit bedroom did he speak.

"What the hell are you doing here?"

"Not now," the doctor said, eyeballing him. "You're a mess.

Let's get you cleaned up."

Anatoly tore his arm out of the doctor's grip. Barely. "I can clean myself up. What's this about?"

"You'll find out," the doctor said. "I'm sorry, by the way."

"For what? What's going on?"

"You'll find out. Get cleaned up."

Anatoly stared at the man for a few moments, realized he would get nothing more out of him, and did as he was told. He gathered some clean clothing—jeans, underwear, and a sweatshirt—and headed into his bathroom, careful to avoid the puddle of vomit occupying the entrance. In ten minutes, he was washed and sitting at his small kitchen table across from the doctor and the admiral. A pot of tea and several mismatched cups rested on the table; the room, Anatoly noted, smelled of old vomit, trash, dirty dishes, and stale sweat.

"What the hell is going on?" Anatoly demanded.

The admiral, he saw, continued to look around disapprovingly for a few moments, and Anatoly felt a surge of embarrassment at his surroundings. That feeling only amplified his anger at the intrusion.

"Unless you two are going to help clean up or pay for a maid, this hell-hole I live in isn't going to get any cleaner just because you don't like it," he growled. "So, tell me why the hell you're both here."

The admiral cleared his throat and nodded. "Anatoly, do you know who I am?"

Anatoly nodded. "Sure. You're the dumbass that runs the Navy."

Anatoly saw the admiral's eyes flare briefly. Borshevsky offered no other response to the insult. "Anatoly, I believe the doctor here has something he wishes to tell you."

Anatoly shifted his gaze to the doctor and noted that the man looked visibly nervous. He worked to force an extra helping of sarcasm in his voice. "Well, Doctor? Don't tell me. You found more cancer? Is that it?"

The doctor turned to look at Borshevsky and Anatoly saw the admiral nod.

"Tell him, Doctor," Borshevsky ordered. "Tell him now, or I

will. And I will make damn certain you are never heard from again."

Anatoly saw the doctor swallow hard. He felt his pulse quicken without knowing exactly why it did so. "Tell me what, Doctor?" he said.

The doctor gulped again and Anatoly was struck by just how nervous the man looked. Gone was the superior attitude he'd displayed in every office visit.

"What, Doctor? What is it you have to tell me?"

"Anatoly, about your cancer…" The doctor stopped, as if he was afraid of what he was saying.

Borshevsky smacked the physician on the back of the head, almost hard enough to send him flying from his chair. "Tell him, you piece of shit."

The doctor righted himself in his chair and, against the reddened face, Anatoly was dumbfounded to see tears forming in his eyes.

"Tell me what?" Anatoly shouted. He could hear his voice shaking, but wasn't sure why that should be. It felt like anger mixed with, what? Terror? But that couldn't be. What was worse than cancer and chemotherapy? He turned to the admiral. "What the hell is going on?"

Borshevsky leapt to his feet, grabbed the shaking physician, and pulled him from the chair. "You aren't dying, Anatoly. At least not from cancer. This piece of shit lied to you."

Anatoly felt time stop. He'd heard the words and his brain was trying to process them. It was a joke, right? Had to be. These two were screwing with him. But… they weren't. Anatoly looked at the doctor and looked at the admiral. The doctor looked terrified and the admiral was seething. Fifty questions flooded into his mind and Anatoly could only ask the stupid one.

"What?"

"It's a lie, Anatoly. A lie. Your cancer is not back. It is not killing you."

Anatoly tried to process that, his mind racing. "But I saw the scans. I saw the lab results." He heard the pitch of his voice change and realized he was nearly shrieking. "I'm going through fucking chemo again!"

"Because this bastard lied to you." Borshevsky shook the doctor like some old rag doll and shoved him against the wall. His head bounced off the plaster and he collapsed onto the floor. "You don't have cancer and you don't need chemo," the admiral said through clenched teeth. "This sonofabitch wanted you to think you did, so he switched everything. Lab results. Scans. Everything."

Anatoly stared at the doctor and blinked. He looked back up at Borshevsky.

"But what if I…" Anatoly started. His pulse was racing and every beat sent new, sharp waves of pain through his skull.

Borshevsky smirked. "What if you got a second opinion? Have you ever tried? For anything? Your request would have been denied and you'd have found yourself sitting right back in this piece of shit's office."

"But chemo…" Anatoly said. "Chemo on a healthy person. That would…"

Borshevsky smiled again. "Yes. Yes, it would."

Anatoly sat perfectly still for a moment. His face, which had been pale as death, flushed bright, crimson red.

"You motherfucker!" Anatoly screamed. He launched himself at the doctor, reaching, struggling, groping for the man's pencil-thin neck. His fists rained down on the much younger doctor, slamming into head, hands, arms, and anywhere else Anatoly could find an opening. A steady stream of obscenities spewed from Anatoly's mouth.

Moments later, Anatoly felt himself ripped away from the fight, dragged up and back by his own shirt. A pair of large, rough hands turned him around and shoved him against the wall and held him there.

"Not now, Anatoly," Borshevsky said. "Not now."

Anatoly's chest was heaving. His lungs burned from the effort he'd exerted. His head was pounding. He struggled against Borshevsky's arms, but found he lacked the strength to free himself.

"Calm down, Anatoly," Borshevsky said. "I have a better way."

Borshevsky removed his hands and Anatoly felt his legs weakening. The adrenaline rush left him as quickly as it had come.

His legs wobbled and gave way, and Anatoly crashed to the floor. His stomach, abused by the chemo, vodka, and exertion, heaved, empty though it was. Anatoly retched over and over, his abs contracting violently as his stomach tried to expel something that wasn't there. When the spasms stopped and he was able to catch his breath, Anatoly looked up. He felt tears start to form in his eyes.

"Why?"

Borshevsky pulled him up and put him back into his chair, and then did the same with the doctor. "This asshole did it because your boss needed a scapegoat." The admiral searched the small kitchen for a towel, located one, and handed it to Anatoly.

Anatoly wiped the spittle from his mouth. "What?" he said hoarsely.

Borshevsky sat down. "You are currently running a cyber campaign against the Americans, yes?"

Anatoly nodded.

"Do you know why, Anatoly?"

"To cause problems. Division. Sow mistrust," Anatoly said.

"But why, Anatoly? To what purpose?" Borshevsky said. "Your job is to create and foment incidents that the American government must pay attention to. Things they have to respond to. You are hitting them on everything they think makes them America. Civil rights. Social justice. Democratic processes, Anatoly. But to what purpose?"

Anatoly hesitated. He wasn't sure. "I… I don't know."

"You can never destroy America doing such things," Borshevsky said. "Sure, you can pit Americans against Americans for a while. But not for long. They always figure something out. They always find some sort of resolution. Some common ground. It may not be perfect, but it works for them."

"So why am I doing this?" Anatoly asked.

Borshevsky smiled. "Because someone needed the Americans so distracted that they would fail to pay attention elsewhere."

Anatoly went silent for a moment. He closed his eyes and forced himself to think. When his eyes opened, he saw Borshevsky leaning forward.

"Still don't see it?" Borshevsky asked.

Anatoly shook his head.

"Your operation is a distraction, Anatoly. It's the left hand of the magician waving around while the right performs the actual trick," Borshevsky said. "Everything revolves around those rigs in the Black Sea."

"That doesn't make any sense. We don't own those and we never will. We've had every proposal rejected," Anatoly countered. "And we can't just take them. The resulting sanctions would make ownership irrelevant."

Borshevsky grabbed one of the cups from the table and eyeballed it. "Mickey Mouse? Where did you get this?"

"Who cares?" Anatoly said. He pointed at the doctor. "What does any of this have to do with what he's done to me?"

Borshevsky poured tea into the cup, held Mickey by the ear, and took a drink. He screwed his face up and swallowed. "This is why I drink coffee."

"Admiral!" Anatoly practically yelled at the man. "Screw the tea. What the hell is going on?"

Borshevsky put the cup down. "You're right, you know. We'll never own those rigs. Unless," the wan smile returned, "there are no other buyers. Every recent incident in the Black Sea was staged. The *Brixton* running over *Neptun Deep*. The hostage crisis on *Trident*. The attempted destruction of *Rapsodia*. Everything you've seen was staged. A single Spetsnaz team, commanded by one Colonel Ilya Gregorovitch Chernitsky and under orders from Director Tolstov, made it all happen."

"Impossible," Anatoly whispered, almost to himself.

Borshevsky leaned forward. "It's not impossible. It's really no different from what you've been doing. Only you are pushing propaganda and false narratives. Constructing arguments based in sheer fantasy. Everything in the Black Sea has a kinetic factor. A tangible, physical aspect. All created by the director and this Spetsnaz colonel."

Anatoly was silent for nearly a minute. "Fomenting a crisis?"

"To drive potential buyers away." Borshevsky nodded. "Create the appearance of instability and insecurity. Drive potential costs up. Make the risks appear to outweigh the rewards for companies in the market for natural gas and oil rigs." He shook his head. "And it's working. Almost every company interested in ownership has withdrawn proposals since this started. That leaves…"

"Us. It leaves us," Anatoly said. "But the Americans have to know, at least suspect…"

Borshevsky was shaking his head again. "No one in the American government is focused on that part of the equation. For a variety of reasons. Your work is helping. The incident with several of the leaders of their Democratic Party turning on the president helped, too. Their president is becoming irrational and angry. He feels he is losing control. Like most powerful men, he understands the importance of legacy and he feels his slipping away. His conversations with his closest aides have grown contentious. Even in places like the Oval Office and situation room."

Anatoly thought about that for a moment. "How can you know this?"

Borshevsky shrugged. "How do you think?"

Anatoly sat bolt upright. "Impossible."

"Not impossible. Improbable, maybe. But not impossible," Borshevsky said. "The man's name is Harlan Alexander, and he works in the situation room. He was recruited by his father after the death of his mother. An event that Director Tolstov's people had a hand in arranging." The last part was a lie, but Borshevsky added it anyway.

Anatoly swallowed hard. "What does this have to do with me?"

"It's all about risk management, Anatoly. For your part in all of this, the president and the director needed someone who could be hung out to dry in the unlikely event that the cyber campaign could be definitively linked to the Kremlin. Who better than an angry man? You have cancer. You got it from that shitstorm at Chernobyl. You are in poor health and you are angry at the system that allowed this to happen. But you're also loyal. You stayed with the system, even after Chernobyl. After what happened to your wife and brother. You are someone who might be inclined to believe the propaganda, to believe that the West had a hand in the evils of your life. And you have a cyber army at your disposal." A shrug. "Who knows what a desperate man like yourself might do with the remainder of your life? An unauthorized cyber war against America might be justified."

"But..."

Borshevsky raised his hand. "It does not matter if it makes sense. Most of the stuff your team sends out into cyberspace doesn't make sense at all, but those crazy assholes in America believe in it." Borshevsky turned to the doctor. "They compromised this shithead and forced him to doctor your medical records. One way or the other, you would not survive this. Either the chemo would kill you, or, possibly, a single bullet to the skull would. They'd call it a suicide, of course."

Anatoly felt his pulse quicken again, felt the rage return.

"Why are you telling me this?" he growled.

"Because, to this point, nothing overly serious has happened. No permanent damage has been done. But the president is close to stepping over a line. He is considering sinking the American warship tailing the *Makarov*. He and the director have convinced each other that this is something they can hide from the Americans. It's bullshit. If they fire on the Americans, someone will know. Someone will find out. The Americans will not take such action lightly. They will retaliate. There will be a war, Anatoly. A war that we cannot win."

Anatoly's head sagged. His face was flushed, but he stayed quiet for several minutes. When he spoke again, he heard the fragility in his own voice.

"What do you want me to do?"

Borshevsky stood and pulled the doctor out of his seat, then turned back to Anatoly. "Get what I've told you to the Americans. Quickly. I cannot refuse to sink the American ship for long. If I do, Barsukov will dismiss me and have someone else give the orders. You need to move fast, Anatoly."

Anatoly stood on his weak legs. He gripped the table for support. He jerked his chin at the doctor.

"What about him?"

Borshevsky grinned. "Oh. I believe his days of practicing medicine are over."

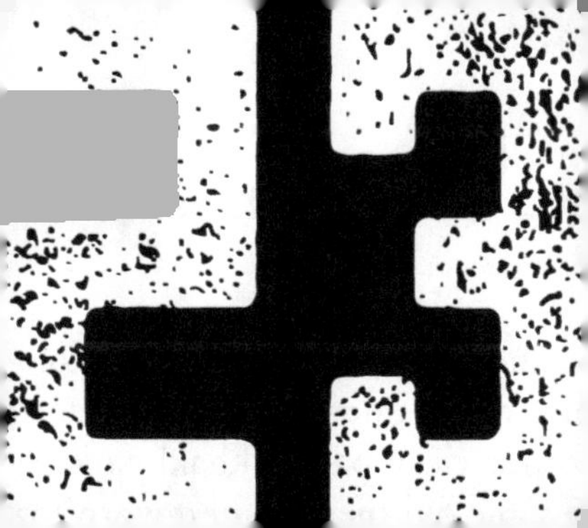

Novokuznetskaya Flats
08 December 2022 | 0830 Local Time
Moscow

Anatoly, feeling vaguely human after a second, longer shower, stood on the street corner just outside the entrance to his apartment building. Dressed in a clean pair of khaki pants, a flannel shirt, an overcoat, and the same old sneakers he'd worn for years, he waited for a taxi. In his pockets were various identification papers and his passport. On his back was a single pack containing a change of clothes and the pictures of his brother and wife.

Anatoly thought about his plan. It wasn't much, but it was bold—bold enough that some might call it stupid. It wasn't even the first idea he'd had.

He'd originally planned on heading to work and having the information Borshevsky had given him transmitted directly to the American government. He likely would have been able to co-opt a member of his team to assist. But he'd not been able to find a way to make that work. The information itself was a problem. It just didn't fit with the rest of the operation and there was, he'd concluded, no way to disguise it. Whoever he tasked to send it would have questions that Anatoly couldn't answer.

He'd run through several other scenarios while cleaning himself up and he just could not find a way to make any of it work.

In the end, he'd decided on this plan. The stupid one. The simplest one. The one that would cost him the life he knew.

Anatoly planned on walking right through the front door of

the American embassy. What, he'd asked himself, was the worst that could happen?

He'd be seen walking into the building. He knew that. Russian intelligence monitored the comings and goings at the cream and tan building on Bolshoy Devyatinsky Lane. The area in front of the building was wide open, perfect for surveillance cameras and personnel. It would have been possible to arrange something covertly, to arrange a brush pass or some other means of passing written information off to one of the American officials as the approached the building, but Anatoly did not think he had that kind of time. Borshevsky had given him the impression that he needed to move as fast as possible, and that meant a direct approach.

So, walking in the front door was the plan he adopted. He'd do it, hand over what information he had, and, if the Americans believed him, accept whatever offer of assistance they extended.

And if they don't believe you? his brain teased. If they toss you out on your ass?

Then, Anatoly, you run. You run for your life.

Where?

Anatoly smiled.

Pripyat?

He laughed at that.

Why the hell not?

He remembered where they'd buried his brother and wife, in lead-lined coffins covered in meters of concrete. There were others there, he knew. Anatoly wasn't sure how many. Mostly soldiers, plant employees, and firefighters who weren't among the official tally of casualties. He probably knew some of them, had probably worked with them. He'd certainly gotten drunk with some of them. Pripyat hadn't had many bars. At least, he thought, not during the liquidation.

Yes, Anatoly. That's where you go to die. With your family. You head to Pripyat. Say goodbye to your family. Tell them you're a traitor. Explain why. And then put a bullet in your head.

"You don't even own a gun," Anatoly muttered. "Idiot."

Fine, his brain said. A rope would do. Better than what those bastards in the FSB will do to you. Better than what your own boss had planned for you.

Anatoly laughed at himself.

Amazing, he thought. The shit you come up with over tea and in the shower.

He'd gone over his plan again and again, trying to poke holes in it. He'd discovered one. He wasn't sure he'd be allowed to go to Chernobyl or Pripyat. He thought he remembered hearing that tourists were being permitted into the area, but that was by request. That anyone would request to visit the place seemed insane to Anatoly. But unless the Americans agreed to listen and help, it was all he had.

A taxi pulled to the curb, the driver waving to Anatoly. Anatoly waved back and stepped to the rear door. He reached out, touched the handle with his fingers and paused.

This is it. No turning back. No matter how ridiculous this idea is.

Anatoly Mikhailovich opened the car door and climbed in.

"Destination, sir?" The driver looked old enough to have fought in the Great Patriotic War.

"Novinsky Passazh, grandfather." Anatoly wasn't about to have the driver take him straight to the American embassy. He chose a nearby mall instead.

The driver nodded once, engaged the meter, and put the car in gear. "Shopping trip?"

Anatoly remembered a time when the KGB had used damn near everyone to spy on the populace, taxi drivers included. His paranoia almost got the better of him. "Yes, Some things for my nieces."

"Ah. Family. Nothing better, young man. Nothing better. I remember bringing gifts back to my nieces after the war." The driver pulled out into traffic, swearing at random drivers for offenses both real and imagined. "Did you serve? Afghanistan, maybe?"

Anatoly shook his head, the gesture lost on his driver. "Not Afghanistan. Chernobyl."

The driver turned his head, swerving slightly. "Mother of God, boy."

Anatoly shrugged. "Where did you serve?"

The driver changed lanes, narrowly missing the rear bumper of a dump truck. "Stalingrad," he hissed. "Until the end."

"And you're still working? At your age?"

The driver nodded. "It's either this or rot away somewhere. I chose this. No sense wasting away, waiting for death."

Wasting away. Waiting for death. That's what I've been doing. What they wanted me to do. What they tricked me into doing.

"Bastards," Anatoly muttered.

"What's that?"

Anatoly looked at the driver. "Nothing. Sorry."

They tricked you, Anatoly. Used you. Planned to discard you. Just like they did with your wife. And your brother.

Anatoly said nothing for a few minutes. His mind raged. He eventually became aware that the old man was still talking.

"Family is good. Good to see family. Good to spend time with them."

"Yes, it is."

And these bastards took mine away.

USS *James E. Williams*
08 December 2022 | 0845 Local Time
Black Sea

Chief Petty Officer Brian Thompson pounded his fist on the door to Carrillo's office, drawing looks from the sailors moving in and out of the ship's galley. He beat on the door once. Twice. Then a third time before it was ripped open.

"Get your ass in here," Carrillo ordered, slamming the door behind Brian. He flopped in his chair and told Brian to stay standing. "What the hell is wrong with you? Beating on my goddamn door like that. I was on a call with the XO."

"Gotta talk to you about him…" Brian started.

"No, you don't." Carrillo stopped Brian mid-sentence. "You need to get the hell off his back."

"No, Logan. I don't," Brian said. He could feel the adrenaline pumping. "And it's not me I need you to listen to."

Carrillo shook his head. "Listen, damnit. I know you two don't see eye to eye, but this has to stop. It's bordering on insubordination." He pointed at the phone on the bulkhead. "What do you suppose that phone call was about?"

"Aw, hell, Logan. Screw the phone call." Brian was nearly yelling. "Becker says that XO was the one fucking with Faulkner."

"I don't give a good goddamn…" Carrillo started. He stopped. "Wait. What?"

"After XO stormed out of Central, Becker asked me what the hell was going on. I told her to mind her own business and she said that my beef with XO had something to do with Faulkner's death. Then she lays out all this shit that Faulkner came to her with. Harassment, Logan. Extra duty. Failing every inspection and spot-check. All sorts of shit."

"Brian, if any of that was legit, you'd know about it," Carrillo said. "Hell, I'd know about it."

"That's crap and you know it," Brian barked. "You know how many chits and forms I see each week? A full third of the crew belongs to my department. No way in hell I notice some of this shit."

Carrillo crossed his arms. Brian continued. "If I'm wrong and Becker's full of shit, you can fry me yourself."

"I don't need to. You're gonna screw yourself just fine," Carrillo pointed out.

"Then what's it look like if you do nothing and Becker is telling the truth?" Brian waved his hand around. "When all this is over, when we sail for home, there's gonna be an investigation into Faulkner's death. They're gonna talk to Becker. They have to. She was his mentor. What the hell do you think she's gonna say?"

Carrillo sat there for a moment.

"I'll tell you exactly how its gonna go, Logan. Becker is gonna tell them what she just told me. Then she's gonna tell them she told me. They're gonna ask what I did with the information and I'm gonna hang it on you. If you don't at least ask the question and Becker is right, you're gonna be the senior man with a secret." Brian leaned forward and put his hands on Carrillo's desk. "When that happens, you can kiss that anchor with your two little stars goodbye."

Carrillo shot out of his seat, yelling, "What the fuck is wrong with you? You think you can come in here and threaten me?"

Brian pulled open the door. "It's not a goddamn threat, Logan. It's what is going to happen. Nothing more. Nothing less." He walked out of the office.

"Where the hell are you going? Get your ass back in here."

Brian stopped and turned. "Or what? What the hell is it you're gonna do?"

Carrillo opened his mouth to respond, but his words were drowned out by the ship's 1MC announcing system.

"General Quarters! General Quarters! All hands man your battle stations. Route to general quarters is forward and up on the starboard side, down and aft on the port side."

"We're not finished with this, Brian," Carrillo snapped, slamming the door and moving off with the flow of sailors rushing through the passage.

Brian moved off with the traffic, cutting through the mess decks. It took two full minutes to get back to Central. When he entered, the room was already full of sailors donning flash gear and assuming their battle stations. On one side of the space, the Damage Control Assistant was busy taking reports on the status of the ship's material condition and readiness of the various repair lockers. At the electric plant console, Becker was busy giving orders to align power from the ship's only running generator to vital loads.

"What the hell happened?" Brian barked. The question was directed at the DCA.

"Weapons malfunction. We just launched a torp," Becker shouted over her shoulder.

Brian's head snapped around and his brain recalled the tags he'd reviewed. He'd never authorized them after getting a note from one of the combat systems chiefs saying they weren't required. "What?"

"You heard me, Chief," Becker yelled. "There's a live torpedo in the water!"

Brian wanted to ask how that was even possible, but he stopped himself and began scanning the consoles. He stopped at the propulsion console. "Cruz, they get that engine up yet?"

Cruz shook his head. "Not yet, Chief. We're dead in the water right now."

**K-561 *Kazan*
08 December 2022 | 0855 Local Time
Black Sea**

"Captain! Torpedo in the water. Bearing two-eight-five!"

Korov's head snapped around and his orders came without thought. "All ahead flank! Right full rudder. Now!"

The helmsman's right hand shot out to the engine order telegraph and he twisted the dial fully clockwise. His left followed suit with the helm.

"Right full rudder aye, Captain," the helmsman's voice rang out. He watched as the engine room answered the ordered speed. "Engine room answers all ahead flank, Captain."

Korov nodded, grabbed onto a nearby railing, and snapped at the officer of the deck. "Battle stations, torpedo."

The junior officer stood still for a moment, his mouth hanging open in shock until Korov barked again. "Move it, sailor!"

In seconds klaxons began sounding throughout the hull and sailors rushed through tight passages and ladders. Korov turned to watch the heading and speed and saw both changing.

"Come on," he muttered, willing the dials to rotate faster.

USS *Key West*
08 December 2022 | 0856 Local Time
Black Sea

"Oh shit." Chief Hughley slapped one side of his headset off. "Conn! Sonar! Torpedo in the water. Bearing three-one-five. It came from the *Williams*."

"Conn, aye," the junior officer answered.

"Not sure what happened, sir. There was nothing and then boom. Sounds like it's heading away. Towards the *Makarov*."

"Conn, aye." The junior officer turned around. "Chief of the watch. Sound battle stations."

It took four seconds for the gonging to start and ten more for Commander Reynes to arrive in the control room.

"Sonar reports the *Williams* just fired on the *Makarov*, Captain."

"What the hell?" Reynes looked around. "Sonar, where's the fish?"

"It's turning, sir. Three-zero-eight. Moving away. Same heading we have for the *Makarov*."

"Christ," Reynes swore. His mind raced. "Where's the *Kazan*?"

"He stomped on the gas, Captain," Chief Hughley said. "He's hightailing it outta Dodge."

Reynes turned to the officer of the deck.

"I didn't order a turn or speed change, Captain. No one knows we're here and the torpedo is racing away. Figured you wanted to stay covert."

Ballsy, Reynes thought. He smiled. "Good call." He turned to check the course and speed. "Where's the *Williams*? Is she moving?"

"*Williams* is about ten thousand yards. Bearing three-one-four.

Makarov is nineteen-thousand yards."

"Sonar, speed for the *Williams*?" Reynes asked.

"Nothing, sir," Chief Hughley said. "Hard to hear right now, but I think she's still just sitting there."

Has to be an accident, Reynes thought. You wouldn't launch and then just sit there. "Shit."

Lieutenant Commander Sandler walked into control. "Was back aft, Captain. What's going on?"

Reynes explained for a few seconds.

"Accident?" Sandler said.

"Only thing that makes sense."

"Think the *Makarov* or *Kazan* will see it that way?"

"Christ, XO. I hope so," Reynes said.

"And if they don't?" Sandler asked. "Do those rules of engagement cover something like this?"

**Frigate *Admiral Makarov*
08 December 2022 | 0857 Local Time
Black Sea**

"Captain!" Gorshkov shrieked. "Torpedo in the water! Bearing two-nine-five. Eight thousand meters and closing!"

"What!" Captain Dashkov's head came around, up and away from the report he'd been editing.

"The tail picked up a launch. American Mark 46."

"Right full rudder. All ahead flank," Dashkov shouted. His brain raced through the numbers, trying to recall the specs on the American weapon. Ten thousand meters? Eleven? He could make fourteen or fifteen knots after the turn on one shaft in this sea. His brain struggled to catch up.

What was that? Seven minutes to clear the torpedo's maximum range and just over that for the torpedo to cover its distance. Outrunning was possible. Maybe. "Gorshkov, sound battle stations."

As the klaxons erupted, Dashkov felt the *Makarov* lurch forward and lean away from the turn he'd ordered.

"Why the hell did they shoot?" Gorshkov yelled.

"Who gives a shit?" Dashkov said. "What weapons are available?"

"Fire control for the A-190 deck gun is up," Gorshkov said.

"None of the systems for a surface-to-surface missile launch are fully repaired."

"And the support systems for the deck gun?"

Gorshkov froze. "I… Weren't they still working on repairs?"

"Find out! Now!"

K-561 *Kazan*
08 December 2022 | 0900 Local Time
Black Sea

"Sonar! Where is the torpedo?" Korov demanded.

"Tracking on the *Makarov*, Captain."

"Just the one?"

"Yes, Captain. Sounded like a Mark 46," Sonar confirmed.

"Distance and bearing to the *Williams*?" Korov asked.

"Bearing now one-nine-five. Fourteen thousand meters and opening, Captain."

Korov paused and thought, searching his memory for specifications. On the torpedo. On the *Williams*. On the *Makarov*. On his own submarine. "Officer of the deck, come to new course one-eight-zero. Slow to five knots."

The officer of the deck relayed the orders as Korov's brain worked feverishly. The Americans had fired on a Russian warship. One he'd been ordered to protect.

Korov walked aft and leaned into the sonar room. He tapped the sonar officer on his shoulder. "What is the *Williams* doing, Yevgeni?"

Belyaev held a hand over one of his earpieces. "Nothing that I can hear, Captain." He looked back over his shoulder. "I don't think he's moved."

Korov walked back into the control room, still working through the situation, thinking through his options.

Why wasn't the *Williams* maneuvering? Could it have been an accident? Did it matter? If the torpedo caught the *Makarov*, wouldn't he have to shoot? *How long do you have, Ivan Sergeyevich? Six minutes? Seven? What if it misses? Do you still fire? Can you afford not to?*

Korov slammed his fist on the chart table. "Goddamnit."

The *Kazan*'s navigator looked over at him. "Captain?"

Korov stood silent, thinking about his orders. He made his decision. "Dima Igorovich, make tubes one and four ready and get me a firing solution on the *Williams*."

**Frigate *Admiral Makarov*
08 December 2022 | 0903 Local Time
Black Sea**

"Gorshkov! Where is the torpedo?" Dashkov looked around the bridge. The helmsman was holding on the ordered course as best he could given the state of the seas and the storm that was lashing the *Makarov*'s weather decks with sheeting, freezing rain. The damaged frigate's indicated speed had increased quickly after the emergent turn, but had topped out at just under fourteen knots. Dashkov ran the numbers in his head for the twentieth time. It was going to be far too close. His ship was not safe.

"Dead aft, Captain!" Gorshkov yelled. Dashkov could see the panic on the man's face, made even more grotesque by the pale red lights on the bridge.

"Time to impact?"

"Sixty seconds, Captain," Gorshkov said. His voice, loud as it was, trembled.

Dashkov's eyes returned to the ship's indicated speed as the frigate bounced on the roiling sea. He watched the digital reading flicker up and down. Thirteen-point-six. Twelve-point-eight. Thirteen-two.

"Come on, damnit," he growled. "Move!"

Dashkov didn't like turning his stern to the weapon. Didn't like presenting the torpedo's seeker head with the noisiest portion of his ship. But he'd had no other appealing alternatives. He'd had no way of knowing at what distance from launch the weapon would arm itself. He'd assumed the worst. That and the *Makarov*'s damaged bow sonar array had made turning toward the incoming threat a poor choice. He'd needed a way to keep tabs on the weapon and that meant using the tail. The rest was simply a matter of time and distance. A race. Which object could reach the eleven-thousand-meter range first? The *Makarov* at thirteen knots or the torpedo at fifty plus?

Dashkov swore again and turned. "Is the gun ready?"

Gorshkov picked up a handset, spoke, and looked up. "Two minutes, Captain. A problem with the high-pressure air system."

Dashkov slammed his fist against the helmsman's console.

**USS *James E. Williams*
08 December 2022 | 0903 Local Time
Black Sea**

Chief Petty Officer Brian Thompson stood in the middle of Central Control watching the propulsion console anxiously, as though it might magically provide some escape. He was not a naval tactician. He'd never stood watch on the bridge or in combat, but he did not imagine that sitting still after launching a torpedo was a great idea.

As if to confirm his thoughts, a messenger from Combat walked into the space and tapped him on the shoulder. Brian turned to the young petty officer.

"Yeah?"

"Captain wants to know the status of the engines."

Hell, Brian thought. So, do I.

A second messenger, this one a fireman from Brian's own department, stuck her head in the space before Brian could answer.

"Top, Chief Guillory says he needs another minute on the turbine. He thinks he's got it and he's waiting for the engine controller to reboot."

Brian nodded. "Get back down there and tell him to have everyone stand clear. I'm emergency starting that engine as soon as I get a ready indication up here."

"Yes, Chief." The sailor's head disappeared and Brian turned to Cruz.

"Cruz, you hear that?"

Petty Officer Cruz had the procedure open and his finger hovering over the start button. He was watching the status screen intently and did not turn to respond. "Yes, Chief. E-start as soon as I get the ready signal."

Brian turned to the Combat messenger. "Tell the captain and the bridge to stand by for engine start."

The sailor didn't move. "What if it doesn't work?"

"They'll figure it out when we don't move," Brian barked. "Get a move on."

The sailor raced out of Central just as Cruz shouted, "Ready signal. Emergency starting, now."

Brian turned to see Cruz punch the button for the start and watched as nothing happened. His head swiveled this way and that before settling on the electric plant console. "Shit. Becker. Give me bleed air! Now!"

Becker swore and punched the button that vented bleed air from the generator gas turbines to the starting air piping system. Brian watched as the indication lights shifted and turned back to Cruz.

"Hit it again, Cruz!"

Cruz hesitated. "But Chief…"

"But hell!" Brian yelled. "Punch it, Cruz! Now!"

Cruz's finger depressed the emergency start button and everyone held their breath as the huge gas turbine began spinning up. They watched the RPMs change, creeping upwards. They saw the fuel pressure change, watched the cans ignite. Temperatures rose. The speed changed. It cleared the minimum necessary to engage the system's clutch and Brian watched as the engine leveled out at its normal operating parameters.

A buzzer sounded and everyone's head snapped to Cruz.

He didn't turn. One hand flipped through the procedure manual and the other dropped to the throttles. "Bridge requests throttle control. Transferring now."

Brian watched for thirty seconds as Cruz worked. "Bridge has positive throttle control. Coming up to two-thirds."

Brian's gaze moved up to a black and orange display above

Cruz's head and he saw the ship's speed slowly increase. He smiled and heard a familiar bayou accent behind him.

"I got folks standin' by at each bearing, pump, and the reduction gears."

Brian turned to see Chief Guillory wiping his hands on a rag and sweating profusely. Brian grinned. "You magnificent son of a bitch."

**Frigate *Admiral Makarov*
08 December 2022 | 0904 Local Time
Black Sea**

"Captain! It's got us!" Gorshkov's voice was almost a scream.

In the split second between hearing the report and reaching for a microphone, Dashkov's brain raged at the injustice of the act and fumed at fate. A smaller, detached part of his brain began to pray. For his ship. For the crew. Even for the damn Americans he had tucked away below decks.

"Brace for impact!" Dashkov yelled into the microphone.

The yelling distorted his words, but the message got across. Throughout the ship, sailors held on, knees and arms bent slightly against the coming explosion.

Dashkov turned to the helmsman. "Left full rudder!" he yelled.

The helmsman had just enough time to turn the frigate's helm two full rotations before the torpedo hit home, dead center on the hub of the starboard propeller. Powered by Otto Fuel II and traveling at more than forty knots, the weapon expended nearly all of its forty-four kilograms of PBXN-103 high explosive against the propeller, its attached shafting, and the hull of the *Makarov* itself. The explosion ripped the screw from the ship and wrenched away the strut and a portion of the hull, exposing fuel storage tanks to the expanding ball of flame. The secondary explosion ripped outwards and upwards, tearing off a seven-meter-wide portion of the *Makarov*'s stern and cracking the hull through to the ship's aft steering compartment.

The stern of the *Makarov* was blown four meters into the air before slamming back into the roiling surface of the sea, flinging sailors and loose gear up, down, and forward.

Captain Dashkov, after ordering his crew to brace for the impact, was flung forward into the chart table. His head hit squarely on its sharp edge and stopped even as the rest of his body continued forward. His neck, folded backwards by the opposing forces, snapped, and he died still clutching the microphone in his left hand even as sirens announcing fires and flooding erupted all around him.

The White House
08 December 2022 | 0209 Local Time
Washington, DC

President Daniel Evans stormed into the White House situation room. He noted the young US Army major who'd assisted with the translation and clapped him on the shoulder before sitting.

"Thank you, Major."

The president turned to his staff, searching for the Secretary of Defense. "Frank, what the hell happened?"

Franklin Tolchanov stood and pointed. "Mr. President, National Military Command Center received a message from the USS *James E. Williams* stating that they have discharged a weapon accidentally and that the weapon, a Mark 46 torpedo, is tracking on the Russian frigate *Makarov*." Tolchanov paused as an aide handed over a message form. "Mr. President, the *Williams* reports that the torpedo struck the *Makarov* and that the frigate is on fire and down at the stern."

"How is this even possible?" Secretary of State Jack Burroughs asked. "Aren't there safeties? Interlocks? Something?"

Evans nodded. "There are." He paused. "That doesn't matter right now. We can investigate later. We need to report this as an accident to Moscow. Barsukov needs to know this was not intentional."

"After the ramming?" Burroughs asked. "No way he buys that."

Evans looked around. "Ophelia? Anything coming from them?"

The Director of National Intelligence shook her head. "It's too early to have gathered any reliable information. I would imagine that Barsukov is getting the same briefing you are right now."

"What will he do?" Evans asked.

"Barsukov?" Burroughs asked with a shrug. "That depends on a lot of factors, and it might not even matter."

Tolchanov sat back down. "What do you mean?"

"This just happened? Right?" Burroughs said. "With modern comms, we're what? Five or six minutes removed from real time?"

"What's your point?" Evans asked, his temper flaring briefly.

Burroughs pointed. "Mr. President, we have the *Williams* and the *Key West* out there. I don't know what the status of either is, but you've given orders that each may fire in self-defense…"

"Or defense of others." Tolchanov finished the sentence and looked at his watch. "Shit. Mr. President, Jack's right. We know there's a Russian sub out there. It's likely that the *Kazan* has the same orders you gave to the *Key West*. If that skipper thinks this was an offensive action and that it might happen again, he could already be lining up a shot on the *Williams*."

To his right, Evans saw Major Alexander flinch. He turned. "Everything all right, Major?"

Alexander nodded. "Yes, Mr. President. My apologies."

Evans turned back. "Wouldn't Barsukov order his boat to stand down?"

Tolchanov shook his head. "Only if he accepts that this was an accident, and even then, it might not matter."

"If the *Kazan*'s gone deep, you mean? Out of comms range?" Evans said. He paused for a few moments to think. "Can we withdraw our ships from the area safely? Disengage?"

"We can send the orders. It'll take time, though, and that's time that the *Kazan* could use to set up and launch his own weapons," Tolchanov reported. "The *Williams*'s commander says he's got one engine up and running on one shaft."

Evans nodded. "Frank, give the order to back away slowly. Jack, try to get Barsukov on the damn phone."

Tolchanov nodded and Burroughs leaned towards one of the phones on the conference table. His hand stopped in mid-air. "Mr. President, it's worth noting that we still have sailors and your nephew on the *Makarov*."

"I know, Jack," Evans said. "I know. Make the call and pray he answers this time. Then get a message to the embassy in Moscow."

US Embassy
08 December 2022 | 0915 Local Time
Moscow

The American ambassador to Russia was a short, stocky man who'd spent half his adult life working for the State Department and the other half teaching, first at Penn and later at Johns Hopkins' School of Advanced International Studies. He was having one hell of a morning. Aside from the normal slate of issues that assaulted him on a day-to-day basis, he had the ongoing tension in the Black Sea to worry him and a steady stream of requests for information from the White House to answer. Therefore, he was not pleased when he was asked to come down to one of the basement-level conference rooms by one of the embassy's lawyers and the CIA's chief of station.

He stormed into the spartan room with the intention of making his displeasure known, but his opening tirade was stopped short when he saw a third man in the room whose face he immediately recognized, but could not quite place.

"Ambassador, this is Mr. Anatoly Shablikov," the COS said. "He's personal assistant to SVR Director Tolstov, and he's asked for asylum in exchange for information. We've been talking for a few minutes and I figured you should hear it."

The ambassador paused, thinking. Yes, he remembered. That reception the previous year. The ambassador took a seat across from Shablikov and tried to keep his face impassive. "Okay, Mr. Shablikov. What can I do for you?"

Anatoly leaned forward in his seat and gestured at the COS and the lawyer. "I have explained to these men that what you believe is happening is not real."

The ambassador didn't blink. "Meaning?"

"First, the events in your country, the dissent and protests and violence…We caused that and I can explain how. It's not important now and can be dealt with later."

The ambassador, face still neutral, nodded. "Okay. What's

important now?"

"You are on the brink of war, sir," Anatoly said. "Or a significant conflict, at least."

The ambassador looked at the COS and got a nod. "Mr. Shablikov, I have a full and busy day ahead of me. Would you mind coming to the point?"

Anatoly nodded. "Sir, the events you are responding to in the Black Sea are not real. They are staged. False flag operations designed to provide my government with the opportunity to legally acquire various rigs that have recently been put up for sale in the area." Anatoly explained for several minutes, repeating, more succinctly, the information about operations in the Black Sea he'd already relayed to the other two men in the room. When he was asked about his motives, Anatoly explained his meeting with Borshevsky and the doctor.

When Anatoly stopped talking, the ambassador leaned forward. "Mr. Shablikov, that is an entertaining story. I'm sure you have some way of corroborating your claims?"

"I'm sorry," Anatoly stuttered. "Corro…"

"Proof, Mr. Shablikov. Proof," the ambassador said. "Can you prove this? Where did this information come from? How can we confirm it?"

"The information about the Black Sea was given to me by Admiral Fyodor Borshevsky. I do not know how you might be able to confirm this. The information about the cyber campaign comes from me. I was the person put in charge of the operation and can provide whatever information you require." Anatoly paused. "Even the address for the facility we have been using."

The ambassador turned to the COS and jerked his head at the door. When he received a nod, the ambassador turned back to Anatoly. "Mr. Shablikov, will you excuse us?"

"Certainly."

The ambassador stood and left the room with the COS. When the door was firmly shut, he shook his head. "What am I supposed to do with this?"

"It's worth a look," the COS said. "We've been able to confirm his identity."

The ambassador held a hand up. "I recognize him. Met him last year at a reception." He paused and looked through the small window in the door. "He seems pretty sure of himself, doesn't he?"

The COS nodded. "You heard why he's pissed. Forcing chemo on a healthy man." A shudder. "Jesus Christ, that's some sick shit if it's true."

The ambassador continued looking through the window. "Any way for you to confirm any of this independently?"

The COS thought for a moment. He was about to speak when one of the embassy staff walked up.

"Mr. Ambassador," she said. "This just came in from Washington." She handed over a note, which the ambassador read twice before looking up and dismissing the staffer.

"Christ."

"What?" the COS asked.

The ambassador handed over the message. "They've started shooting in the Black Sea."

The COS read the message and looked up. He jerked his thumb at the door. "What do you want me to do about this guy?"

The ambassador glanced through the window again. "Keep him here. Try to confirm what he's said and get me that info as fast as you can."

"Yes, sir."

"Anything else?"

"One thing he didn't cover with you in the room," the COS said. "Mr. Shablikov there says that there's a father–son team passing information to the SVR. A Major Harlan Alexander and his dad, Henry. Henry used to be one of ours. Drummed out after an incident while he was COS."

"And the major?"

"He works in the situation room."

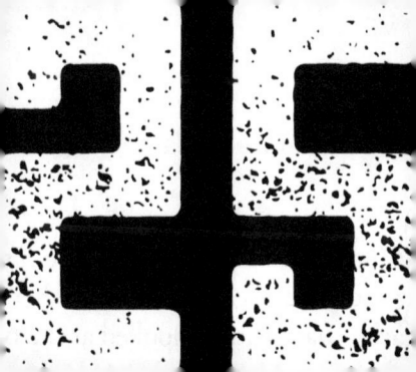

The Kremlin
08 December 2022 | 0930 Local Time
Moscow

Russian president Dmitri Barsukov walked into his office and shed his jacket, tossing it on the edge of his desk rather than pausing to hang it on the nearby coat rack. He looked at the two men in front of him, scowled, and waved both to their seats.

"Admiral Borshevsky," he started. "What is the status of the *Makarov*?"

The admiral settled into his seat, sitting upright and stiffly as was proper. "Reports say that the after portions of the ship are on fire or flooding. The ship has lost propulsion and steering and is operating off emergency generator power."

"How in the hell did this man, Dashkov, let himself get torpedoed by a crippled warship?" Barsukov growled. "First, he gets the ship run over by the American destroyer and now he's let them fire a torpedo up his ass. I would have him shot if we still did such things."

Borshevsky cleared his throat. "Mr. President, that will not be necessary. Captain Dashkov is dead. He was thrown into a table when the torpedo exploded and broke his neck. A senior lieutenant named Gorshkov is attempting to save the ship."

"Gorshkov?" Barsukov raised an eyebrow.

"He is a distant relative of the admiral, yes," Borshevsky

confirmed.

"Whatever." Barsukov waved the matter off. "And what in the hell was the *Kazan* doing when this happened? He was supposed to protect the *Makarov*, yes? Not stand by while a Russian warship was attacked and sunk."

"Mr. President," Borshevsky said. "This does not work like that. The *Kazan* is not one of your bodyguards. His job is not to take the bullet, but rather to listen and observe and warn."

"And retaliate, Admiral," Barsukov said. "I have four messages from the Americans already. One from Evans. Two from Burroughs, their Secretary of State. And one from the ambassador." He held up the notes. "Each one explains that this was an accident and that it would be in everyone's best interests if we agreed to meet and discuss everything that has gone on."

"If I may, Mr. President," Borshevsky said. "I suggest that you do that before this goes any further. We have probably lost the *Makarov*. The reports are not good. The Americans have sustained significant damage to the destroyer *Williams*. The *Kazan* already has orders to fire if fired upon. If he does, if he sinks the American ship, what then? What do you think President Evans will do? What will his advisors say? What will happen?"

"He will take us seriously," Barsukov said. "He has not done so yet. Despite every statement. Despite the rhetoric. Despite my admonitions to back off and let us handle the situation. He has kept that destroyer shadowing the *Makarov*. Even after the collision, he did not order that ship to withdraw. He kept sticking his nose where it doesn't belong. It is fair play to bloody it."

"It has been bloodied, Mr. President," Borshevsky said. "Both sides have lost face. You have what you wanted. Nearly every proposal for rig purchases in the Black Sea has been withdrawn. Our companies will be the only suitors remaining when this settles down. And as far as Evans knows, all we were—are—trying to do is ensure security."

"You don't see it, Admiral. Do you?" Barsukov was shaking his head.

"See what, Mr. President?"

"He knows, Fyodor Kirilovich. Somehow, he knows," Barsukov said.

"What can he possibly know, Mr. President?" Borshevsky asked. "He has domestic troubles. Protests and riots. Certainly, we have pushed inflammatory rhetoric and aided with the collisions of various political groups and police in America, but he can't know we are the driving force behind it. If he does, the director here," Borshevsky waved his hand at Tolstov, "has already planned for that. The blame will fall on this Shablikov fellow."

"That does not bother me, Admiral," Barsukov said. "The operation in the Black Sea does."

"Again, Mr. President. What can he possibly know?" Borshevsky asked. "It is true that no operation can truly be airtight, but this is as close to ideal as possible. There are no loose ends and there has been no evidence that points definitively to us."

"Mr. President, the admiral is correct. Evans cannot possibly know anything. He might suspect us, but there is no evidence that he could produce to tie us to this."

Barsukov turned on Tolstov. "Then why did Evans keep that destroyer shadowing the *Makarov*?"

Tolstov shrugged. "It was purely logical, Mr. President. Especially after we picked up their sailors and the president's nephew. We did discuss these risks. We knew that holding onto the Americans would look suspicious, and we've covered that act in the only way that was logical."

"And neither of you is concerned? With security? With the possibility that the facts will eventually come out?"

"Mr. President, the only thing I am concerned about is the *Kazan* firing on the Americans. That can have only one outcome, and it is contrary to our purposes," Borshevsky opined.

"I disagree, Mr. President," Tolstov countered. "If the *Kazan* does fire, it will be in defense of the *Makarov*. The world would consider it justified, and it helps sell the idea that the Americans are the aggressors here and that we are just trying to ensure the security of the region."

"That's crazy!" Borshevsky raised his voice for the first time.

"The Americans will not sit idly by after we attack one of their warships."

"They've done it before. At least publicly," Tolstov said. He leaned back in his seat. "What did the Americans actually do after the incident with the *Stark*? The *Liberty*?" Tolstov shook his head. "No, Admiral. They will do as they have always done. They will apologize and push this story about an accident. The world will believe our version of events."

"Believe what? That Evans ordered an attack on a ship with five American sailors and his own nephew on board?" Borshevsky looked from Tolstov to Barsukov. "This is insane, Mr. President. Especially if the claim about the accident is true. They would be able to prove such things. There are electronic records of everything that occurs in a ship's combat systems control suite, especially with respect to a weapons launch."

"All the more reason to let the *Kazan* sink the American, Mr. President," Tolstov said.

"What?" Borshevsky turned to the SVR director.

Tolstov shrugged. "If there is no ship, there are no records."

Borshevsky started to speak but was stopped by Barsukov's raised hand. "Your objections are noted, Admiral." The president flashed a gentle smile to ease the blow. "I have no doubt that you argue for what you think is best and, if this was strictly a naval matter, you would be absolutely correct. But this is bigger than that. This is about the survival of Russia. About keeping the economy afloat. Getting Russia and her people off life support and moving forward. Gaining control of those rigs, Admiral…" Barsukov shook his head. "We are talking trillions over the coming decades. Trillions that will inject new life into this nation. That will bring us back from the brink."

Barsukov looked down at his hands and then back up. "Admiral, what is the *Kazan* doing?"

Borshevsky blinked. "Right now? As we speak?"

"Yes."

Borshevsky's eyes flashed to his watch and his brain raced to track the time. *The report was three minutes old when we began the* discussion. We've been talking for four, no, five... Eight minutes in. Maybe nine or ten. Borshevsky swallowed. "The *Kazan* would be tracking the American. Working through rules of engagement and the last set of orders he received. Setting up and locking in a firing solution."

"And how long until *Kazan* could launch?"

"Maybe three or four minutes more, Mr. President. The captain will…" Borshevsky paused.

"Will what, Admiral?"

"He'll want to be sure, Mr. President," Borshevsky said. "Sure of his orders and sure of the shot."

Barsukov nodded. "Very well, Admiral. We will not interfere. The American fired on our ship and the *Kazan* will carry out his duty."

Borshevsky looked from Barsukov to the director, and back. Mother of God, he thought.

USS *Key West*
08 December 2022 | 0932 Local Time
Black Sea

"Conn! Sonar!" Chief Hughley said. "Got prop noises from the *Williams*. She's on the move."

"Conn, aye." About damn time, Reynes thought. He turned towards the sonar chief's voice. "And the *Kazan*?"

There was a lengthy pause in the *Key West*'s attack center. Reynes thought he could hear the men and women in the room breathing.

Quiet as a damn tomb, his mind reported.

"*Kazan* had faded out, Cap'n," Hughley said. "He bugged out when the *Williams* cut that fish loose, made sure it wasn't after him. After that, he started creeping back this way. He pops up every now and again, but nothing solid."

"Aye, Chief. Thanks," Reynes said. He looked to Lieutenant Commander Sandler on his left. "What do you think, XO?"

Sandler paused, his forehead furrowed in thought. "Getting in position for a shot?"

"Explain," Reynes commanded.

"Skipper, you gotta figure he had the same orders we did. Protect the surface ship. Under the last rules of engagement we got, we can shoot in self-defense or to defend the *Williams*." Sandler paused again before going on. "We guess the *Williams*' launch was an accident, but we don't know. Maybe he doesn't know either."

"You think he'll shoot?"

"With what I know and what I don't know, I wouldn't," Sandler said. "But I ain't him." Another pause. "Fifty-fifty he tosses a fish at the *Williams*, Skipper."

Reynes turned back to the displays in front of him and took in the data, transposing it all onto a three-dimensional map in his mind. Locations, tracks, speeds, bearings, depths. Over his shoulder, he called to the sonar chief. "Chief, give me the last good lock you have for the *Kazan*."

Chief Hughley relayed the information and Reynes plugged that into the map in his head. He looked at Sandler. "Fifty-fifty isn't something I'm willing to play with. I want us out of the line of fire in case this bastard shoots." He stopped. "Let's try to sneak around behind him."

"Yes, sir."

Quietly, Reynes thought. Quietly.

USS *James E. Williams*
08 December 2022 | 0940 Local Time
Black Sea

"Chief, got some vibes on the main." Cruz's voice sounded nervous.

Brian looked up from the log book he'd been writing in. He turned to the one of the messengers standing nearby.

"Get me Chief Guillory, quickly."

Brian watched the sailor leave the space and took two steps toward the propulsion console. He leaned over Cruz's shoulder. His eyes scanned the screen for a moment before tracking in on the line with the proper reading. He watched the numbers twitch up and down, tracking vibrations smaller than the human eye could possibly detect. Each rise came dangerously close to the engine's alarm setpoint. Just a few increments higher and the engine's electronic brain would initiate an emergency shutdown.

Brian patted Cruz on the shoulder and let his eyes drift up to the battle override button. It sat there, unlit, with a plastic safety cover in place. Brian froze, thinking. His mind reviewed every regulation and operational order he could think of.

The *Williams* was at battle stations. This was the last engine on the last shaft. He could depress the button. He was nearly certain of that fact. But what did the captain want? They'd launched a torpedo earlier. Whether it had hit anything or not, Brian didn't know.

Did that matter? No.

But pressing the button would override the safety shutdown for vibrations. The engine would just keep going until it tore itself apart. And that, he thought, would leave the ship dead in the water with no engines. Not hitting the button would do the same thing. The vibes would continue bouncing around until something caused it to hit that shutdown mark. And they'd be dead in the water. But with the chance to restart the engine.

"Damnit," Brian swore. He turned to write out a note with his question on a message blank. He'd just picked up the pen when the XO entered the space.

"Where's CHENG?" Caldwell demanded.

Brian started writing. He answered without looking up. "In Combat."

"What's that?"

Brian looked up and saw the XO pointing at the note he was writing. "A question for the captain. About the engines and battle override," Brian explained as he finished the note. He dropped the pen and reached to hand the note to another messenger. The XO snatched it out of his hand.

"Sir, I need that to go to the CO," Brain said. He felt adrenaline dump into his system. He felt his pulse race.

"No, you don't," Caldwell snapped. He pocketed the note. "Put the engines in battle override. My authority."

Brian shook his head. "Sir, you don't have that authority.

Only the EOOW and the CO can order that and only in specific situations. In this case, the last engine on the last shaft belongs to the captain."

Caldwell put his hand on Brian's chest and pushed him aside. "Petty Officer Cruz, place the engine in battle override."

Brian slapped the XO's hand away. "Don't do it, Cruz."

"Cruz," Caldwell barked. "I am your executive officer and I'm ordering you to put the engine in battle override."

"Chief?" Cruz stammered. "What the hell do I do?"

"Sir," Petty Officer Becker said. "It has to be either the EOOW or—"

"Nobody asked you, Becker," Caldwell snapped. "Stay in your damn paygrade."

Brian pointed at the messenger. "Get Master Chief. Now!"

Caldwell turned to tell the sailor to ignore the order, but the undesignated fireman had already hauled ass. He turned on Brian. "What the hell is your problem?"

"Sir, you don't have the authority to make this call," Brian said. He stepped between Caldwell and the console.

"The hell I don't." Caldwell pointed at Cruz over Brian's shoulder. "Battle override or I end your shitty little career."

"Sir," Cruz started. "You can't—"

Caldwell put one hand on Brian's chest and shoved, reaching for the override button with his free arm. Brian stumbled back, but kept his body between the XO and the console. He pushed himself upright and stood toe-to-toe with Caldwell, bracing against the XO's repeated attempts to reach over, under, and around his arms and body.

The XO's finger made contact with the button's safety cover and Brian leaned into the man to keep him from lifting it free.

"Fuck you, Chief," Caldwell snarled. "I'm ordering you to—"

"No, sir. You aren't," Brian said.

Caldwell jabbed a knife hand into Brian's chest. "Who the hell do you think you are?"

Brian pushed the hand away and braced against the console. "Knock it off, sir."

"Or what, Chief?" Caldwell sneered. "Last chance."

"Not gonna happen, sir," Brian started. "Not until the captain—" He didn't see the XO's fist until it was too late. His vision exploded into thousands of tiny points of light. A searing pain ripped through his upper lip and nose. Brian's eyes began watering instantly. He sagged against the console and was vaguely aware that the man who'd just decked him was lining up a second jab. Brian lifted his right arm to block it.

"XO, what in the hell are you doing?" The loud, gruff voice of Master Chief Logan Carrillo filled the room.

"He's refusing to follow orders, Chief," Caldwell barked.

"Orders you can't give on this ship or in this situation," Carrillo said.

Brian's vision cleared a little and he was able to see Carrillo and two of the ship's masters-at-arms standing in the space. He became vaguely aware that something warm and sticky was running down his face. He touched his hand to his nose and felt pain shoot off in every direction. Brian looked at his hand and saw blood.

"Now listen here, Chief," Caldwell said.

"No, you listen," Carrillo snapped. "This is not the time or place, and even if it was, you just assaulted and battered one of my sailors right in front of me." Carrillo turned to the two sailors who'd entered with him. "Escort Lieutenant Caldwell to his cabin and keep him there."

Caldwell stepped away from the three men in front of him. "You don't have the authority to—"

"He may not," said the senior master-at-arms, "but I do, especially after witnessing an act of violence."

Carrillo growled at Caldwell. "I suggest you go with them quickly and quietly, sir. They're here on the captain's orders."

When the XO didn't move, Carrillo leaned into his ear and whispered. "According to a bunch of video recordings I just saw saved on Petty Officer Faulkner's shared drive account, you got lots bigger problems than dealing with me and my chiefs."

Brian watched this and caught portions of what Carrillo

whispered. He saw Caldwell go pale and look around, pointing frantically at each sailor in the room.

"You all saw that!" he shouted. "He threatened me. You're all witnesses."

"I didn't see shit, sir," Cruz said. "'Cept for that part when you threw hands at Chief."

Caldwell spun on Cruz and launched himself at the junior sailor. "Why, you little mother—"

The two masters-at-arms tackled the XO, dragging him to the ground inches from Cruz. The XO fought back for a few moments, kicking and screaming and letting loose a steady stream of curses and threats, before the masters-at-arms got control of the situation. When the struggling finally ceased, they hauled Caldwell to his feet and turned him to face Carrillo.

"Get him outta here," Carrillo growled. "Then let the skipper know."

Caldwell resisted the first attempts to remove him from the space, planting his feet and pushing back against the sailors gripping his arms. It was only after one of the sailors produced a set of zip-strips and showed them to him that the XO allowed himself to be escorted out of the space.

Carrillo watched the XO depart and pulled Brian to the side. "You need a relief?"

Brian found a dirty rag in a back pocket and began dabbing at his bleeding nose. He shook his head. "Maybe just Doc and an icepack." He kept trying to wipe the blood away, folding and refolding the rag as each portion became sodden. "What was that about the shared drive and Faulkner?"

"Had Chief Ibanez check Faulkner's account after what you claimed earlier. Just in case," Carrillo said. "Found a shitload of audio and video files. Ten of which show Caldwell threatening and harassing the kid."

Brian started to say something, but stopped when Chief Guillory walked up.

"What the hell happened to you?"

25

The Kremlin
08 December 2022 | 1000 Local Time
Moscow

SVR Director Igor Romanovich Tolstov was met by one of his aides thirty seconds after stepping out of the president's office. The man, a fiftyish and graying security officer, was carrying a sealed envelope, which he handed over with a note. Tolstov took both items. He tucked the envelope under one arm and unfolded the scrap of paper. He read the message, looked at the bearer, and then read the note again.

"Is this..." Tolstov started to ask.

"Yes, Director," the man said. "Positive identification."

Tolstov stuffed the note into a pocket. "I need a secure space and a phone," he commanded. "Now."

The man stepped out of the way and pointed down the hall. "We have both standing by."

In another forty-five seconds, both men were inside the room and Tolstov was ripping open the envelope. In his haste, he tore the edge off one of the photographs inside, but it did not matter. There were plenty of shots to spare. Tolstov spread them on the table in the center of the room and spent a full minute looking at them.

Thirty frames. All showing Anatoly Mikhailovich Shablikov waltzing through the front door of the American embassy.

Anatoly, you sonofabitch, Tolstov thought. He turned to the security man.

"And there is no reason for his to be there? No appointment of some sort?" It was a stupid question and Tolstov knew it. But it had to be asked.

"No, Director." The security officer shook his head. "None that we could discover. We have no idea why he's there or what he's doing."

Tolstov swore. He was reasonably sure he knew what Anatoly was doing and why. It wasn't a certainty, he told himself. But what in this business ever was?

Tolstov checked the time and date stamps on the photographs and noted that they'd been taken that morning, less than twenty-four hours after he'd described how he'd set up Shablikov to the president. How he'd co-opted the doctor and used Anatoly's previous bout with cancer to frame him as an angry man gone rogue. Just in case the whole operation went sideways. He'd gone into intricate detail on the matter with the president. And to Borshevsky.

Tolstov swore again and picked up the phone. "You are certain this is secure and untraceable?"

The security officer nodded. "Yes, Director."

"Good." Tolstov began dialing the first number in a long chain of cutouts that would end in a small town sixty miles south of Washington, DC.

"Need anything else, Director?"

Tolstov walked the man to the door. "I need to be alone for five minutes." He paused, heard the phone begin ringing. "And I need someone to go arrest that idiot Borshevsky."

"What charge, Director?"

"Treason," Tolstov hissed.

USS *James E. Williams*
08 December 2022 | 1005 Local Time
Black Sea

Brian watched anxiously as the engine vibrations twitched back and forth. His nose ached and he found it difficult to breathe with cotton balls stuffed up each nostril to stem the bleeding. A messenger tapped him on the shoulder and he turned.

"Chief, Cap'n gave in. Gave the order to put the engine in battle override and to tell the bridge just how far they can take it." The messenger handed over the note.

Brian read it, nodded, and turned to the console. "Cruz, place the engine in battle override."

Brian watched as the junior sailor lifted the clear plastic cover and pressed the red button underneath. The button illuminated immediately and the console buzzed a scrolling note to tell everyone what had been done.

Brian noted the action in the log, scribbled a response to the captain and orders to the bridge on the back of the message form, and handed it back to the messenger.

K-561 *Kazan*
08 December 2022 | 1010 Local Time
Black Sea

"Sixty seconds, Captain," the weapons officer reported.

"Very well." Korov acknowledged the information and turned. "Sonar, any additional contacts?"

"No, Captain," Belyaev said. "Only the *Makarov* and the target. The remaining surface traffic is well clear."

"Very well," Korov said. He turned to the table in front of him and reviewed the options in his mind. He had two choices. The *Makarov* had been attacked by the American destroyer and the American was now moving away from the scene. His last orders were clear. Defending the *Makarov* warranted taking the shot.

But it could have been an accident, his mind said. And if it was, and if you still fire…

Korov gripped the table with enough force to turn his knuckles white.

"Captain," the weapons officer said. "We have a firing solution. Tubes one and four ready in all respects."

You don't know it was an accident, Ivan Sergeyevich. You only guess. And you have orders.

"Captain?"

Korov looked up. The weapons officer was staring at him. Waiting. Korov pulled himself erect.

"Flood tubes one and four. Open outer doors."

"Aye, Captain."

The order was relayed and Korov waited.

"Tubes flooded. Outer doors open, Captain."

Korov nodded. "Fire one and four."

USS *Key West*
08 December 2022 | 1011 Local Time
Black Sea

The *Key West* was coming through a slow turn when Chief Hughley's voice boomed. "Conn, Sonar. Torpedoes in the water. Bearing zero-nine-zero."

Reynes shot upright from his spot near the charts. "Left full rudder. All ahead flank. Standby to launch countermeasures," he barked.

The attack center exploded as voices repeated his order and began passing information back to him. Reynes felt the Los Angeles–class submarine lean into the turn. He turned to the weapons console.

"Snapshot. Tube three. Bearing zero-nine-zero."

Brookshire Apartments
08 December 2022 | 0312 Local Time
Alexandria, VA

Major Harlan Alexander stepped through the door, made it two steps down the sidewalk, and stopped. He patted his overcoat pockets down quickly and, not finding what he was looking for, undid a pair of the coat's front buttons and checked the pockets of his pants.

"Damnit."

Harlan stormed back into the house, not pausing to wipe his feet on the mat. His eyes scanned the room, searching. The table by the door was empty. As was the coffee table.

"Where the hell?"

On his third sweep through the room, he saw his cellphone, resting on the arm of a dark brown wingback. Right where he'd left it the night before.

Harlan tiptoed across the room, knowing that he was getting snow and muck on the thick living room rug and not especially caring. He was running late as hell for his early morning watch in the situation room. His brain was already calculating the best route through traffic when he picked up his phone and saw that it was ringing in silent mode. Not recognizing the number, he thumbed the button on the right side, declined the call, and hurried outside to his car.

Harlan was backing out of the driveway when the same number called again, this time appearing on the Mercedes's dash display because of the automatic feature that linked the phone to the car via Bluetooth.

Harlan hit the red button on his steering wheel, declining the call again as he finished backing up and put the car in drive. When the phone rang again and displayed the same number, Harlan slammed his thumb down on the green call button.

"Listen, damnit!" he yelled into the roof-mounted microphone. "Take me off your damn call list. I'm not intere—"

"Shut up and run, boy," Henry Alexander's voice interrupted.

Harlan slammed on the brakes and the Mercedes slid to a halt on the snow and ice. "What?"

"You heard me, boy. Someone snitched," Henry said. "Get a move on. You remember where and how. Get going."

Harlan's mind raced. He searched for the information he needed and came up blank, his mind settling somewhere between anger and panic. Distantly, he noted that the two emotions felt oddly similar.

"But Dad… What? Why?"

"No time, boy. Get a move on."

The call ended. Harlan sat there, the car idling, and tried to dial his father back. The call went to voicemail.

Harlan tried again and got the same result.

He tried a third time and got an automated recording telling him that the number he'd dialed was no longer in service.

Harlan let loose a violent stream of obscenities, threw the Mercedes into gear, and raced off down the slick road.

USS *James E. Williams*
08 December 2022 | 1015 Local Time
Black Sea

"Torpedoes inbound. All hands brace for shock." The wall-mounted speaker above Brian's head roared to life.

As his mind worked to process what he'd just heard and his head swiveled to check the engine's status, the thought that he hadn't known the 1MC announcing system even worked flitted through Brian's consciousness.

"Chief!" Cruz yelled above the clanging alarms. "Bridge just ramped the engine above shutdown vibes."

Brian's eyes shot to the panel above Cruz's head and he saw the ship's speed increasing slowly. As he watched, he felt and saw the ship's course change, the gradual lean to port reflected by the movement of one of the arrows on the rudder angle indicator. The 1MC blared to life again.

"Stream the Nixie."

Christ Almighty, Brian thought. Trying to outrun and outmaneuver a torpedo on one engine and half a rudder.

"Chief?" Cruz yelled. "Vibes getting really bad. What do I do?"

Brian eyes flashed first to the readings and then to the illuminated battle override button.

"Strap yourself in, Cruz."

K-561 *Kazan*
08 December 2022 | 1016 Local Time
Black Sea

"Captain!" Belyaev screamed. "Torpedo in the water. Sounds like an American Mark 48. Bearing zero-eight-zero."

"What?" Korov growled. "From who?"

"Submerged contact, Captain. Same bearing," Belyaev said. "Aspect change. Blade rate for thirty knots. Possibly an American. Los Angeles–class."

Korov swore to himself. He turned and bellowed. "Left full rudder. Ahead flank."

As the order was carried out, he turned to Sonar. "Range to the destroyer, Yevgeni?"

"Our weapons are four thousand meters and closing, Captain. They have acquired and are homing."

"And to the inbound?"

"To the Mark 48," Belyaev said. "Ten thousand meters and closing, Captain."

Korov began doing the math in his head and searched his memory for the specifications and capabilities of the incoming torpedo. The damn thing and its five-hundred-kilogram warhead were racing towards him at better than forty knots. Probably closer to fifty. And the weapon's range was just over twenty nautical miles. Nearly thirty if you went with some of the more recent intelligence reports. At this range he could not outrun the weapon, and it could turn circles around him.

An idea flashed through his mind.

Korov spun around. "Surface the boat! Now!"

USS *Key West*
08 December 2022 | 1017 Local Time
Black Sea

"Sonar," Reynes said, sticking his head into the cramped space. "Talk to me."

"*Kazan*'s weapons are locked on the *Williams*, Skipper." Hughley looked up. "I don't see how they can miss."

"And ours?"

"Hot, straight, and normal, Skipper," Hughley said, pointing at the track on the screen. "Russkie boat bugged out fast, but he's big and noisy. That fish shouldn't—"

The sonar chief stopped talking and held a hand up. He crouched back low over the screen. "Lotsa hull poppin', Skipper. Can hear it even with the fish racing through the water and everyone digging holes at speed." Hughley looked back up at Reynes. "He's making for the roof, Skip."

Reynes nodded. At this range it was the smart choice. The Yasen-class couldn't outrun the 48 and damn sure couldn't out-turn the fish. With a roiling surface, the only attractive option was to try to get lost in the surface capture.

Hell, Reynes thought. It might even work.

He took three steps back into the attack center.

"XO, let's settle her down and clear datum. Bring it back to five knots and let's see what happens."

Lieutenant Commander Sandler relayed the orders. The *Key West* slowed to five knots and began a slow, arcing turn to the northeast.

Side Streets
08 December 2022 | 0319 Local Time
Alexandria, VA

Harlan Alexander raced through the side streets and backroads as fast as the snow and ice would permit. His brain tried desperately to track and hold multiple trains of thought. How had this happened? How had he been discovered?

His eyes flashed back and forth between the mirrors and the roadway, searching for any sign of a tail as he maneuvered through and around traffic towards the congested DC Beltway.

Four blocks from the nearest entrance ramp, Harlan changed lanes abruptly, something that he'd done tens of thousands of times over the years without any concern for the police or the possibility of a citation. This time, just as his car crossed what, except for the snow, would have been a dashed white line, the blue-and-red flashing lights of an unmarked police cruiser lit up the interior of his car.

Harlan felt adrenaline dump into his system and barely resisted the urge to stomp on the gas. He kept edging to the right, certain of what was to come. Sweat formed along his hairline and Harlan found himself clutching at the wheel to keep from trembling. He checked the rearview mirror and saw the squad car moving up behind him and beginning to edge to the right, into the same lane Harlan had just moved into.

Harlan swallowed hard. He looked to his right and saw the open shoulder. He could pull over there and stop.

Or gun it.

Harlan looked in the rearview again. The lights were still flashing and the siren wailing as the cruiser eased in directly behind him.

And kept moving right.

Harlan gulped down air and wiped the sweat from his brow as the police car shifted to the shoulder and sped off in the distance.

Harlan let his hands drop from the wheel and watched them shake and tremble. He clasped them together and tried to control his breathing even as the car behind him began honking.

Harlan looked up and saw the gap in front of him. He put his hands back on the wheel and his foot depressed the gas. After two minutes of stop-and-go traffic, Harlan looked to his right and saw one of the local liquor stores. He looked at his face in the rearview, glanced at his still-trembling hands, and pulled off into the parking lot.

The White House
08 December 2022 | 0320 Local Time
Washington, DC

"What in the hell happened?" Daniel Evans shouted in the situation room. He caught the look Barnes gave him—the one that clearly said he needed to gain control over his temper—and ignored it. He distantly registered that that particular question was becoming his most used phrase of late.

Secretary of Defense Tolchanov was still standing, having walked into the room mere seconds ahead of his commander-in-chief. "We don't have much, Mr. President. Barsukov is ignoring everything we send his way about the accident, and we just got this flash message that *Williams* is attempting to evade two incoming torpedoes."

"From who?" Evans barked. "The *Kazan*?"

Tolchanov nodded. "Seems likely, Mr. President. Only other info we have is a lot of chatter. Signals office is relaying us the intercepts in real time and we're waiting on an interpreter to get here."

"We don't have one standing by?" Evans threw his hands up and looked around. "What the hell, folks?"

Barnes stood and spoke, his voice even and calm. "The gal who was on duty was came down with something midwatch, Mr. President. Vomiting. High fever. She had to get to the hospital."

Evans looked around again. "Where's the major? That one who translated the other day? Can't he do it? Shouldn't he be here?"

One of the military officers against the exterior wall, an Air Force lieutenant-colonel, stepped forward. "Mr. President, Major Alexander has not arrived for duty yet." The officer shrugged. "It's likely he's stuck in traffic, what with the snow and all."

Evans glared at the man for a moment before turning to Barnes and Tolchanov. "Okay, we've got torpedoes in the water tracking a crippled destroyer. What can we do? How much time do we have?"

"Not much we can do for the *Williams*, Mr. President," Tolchanov said. "They either evade or they don't. What we need is guidance for the *Key West*. With the attack on the *Williams*, she will track and fire on the *Kazan*. Those were her last orders. Defense of others. Given the information we have, it is likely that *Key West* has already launched."

Evans slumped into his chair at the head of the cluttered table and reviewed the information he had. *Makarov* was sinking, the victim of an accident. The Russians weren't buying that story and they'd attacked the *Williams* with a cruise missile submarine. He had the *Key West* stalking the area, presumably working to develop a firing solution on the *Kazan*.

If they hadn't already fired a snapshot when the *Kazan* launched, Evans reminded himself. That, as SECDEF had just said, was fairly likely.

"Any word from the *Key West*?" Evans asked. He watched as heads shook and forced himself to think. It was difficult to do with the adrenaline in his system. He could feel and hear his pulse racing in his ears.

Take a deep breath, Evans told himself. And think.

"Can we get a signal to *Key West*?" he asked after a few moments. He thought he knew the answer, but his most up-to-date information on submarine communications was more than a decade old.

"Yes, sir, Mr. President," Tolchanov said. "ELF can transmit fairly deep. Takes a while to download the message, though. Whatever we say needs to be short. And the *Key West* might still miss the transmission."

"If we tell *Key West* to back off, what happens?" Evans asked.

"Depends on whether the *Williams* survives and whether or not the *Key West* has launched against the *Kazan*," Tolchanov said. "Lotta variables, Mr. President. Bottom line is pretty simple. Only way this stops now is if you and Barsukov can pull everyone back."

"And worst case?" Evans said.

"Worst case?" Tolchanov said. "Today ends with four ships on the bottom of the Black Sea and hundreds of dead sailors on both sides."

"And it might not stop there, Mr. President," Barnes interjected. "Especially if Barsukov refuses to listen."

Evans sat still for a moment. "Any word on our people on the *Makarov*?"

Heads shook around the table. Evans nodded and stood. "All this over some damn oil wells." He pointed at Tolchanov. "Get a message to the *Key West* to stand off at a safe distance if she can. She may defend herself, and the *Williams* if she survives, but that's it. Defense only."

Tolchanov nodded.

"What about Barsukov?" Barnes asked.

"We keep trying," Evans said. "Privately and publicly. Get the press corps assembled."

USS *James E. Williams*
08 December 2022 | 1022 Local Time
Black Sea

"Torpedoes inbound. All hands brace for shock!" The voice over the *Williams*'s 1MC system was followed by the clanging and gonging sounds of the ship's collision alarm.

Brian glared at the speaker and repeated the order for everyone in Central Control, wedging himself against one of the space's large computer consoles. His head ached, partially due to the chaos and stress of the moment and, Brian thought, partially because of his more recent run-ins with solid objects.

Brian looked around, saw everyone in the space doing as he was doing. They were all leaning on whatever solid surfaces they could find, legs and arms slightly flexed to help absorb whatever impact might come. Most were looking around, and Brian could see the strain on each face. Jaws seemed to be clenched tight. Every set of eyes looked worried.

Brian took a deep breath as the alarms kept up their interminable racket. His brain began racing. Thinking back to the previous year, when the explosion in Shaft Alley had crippled the ship and killed one of his sailors.

Who's back there now?

Brian blinked. Try as he might, he couldn't remember. He'd written the watchbill. He'd assigned someone to the space. And the torpedoes, Brian thought. Are they chasing us down from behind? They'd have to be. If they struck aft, would he lose another sailor? Had he sent someone else's kid to his or her death?

"Shit." Brian reached for the microphone to tell the sailor to get the hell out of the space. He pressed the button down before remembering that the engineering speaker system had been damaged in the collision.

◆ ◆ ◆

The *Kazan*'s two torpedoes raced after the *Williams*, each weapon's sonar system pinging and listening and guiding the warhead to the target. Hitting the destroyer was a difficult task, even for each weapon's computerized brain. The target was on the surface in heavy seas, rolling and bouncing in the winter storm. Both Russian torpedoes found it difficult to differentiate between the ship itself and the massive shapes formed by the trough of each surface wave. In both cases, the targeting system began to see dozens of possible targets.

The first torpedo chose the biggest target it saw and drove straight into it, leaping out of the water in between two huge waves before crashing back into the sea to search again. This weapon completed the same process three times before a fourth crash into the raging sea broke it apart.

The second torpedo also identified a target and raced towards it, the onboard sonar lashing out and listening as the distance closed. This weapon also found nothing but the empty space between waves and crashed back into the sea to begin another round of circling and searching. The onboard sonar locked onto another possible target and the weapon turned to chase it, covering the short distance in less than ten seconds. The high-speed screws screeched in the roiling water, and the weapon made several minor steering adjustments. The torpedo leapt from the water into the space between two waves less than ten meters from the *Williams*'s starboard side. It raced through the air and collided with the next wave hard enough to detonate the warhead, just seven meter from the hull of the *Williams*.

◆ ◆ ◆

Brian was thrown sideways into the bulkhead by the force of the blast, and something in his brain told him that the hit hadn't been that bad. The lights flickered, went out, then shifted to emergency mode. He looked up just as alarms began wailing. Sailors began yelling information, relaying status as best they could. Ten feet away, he saw the DCA pick up her 1MC handset.

"Hit Alpha. Starboard side. Investigators out!" she ordered.

Brian pulled himself to his feet. His legs felt wobbly. He tried to ignore it.

"Cruz? Becker?"

"Generator is down, Chief," Becker reported. "Lost part of the bus, too."

Brian nodded and turned to Cruz, saw the sailor holding a hand over his face and saw blood covering the keyboard portion of the console.

"Shit. Cruz."

"I'm okay, Chief. Just my nose, I think," Cruz said, scanning. He turned. "We lost the engine, Chief."

Brian snagged his own handset for the ship's announcing system and looked to the DCA. She nodded and twirled a finger to tell him to hurry.

Brian pressed the transmit button. "Engineering casualty. Engineering casualty. Loss of GTM." He repeated the information once more before ordering a casualty response team to the main space and turning control of the 1MC back over to the DCA.

K-561 *Kazan*
08 December 2022 | 1025 Local Time
Black Sea

"A hit, Captain," Belyaev reported.

"And the inbound?" Korov asked, clinging to a handrail as the *Kazan* wallowed violently in the heavy seas. "Where is the inbound?" The ship's motion worried Korov. He knew well what force a raging sea could exert on a metal ship. Great damage could be inflicted by seas like this, especially on the submarine's sail, rudder, and planes. But the choice between the heavy rolls and a circling torpedo was an easy one. Better, he thought, to risk minor damage on the surface than the much heavier damage the weapon hunting them could inflict.

"Circling, Captain," Belyaev said. "Though it is difficult to track with the explosion and the surface noise."

Good, Korov, thought. Sonar impairment works both ways. Just a matter of degrees. He began searching his brain, trying to recall the specifications on the American torpedo and calculate the time until it ran out of fuel.

USS *Key West*
08 December 2022 | 1026 Local Time
Black Sea

"*Williams* took a hit, Skipper," Chief Hughley reported. "Can't tell how bad."

Reynes nodded. "And our fish?"

"Circling," Hughley said. "It's just looking now. Safe bet that *Kazan* is on the surface. Hard to tell with all the noise in the water."

Reynes thought for a moment, calculating the time until the Mark 48 expended its load of fuel. He turned to Sandler.

"XO, what say we get on the other side of this guy?" Reynes stepped up to the chart table and pointed. "We lost him about here. If he's on the roof, he's deaf as a post and he can't come back down until he's certain that fish has given up."

"Gives us a good long while to find a hiding place," Sandler said, looking at the chart. "Wait for everything to settle back down and listen?"

Reynes nodded and glanced at the weapons console. "And get that tube reloaded with another 48."

"Can do," Sandler said, before turning to give the appropriate orders.

Satisfied, Reynes turned back to the sonar room. "Chief, you speak up as soon as you hear something."

The White House
08 December 2022 | 0329 Local Time
Washington, DC

Daniel Evans saw Ophelia Adams enter the situation room and lean over to whisper into Leslie Barnes's ear. That made him curious, but he turned away, intent on getting some sort of answer from the Secretary of Defense.

"Frank, I need to know if that message got through to *Key West* before I talk to the press." Evans looked at his watch. "I've got two…" He stopped speaking when he caught Leslie Barnes standing up out of the corner of his eye. Evans turned to the chief of staff.

"Leslie?"

Barnes cleared his throat. "Uh, Mr. President. We need to continue this discussion in the Oval Office."

"What?"

"Something else has come up, sir," DNI Adams said. "It requires your immediate attention."

"What the hell are you talking about?" Evans pointed at the screens attached to the far wall of the room. "I've got one, possibly two ships shooting it out with the Russian Navy in the Black Sea. What's more important than this?"

Barnes winced. "Not here, Mr. President." He turned to the rest of the table and pointed at the Secretaries of Defense and State. "Frank, Jack. Would you please join us?"

Evans stood and looked from Adams to Barnes, and back. "What is going on?"

Barnes leaned in and whispered in Evans's ear. "Not here, Daniel. This room is no longer secure."

Evans blinked and looked around the room. He saw the uneasy expressions. The curiosity. Each person clearly wondering what could be more important than American and Russian ships shooting at each other.

Evans excused himself and followed Barnes back to the Oval Office. He wanted to ask for more information, but decided against it. Whatever the issue, it was clear that neither Adams or Barnes wanted to discuss it in anything like a public forum.

It took three minutes to make it into the Oval Office. Once everyone was in and the molded door was shut, Evans spun on his advisors.

"What the hell do you mean the situation room isn't secure?"

Barnes looked to Adams and nodded.

"Mr. President," Adams said. "The FBI has secured a warrant for the arrest of Major Harlan Alexander and his father, Henry."

"What?" Evans said. "What for?"

Adams opened a folder she'd been carrying and withdrew several sheets of paper which she passed out to everyone in the room. "The chief of station in Moscow has a source, a walk-in, who has claimed that the Alexanders have been feeding information to Russia for some time now. The source also claims that everything that is happening right now with Russia is part of an operation to enable Russian, state-owned energy companies to purchase a majority of the oil and gas rigs in the Black Sea."

Evans looked down at his sheet of paper and scanned it. He looked back up and poked a finger at it. "This says that they've orchestrated the rig incidents and have engaged in a cyber campaign in order to make my domestic problems worse. Did I read that right?"

"There's more, Daniel," Barnes said. "Keep reading."

Evans raised an eyebrow and looked back down at the paper. When he raised his head again, his face was beet red. "Blackmailing the senators?"

Adams nodded. "That's the claim, Mr. President."

Evans tried to take a breath and calm himself down. "They laundered money into the re-election campaigns for each of these people and threatened to out them?" Evans tossed the paper on the floor. "Are you shitting me? I'm having all of these problems, at home and abroad, because Barsukov can't fix his economy?" Evans stormed around his desk. "He runs Russian finances into the damn ground and this bullshit is his way out?"

"Mr. President…" Barnes started.

Evans cut him off with a raised hand. He turned to Adams. "I am assuming that you believe this information to be reliable?"

"Yes, Mr. President." Adams nodded. "We need to confirm a few things, but the placement of the source suggests that this is genuine."

"Who's the source?" Evans asked.

"Mr. President, you don't normally want to—"

"Do the Russians know we have the source?" Evans asked. "You said he was a walk-in. I assume that means the embassy in Moscow. If he literally walked in, they have to know who he is and what he would say. Correct?"

Adams nodded. "Unless it's an elaborate plant. The chief of station believes he is genuine."

"Why?"

"Because the source claims that he's being treated with chemotherapy for a cancer that he does not have, and the embassy physician confirmed that information after a thorough examination," Adams said.

Holy shit, Evans thought. He paused and took a deep breath.

"Ophelia, if the Russians know this source is at the embassy, I can't screw him over much more than that. Right?" Evans looked from Adams to Jack Burroughs, the Secretary of State. He saw heads shake and smiled grimly.

"Frank." Evans pointed to the Secretary of Defense. "Keep trying to get that message to the *Key West*. Defensive only. As long as the *Kazan* doesn't shoot again, *Key West* is to hold fire."

Evans turned to Adams. "I want you to work on a way to get that source out of Moscow safely, if that is what he wants. I don't care what it takes. I don't want him to have a sudden, unexplained heart attack or accidentally trip out of a third-floor window. Got me?"

After Adams nodded, Evans turned to the Secretary of State. "Jack, I don't give a rat's ass what you have to do, but you get that sonofabitch on the phone. I want to talk to Barsukov and I want that bastard to know what we know."

"Yes, Mr. President." Jack Burroughs nodded. "But it won't be easy."

"If you have to out him on CNN, do it. Coordinate the message with Leslie and Ophelia," Evans ordered. "Any questions?"

"What do you want me to do?" Barnes asked.

Evans walked back around to the front of the Resolute Desk. He squatted and picked up the sheet of paper he'd thrown on the floor. He pointed at it and growled. "I want these senators in here. Yesterday, Leslie."

20

USS *Key West*
08 December 2022 | 1115 Local Time
Black Sea

"Conn. Sonar. Contact bearing one-seven-nine," the *Key West*'s sonar chief announced, his voice quiet and crisp.

"Conn, aye. All Stop. Quick quiet." Reynes gave the order without thinking. It was an automatic, pre-programmed response. It had been close to an hour since they'd fired on the *Kazan* and Reynes had been busy maneuvering, using the noise and chaos generated by the detonations of the *Kazan*'s torpedoes as camouflage.

The helmsman reached forward, turning a dial on his console that told the engine room to stop the *Key West*'s powerful steam turbines. The needle the helmsman controlled shifted from "Ahead 1/3" to "Stop." Seconds later, the needle controlled by the engineers shifted to match.

"Conn. Helm. Maneuvering reports all stop."

Reynes nodded and turned. "Conn, aye. Sonar, info on the contact?"

"Faint, sir. Real faint. Behind us. Tail picked up something."

Key West's executive officer sidled up to the captain. "Come around?"

The captain thought for a moment, reviewing the tactical situation. He had the advantage. The *Kazan* could not stay on the surface forever.

Well, Reynes thought, he could, but it would be a damn miserable experience. Submarines were not made to sit on the surface in any weather. They certainly weren't built to sit on the roof in the middle of a winter storm.

Reynes looked at the XO and shook his head. "Not yet. We wait. If he was coming below the layer, we'd have him. He's just sitting up there, hoping to hell this all ends or we just go away."

That bothered Reynes. After the first slew of shots had been fired, he'd expected a message telling him to stand down while everyone talked this out. But he'd not gotten that message. There had been no declaration of war, not that he'd heard about. Surely, he wouldn't be allowed to continue prosecuting this target indefinitely.

The XO stretched and yawned. "Whatcha think, Skipper? Got a sniff of us?"

"They've been spending big on sonar upgrades. But they've been up there in all that noise while we've been sneaking around. Still…" Reynes turned. "Chief?"

A quiet growl. "He's just sitting up there."

The captain shot an inquisitive look at his second-in-command. "XO?"

"He's gonna have to drop down a bit to really look for us. Big concern is that tail of his. We assume it was out, right? If that's the case, it's possible it was hanging out down here listening." Sandler shrugged. "He's gotta be moving. Wouldn't wanna sit up there at all stop."

"Agree. We give it a few minutes and turn away. Open the distance before we turn back in. Passive search."

The executive officer grinned.

"Fuckin' hide-and-seek world champs."

K-561 *Kazan*
08 December 2022 | 1118 Local Time
Black Sea

Korov was in Sonar three seconds after ordering his submarine stopped. He'd not wanted to do that. A submarine sitting still on the surface in this weather was like a plaything in a child's bathtub. The submarine was rocking violently and Korov could see the effect the motion was having on the crew.

"Talk to me," he said to Belyaev.

"Captain, tail is above the layer." The sonar officer spoke in terse, clipped sentences, just like he'd been taught in school.

"And the contact, Belyaev? Where is the American?"

"Lost the contact, Captain."

The captain turned. "Bearing?"

"Uncertain, Captain. Best estimate is zero-one-zero."

"A submarine?"

"Can't confirm, Captain, but yes. That is my assumption." Belyaev paused. "Though the computer is not classifying the noise as a submarine."

Captain Korov lit a cigarette, his steel-gray eyes locked on the sonar display. It was a habit he'd been unable to break, despite his wife's pleas.

"What are you thinking?" The *Kazan*'s first officer spoke quietly.

"It has to be the American. No one else was out here before the shooting started, and ships do not generally walk into live fire areas for fun," Korov said.

The first officer was skeptical. "Captain, we don't even know that it was a legitimate contact. If the computer couldn't classify it, then it could be anything. Anything."

Korov took a last drag on his cigarette before crushing it out in a built-in ashtray. He nodded. "True Valeri. It could be anything. It could be a whale. It could be shrimp. It could be the water playing tricks with our systems. It could be a fucking unicorn! But it was none of those things. It was a submarine."

The first officer interrupted. "An American, Captain? Where did he come from?"

"Simple, Valeri. Despite what Moscow said, the Americans did have a submarine in the area, and I do not believe that whoever it is just went away after shooting. The Americans must be here somewhere. They know what we've done and their rules of engagement allow them to continue hunting us because of our attack on the destroyer. They can't not respond."

Korov was furious. He hated that his submarine had been found. That he'd been heard. He hated knowing that, even now, he was being actively hunted. He pointed at the sonar displays. "That contact stopped making noise when we changed depths. He heard us."

Being tracked. It's like admitting you're mortal. Flawed. You knew it was possible. But still…

Korov shuddered and turned away from the first officer. "Belyaev. Anything yet?"

"No, Captain. If it's a submarine, I think he's below the layer."

"What was the last bearing, again?"

"Approximately zero-one-zero Captain."

The captain turned to a young officer standing nearby. The man was pale as death. "Navigator, make your course one-eight-zero. Turns for five knots."

"Creep away and turn back in?" The first officer was nodding.

"Yes, Valeri."

DC Beltway
08 December 2022 | 0425 Local Time
Washington, DC

Harlan Alexander had no idea how long he'd been on the road, driving aimlessly through and around Washington. He had no idea where he was going, and the quarter-empty bottle of scotch whisky between his legs hadn't aided in his contemplation. He'd bought the bottle in the hope that the alcohol would calm his nerves and allow him time for thought as he meandered at speed through snarled DC traffic.

That plan, Harlan thought, had failed miserably. Despite the alcohol, he could feel his pulse racing, as if it were trying to outrun the car. Harlan was sweating profusely. He could feel the rivulets rolling down his neck and temples. A distant part of his brain tried to write that off to the heat in the car itself, but a quick glance at the temperature controls told him that this was a lie.

Where the hell do I go?

Harlan told himself that he just didn't know. He and his father had developed plans for this. Just in case. But try as he might, Harlan just couldn't remember any of the details.

Harlan changed lanes, one hand on the wheel and one hand holding the neck of the whisky bottle. An angry honking reminded him that he'd not used his turn signal and Harlan reproached himself. Police didn't usually pull folks in the area over for failure to signal, but it could happen. And if it did…

"Shit." Harlan lifted the bottle as high as he dared and tried to take a discreet swig of the brown liquor. The driver behind him chose that moment to swerve into the next lane and race by, honking madly and, Harlan presumed, middle finger waving wildly.

Harlan started. His body jerked at the noise and he spilled a portion of the whisky on his shirt and pants.

"Goddamnit!" He looked down at his lap and tried to shove the bottle into the center console cup holder.

He felt the Mercedes swerve and looked up to see two lines of brake lights illuminating in front of him as his car straddled two lanes of traffic.

Harlan stomped on the brakes and eased back into his own lane, swearing and praying the whole way.

The car slid to a merciful halt mere feet from the back of a conversion van with an advertisement for electrical services.

He blinked and tried to ease his grip on the wheel. Another honk made him turn to his left. In the vehicle beside him, two blue-haired ladies were glaring, each with a bony middle finger fully extended.

Harlan waved sheepishly at them, mouthed an apology, and turned his attention back inside his own vehicle.

"I need a place to go," he muttered.

As traffic began inching forward again, he racked his brain and tried to think. He looked at the map displayed on the car's console and cocked his head.

Harlan reached out and touched the icon to zoom out on the map. He did it again. And again. He looked at the area. Saw the dizzying array of green and yellow and red lines that covered the map between Baltimore and Washington.

Too many people, he thought. I need something different.

Smaller. Less populated.

He reached out again and used his finger to move the map display around. On impulse, he scrolled north until the traffic patterns disappeared from view.

Pennsylvania.

A small town, maybe?

Harlan thought about that for a moment. He looked at the road, inched forward a few more feet, and looked back at the map. He scrolled a few more times, found a nearly blank area just across the border and clicked on it, setting the destination.

As traffic began inching forward again, Harlan picked up the whisky and took another drink. He put the bottle back between his legs just as the onboard GPS system began announcing the first set of instructions to take him north.

To farm country, Harlan thought.

Why the hell not?

The Kremlin
08 December 2022 | 1133 Local Time
Moscow

Russian president Dmitri Mikhailovich Barsukov sat down behind his desk and looked at his SVR director.

"What in the hell happened and where is Admiral Borshevsky?"

"The admiral has been placed under arrest…" Tolstov began.

"What?" Barsukov's voice boomed. "Arrested by whom? Who gave that order?"

"I did, Mr. President."

"What the hell for?"

Tolstov cleared his throat. "Mr. President, the admiral is the least of our problems right now." He paused. "We have to assume that the Americans know everything. My assistant was seen walking into their embassy. He has no business there. He has never so much as approached that building before, much less entered it."

"What in the hell is he doing there?" Barsukov exploded.

Tolstov did not answer at first. He sat still and watched the president seethe. When he finally did speak, his voice was measured and calm. "He is trying to kill Nightingale, Mr. President."

Barsukov sat for a moment before speaking. "He found out what you've done? From Borshevsky?"

"I have to assume so, Mr. President," Tolstov said. "Nothing else makes sense. The only other people who knew were the doctor and the admiral."

"So, you had them both arrested?"

"The admiral, yes," Tolstov confirmed. "I have not arrested the doctor yet. He has disappeared. We are looking."

Barsukov leaned forward in his seat. "Now what, Igor Romanovich? This operation was supposed to scare off buyers in the Black Sea so that we would have the opportunity to purchase every available platform and make domestic governing so overwhelming for Evans that he could not gather the political backing to do anything about it. Now, I have lost one of our frigates, which, I remind you, may yet sink with several Americans on board, including their president's nephew. Our submarine in the area has attacked and crippled an American destroyer and is now in a life-and-death battle with an American submarine. A battle, Igor, that we've been unwilling to stop."

"Mr. President," Tolstov said, noting that the president had used the word 'unwilling,' not 'unable.' "We have met several parameters of the operation. We have introduced instability in the American public and we are, in most cases, the only remaining potential buyer for most of the target oil and gas platforms."

"Which means nothing, Igor Romanovich," Barsukov snapped. "Nothing."

"What do you mean?"

"Do you think that the American public will settle down when it comes out that we instigated everything? And if Shablikov tells them that he orchestrated the compromise of the senators, what happens then?" Barsukov shook his head gravely. "They will come after us. Economically. Politically. Maybe even militarily."

Tolstov thought for a moment. "Mr. President, I understand your concerns, but I do not think that you understand the American public as well as I do. Collectively, they are an uneducated rabble. Their herd mentality makes them, has always made them, predictable. True, they value information, but they are decidedly inept at validating what information they do get. On the whole, the American public tends to just read or listen and then accept. This is especially true on the fringes of their society, which is where the loudest voices exist."

"So, what is it you are saying? That nothing Shablikov can say will matter?"

"Exactly, Mr. President." Tolstov nodded. "The American left will latch onto his claims. The right will oppose such information as propaganda. It won't much matter what the facts are. Each side will pursue their version of the truth, or at least the truth that is most palatable to them."

"That's crazy." Barsukov stared at him incredulously.

"To our way of thinking, yes," Tolstov said. "But it is true even so."

"So, what are you telling me?" Barsukov asked.

"I am telling you that all is not lost. The American public is broken. They are vulnerable. We have found something that we can use in the near future. Something that might be more valuable than oil or gas. We have found a way to crucify the Americans. To turn them on each other with a vehemence they've not felt for almost two hundred years. We can create a civil war in the United States."

Barsukov swallowed. Hard. He shook his head. "No. This needs to stop. I am—"

Tolstov's thin smile stopped Barsukov cold.

"What?"

"You were going to say that you are ordering me to stop. Yes?"

Barsukov nodded. "Yes."

"No." Tolstov stood.

"No?" Barsukov began to stand out of his own chair. "No? Just who do you think you are?"

Tolstov leaned forward, his thin smile twisting, morphing into something more dangerous. "I am the man who put you in that seat, who elevated you to the presidency."

Barsukov felt his blood run cold, felt his legs weaken. "What are you saying? What is this madness?"

"Your predecessor had a similar opportunity to the situation I have presented to you. And he declined. He lacked the guts to go through with it. He lacked the ambition. He was a coward. And I rid myself of him."

"What…but he died of a…?"

Tolstov walked to the door and set his hand on the knob. Before leaving, he turned back to the president. "Do you really believe that your predecessor suffered a massive heart attack? You knew him quite well. Tell me, Dmitri, does that seem likely in his case?"

Tolstov opened the door and left the room.

Barsukov began shaking uncontrollably.

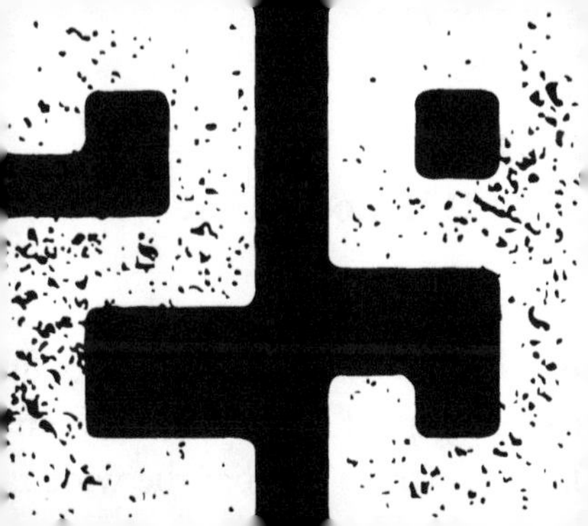

**USS *James E. Williams*
08 December 2022 | 1135 Local Time
Black Sea**

Brian watched in fascination as warning lights flashed. He heard the sirens and the yelling of sailors as they attempted to pass information back and forth to combat the wide range of damage. Brian tried to keep track of it all. The engines were all down hard. The shock of the explosion had finally killed the last remaining propulsion engine only moments before the ship's generators had also failed, plunging the ship into an eerie darkness.

Brian had assumed that the generators had simply tripped because of the vibrations induced by the explosion, but Petty Officer Becker was having no success restarting any of the units and she'd spent the last ten minutes reading through a growing list of faults. Brian watched the young petty officer work, trying to clear what she could remotely and scribbling written instructions for messengers to take to the various space watches in an effort to restore at least one of the units to operating status.

"Chief?"

Brian blinked and turned his head to see Becker looking at him. "Yeah?"

"This goes quicker if I run down there myself." She waved a hand at the console. "I can stop by Repair Five and pick up some help, if that's okay."

Brian nodded. "Give me a sec."

He turned and walked the four steps to where the DCA and several sailors were conversing and marking up the ship's damage control boards, tracking the status of each issue the ship was currently fighting. Brian let his eyes trace over the boards. He saw several fires annotated, mostly alpha ones. There were more than twenty reports of flooding, including, Brian saw, what appeared to be a re-opening of the hull fracture just forward of Central Control that was dumping more than forty gallons per minute into the *Williams*'s starboard-side passageway. There was an annotation listed on that casualty that indicated five inches of water on the deck and rising.

Brian tapped the DCA on the shoulder. When she turned, Brian could see the stress on her face and immediately felt guilty about possibly adding to it.

"Ma'am, I need two of my folks from Repair Five to help Becker get the generators online."

The DCA nodded, glancing at the charts behind her. She paused for a moment before turning back. "Take who you need, check them out with the locker officer and locker leader. Working in the dark blows."

"Thanks." Brian turned back to Becker and relayed the instructions. "I've got the console."

After Becker left, Brian turned his attention to the ship's lack of propulsion.

USS *Key West*
08 December 2022 | 1140 Local Time
Black Sea

Commander Reynes stared at the bulkhead, eyes scanning *Key West*'s massive array of gauges and dials, taking in everything without really seeing it. His mind was still in Sonar.

"Talk to me, Chief."

"Nothing, sir. Just the faint creaking and popping," Hughley reported. "Never heard plant or screw noises."

"Best guess, Chief?"

"He came down a bit from the surface, Cap'n. Probably trying to ease the ride a bit."

Lieutenant Commander Will Sandler entered the small space and stood next to the captain, mumbling almost to himself. "Surface capture. Don't know if that's smart or not."

Reynes turned. He could feel the butterflies kicking around, could feel the adrenaline pumping. "Explain."

"Well, Captain, if he stays up there, it makes him damn hard to find. He's covered by a thermocline layer from below and all the damn noise the surface is making with that storm topside. Either way, our sonar won't hear shit. But neither will his."

The captain raised an eyebrow. "And?"

A shrug. "And, if he heard us, he's long gone by now. I would be. The ride up there might suck a little more, but he could be twenty thousand yards away by now. Maybe more."

"And do you think he stayed up there because he heard us?"

The executive officer shook his head. "I don't know. He had to go up to avoid the fish. After that, who knows. Maybe he heard us and decided to stay hidden up there. Maybe he's just staying up to catch message traffic or some shit. But that doesn't seem likely. Doesn't much matter either way. He's up there. Or was. And if he's still there, he's tucked away in a nice little soundproof envelope."

Commander Reynes nodded. "Ideas?"

"We could sneak up there. Surprise the shit out of him."

Reynes thought for a moment, trying to recall the capabilities of the Russian sonar tails. "We could. As long as his tail is up there with him. If he's still trolling beneath the layer, he'll hear us creaking on the way up."

"True." The executive officer paused. "Ain't war grand?"

The captain chuckled and glanced at the executive officer, wondering if anything ever bothered him. "Enjoying yourself, XO?"

A shake of the head. "Not really. But being angry all the time was gonna kill me."

"I heard something like that from my wife before we left."

"My ex-wife told me that."

Reynes raised an eyebrow again. The XO had suffered through two divorces, both amicable. Submarine life tended to be hard on families. "Which one?"

"Both, actually."

The captain chuckled again and turned. "Sonar?"

"Nothing new, sir. Just whales and fish and a whole shitpot full of surface noise," Hughley said.

"Thanks, Chief. Keep listening."

"Yes, sir."

The captain turned back to the executive officer. "You're gonna command one of these boats soon. Suggestions?"

"MOSS."

"MOSS?" Reynes smiled. Mobile Submarine Simulator. Effectively a Mark 48 torpedo with a sound transducer instead of a warhead.

The XO knew his shit. No question. A bit aggressive. But what young submarine officer wasn't? Attack boat officers were supposed to be aggressive, especially if they wanted command of their own submarine. What was the old toast? To sickly seasons and bloody wars. Two sure routes to promotion.

"Sure, boss. We program one of the simulators to sound like us at, say, five or six knots, kick it out of tube four, and set it to run up above the layer."

"Lure him back down below the layer where we can track him? Not bad, XO." The captain thought for a few seconds. "Better make it twelve knots. We don't want to be obvious, but we want him to hear it. Set it up to break the layer on the other side of the contact."

The captain called to Sonar. "Chief. Distance to contact?"

"Best guess is ten thousand yards, Cap'n," Hughley reported. "That's iffy, though."

"Thanks, Chief." Reynes looked back at Sandler. "XO?"

"Sir?"

"Set up the MOSS. Have it run out twelve thousand yards on the last known bearing before it goes shallow. I want that simulator on the other side of the contact before it starts radiating. Make damn certain it sounds like us on a search pattern."

"Got it." The executive officer grinned.

"Get to work, XO," Reynes commanded.

**K-561 *Kazan*
08 December 2022 | 1146 Local Time
Black Sea**

Captain Korov was losing his temper. He could feel his face flushing, but kept his voice under control. Barely. "Goddamnit, Sonar! Where the hell did he go?"

"I don't know, Captain. We're deaf up here. The heavy seas are interfering with our systems, and nothing is penetrating the layer."

The first officer approached, whispering, "Captain, stream the tail below the layer. If that contact was an American submarine, we might catch wind of it that way."

Mikhail Gregorovich Alexandrov spoke. Anger was evident in his voice. "Why do you both persist in this? For that to have been an American submarine, at the location you say, means that he would have been tracking us."

Korov turned. He wanted to strike the man in front of him. To plow his fist into the man's fat, ignorant face. He growled instead. "Your point?"

"This boat cannot be tracked! It is technically superior to anything the Americans have. It is—"

"Spare me the rhetoric, Alexandrov. This boat can be tracked. Our own sonar systems can find it. Our own ships have found it. Three times on trials alone, and two more times since joining the fleet."

Not since I have been the captain.

"But those are our systems. Our ships! We know how. They don't. The Americans cannot compete with our…" The political officer was pointing now, gesturing at the world outside the *Kazan*'s pressure hull.

The captain raised his hand, stopping the political officer cold. He didn't have time for this. "Alexandrov. Do you know where we got the data to build this technological marvel?"

"From our scientists and engineers. Where else?"

"And do you know where they got their information? Where did they get the fundamental design data behind the new sonar systems? The new coolant pumps? Do you know that?"

"From our intelligence services, of course."

"And, Alexandrov, has that addled mind of yours ever wondered why a spy agency is giving engineers such data?" Korov scanned the *Kazan*'s control room, running his eyes over the displays.

"They have scientific sections. Research and Development. Obviously."

The captain turned from the gauge board, faced the political officer. "Are you serious?"

Alexandrov looked baffled. Korov stepped closer, his face inches from the other man's nose. "The data used to build this boat was developed from the American Los Angeles class," he growled, "a design that is older than every single sailor on this whole goddamned boat."

Alexandrov's mouth flapped open and shut, his eyes wide. "That's... That's...."

"That's?"

"That's not true."

"Yes, it is, you whelp! Your precious spies stole an obsolete American design and we used it to build this. Yes, we improved the technology. But they have too. They've been improving that design for more than three decades now. The advantages you speak of do not exist. Whoever it is out there is at least our equal. This submarine is not invincible. It can be found. By anyone with the skill to look." Korov paused.

You sound defeatist, Ivan Sergeyevich. In front of a political rat. Fix it. Or don't.

Korov forced himself to calm down. "Now, Mikhail Gregorovich, I have a submarine to find. You are dismissed."

Alexandrov's face flushed as he left the attack center.

The first officer whispered, "Captain, is that true? That we stole obsolete data from—"

"Of course it's true. This boat's original design was obsolete before idiots like that decided to build it."

The first officer considered that and then returned to the problem at hand. "Captain, the tail?"

"Make it so."

The White House
08 December 2022 | 0455 Local Time
Washington, DC

"I'm sorry, Mr. President," the executive secretary said. "They're saying that President Barsukov is unavailable at the moment."

Daniel Evans looked up from the speakerphone on his desk and cocked his head. He spoke while staring at the staffers in the room with him. "Did they say when he'd be available?"

"No, Mr. President."

Evans blinked. "Thank you." He punched the button to end the call. "We've got two surface ships damaged and two submarines running around trying to kill each other off, mostly because the Russian boat keeps launching fish. I can't get the Russian to stop, and I'm not going to tell *Key West* she can't defend herself. The only way to prevent the loss of either sub is to talk to the Russians and I can't get Barsukov on the phone. What's he playing at?"

DNI Adams spoke first. "Depends. He has to know, or at least suspect, what Shablikov has told us. If those claims are true, and he's not taking calls..." Adams shook her head. "Maybe there's something we don't know. Something that is enabling him to think that whatever we know doesn't really matter."

"What do you mean?" Chief of Staff Barnes asked. "How can he possibly think that none of this matters?"

"Leslie." Ophelia turned, holding up the transcript of Shablikov's interview. "This is all hearsay."

"What?" Evans said, glancing down at his own copy.

Adams looked around at everyone in the room. "Gentlemen, all this is, right now, is the testimony of an angry man. It's he-said, he-said, on an epic scale." She paused. "But there is no hard proof.

Sure, Shablikov provided a highly detailed sketch of everything. Dates. Times. Locations. Even the address of the cyber warfare facility. But it is still the word of an angry man against that of the Russian government."

"Are you saying they can just pretend that this man is pissed and lying?" Barnes asked. "Couldn't we track down the servers used? Wouldn't that corroborate part of this?"

Adams shook her head. "Theoretically, yes. Tracing was the first thing I ordered before I delivered this information. But it's highly probable that that facility is already being shut down and dismantled. That probably happened as soon as the Russians found out Shablikov waltzed into our embassy."

"So, they just unplug everything and that's it?" Evans asked. "Aren't there historical records of IP addresses or something?"

Adams nodded at that. "That's true, but proving this without the actual servers, being able to point to exactly who did these things and then linking Barsukov and, probably, the SVR to the op is like trying to prove murder without a body. There will always be doubt, even among folks who are highly skilled programmers."

Evans lifted his head, looking up from the report. "What's that mean?"

"Mr. President," Adams said. "Do you know how to program or code?"

"No." Evans shook his head.

"If you weren't the president and I told you this story, you'd either believe me or not. In either case, if I attempted to provide you proof, would you necessarily believe it? Would you even understand what I was showing you?"

Evans considered that for a moment, frowning.

"You're saying that they'll just claim we made all this up?" Barnes asked, catching on. "That we doctored this information to implicate Barsukov and the SVR?"

"It's what I would do," Adams said.

"But Americans wouldn't…" Barnes stopped himself. "Sonofabitch."

"What?" Evans asked.

"That's it," Barnes said, turning to Adams. "Isn't it? It's that simple."

"What's that simple?" Evans asked, still lost.

Barnes pointed at the report on the Resolute Desk. "Mr. President, this Shablikov fellow claims that the purpose of the operation on this side was to erode public and congressional support for you. They wanted to inhibit your ability to get things done. To make it so damn hard to do your job at home that the mere thought of interfering in Russian purchases of Black Sea rigs would be either impossible or, at least, way off the radar."

Evans looked from Barnes, to the report, and back at Barnes. He blinked.

"Mr. President," Barnes said. "Americans will believe the Russian side of this story. Some of them, anyway. Enough to make your life miserable."

"But this is nuts, Leslie," Evans protested. "They can't possibly…"

"Why not, Daniel?" Barnes asked. "Over the last couple of years, the American public has demonstrated an alarming tendency to believe wild and crazy stuff. Hell, sir, a goodly portion of the nation convinced themselves that the coronavirus wasn't real or that it was something the political left and NSA made up so that we could stick folks with vaccines loaded with tracking devices."

Evans frowned again and Barnes continued. "Think about it, Daniel. Over the last couple of years, near-irreparable divisions have erupted in the voting public. Things that that report says the Russians exacerbated over the last few weeks. All of which has one very specific impact on American politics."

Evans thought for a moment. His eyes traced from the report to the faces of Barnes and Adams and back. When he finally spoke, his voice was low and quiet. Almost a whisper.

"It's about trust," Evans said. "They used existing problems to erode trust. I can tell our side of this story and the only people who will believe it are the folks who still trust this office. Everyone else will hear it and look elsewhere for answers." Evans jabbed a finger at the report. "And these bastards have proven that they can influence some of those sources." He took a deep breath and exhaled, confronting a new reality. "They broke us, didn't they?"

"They have corrupted how the American public thinks, Mr. President," Barnes said. "You are not going to spend the rest of your presidency in a world that can easily be separated into truth and fiction. Those are ideal concepts that are becoming irrelevant. You will have to navigate a political universe that is based on beliefs and emotions and opinions. You may know the truth, but from now on, facts will be less important to voters than a perception-driven tribalism."

Evans grimaced. For a man who'd dealt largely in hard data and verifiable information for his entire adult life, that was a huge idea to absorb.

"What do we do first?"

Highway 45 North
08 December 2022 | 0501 Local Time
Maryland-Pennsylvania Border

Harlan Alexander followed the directions dictated by the soft, computerized female voice from the car's GPS and turned off the freeway onto one of the many country highways crossing north into Pennsylvania. The road, he saw, was surprisingly clear of snow and ice, and as he merged from the entrance ramp, Harlan edged the speed of his vehicle up a few miles per hour above the posted limit of fifty-five.

He'd tried dialing his father's cell phone three more times in the past forty minutes and had received the same message each time. The number he was trying to reach was no longer in service.

And the phone, Harlan finally admitted to himself, was

probably lying at the bottom of the Patuxent River.

"Shit," Harlan muttered.

He grabbed the bottle of liquor and took a quick swig before using the buttons on the steering wheel to bump the speed up closer to seventy.

38

**USS *Key West*
08 December 2022 | 1208 Local Time
Black Sea**

"Captain, MOSS is ready in all respects." The executive officer was smiling.
But it's a nervous smile. He must be nervous. I am.
Reynes thought about that and considered his next action. Launching a simulator was a risk, but it was a manageable one.
Launching anything from a torpedo tube would generate a mechanical transient. It would make noise that a submarine could theoretically hear. If that happened, this plan would go to shit immediately and it was entirely within the realm of possibility that the Russian skipper would fire a snapshot before trying to evade. But if the Russian boat was still up in the surface capture, the chances of him hearing the launch would drop precipitously. In that event, the next thing the Russian heard would be the simulated sound of the *Key West* sneaking around at twelve knots. After that…
He's left with two choices. Chase it. Works in my favor. Ignore it. Which means they'll know we're here somewhere.
Reynes made his decision. "Weps, open outer door. Flood tube four."
A pause, then near-silence as the order was relayed in whispers. Confirmation came quickly.
"Outer door open. Tube flooded."
Reynes nodded. "Fire tube four."

"Fire tube four, aye."

The submarine shuddered as the MOSS was ejected from the ship and began its run.

The report came quickly. "Tube four fired. MOSS normal in all respects."

"Close outer door." Reynes turned. "XO?"

"Sir?"

"I want tube four loaded with another ADCAP."

"Yes, sir."

The executive officer turned to relay the order to the torpedo room. The captain went back to staring at the tactical plot. His eyes traced the chart, calculating and measuring. He turned and called over his shoulder.

"Sonar?"

"Sir?"

"Estimated run time on the MOSS?"

"Just over eight minutes Cap'n," Hughley reported.

"Thank you, Chief."

Reynes glanced at his watch as the executive officer returned. "Captain, about five minutes to reload tube four."

Reynes nodded his acknowledgment. "Get the ship into position, XO."

A curt nod. "Yes, sir."

K-561 *Kazan*
08 December 2022 | 1210 Local Time
Black Sea

Korov was furious. He'd lost the contact, if he'd ever had it, and now his sonar officer was giving him more bad news.

"The tail will not deploy, Captain."

"I heard you the first time. Why not?" Korov growled into his handset. He knew it was unfair to snarl at the man, but he needed to growl at someone.

"I don't know, Captain," Belyaev responded.

The first officer stepped in, his voice calm and quiet. "Captain, with your permission, I will help Yevgeni Stepanovich troubleshoot the tail."

Korov turned on the first officer. "I need that tail working, Valeri. Now."

"I'll handle it, Captain."

The first officer walked away as Korov spoke into the phone, calmer now, but not by much. "Sonar, the first officer is on his way to assist you. I need that tail. I need information."

"Yes, Captain. We are working on it."

"Is there anything else you can tell me?" Korov asked.

"No, Captain. The surface noise is still playing hell with our systems."

"Very well, Yevgeni. Report back in two minutes."

USS *James E. Williams*
08 December 2022 | 1212 Local Time
Black Sea

Brian Thompson hovered over the electric plant console and scanned the three handwritten notes he'd just been given. Each piece of paper contained a short list of issues that prevented the generators from starting. Generator number two had the fewest problems, but Becker had noted that two of the five issues were not easily repairable. Generators one and three had similar numbers of problems, but Becker was reporting that three would be the easiest and fastest repair. He considered the lists and looked up at the messenger.

"Is she sure?"

"Seems so, Chief."

Brian nodded. "Tell her to hit up number three first. If she needs parts, let me know as soon as possible."

"Roger that, Chief." The messenger turned on his heels and left the space, heading up through the hatch in the overhead because the starboard-side flooding was almost knee-deep outside the door to Central.

Brian watched the sailor leave and turned to where the DCA was still working through the thirty-odd casualties that were threatening the ship. As she worked, Brian scanned the charts again.

Two of the fires had spread and two more were threatening to. Smoke had forced the evacuation of several compartments, and the flooding along the starboard passageway was within inches of forcing all of Repair Five to relocate somewhere other than the mess decks.

"Chief." The DCA had grabbed Brian's arm. "Chief?"

Brian blinked. "Yeah?"

"I need power, Chief." She began pointing at the diagrams. "Without power, I have nothing but CO_2 bottles to fight fires with. We also can't de-smoke these compartments or recharge the SCBA bottles."

Brian swore to himself. He'd forgotten about that. The ship had a limited number of bottles. Until power was restored, there was no way to replenish each bottle's air supply. If they ran out of bottles with fires raging out of control…

"Becker is working on it," Brian said. "I don't know how long."

The DCA looked at the charts and back at Brian. "We're gonna start losing spaces fast if something doesn't change." She pointed. "These two fires have already spread. This one is in four spaces now. This one isn't far behind."

"What about the flooding?" Brian asked.

"They've got a box patch in place on the hull fracture. Down to maybe five gallons per minute. We have a bucket brigade out through the hangar and the deck drains are open. It's manageable unless that crack gets bigger. With the way we're getting thrown around, that's a distinct possibility."

Brian's eyes lit up. "Can you get to both ends of the crack?"

"What?"

Brian's mind raced. "I need one of the machinists from Repair Five."

"Which one?"

"Doesn't matter. Have them meet me at the box patch." Brian pointed at the space's aft door. "I need to go through there. It's gonna let in water…"

The DCA pointed at two sailors. "You two. Make damn certain that door shuts after Chief leaves."

The pair nodded and moved to the door with Brian. He pointed at the taller one. "I want you to open the door, let me through, and slam it shut behind me." Brian pointed at the shorter one. "You help him shut it. Shouldn't be hard. Just make sure it's shut tight."

Brian got a pair of nods and moved to the side so the door could be opened. He looked at both sailors.

"On three?"

Highway 45 North
08 December 2022 | 0513 Local Time
Pennsylvania

Harlan Alexander glared at the bottle in his right hand, still steering with his left. It took a few moments for him to realize that he'd consumed the entire bottle.

Not the whole bottle, he corrected himself. You did spill some all over yourself. Twice.

That he'd not driven completely off the road or been pulled over yet was something just shy of miraculous. He knew he was swerving. With his vision slightly blurred, he'd ventured across the centerline and onto the rough gravel shoulder of the back roads more times than he could count. If anyone had seen him, especially a cop, he'd have been flagged immediately. But he hadn't been seen. In truth, he'd not seen a car, a person, or even a light since he'd crossed into Pennsylvania.

Harlan wasn't quite sure where he was. His mind had started wandering, shifting from topic to topic almost as quickly as the Mercedes shifted up and down through the gears. He'd thought about what he'd done. His father. Food. Whatever song had been playing. Fantastical arguments justifying his actions. His intoxicated brain had hummed along, skipping around until he'd become aware that the GPS system was admonishing him for missing several turns. He'd turned the destination directions off at that point, choosing to just meander while occasionally checking to see that the dash's compass display indicated that he was still moving roughly north.

Harlan tossed the bottle onto the passenger seat, not really caring if whatever remnants might be left dribbled out onto the immaculate leather. He returned his right hand to the wheel and checked the road just in time to maneuver around a curve at more than twice the legal speed limit. A song began that he didn't particularly care for, and Harlan looked down at the center console, searching for the icon on the touch screen that would skip the track.

While he was fiddling with the playlist, Harlan missed two signs. The first would have welcomed him to New Freedom, Pennsylvania. The second would have told him of a slight curve in the road ahead with a warning to lower his speed to twenty-five miles per hour.

Harlan skipped the song and raised his eyes to the windshield in time to see the road veering away to the left and a large, darkened structure looming in his dimly lit path. His right foot moved to slam on the brake and his hand yanked hard left on the wheel, over-correcting and sending the Mercedes too far left as the car tried to decelerate.

Harlan and his car slammed into a stout brick wall at more than forty miles per hour. When the airbag exploded in Harlan's face, he saw stars for a split second before his world went dark.

USS *James E. Williams*
08 December 2022 | 1214 Local Time
Black Sea

Brian Thompson waded through freezing water that was at least calf deep. He felt it soaking up the legs of his coveralls and running down inside his boots. He moved outboard from Central Control and turned to his left, heading forward for thirty feet to join the group of sailors struggling to contain the leaking hull fracture.

In the dim light of several handheld flashlights and battle lanterns, Brian could see the box patch and noted that the sailors had erected mechanical shoring to hold the patch in place. He saw the water still streaming in from the portions of the crack that were uncovered by the bulky repair patch.

"Where's the team lead?"

"Here, Chief." A sailor waved a flashlight.

Brian leaned closer, fighting to be heard in the chaos of repair work and dewatering. "Is it getting worse?"

The sailor nodded in the dark and gestured with the flashlight. "It was contained before. The whole crack was covered by the box. Those last two rolls…"

Another sailor, this one wearing red coveralls, walked up, sloshing through the cold water and cursing. "Chief? I was told you wanted to see me?"

Brian turned to one of the sailors nearby and grabbed his battle lantern. He pointed it at the crack. "Do we have anything that can drill through the hull?"

The machinist leaned closer, pushing two others out of his way. "Without power? Hell, Chief. I don't know."

"This crack's gonna keep getting worse in these seas. We need to find a way to drill both ends. The crack can't expand after that. Not easily, anyway."

The sailor shook his head. "Without electricity, I just don't know, Chief. Lemme see what I can come up with."

Brian patted the sailor on the shoulder. "Grab whoever you need for this. Clear it with the locker officer." Brian turned to head back to Central.

"Where are you going?"

"To see what I can do to get power restored."

USS *Key West*
08 December 2022 | 1214 Local Time
Black Sea

Commander Reynes turned to see the executive officer approaching.

"Captain, we are in position."

Reynes nodded. "Thank you, XO. Tracking party ready?"

"They are."

"Good." Reynes turned and called over his shoulder. "Sonar?"

"Sir?"

"Run time left before the MOSS goes active?"

"Three minutes, seven seconds sir," Hughley said.

The captain looked around. No one was watching him. Each sailor was focused on his or her task.

Professionals. Experts.

He smiled and reached for the breast pocket of his coveralls. The executive officer noticed the gesture. "Thought you quit."

"I did." Reynes grinned sheepishly. "Last year. Seems like time for a smoke, though."

"I won't disagree. But you decided it was a smoke-free boat," Sandler chided.

Reynes glanced sideways at the executive officer. "Thanks for reminding me."

"No problem," Sandler said. "Part of the job, boss."

"Jackass."

The executive officer laughed, reached into his own pocket. A pack of cigarettes and a lighter appeared. He smiled. "You should be nice. I have smokes."

"Asshole."

"That's better, Captain."

Reynes turned to the executive officer, an eyebrow arched. "Wait a second. If I ordered a smoke-free ship, why do you carry smokes?"

A shrug. "Well, I usually save them for port visits."

"And you have them now because?" Reynes asked.

"Call it a hunch, Skipper. Figured that order might get rescinded soon. We're a ship of war, in a shooting match with another submarine. Smokes go with the territory. Fits the image."

"Like all the movies where the commander calmly lights up before launching the torpedoes? Attack center full of haze?"

"Something like that." Sandler nodded.

The captain shook his head, turned. "Sonar. Run time remaining?"

"Ninety seconds, Cap'n."

Ninety seconds. A minute and a half. And then what? If they're there. And if they bite. You shoot. Right? And send a hundred Russian sailors to Davy Jones? Can you do that? Can you kill a hundred people?

Reynes looked around at his crew again. Saw the young faces. Thought of their families and friends and loved ones.

Can you do it, Scott? Can you pull the trigger on a hundred souls?

Reynes looked around again. He saw a few faces glance his way. Remembered that the Russian boat had already hit one American warship and had sure as hell tried to put a fish into his command. He thought about the question again.

Can you shoot at and sink a Russian warship and live with yourself?

Reynes smiled grimly.

Goddamn right, I can.

Reynes turned back to the executive officer. "Give me a cigarette, you jackass. Lamp is lit."

K-561 *Kazan*
08 December 2022 | 1215 Local Time
Black Sea

Korov gripped the handset so tight his knuckles went white. The voice on the other end was shaking and nervous. "No luck, Captain. Tail is out of commission. We've run diagnostics. Nothing. Likely a problem with the winch. A ruptured seal that shorted out the motor."

Korov struggled to keep his anger in check. "Tell the first officer to get back up here."

"Yes, Captain."

Korov hung up the phone. Nothing was going right. He couldn't risk going below the layer until he knew what was down there. He couldn't find out what was there because the tail had malfunctioned. That and the fact that the rest of his sonar system could hear only the crashing and rolling of the sea above him. To top it all off, the political officer was back, sitting in the corner with a notebook and documenting everything for some report to Moscow.

Korov glared at the short, fat, balding man and, for the first time, noted the sheer size of the man's waistline. A distant part of his mind wondered how in the hell he'd fit through the submarine's access hatches.

Not now, Ivan Sergeyevich. Not now.

Korov turned back to his consoles. "Fuck."

"Sir?"

The captain turned, saw the first officer approaching. "Nothing."

"Captain, if we cannot change depth and we cannot hear, might we be able to creep away?" the first officer offered.

"Creep away?" Korov was thinking through his options. He didn't like the sound of that one.

"Yes, Captain. If we can't hear the American, he can't hear us. We use the surface capture to increase speed and move. We can put forty thousand yards behind us in no time, even in this sea."

He gestured at the rolling hull, at the sailors rocking back and forth in a steady, disconcerting rhythm.

"We can't do that. We have orders to remain here. What if we leave and the American has orders to finish off the *Makarov*?" Korov shook his head. "No, Valeri, we cannot leave. We have a mission. We need a break."

"Captain, we cannot plan for such things."

"I know. We wait here. Fifteen minutes. Then, if we hear nothing, we work our way below the layer. Slowly. Quietly."

"He might hear us."

"Might? No." Korov shook his head. "He will hear us. Any sonar officer fresh from training can hear hull popping. We have no other choice. We must find him."

The first officer nodded. "Your orders, Captain?"

"Make sure battle stations are manned and ready and the tubes are loaded."

"Yes, Captain."

Intersection—Main Street and Southwood Road
08 December 2022 | 0516 Local Time
New Freedom, PA

Harlan Alexander's eyes snapped open, and his brain registered its first coherent thought in more than a minute.

Fucking Mondays.

The thought rampaged through Harlan's mind. The notion, and the rage that came with it, wasn't the result of Harlan's normal thought process. It was a knee-jerk reaction—the instinctual response of his subconscious to the stimuli around him.

His brain wandered through his life's recent events and marveled at all of it. Until today, everything he'd ever done had been regimented. Even, to a certain extent, his spying. But today, beginning with the phone call from his father, had been a wholly different experience.

He'd flown by the seat of his pants for the first time since high school. He'd obeyed whatever decision his gut made, his shitty instincts—and the alcohol, he admitted—digging him deeper and deeper into trouble even as his brain screamed for the lunacy to stop. Blaming this on a fucked-up case of the Mondays was pure instinct, and, like every other instinct he'd had today, this one was dead fucking wrong.

Mostly because it wasn't Monday.

It was just the long parade of I-can't-believe-that-shit-just-happened kind of events Harlan had endured over the past few hours that made it seem like a Monday. One never-ending shitstorm of a day.

Harlan's thin hands clutched the steering wheel, a bony, white-knuckled death-grip that was only one of the visible indications that this day had well and truly gone to hell in a handbasket.

Harlan's arms were tense, muscles flexed against an impact that was already more than a minute in the past. Those tense arms, the sinew and tendons pressing through the thin layer of fat and skin, connected to Harlan's taut shoulders and strained neck—each of which were also still braced to protect against the massive physical forces that the immutable laws of science mandated to be present when a two-thousand-pound car collides with a ninety-thousand-pound building at nearly double the posted speed limit.

Ninety seconds after impact, the first audible word escaped from Harlan's clenched jaw, falling onto the semi-deflated airbag, which drooped from the steering column like the world's most depressing birthday balloon. That the damn thing hadn't blown his arms to the sides, dislocating them in the process, surprised him, but only for the fleeting nanosecond it took for the thought to form and dissipate.

"Fuuuck."

Harlan stared straight ahead through the spiderwebbed windshield of what had been, until around two minutes ago, a moderately expensive sports car. The hood, normally a smooth, white sheet of pressed metal, was folded and creased at various angles, driven up and back into his field of view like some weird mountain-scape diorama. Wisps of steam, coming from whatever was left of his radiator, drifted up and evaporated into an ungodly cold sky that was threatening to shit another round of snow that the forecast had been calling for.

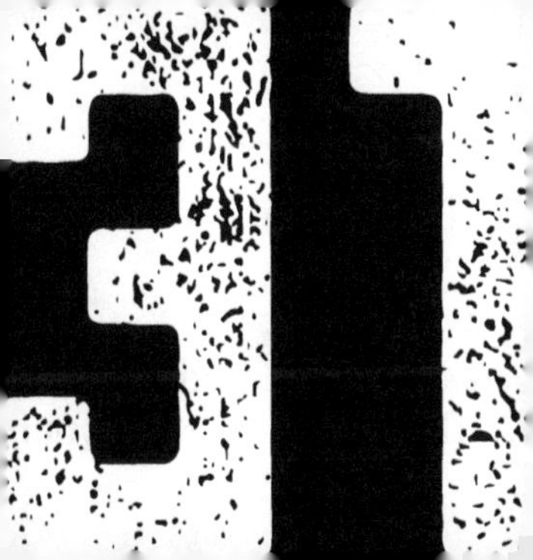

**USS *Key West*
08 December 2022 | 1218 Local Time
Black Sea**

"MOSS just went active, Cap'n. Heading up through the layer."
    Reynes nodded. "Thanks, Chief. Keep your ears open."
    "Always, Cap'n."
    "XO."
    "Sir?"
    "We ready?"
    "Yes, sir. Tubes one through four loaded with ADCAPs, tracking party standing by, battle stations manned."
    Reynes nodded. "All stop."
    The order was passed. The helmsman answered, rotating the engine order telegraph to the correct position.
    "All stop, aye."
    The telegraph clicked as the engine room answered the order. The helmsman spoke again.
    "Engine room answers all stop."
    The captain looked around. Every face was set. Jaws clenched. "Breathe, folks."

**K-561
08 December 2022 | 1219 Local Time
Black Sea**

Korov's head snapped around. The sonar officer's voice was crisp and clear. "Captain, sonar contact. Steam plant noises and propeller noises. Bearing two-zero-zero."

The captain smiled, spoke quickly. "Sonar. Distance to contact?"

"Two thousand yards and opening, Captain."

"Speed?"

"Blade rate indicates turns for twelve knots."

The captain turned to his first officer; a grin plastered across his face. "A break, my friend. The American was impatient and came up for a look."

The first officer looked up from the tactical plot. "He's behind us, Captain. And moving away quickly."

"That he is. New course one-nine-five. Make turns for fourteen knots."

"Yes, Captain."

USS *James E. Williams*
08 December 2022 | 1222 Local Time
Black Sea

Brian had been shivering for a few minutes and had begun pacing back and forth in Central in an effort to keep himself warm. Normally, without power to run the ship's five air conditioning plants and sprawling ventilation systems, a dark ship would slowly grow warmer and warmer, eventually reaching the point where it felt like you were trying to live and work inside an Easy-Bake Oven.

But not here. Not during a winter in the Black Sea. It was cold as hell outside and that chill was creeping into the ship.

Something else to worry about, Brian thought as he turned to examine the status of damage control efforts.

The newest updates to the boards and charts showed that four fires were now out of control and one that had been thought to be out had re-flashed and was now threatening the starboard side of the *Williams*'s Combat Information Center.

Between the fires and smoke, there were now more than fifty compartments on the ship that were inaccessible, and, unless something changed, that number would continue to grow.

This, thought Brian, is how you lose an entire ship. Not one big problem, but hundreds of smaller ones that piled on top of each other until the abilities of the crew and the capacities of the ship's damage control systems were so overwhelmed that nothing else could be done.

Thankfully, Brian thought, these damn ships were built with a lot of damage control capacity.

His eyes traced to the ship's clinometer and he watched the bubble swing wildly as the ship was tossed back and forth, trying to gauge the mid-point, attempting to determine the list caused by the flooding issues on the starboard side.

A degree maybe. Two?

"Chief?"

Brian felt a tap on his shoulder and turned. A messenger shoved a note into his hands and Brian opened it. He looked up.

"Two minutes?"

"That's what Becker says, Chief. Two more minutes to reset everything. She said the damage wasn't nearly as bad as she'd thought."

Brian handed the note back to the messenger. "Take this to the skipper. He should still be in Combat."

The sailor nodded, folded the note away, and headed for the escape hatch. Brian relayed the information to the DCA before taking a seat at the electric plant control console and pulling out the procedure for generator start-up.

Intersection—Main Street and Southwood Road
08 December 2022 | 0525 Local Time
New Freedom, PA

Harlan was still staring forward when a knock six inches from his ear shattered the silence. Without peeling his grip from the wheel, he turned his head.

There was a man there. Harlan could make out the vague outline of a face staring through the steamed-up, and intact, driver-side window. The mouth on the figure appeared to be moving, but Harlan couldn't hear anything but his own pulse—the sound of his adrenaline-fueled heart pounding away echoing through his skull.

The dull booming in his ears continued for what seemed like an eternity as his body processed the fight-or-flight chemical—trying to ease him back into the normal flow of time. Harlan's hearing returned, slowly, as his body began to register the aches and pains commensurate with a fifty-mile-per-hour collision.

"Hey buddy. You 'kay?" The voice was muffled and soft.

Harlan stared at the man, his brain chewing on the words, searching through a lifetime of collected vocabulary for the appropriate response.

"You 'kay, man?"

As the adrenaline continued to subside, Harlan began to shake. Various parts of his body began yelling at him, scorching bundles of nerves that indicated the location and general severity of his injuries. His neck was sore, as were his arms and legs. The opening flickers of something like a rope burn began to blaze a diagonal line across his chest. Harlan looked away from the man at his door, detaching his fingers from the wheel as his hands began to shake violently. He stuck the rogue appendages in his armpits, because he didn't know what else to do with them. Harlan squeezed his arms across his body, aware again of a voice and knocking to his left. He turned to see the man reaching for the door handle.

The man at the window pulled and tugged while Harlan sat there, shuddering. The door proved immovable; it was jammed, covered by a portion of the car's frame that should have been two feet forward of its current location.

The knocking resumed. Harlan looked again.

"Hey man. Door's stuck. You 'kay?"

Harlan understood the words now. He nodded. The man yelled a bit louder.

"Got to get out, man. I smell gas." The blurred figure pointed to where his nose should be.

Gas? Harlan's brain shifted focus, ignoring the shakes and kick-starting his sense of smell. Above the faint odors of clean leather and barrel-aged whisky, the unmistakable aroma of gasoline drifted into his consciousness.

Harlan's eyes shot fully open. In every action movie he'd ever watched, this was the moment when the car exploded, blowing whatever poor bastard was trapped inside to hell and gone.

He fumbled for the seatbelt release as his eyes traced around the car. He noted that the electrical system was still functioning as he tried to open the door. He gave it three good shoves as the man outside rapped on the windows.

Nothing. The door wouldn't move. He looked to the passenger-side door as the knocking intensified. All other smells vanished as his mind focused on the threat most likely to incinerate him. Harlan leaned across the center console, working that door handle with an outstretched arm. He could still hear the shadow beating on the window. That angered him. *Christ, dude, I'm trying to get out!*

The passenger door wasn't working. Harlan tried to think. The beating on the driver's side window continued, the cadence a timer ticking down to the moment when the car would vaporize with him inside. Harlan turned to yell at the hazy stranger, then stopped as he saw the vague outline of a finger pointing up. The voice came back to him now.

"The roof. Out the roof!"

Harlan looked up. The sunroof! He reached out and mashed the button to send the smoke-colored glass rearward—watching as the last luxury option he'd selected for this car inched open and stopped. Harlan mashed the button again. The glass moved a few more inches and stopped again.

"Come on!" Harlan screeched. "Open, you piece of shit!" He pressed the button again, visions of a fiery death dancing through his mind. The sunroof opened fully, grinding to a halt against the rubber stops.

Harlan struggled upwards into the frozen night, eager to escape the car that had to be burning by now. He had never been a particularly athletic man; his bruised and battered limbs fought his every effort to extract himself from the wrecked vehicle.

It took four tries before Harlan made it to the roof of his once pristine car. The smell of fuel was stronger out here. Much stronger. That realization panicked him, and, forgetting where he was, he attempted to stand and run. As soon as the hardened leather soles of his dress shoes made contact with the slick metal roof of the car, his feet went out from under him.

He landed in a pile on the frozen sidewalk amid the first flakes of snow with the temerity to stick. Despite the subzero temperatures of the air and the concrete, he could feel a warmth on his face—a sensation he figured to be road rash from his unceremonious tumble off the wreck.

The wreck! Shit!

Harlan hauled himself up onto his hands and knees and worked to scramble away from the car. His irrational brain told him that there could be only mere seconds before the explosion, and he needed to put some distance between himself and the mangled two-seater. In his mad, crab-like dash, he brushed past the blurry stranger.

USS *Key West*
08 December 2022 | 1226 Local Time
Black Sea

"MOSS is programmed to come back below the layer, Captain," *Key West*'s sonar chief announced.

A nod that the sonarman couldn't see. "How long?"

"Twelve minutes into the run. Call it forty-five seconds from now."

Another unseen nod. "Thanks, Chief."

"Yes, sir."

Reynes turned to the executive officer. "Will he bite?"

"Even money he follows it below the layer."

"That good?"

"Better odds than I got on the Red Sox winnin' the Series next year."

Reynes put out his cigarette. "XO, have you ever been wrong?"

"About work or baseball?"

"Either."

A nervous grin. "Sure, boss. I'm wrong on baseball all the time."

"Evens out at work?"

"Yes, sir."

The sonar chief's voice rang out. "Conn, Sonar. MOSS is going deep. Just cleared the layer."

Reynes rolled his neck, needing it to pop. He took a deep breath. "Conn, aye. Heads up, folks. Game time."

K-561 *Kazan*
08 December 2022 | 1227 Local Time
Black Sea

"Captain, contact dropped below the layer." Korov was watching the plot intensely.

Where are you going, friend?

The captain turned to the navigator. "Follow him. Make your depth one-five-zero meters."

"Make my depth one-five-zero meters."

The captain, satisfied, turned back to the first officer. "I want a firing solution on this fool. Tubes two and three."

"Yes, Captain."

The submarine angled down at the bow and slipped into the deep.

USS *James E. Williams*
08 December 2022 | 1228 Local Time
Black Sea

Brian was staring intently at the screen when he saw one of the status lines change from remote to local control. He looked at it for a moment, confused.

Why would Becker put the generator in local?

He reached over to pull the comms microphone out of its holder and then smiled. Without comms, Becker couldn't talk to Central and a coordinated remote start could not occur. She was going to start the generator at the local panel and then shift everything back to remote control.

Brian leaned closer to the screen and yelled over his shoulder. "DCA, stand by for generator start."

Brian watched the engine status change, saw the 'start initiated' warning. He watched as the generator appeared to gather RPMs for a brief moment before everything zeroed out and several warning lights began flashing to indicate a failed start.

"Damnit!" Brian slammed his fist into the console.

USS *Key West*
08 December 2022 | 1229 Local Time
Black Sea

"Conn, Sonar. Submerged contact bearing zero-zero-one. Turns for fourteen knots. Moving left to right."

Reynes looked up from the tactical plot. "Conn, aye. Got a classification, Chief?"

"Working on it, sir."

"Let me know as soon as you have something." He turned. "XO?"

"Sir. Tracking party is on it. Should have a firing solution in two minutes."

"Thank you, XO."

"Conn, Sonar. Hull-popping noises stopped. Contact steady on course zero-zero-five. Range to contact is six thousand yards and opening. Computer designates contact as Yasen-class. It's the *Kazan*, Captain."

"Great job, Chief. XO?"

"Just who we were looking for. " A brief grin.

"Firing solution?" Reynes barked.

"Ready, Captain."

"Warm up tubes one and four." The order came naturally. Easier than Reynes expected.

"Aye, aye, sir."

K-561 *Kazan*
08 December 2022 | 1231 Local Time
Black Sea

"Captain, tubes two and three ready."

Korov grinned. "Very well. Open the outer doors."

The captain waited as his first officer passed on the order.

You've trained for this. Years of drills. Exercises. Lectures. Repetition. Practice. For this moment. Hunting another submarine. Not like shooting surface ships. Prey that can't shoot back. This is hunting. A steel wolf pelt to hang over the mantel.

"Outer doors open, Captain."

"Fire two!"

"Firing two."

The ship shuddered.

"Two away, Captain."

"Fire three!"

Intersection—Main Street and Southwood Road
08 December 2022 | 0532 Local Time
New Freedom, PA

Harlan figured he'd traveled a good fifty yards before deeming himself safe. His hands and knees were on fire, the skin on them torn away during his undignified escape across the rough, hardened concrete. Exhausted and injured, Harlan flopped onto his back and waited for the explosion.

Nothing happened. He listened, confused by the silence. Where was the deafening boom and the roar of a fuel-fired inferno? That should've happened by now, right? But there was nothing. All he felt was cold and aching. All he heard was an odd zip-zopping, shuffling noise that his mind struggled to place until the blurry stranger's face appeared over him again.

"Shit, man. You 'kay?"

The stranger's face came into focus. It was old and creased, folded and weather-beaten. Wisps of gray hair stuck out at odd angles from what Harlan thought to be at least three different knit caps—the most visible of which was brown and red and…

"Is that Rudolph?"

The creases at the bottom of the face moved, waves of frozen lava splitting open in a wide grin.

"You fine," the face pronounced.

A hand was extended. Harlan blinked and took it. The stranger helped him, slowly and gingerly, to a sitting position.

"What happened?" Harlan asked.

The face cocked quizzically in front of Harlan as the stranger squatted down. Harlan looked at him. The man was covered in dirt and appeared to be wearing several layers of clothes. Harlan could make out at least two sweaters; the outermost one looked like it might have been purple at some point. The stranger was also wearing at least two overcoats—one brown and one orange, both full of holes and poorly patched in places. As Harlan took in the rest of the man in front of him, the stranger spoke.

"Smacked that buildin'. Smacked it good." The voice, an odd combination of rough English and smooth bass, sounded like it belonged to a connoisseur of tragedy.

Harlan wasn't listening. He was focused on the man's pants. Curiosity got the better of him.

"Are those snow pants?" Harlan hadn't seen snow pants since childhood, not like these, anyway.

The face looked down and back up and cracked into a massive smile again.

"Yep. Don't make 'em like this no more. Nope."

Harlan shook his head, his battered neck reminding him that it was stupid to do so. The stranger spoke again.

"Why'd you jump off the car? Ain't that much hurry. A man could hurt hisself that way."

Harlan nodded. "Smelled gas. Thought the car would explode."

The wide smile returned, accompanied by a fatherly look that was part disbelief and part amusement. "Cars don't 'splode, man. Catch fire maybe. But 'slpode? Nah." The stranger shook his head like a disappointed professor. "Hell, man. Your car ain't even burnin'."

What? Harlan looked over at the wrecked vehicle. The stranger was right; it wasn't on fire, wasn't even smoking. It simply sat, what was left of the front end touching a concrete wall, one headlight—still on—hanging by a cable like a dislocated eye falling out of its socket.

"Can you help me up?" Harlan asked.

"You sure?"

Harlan nodded and held up an arm. He was sure. If the car wasn't on fire, he could get his wallet and cell phone.

A surprisingly strong hand—Harlan hadn't noticed that before—grasped his and pulled, evenly and slowly, as Harlan struggled to stand erect, wobbling like a newborn colt.

As he pulled himself upright, he was assaulted by a violent urge to vomit, a condition exacerbated by a sickening swirling feeling that threatened to tip him right back over onto the frozen pavement. With his arms out, waving and wiggling to counteract the pulling and tugging of gravity from every point on the compass, Harlan couldn't quite decide whether the sensation was the result of a badly jumbled collection of inner ear bones or the entire bottle of whisky he'd consumed over the past few hours.

**USS *James E. Williams*
08 December 2022 | 1233 Local Time
Black Sea**

Brian watched as the generator began a motor and reset cycle. He instinctively reached for the microphone again and actually pulled it off the rack before remembering that it didn't work.

He looked over his shoulder at the starboard side of Central and squinted through the dark to see the progression of damage the DCA was trying to track and combat. He couldn't see well, but it appeared that several more markers had gone up, indicating additional spaces consumed by out-of-control fires and heavy smoke. As he scanned, he heard one messenger report that the flooding in the starboard-side passage was nearly twenty inches deep.

Brian turned back to the panel in front of him, wondering just how much longer it would last on battery backup.

"Chief?" the DCA called.

"Yeah?" Brian didn't turn.

"Anything?"

Brian watched the motor purge end and shook his head. "Nothing yet. Becker just motored the generator to clear any old fuel. She can restart as soon as all the start permissives clear. Maybe another minute or so."

"I need power, Chief."

I know, Ma'am, Brian thought. I know.

32

USS *Key West*
08 December 2022 | 1233 Local Time
Black Sea

The sonar chief yelled. "Conn, Sonar! Transient! Transient! Torpedoes in the water!"
"At us?"
"No, sir! At the MOSS! They shot at the MOSS!"
Reynes turned. "XO?"
"Tubes one and four ready in all respects."
"Open the outer doors. Flood tubes one and four."
A pause. The report came.
"Outer doors open. Tubes flooded."
Reynes paused.
Can you do this, Scott? Can you kill one hundred men?
The captain of the USS *Key West* looked around.
One hundred men like yours? No. Not like yours. These one hundred men have helped kill innocents. They're different. You're different.
Reynes blinked.
What's different? They're following orders. So are you. That argument didn't work at Nuremberg. So, what's different? Nothing. It's them or you. His crew or yours.
Commander Scott Reynes leveled his gaze at the XO.
"Fire one and four."
The XO answered. "Firing one and four."
Reynes turned to the helm. "Make turns for six knots."
The helmsman answered. "Make turns for six knots, aye."

The submarine shuddered as two torpedoes were ejected into the ocean, their motors propelling them forward rapidly. Sonar announced the start of the run. "Conn, Sonar, both fish running hot, straight, and normal."

"Conn, aye. XO, close the outer doors. Reload one and four."

"Aye, aye, Captain."

K-561 *Kazan*
08 December 2022 | 1234 Local Time
Black Sea

The *Kazan*'s sonar officer screamed. "Captain! Transients! Aft!"

"What!?"

"Torpedoes in the water! Bearings one-seven-zero and one-seven-five!"

Korov's response was automatic. "Flank speed! Right full rudder. Make your depth two-zero-zero meters!"

The navigator acknowledged the order. In the corner, the political officer stopped writing and went pale.

"Sonar!" the captain barked, instinct and years of drills taking over. "Where are the torpedoes?"

"Three thousand meters and closing, Captain!"

"Active?"

"Yes, Captain!"

"Time to impact?"

USS *James E. Williams*
08 December 2022 | 1235 Local Time
Black Sea

Brian watched as the generator status changed again. Without thinking, he folded his hands and began muttering a brief prayer.

Brian closed his eyes, expecting to hear the buzzing of alarms that would announce a second failed start. Time seemed to stop. He heard…

Nothing.

Brian opened his eyes and traced the screen, tracking the readings. RPMs. Fuel Pressure. Flame On.

Brian stared at the data. He read the list once. Then a second time.

I'll be damned.

He turned and shouted at the DCA. "Becker did it! Holy fucking shit. She did it."

"What?"

"Number three generator online. Paralleling to the bus in two minutes."

Brian's heart raced as adrenaline dumped into his system. His hands shook almost uncontrollably as he worked the console, verifying phase alignments and load shed settings so that power went to vital gear only.

Intersection—Main Street and Southwood Road
08 December 2022 | 0536 Local Time
New Freedom, PA

Harlan closed his eyes and took a few deep breaths, sucking in lungfuls of ice-cold air. The whirling inside his body slowed and the watery, pre-puking sensation in his mouth eased—not gone, but not nearly as threatening. He opened his eyes and caught the stranger looking at him.

"You gon' be all right?"

"I'm fine."

The man shrugged and used the grimy sleeve of his outermost overcoat to wipe his nose. "You don' smell fine," the man noted. "Smell like you been imbibin' a bit."

Harlan turned, briefly angered by the poorly veiled accusation, and caught the hopeful look on the man's face. He shoved the anger back down inside and shrugged apologetically.

"Sorry, man. Fresh out."

"Sheet."

Harlan flashed a wan smile and took a first step, paying close attention to the previously simple mechanics of placing one foot in front of the other.

"Take it easy, my man. You wobblin' like Smelly Bob."

Harlan shuffled forward a bit, the stranger at his side like some training wheel for drunks.

"Who's Smelly Bob?" Even inebriated and injured, Harlan couldn't not ask about such a moniker.

"A fren'. Betcha wanna know why I call him Smelly Bob."

Harlan continued his shuffle. Left. Pause. Right. Pause. Repeat. "I can guess."

"You'd be wrong," the man noted. "Where you goin'?"

"Back to the car. Wallet and phone."

Step. Pause. Step. Pause.

"You sure? Still smells like gas."

Harlan stopped, looked up from his feet. He took in the scene for the first time, sniffing the air as an increasing number of snowflakes fluttered through the air, a collection of crystalline butterflies cavorting in the cold.

In front of him, still more than thirty yards away, what was left of his car lay against the heavy concrete wall of what looked like an old warehouse. As his nostrils pulled in the frozen, fresh scent of clean snow and a hint of petroleum vapor, he examined the rest of his surroundings. The building that had demolished his car wasn't actually a building anymore. He'd collided with the only undamaged wall of an edifice that had clearly been consumed by fire in the recent past. Even in the dark—there was only one flickering streetlight—Harlan could make out the charred remains of the structure.

To the right, the road Harlan had been using trailed off into the distance, disappearing into nothingness. No lights. No homes. No buildings. *Cornfields? Do they have cornfields in December? Is it just a field during the winter?* Harlan wasn't sure. He turned the other way, his neck bitching about the movement.

To his left, past the onlooking face of the stranger, an empty street stretched on into the night, each side of the roadway lined with two-story shops and crumbling stores, the detritus of a mid-twentieth-century American small town.

Something was wrong, but Harlan couldn't quite put his finger on it. He looked right again. Then left. His neck whined. His brain joined in as inertia bounced it off the inside of his skull. What was missing? It hit him. He looked to the stranger.

"Where is everyone?"

"Sheet, man. Ain't nobody here 'cept you an' me. And Smelly Bob."

"No one?"

"Nope. Just us. And Smelly Bob's big ass."

"Where's Bob?" Harlan couldn't bring himself to call the man names, not having met him yet.

A shrug. "Home. Drunk. Stinkin' up the place."

Harlan resumed his aching shuffle. "Where's home?"

The man let out a booming laugh that startled Harlan, zapping his already twitchy nerves. "Wherever we want. Ain't no one here. Last decent folk left 'bout ten years back."

Harlan was concentrating on his feet again, but the thought dug its way in between the pain and the remnants of the whisky. A ghost town? He briefly considered the matter before his brain lost track of his feet and he began to fall. The vise-like grip of his human training wheel saved Harlan from further damaging his face.

"Thanks. What's your name?" Harlan hadn't even though about asking that yet.

"Mom called me Frank. Smelly Bob calls me Fat Tim."

"And your dad?"

Tim shrugged.

"What do I call you?" Harlan wondered how men like this got these nicknames.

"Whatever you want."

"Tim?"

"Sure."

Harlan began tipping over again. The strong hand of Tim held him up.

"Say, man. Want me to get your things?"

Harlan shook his head, his brain recoiling at the idea. The phone was a thirteen-hundred-dollar piece of high-tech gear, and his wallet had about five hundred in cash stuffed inside. No way in hell this guy was touching either. "I'll make it."

"M'kay, man, but you look like hell."

"Thanks." Harlan was concentrating too hard to roll his eyes.

"No problem."

Harlan looked up. He'd made it maybe ten more yards. His brain, and the rest of his battered body, was pissed about the events of the past several minutes and positively seething about the need to crawl back inside the car and out again. Harlan set his jaw against the aches and pains and led off again with his left foot.

He'd taken two steps, pain coursing through him and the aroma of gasoline overpowering his scuffed-up nose, when he felt Tim grab him from behind. Harlan's brain screamed "robbery!" for no reason other than that was what instinct told him was going to happen.

Harlan turned on Tim and swung. The comically slow punch landed on a solid shoulder like a fly colliding with a freight train. Tim, startled, let go. Harlan swung again, knocking himself off balance and landing in a heap at Tim's feet.

"What's that for?" Tim didn't look angry, just confused.

Harlan panted, lying helpless on the cold pavement. "Just get it over with."

"What?"

"You're gonna rob me now, right?"

"What for?"

Harlan gestured weakly. "Because."

"Man, I ain't gonna rob your drunk ass." He sounded more hurt than angry.

"What the hell did you grab me for?" The volume of his own voice startled him.

"Keep you safe."

"From what?" Now Harlan was confused.

"That." Tim was pointing. Harlan rolled to his side and lifted his head. At first, he saw nothing. Then, as he watched, he saw an army of pale blue flames begin to lick the underside of his wrecked car. With a groan, he dropped his face to the asphalt, a convenient patch of clear, black ice cooling the road rash.

"Fuck."

"Sorry, man. That's a bum-ass deal."

USS *Key West*
08 December 2022 | 1237 Local Time
Black Sea

Key West's sonar chief reported. "Two minutes to impact, Captain."

Reynes nodded. "Both fish active?"

"Yes, Captain. Both have the target."
"God help them."

K-561 *Kazan*
08 December 2022 | 1237 Local Time
Black Sea

Korov bellowed at the sonar officer. "Where are our torpedoes?"

"Circling, Captain."

"A decoy?"

"Yes, Captain."

Korov cursed and turned to the course indicator in front of the helmsman's face, watching the maddeningly slow rotation. He did the math, calculating the time needed to make the turn and fire a snapshot back down the American torpedoes' line of bearing.

Shit, Ivan Sergeyevich. No time. Surface!

Korov barked, "Emergency surface! Now!"

USS *Key West*
08 December 2022 | 1238 Local Time
Black Sea

Key West's sonar chief sounded calm. "Conn, Sonar. Tanks blowing. He's heading up."

"Depth?" Reynes turned his head for the answer.

"Five hundred feet and rising."

"Time to impact?"

"Twenty seconds."

The executive officer did the math. He turned and spoke quietly. "He'll never make it. Will he?"

K-561 *Kazan*
08 December 2022 | 1238 Local Time
Black Sea

Korov leaned forward at an obscene angle as his submarine rose towards the surface, urging the boat higher, to the last possibility of safety. He kept one eye on the depth gauge, watching the needle resist movement.

The navigator's voice rang out, panicked. "One-three-zero meters."

"Where are the torpedoes?" Korov yelled.

"One-two-zero meters. Impact in five seconds."

God help us.

Intersection—Main Street and Southwood Road
08 December 2022 | 0539 Local Time
New Freedom, PA

Harlan wasn't quite sure how long he lay there with his injured face cooling on the road ice. It felt like hours. Time had returned to normal, and so, for the most part, had his thought processes.

He was no longer worried about the car exploding—that concern had been alleviated when he'd taken the time to think.

Sure, the car was on fire now—well, smoldering, technically. Yes, that was troubling—but only from legal and insurance standpoints. The upside was that the leak meant that the gas tank had a rupture. Since it wasn't a contained vessel, pressure couldn't build fast enough to cause an explosion.

See what happens when you listen to me, Harlan? I keep you rational.

Where were you the last twelve hours?

You ignored me, shithead. And you were drunk.

Point.

Harlan conceded the argument to his subconscious and opened his eyes. A pair of mismatched shoes—one that looked like a raggedy-ass rip-off of a high-top Chuck, and the other…

"Tim?"

"Yeah?"

"Is that a Reebok Pump?"

From Harlan's vantage point, he could see that Tim's snow-pant leg was pulled up slightly, like the guy was a hitchhiker trying to show some leg to prospective rides.

"Shore is." Tim was smiling. Had to be. His voice just dripped with happiness and pride. *The man clearly loves his one Reebok.*

Harlan moved his head a few inches. Again, his neck screeched in rage. He could see his car now, what was left of it—a crispy, black, smoking ruin lying against that concrete wall. Apparently, this particular model of sportscar burned like kindling. Harlan tried to shove himself upright and was assisted again by the solid grip of Tim.

"Man, that thing went fast." Tim had his head turned, inspecting the wreck. Harlan looked from Tim to the charred remains and back again.

"Yeah. That wasn't in the brochure." Harlan held a hand out. "Help me up?"

"Long as you don't hit me agin."

"Sorry."

Harlan was hauled to a standing position, still wobbling and unsteady as a newborn calf.

"Whatchoo gonna do now?"

The question was reasonable and hung in the air like a wisp of warm breath. Harlan looked over at the wreck again. No way the phone or wallet had survived that. He turned back to Tim.

"I'm open to suggestions."

Harlan watched as Tim eyeballed him and decided the man's stare was unsettling. Harlan felt his stomach clench. *I'm hoping for a lifeline from a guy in snow pants and one Reebok Pump. Shit.*

"'Spose I could take you to meet Smelly Bob. He don't much like guests, but I don't guess you wanna be here when the troopers show?"

"Troopers?"

"Yeah. Troopers. State pigs. The po-po."

Harlan's head swiveled in every direction, an instinctive reaction that really pissed off his neck. His hand flew to the pain, squeezing at the muscles there. Images of police, sirens squealing and lights blazing, shoving him into the back of a squad car in handcuffs got the adrenaline pumping again. He looked at Tim, saw that judging look again. *Play it cool, Harlan. Cool.*

"Cops come through here?"

Tim nodded. "'Bout four times a night. This here's a shortcut to the barracks."

"How far?"

"Twenty miles. Down that way." A thumb jerked over a shoulder. Harlan considered his options.

"I'd like to meet Smelly Bob."

"And not be here when the po-po show?"

Harlan nodded. "That too."

Tim shrugged and began walking, motioning for Harlan to follow. "'Spect not, smellin' as you do."

"That obvious?"

"Johnnie Walker? Blue Label?"

Harlan stopped dead in his tracks, hand still rubbing his neck. Tim turned. "What?"

"You can smell the make of the scotch?"

A smile. "You got a name?"

Harlan paused. And lied. "Harold."

"Harold?"

"Yeah."

"Harry?"

A painful half-shrug. "Sure."

"Well, Harry. You don't get like me 'less you got problems."

"What do you mean?"

"Mr. Walker and I, well, we have some hist'ry."

Harlan nodded. "Sorry."

"For what?"

Harlan wasn't sure what for and said as much. Tim was eyeballing him again, as if he was some stray at a pound. Finally, he turned and started walking again.

"C'mon, Harry. Ain't too far."

Harlan stepped off after him, following a complete stranger into the darkness.

USS *Key West*
08 December 2022 | 1239 Local Time
Black Sea

"Got him, Cap'n!" Chief Hughley yelled. "Detonation against the hull. No break-up noises."

Reynes looked towards the sonar space. "Is he going to make the surface, Chief?"

"Hard to say," Hughley said. "Water's disrupted. Shitload of noise."

"Best guess?"

"I don't think we killed him, Cap'n," Hughley said. "If he was below the disturbed area, I'd hear him by now."

"Thank you, Chief." Reynes turned to look the executive officer. "Get us up to periscope depth and get a message off."

K-561 *Kazan*
08 December 2022 | 1239 Local Time
Black Sea

Korov was barking orders as fast as his mind could process information. The American Mark 48 had struck just forward of the *Kazan*'s stern tube, the explosion lancing through one of the submarine's baffled ballast tanks. Because the warhead hit several meters from the nearest weld, the ship's internal hull had suffered only two minor cracks, through which seawater was flowing into the engine room.

"Full rise on the planes. Vent the ballast tanks," Korov barked. "Get us on the surface."

He watched as sailors moved to carry out his orders and snatched up a nearby phone. It took three seconds for someone to pick up.

"Damage report," Korov commanded.

"Two leaks, Captain," one of the engineers responded. "The pumps are keeping pace. Barely."

"And the engines?" Korov asked, eyeballing the ship's speed indication by the helmsman as it drooped closer to zero.

"Secured, Captain," the engineer said. "The explosion appears to have damaged the drive train. The grinding in the reduction gears… I've heard nothing like it before."

Korov nodded, thinking. If that was true, his submarine was going nowhere. And there wasn't a damn thing he could do about it.

"Very well," Korov said. "Keep me informed."

He hung up the phone and turned to his first officer.

"Go to radio, Valeri. Get word to Moscow and fleet headquarters. *Kazan* is damaged and adrift. Require assistance."

**USS *James E. Williams*
08 December 2022 | 1302 Local Time
Black Sea**

Brian Thompson collapsed into his seat in Central Control. His head ached and he was shaking almost uncontrollably. The ship, he figured, would survive. Power had been restored. Becker had fixed one of the engines and then had spent nearly thirty minutes aligning power to the most critical equipment on the ship. The flooding in the starboard-side passageway was under control, especially after the machinist had been able to drill both ends of the fracture to keep it from growing as the *Williams* heaved back and forth between swells. All but one of the fires were out and that last one was coming under control slowly. De-smoking the ship was in progress, and that was an exercise that would last hours, if not days.

Brian looked around. Central Control was still chaos. There was no other word for it. Messengers streamed in and out through the hatch in the ceiling. Alarms still flashed incessantly, though the buzzing noises usually accompanying the warnings had long since been silenced. Some people, mostly the newer crew members, were smiling, aware that they'd won somehow. Cognizant that the sea would not take their ship. The older members of the crew, Brian saw, were not smiling. They'd been through this before.

Brian's mind wandered. The last time, back when that contractor had stowed explosives in the emergency shaft seals, they'd lost a sailor. Gearhart.

But it could have been worse. Only one of the explosive charges had gone off. Investigators had found that the leaking seal had corroded away the explosive's signal receiver, preventing the radio signal that had detonated the starboard charge.

Our broke-ass gear saved our bacon, Brian thought. And we lost just the one sailor.

It could have been worse.

Just like this one.

Despite everything, Senior Chief Martin had reported no major casualties. A few bumps and bruises and minor scrapes, but no serious wounds and no deaths.

We were torpedoed and no one died.

"Jesus Christ," Brian muttered.

The White House
08 December 2022 | 0615 Local Time
Washington, DC

"Talk to me." President Daniel Evans replaced the phone and rose behind his desk in the Oval Office. He looked at the men and women standing in front of him. "What happened?"

Secretary of Defense Frank Tolchanov handed him a sheet of paper. "The submarines took two more shots each. Both Russian torpedoes missed. They were targeted on a simulator rather than the *Key West*."

"And the *Key West*'s fish?" Evans asked.

"One hit," Tolchanov said. "*Key West* reports *Kazan* surfaced. Extent of damage unknown. *Key West* is remaining on station to monitor events and render assistance if ordered. Though," Tolchanov added, "I'm not sure what help a submarine will be in those seas."

"Good point." Evans nodded. "And the two surface ships?"

Tolchanov read from another piece of paper. "The *Williams* is nearly dead in the water. They have no propulsion and only one generator. Flooding is under control. Only one fire remaining. Everything else is out and the crew is trying to de-smoke the ship."

"What about the *Makarov*?"

"They got lucky," Tolchanov said. "*Williams* still has eyeballs on the *Makarov* and says that the Russian frigate is down at the stern, enough that no part of the flight deck is visible."

Evans held a hand out and Tolchanov handed over the rest of the message traffic. Evans scanned it and handed it back.

Tolchanov took the papers and pointed at the phone. "What did Barsukov say?"

"They will withdraw their blockade, effective immediately," Evans said. "We can send other ships into the Black Sea to render assistance in about an hour or so."

"Anything about our folks on the *Makarov*?" Secretary of State Jack Burroughs asked.

"Barsukov claims that the sailors are fine. Scrapes, bruises, and one hyperextended knee, but that's it," Evans said.

"And Jonathan?" Director of National Intelligence Adams asked.

Evans took a deep breath and shook his head.

"I'm so sorry, Mr. President," Tolchanov said.

Evans nodded. "Thank you, Frank." He looked around the room. "Listen, folks, I'll be fine. We'll tell my family and we'll get through it, but I have things I need to do right now. Things that are much bigger than the death of one man. I need to know why the sudden reversal. Barsukov has refused to talk to me throughout this crisis. In every case he's answered my calls by going on television for a press conference. Now, out of the blue, he's answering the phone and pulling his forces back. He's even letting us waltz Shablikov onto the next flight out of Moscow. Why?"

"Maybe he's worried about the optics," Burroughs offered. "Losing two of Russia's most advanced warships in a couple of days has to be a blow, doesn't it?"

Tolchanov shook his head. "I disagree. They have plenty more, and he's not really lost them. Not yet. As long as they're floating, he'll drag them into a yard for repairs. Depending on the damage," Tolchanov shrugged, "we could see both back in service by the end of the year." He shook his head. "No. It's got to be something else."

"I agree, Frank," Evans said. "But what? What's he playing at?"

"Mr. President." Adams cleared her throat. "There's always the other half of this op."

Evans turned. "The cyber campaign?"

"That," Adams nodded. "And the thing with the Senate. They've proved that they have the ability to corrupt public perception and co-opt American legislators. Without this information from Shablikov, we might have suspected Russian interference, but we may never have known the true scope of the operation."

Chief of Staff Leslie Barnes spoke for the first time. "But if we know the scope, how does this leave them with anything? Why would they just change their minds about the Black Sea portion of this?"

"What if we and this Shablikov guy are wrong about the scope?" Adams asked. "What if it's bigger than this?" She shook her head. "No, that's not right. What if Barsukov and Tolstov inadvertently found that they had the power to influence vast portions of the American public? To coerce legislators with near impunity?"

The room went silent and Evans saw his senior advisors eye each other warily.

"It's not exactly crazy, is it?" Barnes asked. "I mean, look at what they've done. Turn on any two channels and you get both sides of mainstream America railing and yelling and screaming at each other. Happens in public. In the House. In the Senate. Last time we had anything resembling bi-partisanship was the Middle East withdrawal. Since then, the gap between the parties has gotten bigger and uglier." Barnes paused for a moment and turned to the president. "If they think they can continue to exploit that divide, that may be more valuable than a handful of oil rigs."

"Mr. President," Tolchanov said. "This op the Russians ran—Shablikov said it was called Nightingale. You know where they got the name?"

Evans shook his head.

"It's an old Russian folktale," Tolchanov said. "Granny used to tell it to me. Nightingale the Robber. Half man. Half bird. Could lay waste to anything and everything with a whistle. Grasses would tangle. Walls and trees would collapse. Folks would perish just hearing it. Got himself shot down and captured one day by an old Cossack cavalryman. Ilya Muromets, I think. Something like that. Anyway, whenever this Nightingale wanted something from someone, he'd whistle, destroy everyone, and take what he liked."

Evans grunted. "Sounds familiar. What happened to Nightingale?"

"The old Cossack beheaded him." Tolchanov smiled.

"If only it were that easy." Evans smiled back. He looked around at his staff. "Anything else?"

"Yes, Mr. President." Adams cleared her throat. "The Alexanders. FBI picked up Henry Alexander trying to get on a boat. Little private yacht basin in Solomons, Maryland. He's not saying much, but that's to be expected."

Evans nodded. "And the kid?" The president winced. Calling an Army major a kid was somehow grating, no matter what he'd done. "Major Alexander, I mean."

Adams shook her head. "No luck yet. It's like he just vanished. Off the grid. FBI has a single credit card purchase at a liquor store in DC. After that, zilch."

Evans nodded.

"Don't worry, Mr. President," Adams said. "We'll find him."

Intersection—Main Street and Southwood Road
08 December 2022 | 0633 Local Time
New Freedom, PA

Harlan and his guide had only walked about halfway up the main street —the only street, Harlan noted—when Harlan noted two things. The snow was beginning to pick up, and Tim seemed to be limping, an awkward amble that made it look like the man had a lame left leg.

The snowfall troubled Harlan. Here he was, running—okay, hobbling—away from the scene of an accident and it was snowing. He could picture some enterprising young sheriff just following the tracks he was surely leaving behind him. There wasn't a whole lot he could do about that, but he'd watched enough cop shows on television to know it wasn't good for him.

One thing at a time, Harlan.

"Tim? You okay?"

"Shore. Why?"

Harlan pointed out the limp. Tim didn't even slacken his pace as he patted the gimpy leg.

"Busted it up in the Army."

"Shit, man. Sorry."

"What for?"

Harlan shrugged. "Seems a man who takes a bullet for his countr—"

Tim began laughing, his booming chuckles keeping an odd rhythm with his step-drag-step-drag gait. "Sheet, Harry. I ain't take a bullet."

"Oh."

"I crashed me a water buffalo."

Water buffalo? "How do you crash a water buffalo? Like bull riding?"

Tim laughed harder, like a jolly damn homeless Santa. "A truck, Harry. Big-ass truck with a water tank on it."

Harlan felt his face flush slightly and changed the subject. "Tim?"

"Yeah?"

"Where the hell am I?"

Without answering, Tim turned to his left and shuffled down an alley between two buildings that had been a hardware emporium and the local pharmacy.

"This here town is called Raintree." Tim turned right around the end of the pharmacy. "My place ain't much further."

"And where is Raintree, exactly?"

Tim stopped and turned, eyes a bit wide. "Sheet, Harry. You don't know what state you're in? How much booze you drink today?"

A sheepish grin spread across Harlan's face. *Not enough, apparently.* "More than was good for me."

"Sheet. And you still standin'? You drink lots, huh?"

"Actually, no. I never drink."

"I see. Special oh-casion?" Tim turned. "Let's get movin'. Snow's really comin' down."

Thank God. "Lead on, my good man."

After a few more twists and turns, and a painful climb up a set of rickety, weather-beaten stairs, Tim announced their arrival at his abode. The man with the mismatched everything worked a section of wire hanger that apparently served as the lock and flung the door open like some broke-ass Robin Leach. In his head, Harlan could hear the intro.

Hello, and welcome to Lifestyles of the Broke and Penniless. I'm Fat Tim and you're not!

"Don't think Smelly Bob's aroun'."

Harlan stepped in and glanced around. "How do you know?"

"Can't really wire hisself in, can he?" There was a hint of amusement in the chide. "You ain't one fer roughin' it, is ya?" Tim shut the door behind them.

Harlan shook his head.

"Never been campin'?"

Another shake of the head.

Tim barked with laughter. "I'll be damned. Rescued me a greenhorn."

Harlan grinned and looked for a place to sit. He saw none. They appeared to be in a loft above one of the stores on the main street. Odds and ends filled the room. A single, bare bulb lit the space, screwed into a naked socket. Harlan looked at the bulb for a full thirty seconds. Something odd struck him about it.

A light bulb? That works? The light on the street worked, too. But the town's been abandoned. How?

"Tim?"

"Yeah?"

"You have electricity?"

"Yep. Sometimes."

"How?"

"Whatcha mean?"

Harlan looked around. "Town's been abandoned awhile, right?"

"Yep."

"Didn't the power company cut the town off?"

Tim laughed. "'Spose they did, but only at the switch."

Harlan was lost. "At the switch?"

"Yeah. They just turned the town off. Substation's 'bout four miles down the road you came in on."

"And?"

"And Smelly Bob used to work for the power comp'ny. He just went down and turned it back on."

Oh. "That's convenient."

Tim nodded agreement and began digging through a box. "You better cop a squat, man. You don't look so good."

Harlan again looked around for a seat. Tim noticed the look. "Jus' pick out a spot of hardwood. Ain't no chairs."

Harlan used the wall to ease himself to the floor. *Gravity is such a helpful damn concept.*

A flicker of light began to grow around Tim, and Harlan leaned to one side to see what was happening. Tim stood and looked at him.

"'Spect you're hungry. Chili okay?"

"Is it vegan?" The words shot out of his mouth before he could stop them.

Tim looked at the can and back at Harlan. "Says Hormel on the can."

Smooth, Harlan. Real fucking smooth.

"So where is New Freedom?"

Tim worked the pointed end of an old, rusted bottle opener against the tops of two cans of the non-vegan chili and placed the vented containers on a kitchen stove that had Harlan's undivided attention at the moment.

The stove—grill was more appropriate—appeared to be an overturned shopping cart, under which sat a five-gallon steel pot to contain the fire Tim had lit just minutes ago. Harlan began to worry about it burning through the splintered wooden floor until he looked closer and saw that the pot—flames and all—sat on a pile of neatly arranged bricks. *I'll be damned. Genius.*

"Well, Harry, you in Southeast Pennsylvania." Tim's eyes rolled up in thought for a moment. "'Bout two hours from DC. This here ain't actually part of New Freedom. That's about fifteen minutes up the road. But it's close enough."

Harlan's body was starting to tighten up. He could feel the bruises beginning to form—especially across his chest. He was sore, but not cripplingly so. He was sure that would change. His head was pounding like some mad drummer had taken up residence there. He thought wistfully of his bottle of Tylenol, which was probably char-flavored by now. His eyes moved to the box that had produced the chili.

"Tim, any chance you got some aspirin in that box?"

A head shake. "Nah."

Shit.

"Might be some left in the drugstore. Maybe the gen'ral store."

"No shit?"

A shrug. "Prob'ly. Want I should go look after chow?"

Fuckin'-A, Tim. One lobe of Harlan's brain did a fist pump. "Sure. I can go with you."

"Nah. Don't wanna put the fire out. You stay here and mind it." Tim checked on the cans of chili. "Bout ten more minutes."

Harlan nodded, closed his eyes, and slumped back against the wall. The little makeshift stove was beginning to heat the room and the warmth was beginning to poke and probe its way into his muscles. For the most part, it felt great. Harlan could feel the tightness easing off a bit, a sensation he likened to those first thirty seconds in a hot tub. The various aches began to fade slightly, and Harlan felt himself relaxing for the first time in hours.

He was certain that he was being looked for; his father's warning left no doubt about that. But maybe, with a little luck, he could pull this off.

Stay here for a bit, Harlan. Rest up for a couple of days. Maybe head back down to DC, waltz right in the front doors of the Russian embassy?

It wasn't perfect, and Harlan's stomach turned at the prospect of spending the rest of his life in Russia.

But what else is there? What's the alternative? A nice, cozy cell out in Leavenworth or Terre Haute? Fuck that.

When Harlan opened his eyes, he found Tim watching him.

"Where you coming from, Harry?"

"New York," Harlan lied.

"Ain't never been there. What you doin' out here?"

"Just driving."

"Ain't nobody just drives out here." Harlan saw that the look was back. He was being evaluated. By a bum.

A bum that saved your ass, Harlan.

"I'm taking some time off work. Need to clear my head. Too much going on. Know what I mean?"

Tim was checking the chili again. "Shore. I get it. Life gets tough, you gotta jus' get away. I get it."

"Really?" asked Harlan, surprised.

"Shore. Know what I did back then? Back when work got hard? Before I came here?"

Harlan shook his head.

"Hawaii."

Harlan blinked. "Hawaii?"

"Aw, yeah, man. White, sandy beaches. Nice drinks. Sunlight. Hawaii. Any time it got tough, that's where I'd be."

"Serious?" Harlan hadn't thought about that.

"Hell naw, man." Tim's voice changed, and Harlan snapped back to reality. "Folks like me ain't going to Hawaii when it gets tough. You lost your mind?"

Harlan felt the blood rush into his cheeks. He'd not been reproached by anyone in a very long time, certainly not by some damn street bum.

The knock on the door didn't even make Harlan look up.

"Probably Smelly Bob," Tim said, pushing himself to his feet.

Harlan nodded, leaned back, and closed his eyes.

Wait a minute, Harlan thought, why would Smelly Bob need to knock?

"Oh, shit!" Harlan's eyes shot open and he clambered to his feet just in time to hear a booming voice yell, "FBI!"

Harlan's hands shot into the air as four special agents rolled into the room. They barked instructions that he followed to the letter, and, in less than three minutes, Harlan found himself handcuffed and Mirandized and seated in the back of a black mini-van sporting government license plates.

He turned to the agent on his left.

"How?"

The agent smiled at him. "Your car wreck."

Harlan thought for a moment. "The fire?"

The agent shook his head. "No. Mbrace. Works just like OnStar.

Sent out the emergency message when you smacked that building."

Great, Harlan thought. Even my car sold me out.

USS *James E. Williams*
09 December 2022 | 0500 Local Time
Black Sea

Brian Thompson sat staring at the monitor on his desk without really seeing it. His eyes registered the shapes and icons residing on the screen, and he tried to focus on them. His head was still killing him and his whole body ached. He'd just come off watch and the ship was relatively stable. Becker and her team had managed to get a second generator online. The fires were out, though de-smoking would take some hours. They'd tried to conduct flight quarters to assist in rescuing the crews of the two Russian warships bobbing a few miles away on the surface, but the rolling seas had largely prevented that. Not that it mattered, according to the captain. Tugs and support ships from both navies had arrived on scene around midnight to render assistance.

Brian tried to focus on work. Despite everything that had happened, there was still a pile of admin that never seemed to go away. Brian pulled a folder to him and tried to read through the eval inside.

He couldn't do it. His brain kept reliving everything he'd been through in his time on the *Williams*. The events of the previous year. The interdiction of the Pakistani nuke. The explosion in Shaft Alley. The death of Petty Officer Gearhart.

And this time?

Faulkner's suicide. Insubordination with the XO. The collision. And the torpedo.

Brian swallowed hard. Felt the anger surge. Felt his pulse quicken and his face flush. He tried to think about whatever it was that would come next. Told himself that it would be worth it. Just another year or so. Then he'd transfer back to shore for three or four years. He would be home, wherever that might be. His eventual retirement pay would be higher.

Just another year. Maybe.

As long as he had time left on his contract, it was possible that he could stay on the *Williams*. An extension. Involuntary. It wasn't unheard of. The idea had been floated several times in the past few months.

Two more years, Brian thought. If I stay in, re-enlist to get back to shore duty, I could have two more years here.

Brian looked at two icons on his screen.

Is it worth it? More of this in exchange for a couple hundred extra dollars in retirement pay?

Brian clicked on the left icon, watched it open, and clicked on the centermost box. When the cursor appeared, Brian began typing. When he was done, he stared at the screen and read the words.

"Respectfully request permission to retire from active duty effective February 1, 2023."

DOUBLE ‡ DAGGER
— www.doubledagger.ca —

Double Dagger Books is Canada's only military-focused publisher. Conflict and warfare have shaped human history since before we began to record it. The earliest stories that we know of, passed on as oral tradition, speak of war, and more importantly, the essential elements of the human condition that are revealed under its pressure.

We are dedicated to publishing material that, while rooted in conflict, transcend the idea of "war" as merely a genre. Fiction, non-fiction, and stuff that defies categorization, we want to read it all.

Because if you want peace, study war.

INTERDICTION

A MILITARY THRILLER

MATT HARDMAN

INTERDICTION
by Matt Hardman

The world of private security is a lucrative one, a collection of corporate armies built to compete in what has become a thirty billion dollar a year industry. Staffed largely by regular military and special forces veterans, these companies provide services to governments and the corporate world.

What would happen if one of the world's most powerful private security firms went rogue?

Daniel Evans has just been sworn in as the 46th President of the United States and his first major initiative is to fulfill his biggest campaign promise—the complete withdrawal of all American military personnel from the Middle East.

Nicholas DeGuerra is the CEO of TitanX Security, the world's largest private security company. He's a self-made man, a former Delta operator turned businessman who knows that the new president's policy is a threat to his financial security. He's just launched a desperate operation to save his company and his fortune.

Brian Thompson is a United States Navy Chief nearing retirement and looking forward to life after the military. A staffing shortage puts him onboard USS James E. Williams, an aging destroyer deployed to the Horn of Africa.

When a Pakistani nuke is stolen, the President of the United States sends Thompson and the USS Williams on a last-ditch interdiction mission to intercept the weapon and derail DeGuerra's plan.

DEAD SPY, COLD GRAVE

MICHAEL J GOODSPEED

DEAD SPY, COLD GRAVE
by Michael J. Goodspeed

1951.

A growing Soviet threat.

A volatile nuclear arms race.

A dead body in the snow.

Canada's newly formed Special Branch is tasked to investigate the murder of a Soviet diplomat whose naked body is dumped on the American Ambassador's lawn.

With the Soviets refusing to cooperate, and growing pressure from allies to hand over the reins of the investigation, Inspector Declan Connelly and Canada's fledgling security service find themselves in an international tangle of early Cold War treachery and duplicity.

Dead Spy, Cold Grave is a gripping story of spies, moles and murderers, but also the complications of being a small, inexperienced player in the deadly struggle for nuclear dominance.

Michael Goodspeed has had a lengthy career as an Army officer as well as having been a video producer and worked in the telecommunications industry. He has degrees in English Literature and History, Business Administration, and Strategic Studies. He has lived and worked across the Americas, Europe, the Middle East, and Africa. He is the author of numerous articles for scholarly journals and newspapers and has had four books published: two social histories and two historical novels. He divides his time between Toronto and a lake in Northern Ontario.

Matt Hardman is a retired U.S. Navy Chief Petty Officer who currently works as a marine engineering consultant to the Navy's DDG 51 Shipbuilding Program Office. While on active duty, he served onboard a submarine, two aircraft carriers, two amphibious transports, one submarine tender, and one destroyer. During his final tour of duty, he served as the Engineering Department Chief, or "Top Snipe," for the USS James E. Williams (DDG 95). He holds a bachelor's in Intelligence Studies and Counterintelligence from American Military University and a Master's in Writing from Johns Hopkins University.

Matt Hardman is also a husband and father of six children and currently resides in Calvert County, Maryland.